The
HOUSE
of
HAWTHORNE

OTHER NOVELS BY ERIKA ROBUCK

Receive Me Falling

Hemingway's Girl

Call Me Zelda

Fallen Beauty

The
HOUSE
of
HAWTHORNE

Erika Robuck

 NEW AMERICAN LIBRARY

New American Library
Published by the Penguin Group
Penguin Group (USA) LLC, 375 Hudson Street,
New York, New York 10014

USA | Canada | UK |Ireland | Australia | New Zealand | India | South Africa | China
penguin.com
A Penguin Random House Company

First published by New American Library,
a division of Penguin Group (USA) LLC

First Printing, May 2015

 REGISTERED TRADEMARK—MARCA REGISTRADA

LIBRARY OF CONGRESS CATALOGING-IN-PUBLICATION DATA:
Robuck, Erika.
The house of Hawthorne/Erika Robuck.
p. cm.
ISBN 978-0-451-41891-3
1. Hawthorne, Nathaniel, 1804–1864—Fiction. 2. Hawthorne, Sophia Peabody, 1809–
1871—Fiction. 3. Authors, American—19th century—Fiction. 4. Women artists—United
States—19th century—Fiction. I. Title.
PS3618.O338H68 2015
813'.6—dc23   014026205

Printed in the United States of America
10 9 8 7 6 5 4 3 2 1

Set in Adobe Caslon Pro
Designed by Alissa Theodor

As ever, for my love, Scott

Lift Not the Painted Veil

Lift not the painted veil which those who live
Call Life: though unreal shapes be pictured there,
And it but mimic all we would believe
With colours idly spread,—behind, lurk Fear
And Hope, twin Destinies; who ever weave
Their shadows, o'er the chasm, sightless and drear.
I knew one who had lifted it—he sought,
For his lost heart was tender, things to love,
But found them not, alas! nor was there aught
The world contains, the which he could approve.
Through the unheeding many he did move,
A splendour among shadows, a bright blot
Upon this gloomy scene, a Spirit that strove
For truth, and like the Preacher found it not.

—PERCY BYSSHE SHELLEY

Time flies over us, but leaves its shadow behind.

—NATHANIEL HAWTHORNE, *THE MARBLE FAUN*

The
HOUSE
of
HAWTHORNE

Spring 1864
Concord, Massachusetts

In the second-floor storage room where we never go, someone has wound the music box. Its eerie tinkling peels away the years like a bride's clothing, inviting the memory of my first night as Nathaniel Hawthorne's wife. As soon as the image enters my mind, it drifts away—delicate, elusive, and almost impossible to grasp, like a butterfly on the banks of Walden Pond. I open the oak door and enter the room, but only silence waits. The music box rests undisturbed on a table beneath a layer of dust.

"Naughty ghost," I say. "Do not make mischief today, of all days."

I walk to the window and look down toward the pine path, the well-worn trail between our home and the Alcotts'. There in the dark tangle of evergreens, where breezes whisper down the hill, a retreat of a half hour's time renews my brooding husband. I have patted the pines' sturdy trunks, thanking them for giving

Nathaniel these moments of peace, and have sensed their replies in the fragrant sighing of their branches. He soon emerges, stooped and white haired. Even years after his swift aging during our difficulties in Italy, it is still jarring to see Nathaniel so altered in appearance. In my mind and heart he is ever my young summer husband.

In spite of my wish to meet him when he comes into the house, a presence in this room seems to insist that I remain here. Could it be one of the women Nathaniel's ancestors judged for a witch and condemned to hang, or one of our deceased friends or relations? The remembrance of our dead loved ones paralyzes me so that I do not step into the hallway even when I hear Nathaniel's footfall reach the landing and then climb the narrow stairs to the sky parlor. As we both approach six decades of life, he often tells me that I am his earthly savior—a gift from God to bring light to him, who is so apt to see dark. He has fought the coil and stain of the black weeds of his forefathers, even changing the spelling of his surname, to ascend from the bones they left scattered about Salem graveyards. He is still climbing, trying to rise above them.

Nathaniel's need for elevation inspired the tower he had erected on the third floor of our home, the Wayside, in Concord, Massachusetts, fashioned after the mossy castle lookout where we once summered in Florence. The Wayside is the only home we have ever owned. It is the place where we finally unpacked all the trunks, where the wall colors have faded around portraits, where the dear rooms have embraced our family. The Wayside creaks and heaves sighs like an old, fat grandmama who has sat vigil for so many years that she has coughed the dust of British soldiers' boots marching to the commencing battles of the Revolutionary War, has harbored frightened runaway Negroes on their North Star quests, and now hosts this stubborn ghost who enjoys giving us a fright.

I know the secrets in her, this house. There is a floorboard in this room that can be lifted, where a mahogany letterbox holds the papers Nathaniel insisted I cut out and burn from our journals and epistles. I imagine how they must quiver, eager to escape and breathe. Once Nathaniel has left on his journey, perhaps I will go through the artifacts. I should look forward to this airing of my spirit, like pinning clean laundry to the line, but I have a place Nathaniel has inserted into me like a grafting on a tree that says these things should stay private.

The floorboards creak above my head in the sad cadence of the man who haunts his writing space. The room is ten by ten feet, and a trapdoor allows him entrance and solitude, but the tower where he wanted to escape from civilization sticks like a belfry above our house, the tin roof giving no insulation from heat or cold, the windows illuminating his dark silhouette for every neighbor and traveler to see by the light of the astral lamp. The sky parlor was to be his respite, but like all places where Nathaniel thinks he will finally find peace and *home*, it has disappointed him.

Knowing that Nathaniel will remain upstairs until our carriage to Boston comes, and that our children are away or occupied, I cannot resist the letterbox. I count four planks from the window and reach my finger into the small knot in the wood to pry it loose. A musty smell emerges on a puff of old dust, making me sneeze. I wait to be sure my husband does not come in and worry over my health, which has plagued us so often these years.

When I am convinced he still walks in the tower, I lift the box with the courtship letters, the marriage journal, the sketches, and pressed flowers brought back from the places we traveled. A dried paintbrush holds the residue of a long-ago color—the emerald green of an Italian forest on a canvas I painted for Nathaniel, which he used to hide behind a black veil. The flowers are faded like old tapestries hung too long in the sun, and include a night-blooming cereus from my maiden days in Cuba, a white pond lily from the Concord River, and a red poppy from Florence. Under the flowers is a sketch I drew in the days of fevered, falling-in-love inspiration, of a butterfly emerging from a chrysalis. One wing is unfurled, welcoming the breath of spring zephyrs into its body. The other is curled and wet, waiting to escape its confinement.

The chime of the parlor's clock reminds me that we have but an hour before the carriage arrives. I have packed Nathaniel's belongings, so I may spend time with these artifacts from our past that are calling to me, urging me to look for something that I do not know is missing. I hold on to a small hope that this spring-time journey to New Hampshire that Nathaniel will make with his dearest friend, former president Franklin Pierce, might restore my husband's vitality. I will escort him to Boston by carriage, where he and Franklin will then catch a train north, making stops along the way. I pray that if Nathaniel uses this excursion to reflect on how far he has come, how unlike his ancestors he is, and what a rich and fascinating life of experience he has given us, perhaps he will no longer despair.

A dark eye peers out from under the butterfly sketch, giving me a strange thrill. I drew the son of a plantation owner before I met Nathaniel. It was during the year and a half I spent in Cuba, in my maiden days, when I discovered my capacity for love. In spite of that time of passion and growth, I was injured in my soul from Cuba, and I wonder whether it would have been better if I had never gone. I run my finger over the portrait's lips, imagining what the planter's life has been since I left him thirty years ago. My senses are aroused, and I can nearly smell the robust fragrance of Cuban coffee, feel the waxy tropical foliage, hear the melancholy melody brought forth from the planter's long, dark fingers on the piano keys.

Nathaniel's cough startles me. I am aware that another man's likeness is under my hand while my husband stands across the room. Ridiculous though it is, I feel as guilty as if I were caught with a lover. I turn the paper facedown in the letterbox, hoping Nathaniel will not ask about its contents, arrange my face into a smile, and say, "Are you nearly ready, my love?"

He is midgrimace from the pain in his stomach, but upon my address, Nathaniel's shoulders relax and his lips form a smile. I leave my memories and cross the room to him, wrapping my arms around him. Nathaniel's coat is damp with sweat, and the heat coming from him frightens me.

"You are feverish," I say. "You must go to bed. Stay with me."

"I would like nothing better, my dove," he says. "But this is a journey I must make."

"Then let me come with you," I say, knowing such a wish is impossible. I have asked no one to care for the children, and we haven't the money for both of us to travel at this time.

"You must stay and keep our children well, and our hearths glowing."

"For your return," I say.

He does not answer, but brushes a lock of gray hair from my forehead.

"See that you come back to me," I say. "I cannot bear this earth long without my companion."

"Nor I," he says.

I kiss Nathaniel, and when he pulls away his gaze falls on the box and rests there. I hold my breath, wondering whether he will ask about it, but he grimaces again, his pain appearing to distract him from any questions. He leaves to descend to the first floor and wait for the carriage, and I take one last look at the papers before putting them back into hiding, but the artifacts seem to shiver, to urge, and I am unable to part from them.

What do you want of me? I think. *Am I to draw again? To paint? Is it even possible to resurrect the artist in me, whom I have neglected these many years?*

Light coming in through the window falls on the *Cuba Journal*. I turn its pages, and imagine Nathaniel reading it in solitude as a young man, coming to know me safely in print before courting me in the flesh. I wonder which of my words kindled his heart's fire and his writer's pen. Was it my acceptance of the possibility of love, or the vivid portraiture of my words that inspired his? Did Nathaniel sense that a woman so open to newness in the society of others could serve as an interpreter of the world for him?

I begin reading and soon lose track of time. It is as if the decades dissolve and I am back in that exotic land, immersed in the words of my own hand, in worlds crafted from my writings, that conjure a full palette of scenery, society, passion, and tragedy.

My wordsmith is wary of words, and finds them inadequate because they fail him, but I am more trusting. Burrowed in my journal is the story that wants me to remember that traveling to Cuba allowed me to emerge from my maidenhood to become the woman—the artist—who would wed Nathaniel Hawthorne.

1

Winter 1833–34
Cuba

Forty-five miles of carriage ride over rutted, red-dirt roads is as awful an experience as one would imagine, even in a Cuban *volante*, which has some spring to it. But when our *calesaro* points his finger down an avenue of palms, as grand as the columns of a Grecian temple, I forget all my discomfort.

"*Niñas*, La Recompensa!"

Recompense, reward. Can a slave plantation be such a thing?

My doctor has sent me to rest in Cuba's tropical climate with my sister Mary, who will educate the children of the plantation owners for our keep. If I become well, I may instruct them in art. Madame Morrell is an old friend of Mother's, and her husband, Dr. Morrell, will see to my health. The leeches, the opium, and the arsenic have not cured me of my recurring headaches, so this is a last resort. For fifteen years, my art and my infirmity have progressed in equal measure, with illness almost always following inspiration. When it was apparent early on that my pencils and paints could copy even the most powerful masters, my mother and my eldest sister, Elizabeth, saw to my education in the arts and humanities, under the tutelage of the most gifted artists of our time, and most recently with Washington Allston himself. Mr. Allston has been giving me instruction by allowing me to copy his landscapes; my efforts now adorn the parlors of our well-to-do Boston and Salem neighbors, and at twenty-four years of age, I have made a little money and a name for myself through exhibits and commissions. It was he who told me to record all I see in Cuba in the most exact sensory detail, so that I may create original art when I return. Just the thought of bringing my own imagination to life sets off the pulsing in my temples.

Two slaves, a man and a young boy, emerge from the shadows, wearing tattered brown cloth as skirts. In the setting sun, their features are difficult to see, except for the whites of their eyes. When I draw closer, the boy glances at the basket of oranges we have brought for the Morrells from the last outpost. His father turns the key to open the lock, and they pull wide the iron gates. The noise from the rusted hinges drives a spike into my aching skull, and I flinch. Mary wraps her arm around my waist.

"Almost there, Sophy," she says.

After thousands of miles, weeks away from Mother and Father in Boston, an ocean voyage, a short stay in Havana, and travels across foreign soil, we are indeed almost there. My health aboard the ship was surprisingly good. The ocean muffled the noise of humanity, which so plagues me, and the magnificence of the sapphire waters, silvery clouds, and amethyst sunsets provided enough inspiration for me to fill many pages of my journal. Even the incessant bells of Havana and the shouts of slaves and military men did not oppress me as much as this scraping gate. Once it is open, the slaves stand aside with heads bowed, and commend us to God as we pass. I am so touched by their prayers that I reach into the basket and pass two oranges to the boy. His teeth flash in his smile.

"*Gracias, señorita. ¡Gracias! ¡Gracias!*"

As the *volante* proceeds down the drive, his small voice is muffled by the squawking of tropical birds. The tall palms invite me to sit straighter in my seat as I gaze up at their fronds, which ripple in the breeze like fingers waving to us. Even among the evening shadows, I can see the brilliance of the hibiscus, the coffee plants, the delicate laurustinus, and succulent orange trees. A recent rain shower has made the emerald leaves glisten like diamonds, and a rich, earthy smell and the fragrant exhalations of the soaked flowers fill my senses.

"I have never observed such colors in nature," I say. "It is a pity the birds do not sing prettily, but I suppose it would be unfair for nature to apportion gifts so abundantly on just one creature. Though you, Mary, are the exception."

Mary smiles, her skin a becoming shade of the fairest pink rose. I see that her ease has been restored now that we are on dry land. She was ill on the ship from seasickness, and it was a strange thing to be the sister in bloom, if only for a short time.

We reach the end of the drive and stop before a cracked, vine-covered fountain that still bubbles, though it appears as ancient as a ruin. It is bordered in pink roses, and tiny lizards slip in and out of its fissures. The gurgling of the fountain is an antidote to the screeching metal of the gate.

As we are helped down from the *volante* by the *calesaro*, Madame Morrell emerges with open arms from the long, rambling, lantern-lit plantation house. Her dark beauty and stately posture cause a twitch in my artist's fingers, tingling with the anticipation of all they will record of this new world.

"My children," she says, though she does not look more than a decade older than twenty-seven-year-old Mary. "Praise God for your safe delivery. I had dreams your dear heads rested at the ocean's bottom, and I had the duty of sending notes to your mother about your demises. But, oh, your beauty and freshness! How is it possible you have been traveling for weeks and yet are so neat?"

"You are very kind," says Mary. "You must not see the layer of dirt covering us because night has fallen."

"I am sure you would love nothing more than to recline in a warm bath, take your dinner, and sleep for days, which is exactly what we have prepared for you."

"That sounds like heaven, thank you," I say.

I present the orange basket to Madame Morrell, and she receives it with great warmth and gratitude. Her manners are like those of a queen.

"I will have Tekla use these for your *naranjada*, or orange water," she says.

An ancient, wiry slave woman appears and takes the fruit,

bowing and thanking us profusely. Madame Morrell kisses Tekla's wrinkled cheek before sending her away and turning back to me.

"If I did not know you were coming for your health," she says to me, "I would not believe you had been ill a day in your life, though your mother wrote how you have suffered."

"It is a miracle," says Mary. "Since the moment we set sail, Sophy has been a new creature. She is considering employment on the brigs once we have fulfilled our contract with you."

Madame Morrell smiles, but then her face becomes serious.

"The doctor sends his apologies that he is not able to greet you. We had a terrible accident when our *volante* turned over yesterday. Though he is much battered and bruised, I am well. He promises that as soon as he is better, Sophia's health will be his utmost concern."

"Thank heavens you are uninjured," says Mary. "We hope he heals soon."

"The air of the journey has already done much to restore me," I say. "Please tell the doctor to worry only after himself."

"I will pass along your well wishes," says Madame Morrell as she leads us into the house and down a wide hall, plain and elegant in its arrangement. The rosewood sideboards are decorated with fresh flowers, and mirrors and tapestries adorn the walls. Candles and glowing gourds provide the lighting, and give La Recompensa an enchanting aspect. I step closer to examine these strange lanterns, and Madame Morrell lifts the lid to reveal luminous bugs.

"Curculios," says Madame Morrell. "Like large fireflies."

Mary recoils from the beetles, but I am fascinated.

"Everything is so new here," I say. "How are we so fortunate to find employment in heaven?"

Madame Morrell gives me a troubled look that she arranges into a tight smile, but she does not address my comment. I wonder what I have said that makes her face look so dark.

I am at a loss for words when a slave woman, who must be younger than me but whose eyes reveal a longer lifetime of experiences, helps me to remove my clothing and wash in a wide tub. I watch through a crack in our adjoining doorway as Mary endures her bath. She protested such treatment earlier, but when her girl looked as if she would cry, Madame Morrell had to explain that to refuse their service is an insult. They heartily wish to please.

Once I am clean, my girl dries me, helps me into my chemise, and plaits my auburn hair. We will sleep suspended in beds called hammocks that are elevated above the ground and can be swayed like a baby's cradle. They are lined in the softest fabrics, and are surrounded by nets to keep out the pesky tropical insects. My girl tucks me in more snugly than my mother ever has, and I know I must look very strange and wide-eyed to her. As she goes to leave, I reach through the netting for her arm, and grasp it to thank her, but she flinches so severely that I pull away.

"*Gracias*, Josepha," I say.

She nods and whispers many welcomes and blessings from God as she leaves me alone in my room.

I lie awake trying to align myself to the customs of this place.

How unused to luxury we Peabody sisters are! Our family has moved from Salem to Boston to Concord and back like vagabonds, because our dear father has no business sense to support his medical practice and his six children. My sisters and I earn our keep through educating students, making art, and even publishing books, with Mother overseeing and contributing to our efforts. She is the captain of our family ship, with Father a strange and inconsistent mate. It is as if he wishes to be in charge, but he cannot sustain the energy required to do so. Our family is respected in society, in spite of our unfortunate financial situation, because of the superior teaching abilities of Mother and Elizabeth. Both are quite outspoken and liberal, and I cannot imagine what they would say to see Mary and me being served by slaves and indulging in the luxury of a plantation. I am willing and able to adopt the customs of this place because I have promised Mother for the sake of my health, though I do not know whether she realized the extent to which I would have to live like my hosts. I have an internal strength that has been cultivated through years of physical suffering, and which allows me to endure in ways others cannot. Through the wall I hear Mary sniffling, her heart bruised by being waited upon by slaves, and I worry that my sister might not have the fortitude to survive this stay.

I awake with a clenched stomach, soaked in sweat, and worry that I have caught the dreaded cholera that has been infecting so many at home. But after a short time, my head cools and my stomach loosens.

The nightmare that woke me reasserts itself. It was of a beggar girl, a figure who has haunted me since my youth. I know not whether she is flesh or spirit, she who plagues me at every turn. It seems she has followed me to Cuba. I shall never forget her first appearance in my life. I was just a child, not yet in corsets, and the buoyant joy of freedom beckoned me. My grandmother had left the front door and windows of her Salem dwelling open that day to allow in the breeze, and it seemed as if angels and sprites called to me. I placed my pencils and sketch papers on the desk and slipped out while Grandmama was occupied. I thought I would venture just as far as the gate, no more, but a cardinal hopped along the path, so I followed him for a bit to study him for later sketches. Then I smelled the brine from the ocean, and wanted to study the sea for a painting. Before I knew it, and not properly dressed for an outing, I had crested Gallows Hill, where so many unfortunate females had hanged so long ago, but which now appeared to me as an Elysian plateau. I stood over Salem, the world and sea at my feet, warm from my awakening senses. Before long, I turned to go home so Grandmama would not notice my absence, but was startled by a girl in tattered clothing, with dirt on her cheeks. She stood not ten feet from me, and seemed to have an aura of darkness about her. I wanted to feel charity for the poor wretch, but her stern gaze made me afraid, so I looked at the ground and turned to leave.

"Curtsy," she said.

I could not help but turn. "Pardon me?"

"You will curtsy to me."

Indignant, I said, "I will not."

She made a move at me with fingers like claws and threatened me bodily, at which time I ran from her as fast as I could, all the way home, horrified that I had left safety for the dangers of the world of which the elder women in my family so often spoke. I saw the same girl out my window another day and again she threatened me, and though I have not seen her since, I often imagine her during times of distress. But why has the beggar girl returned when I am so happy? Is it because this freedom is like that which I experienced when I ran away? Was her image a warning? Should I stay always at my mother's skirts?

A sound from some strange animal distracts me from my fretting. At first I think it is a cow that has wandered out of the grazing plain and gotten its leg stuck in the brambles along the lime hedges, but then the sound turns high, like a crying cat.

My chamber faces the back of the house, overlooking the coffee fields. The windows have no glass, since it is far too expensive, and impractical in the strong tempests, but I do have shutters that are closed to the damp night air. Madame Morrell believes that taking in the evening breezes and fragrances from nocturnal flowers is dangerous to a lady's health, but I recognize that as superstition.

I slip out of my hammock and step across the layers of moonlight gleaming through the shutters on the polished wood floor to peek out the window. Before my hand reaches the clasp, I hear the unmistakable slashing sound of a whip, followed by a groan that I know now comes from no animal, but from a human. I am immobilized, and do not want to see what is beyond the window, but dark curiosity causes me to lift my hand. When I hear another slash and cry, I bring my knuckles to my mouth and decide that I must not look, but I hear the door to Mary's room open, and she is at my side.

"It is a nightmare," she whispers. "I cannot sleep for the terrible whipping that poor Negro endures."

She reaches for the shutters, but I stop her.

"This is going to be a very long stay here if we look on those things that are not our business," I warn.

"How can you say such a thing?" Mary steps from me to open the shutters.

She draws in her breath and I cannot help but look, though I regret my action.

Moonlight and torch fire illuminate the hellish scene. A Negro is tied to a post while a slave woman and children watch in tears. The *mayoral*, or overseer, continues to apply the whip, though it is clear by the way the slave hangs at the post with blood pouring over the dirt that his lesson is learned. As if this horror is not enough, I notice Madame Morrell clutching the arm of a man who must be the doctor himself, standing on the gallery and watching. He flinches with every crack of the whip while she sobs at his side, but he does nothing to intervene. I cannot help but cry out, and before I can cover my mouth, Madame Morrell turns and sees us in the window. Within moments, she rushes to our chambers and wraps her arms around us, staining our night-clothes with her tears.

"My children, I am so sorry you have to witness this, and so soon after your arrival," she cries. "This is something I myself have not seen in years—my doting father and husband have always spared this cruel necessity from me—but our temporary *mayoral* does not understand our ways."

"Why does the doctor not stop him?" asks Mary.

"He will stop him soon, once the punishment is complete. And I will insist he never watch again. I hate for Dr. Morrell to be so disturbed."

How strange and terrible that Madame is more worried over troubling the doctor than the physical well-being of her slaves. I look at Mary, who has begun pacing.

"Punishment?" says Mary. "Cruel necessity? What could the poor man have done?"

"It could be because of the *volante* accident. He was driving."

"How could an accident necessitate the murder going on outside?"

We turn our heads back to the horror, where the doctor has called out and the whip has ceased to pollute the air with its gruesome noise. Mary joins me back at the window with Madame Morrell, and we watch as the woman and children of the ravaged man lift him and carry him into a long, low hut. Madame Morrell crosses herself.

"The doctor will care for him well in the infirmary," she says. "La Recompensa has the finest slave hospital in Cuba. We have the best-treated slaves. I wish you could understand."

I am sickened by what she has called the best care of slaves on the island, and it feels as if a fire that began on a fuse in my breast has climbed up to my skull and exploded. I clutch my head and nearly fall, but Mary is at my side and escorts me to my hammock.

"You should not have seen this," she says. "I am sorry for opening the shutters."

Madame Morrell calls to her slave, old Tekla, who comes in, exclaiming her sadness in rapid Spanish. Madame Morrell silences her and requests she bring dampened palm leaves to wrap around my head to ease the ache. I want to tell her that the origin of this pain is not in my head, but in my heart.

2

I do not sleep well for the rest of the night, and entertain horrid visions of what I saw. I cry into my sheets for my mother, terrified of this foreign place, of being so far from home amid savages—both slave and noble. The ache in my head does not subside, and I feel the crushing dejection of certainty that I will never outrun my infirmity—that it is a plague upon my spirit I will have to endure for a lifetime. Just when my despair reaches its utmost, my dark room begins to glow the richest shade of lavender. I watch the walls in wonder as the lavender warms to dusty pink, and I hear the bong of a faraway bell. I unwrap the leaves from my head and place them on my bed as I cross the room to open the shutters to the sunrise.

From this vantage in the morning light, I can fully take in the magnificent view from La Recompensa: the wide green lawns and livestock-covered plains, the foliage bursting with flowers of unimaginable color and size, and the columnlike palms. My view crosses an expanse of dark and enticing forest that crawls up the grand mountains that stand proud on the horizon, under a sky that has the appearance of the pearly interior of a great conch shell. It is as if God is reassuring me after the hell of last night that all will be well and justice will prevail. When I see the poor slaves emerging from their huts, filing off to work in fields and forests, the ache in my chest returns, and I pray the sunrise fills them with the same renewal it does me. I know their eternal rest will far outlast their small season of hell on earth, and it is the only comfort I take in their existence.

My eyes find the post, stained from last night's whipping. I force myself to look at the sullied ground, but I see the red dirt has absorbed the man's blood. It occurs to me that the crimson dust of this land did not come from God, but from the punishments of the brutal plantation owners who have invaded His paradise.

I did not think my head would allow it, but after a breakfast of the most succulent oranges and fluffiest eggs imaginable, I have ridden on horseback around the plantation with my escort, Eduardo, one of the Morrells' three children. Eduardo, just twelve years old, takes his duty very seriously. With care, he lifts low-hanging vines, points out the slightest elevations of land, and instructs me on the vegetation I ensure him is all new to my eyes. He delights in my rapturous discoveries, and seems intent on finding new treasures to elicit greater and wilder exclamations. Upon our return, the slave in charge of the horses, Urbano, stables mine and bows to me. He speaks in the Spanish still so uncooperative to my ear, but I understand the name of the horse I have ridden, Rosillo, and he gestures from the large steed to me.

"He says Rosillo is for you, Mees Sofeea," says Eduardo, in the most darling English. Madame Morrell's children speak the Spanish of the doctor's land, and the English and French of New Orleans, Madame Morrell's place of origin. I am in awe of the way she can converse with me in English in one breath, instruct Tekla in Spanish in another, and give her attention to her daughter Louisa's French studies in yet another.

Madame Morrell sits on the gallery watching over us like a benevolent angel. Her face is handsome and complicated. While a gentle smile rests on her lips, her forehead betrays her inner anguish. Mary has told me that Madame Morrell lost her devoted father and an infant daughter many years ago, and that she carries those losses with her always. The way Madame Morrell pats Tekla's arm, I can see that she also shares in the misery of her slaves, though not enough to make a difference in their lives.

The slave woman from last night who witnessed the brutalizing of her man, and the little ones who must be her children, now kneel at Madame Morrell's feet and bow their heads. She places her hands on each one of them, tears falling down her face, and as I draw nearer, I hear that she is blessing them. I place my hand over my heart, enchanted and troubled by this woman and the social order in this strange place. I lower my head to the slaves as they file away down the stairs, and Madame Morrell stands to meet me.

"You are the picture of Santa Ana, a patron saint of horse-women," she says.

I laugh at the thought of being compared to a Catholic any-thing, even something as noble as a saint, but I dare not say such a thing out loud, and take the compliment as it is meant.

"*Gracias*, Madame Morrell," I say.

"You delight us when you speak the language," she says. "And you will have ample opportunities to please our society. We shall have our first visitors tonight."

Mary joins us on the gallery, looking fresh and lovely in spite of the way her face now mirrors our hostess's, divided between pleasure and pain.

"How delightful," says Mary. "Would you like me to start the children's lessons today?"

"No, thank you," says Madame Morrell. "I want the two of you to experience La Recompensa anew, and to allow that terri-ble nightmare to dissipate before you begin your work."

"It will hardly feel like work," I say. "Your children are trea-sures, and I am feeling so well this morning, I could instruct an entire schoolroom of young artists."

"Your words fill my ears with joy," says Madame Morrell. "The two of you do your parents honor, and I will sit this very afternoon to write them about you. But for now, both of you should rest and complete your toilet. When we dine this evening, you will have your first introduction to the Layas sons, neighbor-ing planters of impeccable manners and taste."

I glance at Mary and see her stiffen. Does Madame Morrell mean to make matches for us with Spaniard slave owners in spite of the personal anguish it has brought her, or does she simply hope that we amuse ourselves while in exile here in Cuba? At any rate, I hardly think a Spaniard could capture my interest, no matter how impeccable his manners.

Josepha is a genius at hairstyling. She papers my locks, curls them with hot tongs, and arranges the ringlets so becomingly, I feel a flash of hope that I might take her home to New England when we return, where I could employ her as a servant. Of course, I soon realize my lack of money and her dear child would prevent such an arrangement, but it is a delightful indulgence of thought, nonetheless.

"*Usted tiene el cabello suave,*" she says in her soft, raspy voice. Josepha takes great care in instructing me in the language. Not all of the slaves speak it, especially those just arrived from Africa, but according to Madame Morrell, Josepha has been here for many years.

"*Cabello.*" She lifts my hair and points to it. I repeat.

She rubs a coil of my hair to her face and closes her eyes. "*Suave.*"

"*Suave,*" I say. "Soft."

I instruct her back. She likes this.

"Soft," she says, clipping the word in a strange way. I love how she pronounces our words, though she is rather stupid about remembering them.

I enjoy this language of senses we share, and record the words in my journal so I will have them when I return home and paint.

I feel a sudden longing to do so here, and wonder whether I can have Elizabeth send my oils to me. I will surprise her by asking for them in my next letter. Painting always ignites my flares of infirmity and sensitivity like nothing else. Something about the concentration of all that color and power on the point of a brush, instilling life on a canvas with each motion, brings me such ecstasy and torture. I am left breathless at the thought.

I place my hand to my throat and look back in the mirror. This flush has given my complexion a glow, and I admire the way my hair has been set, the aloe Josepha has brushed over my lips to make them shine, and the grass green of my dressing-up gown, the only elegant clothing I own. Mary and I were embarrassed to admit our poverty, and pretended it was economy of packing that allowed us only one fancy dress each. If Madame Morrell understood our true meaning, she was too well mannered to admit it, and insisted that we will have new gowns for balls and dinners, three each at her expense. Her guilt over what we witnessed no doubt contributed to her generosity on the subject.

The air changes with the introduction of male voices, and I feel a curious lifting in my chest. Though I have no real interest in plantation owners and their sons, I will be polite. Perhaps they will provide amusement for me while I am in Cuba.

The late-afternoon light has made a golden dream of the salon, where Madame Morrell sits at the piano playing a song as sad and elegant as herself. I am entranced by her figure in a billowing crimson gown, framed by the rays of the sun slipping through filmy curtains dancing in the breeze. The scent of jasmine has filled the room from where it climbs around the doorways of La Recompensa, and I might be walking the landscape of an opium haze, which I recall fondly from when I regularly took the drug while under a doctor's care.

Dr. Morrell, now more recovered from the *volante* accident, sits in a chair by the doors leading to the gallery. He is a lanky man with the appearance of a grand portrait that has faded. I am surprised to see a man who has lived so long in the tropics look so pale, and recall that Madame Morrell said his stomach is a constant plague to his constitution. I hope his poor health is not an indication of what may be in store for us.

The children hurry to embrace me, as if they have known me since birth. I am so charmed by these little ones that for the first time, I wonder what it would be like to have a child of my own, though I quickly banish the thought. If childbearing did not kill me, caring for another while trying to tend to my own fragile health would be my undoing. Since my girlhood, Mother has counseled me that to become a wife and, as inevitably follows, a mother would destroy my delicate sensibilities and burden my artist's soul. I met this proclamation with a sullen heart at first, until I realized it granted me freedom to act as I wished with anyone I wished, knowing I could never possibly consummate a union. It would shatter my delicate sphere like glass.

Madame Morrell's song has ended, and when I rise from little five-year-old Carlito's kisses, the two young men standing at the fireplace clap their gloved hands, calling my attention to their eager gazes. Madame Morrell loops her arms through mine and Mary's, and escorts us across the room. We answer their deep bows with our curtsies.

"Don Manuel *y* Don Fernando Layas: *Bienvenidas a señoritas* Mary *y* Sophia Peabody *de* Massachusetts."

"*Encantada de conocerte,*" says Don Manuel.

"*Yo también,*" I say.

The brothers smile, and old Tekla leads the children in a round of applause. It is amusing how delightful they find my crude attempts at speaking Spanish. At my mother's instruction, I am fluent in some of the romance languages, so I will catch on quickly. I cannot help but hold the gaze of the younger brother, Don Fernando, whose dark eyes are lashed more beautifully than any female's, like black moons in a white night sky.

Madame Morrell has left us to welcome a neighboring family that has just arrived. Don Fernando and I continue to gaze at each other until Mary slides her arm around my waist and pulls me toward the dining room, where the cook, Tomás, has announced dinner.

The opium dream continues through the rest of the night.

While I am enchanted by these people, I am separate from them because I cannot understand all that is said. Madame Morrell is a patient and enthusiastic translator, and has done an admirable job weaving Mary and me into the conversations. I long for the day when I will be able to comprehend the words without her intercession, and I am hopeful it will come soon, because I already feel as if I have a small grasp of some of their often used words and phrases. While this separation of culture and language clearly makes Mary ill at ease, I find a certain power in it. It is obvious from Manuel's and especially Fernando's many glances and smiles that I am a novelty to them, a new species of flower they would like to pluck and study.

For all of the language confusion at dinner, afterward the company is quiet, and would prefer to listen to music than converse. The guests take turns at the piano, with and without singing, and I am at ease in the language of music, which we can all understand. When Fernando performs, his diffidence captivates me so that I long to sketch him. I will ask his permission, of course, but we must be in closer acquaintance before I do so. For most of the song he does not look at me, but at the climax it seems he has worked up enough courage to capture my gaze. I am glad the room is dimly lit, or I would be embarrassed at the flush I know infuses my cheeks.

Louisa, the Morrells' sixteen-year-old daughter, starts the dance while Madame Morrell plays, and Mary and I recline together to take in the spectacle. It is interesting that the Spanish decorum that prevents unmarried men and women from touching hands in public so delights in joining them in dancing. They waltz with the fluidity of ocean swells, and in spite of the sparest contact, great passion is conveyed in the motion. The noise of the piano and the dramatic atmosphere begin to destroy the peace in my head, however, so I retreat to a chair next to Dr. Morrell's at the window. I cannot be more shocked when I see Mary join in the dance at Manuel's and Louisa's urging, and I am both delighted and jealous to see her laughing, turning, and collecting their attention. Mary might not have a grasp of the language, but she certainly blooms to the music. If Mother knew she was dancing, and I was in proximity of such sound and exertion, she would faint. Finally, when Fernando escorts Mary in another waltz, I stand and walk outside to the gallery. I cannot endure the closeness of the room for another minute.

No one seems to notice I have left, and that is for the best. I have overexerted my good humors this evening, and will pay for it tomorrow. I stand at the railing and gaze out over the landscape, taking deep breaths from the flowers' exhalations and making mental portraits of the moon-stained mountains. In almost no time, I am transported to my inner world—a place where all my life I have retreated from infirmity of body and circumstance— and exist alone in Cuba as a small creature in a plain of many. The earth seems to pulse up through the foundations of the house to my feet, removing my separation from nature's soul and restoring me to balance. I am shaken when a deep voice in my ear breaks the spell.

"Ven conmigo."

I turn my head to see Don Fernando, a marble figure glowing in the luminous night. He gestures with his head, indicating that I am to follow him, and we creep to the other end of the gallery, where a tall shrub, almost as big as a tree, has grown to meet the house. He points to a lime-size reddish knob, one of many that hang from the shrub, and I turn my attention to the strange growth. After a few moments, the knob stirs and begins to open. The tightly clamped petals and coils of the flower begin to unroll, and it is as if she has thrown her arms and legs open wide to bathe in the moonlight. At her full bloom, the white flower is nearly as large as my face and emits a fragrance of delicate sweetness.

"Beautiful!" I say, tearing my eyes from it. Fernando is not looking at the flower, but at me. I step toward him, and seem to have frightened him, because he looks down at his boots.

"*Sí.*"

His shyness is endearing, and I would wrap my arms around him in gratitude and affection if I could for sharing this lovely spectacle of nature with me. All I can do, though, is offer, "*Gracias*, Don Fernando," to which he bows and escorts me back to the salon, where the party has begun to disperse.

Later that night, alone in my room, I write to Mother, describing the good company and the music, and the new things I am learning about myself in this place.

3

The weeks have settled into a pattern of the utmost sweetness and industry. The days are spent studying Spanish and instructing the children, and even some of the slaves, in drawing. We take our benches and sketch papers around the plantation, capturing nature's splendor and picnicking in the shade of the ceiba trees, which become my new fascination. God made the ceiba on a different scale from the rest of creation. Its grandeur begins at its roots, like thick horses' necks that reach from the ground to my low height, where they connect with their massive trunk, at odds with the delicate canopy of leaves. I cannot keep my hands from the knobby bark, and imagine the trees are old men, great and grumpy, but with a softness that allows us to poke fun at their unusual forms.

A hibiscus plant, with blossoms as red as a ruby, beckons me. I lean in to inhale, allowing its breath to fill my lungs. "My dear sister," I say. "Forgive me for plucking you for my amusement, and know you will be cherished while you perish tucked behind my ear."

The laughter of my companions calls my attention back to them.

"Mees Sofeea," says Carlito, "I fink ju make me waf." And he does "waf" and "waf" at every little thing I say, especially when I address the plants. Then he kisses me from one side of my face to the other, and laughs some more.

I hope Carlito never loses his joy, but I see how his father and mother are so plagued by their exploitation of the slaves, and my heart aches that this child will inherit such a legacy. I pray that even if he grows up in poverty, he never owns a single slave. I am certain slavery is what has made his father so ill.

It is ironic that Dr. Morrell has pledged to make me well when he so withers. He sits watching over us with his green eyes, his gaunt and erudite features a mask of intelligence and gallantry overlaid with such sadness that I cannot look on him for long. It is clear to me that to die in poverty away from this corrupt Eden would be better than to perish in wealth amid its contradictions. But how can I judge him? The moment I turn my back from a slave to the botanical abundance and luxurious bosom of La Recompensa, I find myself justifying my time here, indulging in its richness, philosophizing about the divine justice the slaves will eventually enjoy. Yet even as I turn from it, I feel the cold cloud of the institution shadowing every avenue and gallery.

In this place of my rehabilitation, these horrors can never

allow full rest. Mother begs it of me in her letters, but she cannot understand what we see. I promise her that I will try. After all, I have poisoned every inch of my body in an effort to eradicate my headaches: I have endured leeches and bloodletting; I have prayed until my knees bled; and I have traveled thousands of miles away from my home to a foreign land in search of a cure. I owe it to her to maintain my health.

Distractions help, and I am finding Fernando a welcome one.

Early one morning he asks whether Mary and I would like to ride with him. Mary is not the horsewoman that I am, and declines, but I accept with enthusiasm. I ride Rosillo every day, and having a companion more my age than little Eduardo will be pleasing. Eduardo will still accompany us, of course—Madame Morrell would not think it proper for Fernando and me to ride alone—and he will translate for us.

The slaves commend us to God as we pass on our mounts, and I feel sadness at their kindness. They are surely angels to endure the suffering they do, while always ready to offer us blessings in such heartfelt voices. I return their commendations and offer my thanks, and they too seem affected by my attention. Perhaps this small interaction can offer the slightest balm to their weary souls.

"*Muy amable*," says Fernando, gesturing from me to the slaves.

"*Amable*," I say, searching my mind for the translation.

Eduardo calls back to me. "Very kind."

I smile, and bow my head to Fernando in thanks.

We have reached a vista—one of many along the border of La Recompensa—that offers views grander than any I have seen on earth, and which I intend to commit to canvas in the future. I long to allow my heart to soar to the elevations of the mountains of San Marcos, but the slaves I saw on our way will not allow me a full appreciation of the moment. Fernando glances back at the slaves nearest us, toiling amid the coffee plants, and then back at me.

"*¿Es triste, no?*" he says with a furrowed brow.

I know *triste* in French is "sad," and I can see that is what he means by his face. I am surprised that the son of a planter would speak such a thing.

"*Triste*, sad."

"Sad," he says.

"*Sí*," I say.

"*No me gusta.*"

"He does not like it," says Eduardo, in a voice mature beyond his years. "I do not like it either. I want to go to America with you, Miss Sophia."

"I wish I could take you both with me," I say.

Eduardo translates, and Fernando gives me such a look of longing, I must turn away.

We ride to the trail nearest us and look back over La Recompensa like kings and queens, with the rising sun at our backs. A tiny bird slips from the foliage leading to the forest and looks as if she has been born of the palm leaves. I am transfixed by such an arrangement of greens, and she shows off by coming to rest on a flower of the most brilliant purple. Mr. Allston would be fixated by this rare shade of indigo in nature, and I commit it to memory to note it in my journal.

I hear Fernando ask Eduardo a question in Spanish, followed by his careful pronunciation. Then Fernando turns to me.

"You draw bird," Fernando says.

I delight in hearing my language in his voice, and the fact that he knows of my sketching talents.

"I draw Fernando," I say.

He laughs and shakes his head, waving me off.

I raise my eyebrow and nod. "*Sí*, Fernando. I draw you. After dinner tonight."

He looks at Eduardo. "*Cena?*"

"*Sí*, you will dine with us," I say to him. "And I will draw you."

Fernando picks a flower for my hair. On the way back from our ride, a fresh morning shower mists over us, turning the air alive with diamond droplets. Fernando worries that I will be upset to get wet, but to his delight I laugh and turn Rosillo in circles in the rain.

Fernando sits in profile against the whitewashed wall, fidgeting and uncomfortable in the humid room, while I begin to sketch him. After a short time, he covers his head with a napkin. Silly man—what is he doing?

Eduardo tells me that Fernando is embarrassed and does not wish to sit for a portrait any longer. I am about to protest when Louisa announces it is time for dancing. I am forced to abandon the dark eyes I have drawn—black orbs with lashes floating on the paper. I leave my sketch on the table and join the company. Fernando comes to my side and gives me a little nudge that sends me off balance and into a fit of giggles while he rights me. I pretend to chastise him.

I have grown fond of Fernando. I think of him when I wake, when I ride, and when I go to bed at night, and must admit that I feel lost in the hours between his visits. Mary often becomes frustrated with me because she must ever call me out of my fantasies while she attempts to speak to me of plantation matters. I offer my apologies—I am as surprised as she at what is awakening in me—but I cannot stop the wanderings of my imagination.

I feel the weight of someone's gaze and turn to see that Mary stares at me from across the room. Her brow is furrowed and her arms are crossed. She must have seen my flirtation with Fernando and disapproves. My impulse is to go and stand next to her, but something in me rebels. I am twenty-four years old and have every right to further my acquaintance with this man. I know it will never lead anywhere, so I might as well enjoy myself. I have nearly worked myself up to join the dancing when a low and ominous rumbling of thunder beckons us to the piazza. Over the mountain the sickle moon is obscured by clouds, and a sound begins—a rushing so distinct and terrifying, it seems as if biblical floodwaters will consume us. When she sees my fear, Madame Morrell tells me not to worry.

"Listen," she says. "The storm will not reach us. We can enjoy it from here."

"Pardon," says Manuel, who has joined Fernando tonight. He speaks to Dr. Morrell in Spanish, and when he and his brother separate to retrieve their hats and gloves, I see that they will go home to be safe. I am low in spirits now that Fernando is leaving. He sees and comes to me, bowing before me.

"*Buenas noches*, Sophia," he says, placing his hand over his heart.

He looks so distraught at departing that I hurry to where the withering hibiscus he plucked earlier adorns the mantel. I bring it to him and place it in his hands, allowing my fingers to caress the soft leather of his gloves. He pulls in his breath and hurries away, after his brother. When I turn back to the room, Mary's dark look chills my warmth. I stand straight, pick up my sketch papers, and retire to my chamber.

Without Fernando, I am unable to complete his sketch, so I attempt to record the bird we saw earlier. I want to show how it seemed born from the leaves, but with only the light of a candle, my eyes become weary, and my head begins to throb. I know I should stop drawing, but I am possessed, and do not sleep until the bird sketch is complete.

In the ensuing days, I am plagued with such headaches that I fear Madame Morrell will have to send a letter announcing my tragic death to Mother after all. My pain keeps me in my room, so that I am not able to take my morning ride, or speak with Manuel and Fernando on their now daily visits.

On a fresh morning without mist—the first in nearly a week when I have not woken with a headache—I think I will stay in my room and try to paint the bird using some of the oils Elizabeth sent, accompanied by a note from Mother with a thousand cautions about overexerting myself. It is a foolish venture, however, because the moment my hand touches the green to the canvas, my vision seems to explode, and I see only searing red everywhere I look.

Josepha becomes flustered when I am ill. She is like a doting mother, and in my delirium, I often mistake her for Mother until I note her slender form and her soft brown skin. Tekla abuses poor Josepha for her stupidity, but Josepha must be exhausted from caring for me and the house all day, and her son all night. The poor creature never gets a moment's peace. I try to give her rests, but this seems to upset her as much as Tekla's admonitions.

I wish I could rouse myself when I hear Fernando's voice in the hall. I think he elevates its usual quiet for my benefit, and I send Josepha to him with apologies for my ill health, and the hope to see him soon. She is back shortly with Louisa.

"Fernando wishes you to know," says Louisa, "that he has been practicing a song on the piano to play for your pleasure as soon as the noise does not vex you."

I am touched that he would do such a thing.

"Please send him my thanks and promises to rest so I am able to hear it as soon as possible."

Louisa leaves, and I think of Fernando with a growing thrill until I remember that I was about to write Mother a letter. When I see that I have no more writing paper, I creep into Mary's room to borrow a page. Her room is tidy and smells like fresh linen. Her dresses hang ordered and straight in the wardrobe, which has been left open to allow the air to flow. When I reach Mary's desk, I see that she must have had to abandon her own letter this morning in a hurry. The ink is not capped and the papers fan over the wood in disarray. I see a letter in another's hand peeking out, and after a quick glance over my shoulder to see that no one is nearby, I scan it to ascertain that Horace Mann—the widower who won Mary's heart back in Massachusetts, but who is taking agonizingly long to recognize it—has written her a letter as sterile as one would to a sister. I feel for Mary, who must endure this treatment. It is no wonder she seems suspicious and even jealous of the attentions Fernando pays me. I resolve to embrace Mary to comfort her the moment I see her.

As I retrieve a fresh page, the sight of my name scribbled on the letter she is writing to Mother draws my attention. It is difficult to control my rising anger as I take in the words: *A quivering tinderbox . . . one who cannot control her raptures . . . bears all she sees miraculously well . . . Continue to allow Elizabeth to share Sophia's Cuba letters with the public . . . will see to it that she marries no local planter.*

How dare she! A tinderbox! Marry a planter? And encouraging my mother to allow the public reading of my letters, which I did not know about when I poured out my effusive descriptions of Fernando and flowers and all manner of achingly lovely sights and sounds!

I do not care that Mary will know I read her letter, and scribble in my own handwriting that I do *not* appreciate the sharing of my private thoughts for every gossip to ponder; I am no tinderbox; I keep my sufferings to myself instead of plaguing my company with them; and I will *not* marry a Spaniard— though my hand trembles in rebellion of the very words I write.

I circle my addition to Mary's libelous scrap and sign it prominently so my mother will not miss my frustration, and Mary will see that I have read it.

Once I am back in my room, I summon Josepha to help me with my toilet and do my best to ignore the lingering ache that extends around my ears. I must appear tonight to ensure that Mary is not spreading her venom in this household where I am rehabilitating, learning about the world, and finding a key to a thing that has been locked inside me for so long it is almost frenzied to emerge. I begin to realize it is those around me who wish to suppress it, because they fear what will happen if I allow my full power to be realized. They have wanted my sterility to keep my passions at bay, and have even encouraged me in my infirmities because they wish to contain me. No more!

I take extra care with my preparations, and for that I am late to the table. When I enter, the men rise and the women bow their heads to me, though Mary will not meet my eyes. Josepha pushes my chair in behind me, and the family resumes dinner, though in a heavy silence. I wait for their inquiries after my health, but find the adult conversation—in French, for it is dinnertime— formal, distracted, and well outside of me.

The children are excited because on a previous night neighbors brought a lovely set of turtledoves, and Tomás fashioned a large cage for them out of rattans and cornstalks on the piazza. The female laid an egg, and the children are betting when it will hatch and whether they will be awake to see it. They imitate the lovely cooing sounds, which upon recollection I realize brought me some comfort during my infirmity. I mention this, but no one seems to care except Eduardo, who tells me how glad he is to have me at the table. The children beg to be dismissed early, and Madame Morrell surprises me by agreeing. Before Mary rises to join them, I place my napkin on the table.

"Mary, allow yourself some rest," I say. "I will mind the children, and you may return to your letters."

Her face becomes pale, and as I stand to walk to the piazza, I give her my iciest stare.

Outside, the Morrell children crowd with a group of slave children around a dove they have let out of the cage. They take turns passing her from one small hand to the next, with Josepha cautioning them from nearby. The dove's gentle nature and softness bring smiles to each face when she allows them to pet her.

I kneel next to Josepha's son, a tiny one of not four years old, who flits about with the eagerness of a hummingbird. He places his little brown hand on my arm and speaks rapid Spanish I cannot understand in words, but feel in my spirit. When the dove comes to him, Josepha crouches at his other side and places her hand on his back. He quiets while he holds the dove, and I think that I will write to Mother about the doves and the children, and how even the wiggliest of them understands when nature requires stillness. I will try not to mention Fernando, so I do not stoke the fires Mary has started.

I kiss little heads and stand to venture into the garden at night while Madame Morrell is not watching. Her cautions about the night fragrances harming one's elements are exhausting, especially when I feel as if I need the sweet aroma of the flowers to balance the poison from Mary's sphere. I am about to step off the piazza when I spot a feral cat watching the scene from the railing. As I shoo him off into the shadows, I cannot help but shiver at the thought that just inches away from such innocent pleasure lurks something dark, waiting to destroy it.

4

Silence has taught me something of its power.

Mary comes to me to ask my forgiveness, and while I had intended to make her suffer a bit longer, the combination of her repentance and the golden beams of sunset turning the very air of my room into a jeweled paradise dispel every ounce of ill will I held toward her.

Fernando and his brother, Manuel, have come, further lifting my mood. Fernando is delighted to see me in bloom, and presents me with a bellflower that I know I will paint. Then he sits at the piano and, after experimenting with various chords, begins to play a melody as pure and sweet as a dove's song, bringing as much pleasure to us in the room as the bird did to the children. We gather around him, and I think that music must be a way to enter holy conversation with one another and with God. When the piece ends, various groups of Morrells and neighbors draw together in quiet conversation, and Fernando approaches me at the piazza doors. I know I make a pretty scene for him, with the gentle night breeze stirring my lilac satin gown. It is the first of the dresses promised to me from Madame Morrell, and I have never worn so becoming a frock. I hold the bellflower and inhale its fragrance.

"*¿Te gusta la noche?*" Fernando says, while pointing out at the night.

"*Sí,*" I say.

"*¿Cabalgas conmigo?*" He makes a riding motion with his hands.

"Tonight?" I have never ridden in the night, and I think there has never been such a magical suggestion. I scan the room for Eduardo, and motion for him to join us.

"May we ride, Eduardo? Under the moon and the stars?"

He hurries to ask his father, who agrees with a nod of the head. Madame Morrell looks as if she would rather we did not, but Manuel and Louisa have heard, and will join us. It will be a night-riding party! I encourage Mary to come, and to my surprise she agrees. Within a half hour, we are galloping down the avenue toward the mountains. The ladies here do not wear bonnets, and my ringlets have fallen by the time we reach the border of La Recompensa, but I pay no heed. I feel as if I have no cares. Oh, to ride in the night; I am restored! I lean in to embrace the neck of Rosillo, and squeeze my eyes shut, inhaling the scent of his exertion mingled with the garden's intoxicating fragrance.

"Miss Sophia, look!" calls Eduardo, pointing up to the sky that seems to pass us as if the world were turning at double speed.

"Beautiful!" he says, pronouncing each syllable, and making us all laugh. Fernando and Manuel echo him, to our delight, and we begin calling out the English names for the celestial bodies while they imitate us. Mary smiles as never before. She is so much more at ease when her native tongue is being spoken.

We continue on, following our eager guide, Eduardo, and end up at the base of a cataract, gleaming in the night. By day the spray of this waterfall sparkles with the brilliance of jewels, but in the darkness the drops are not discernible; the water is one fluid, silvery being, pouring forth in a deluge. I drink in great gulps of air, inhaling its freshness, and entering communion with divinity itself.

There is heat at my side in the cool of the night, and it is Fernando. He allows his leg to rest against mine and leans in to me.

"You draw me again," he says.

"I draw you. *Mañana.*"

"*Sí,*" he whispers, so close to my ear that if I tilted toward him, his lips would be on it. I am about to do just such a thing when he withdraws from me into the shadows. I breathe in to quiet my throbbing heart, and spot a night-blooming cereus opening in the moon's light. Once she is in full splendor, I detach her from her vine with apologies to the stalk, and press her in the bosom of my bodice. As we ride back to La Recompensa, I feel her petals on my skin.

I am no woman of letters, but I did once write a poem. It is called "To the Unknown Yet Known," and addresses the lover I imagine waiting for me. Every once in a while, I am stirred by the shadowy form of a man who I feel was made for me, and I for him. It would terrify Mother to hear such a thing—for she more than any other perpetuates the idea that as a holy artist I must remain alone—but the vision is so strong and seems to come from outside my mind, rather than from within, that I feel I am being told some sacred truth. The lines I penned were born in this vision, and give ode to the artist who awaits me, and whose sweet music will accompany my painting in an artists' marriage of the highest order. It concludes with my heart's knowledge that all good I do is for him, and his for me, though we may never meet on this earth.

As the night ride concludes, I allow myself to ask my soul whether Don Fernando is the man I prophesied. I face this question that I have been suppressing because of outward circumstances, but I receive no answer or certainty. It is true I imagined a writer or fellow painter with whom I could live in blissful cocreation, but is not Fernando an artist with music? Does he not make melodies as striking as any collection of words on a page, and naturally, because he was not formally trained?

This thought troubles me, because I could never assimilate myself to plantation life. On the other hand, I cannot deny my love and my destiny. Doing so would deny the very will of God. Perhaps I am here with Mary to change these planters. Fernando is a willing man. He does not suppress his own hatred of the slave system, though he is chained to it by family connection. Perhaps I can help him break away from his own form of enslavement.

As we dismount our horses, I see Dr. and Madame Morrell framed in the light from the salon where they sit on the piazza.

She leans her head on his shoulder, and his cheek rests against her hair. Their arms are interwoven, and I see her laugh at something he has whispered to her. While I watch them, I feel a hollow longing, and wonder whether I will ever rest my head on the shoulder of a holy, earthly companion. For the first time perhaps ever, I begin to covet such a union more than I do my artistic solitude.

5

I do not know where the days go. I teach art to the Morrell and slave children, who make wonderful progress. We spend most nights dining with neighbors at La Recompensa or at other plantations, and almost always with the Layas brothers. My Spanish and Fernando's English improve, and we now converse without needing a translator. I painted the night flower, which left me with a three-day headache, and I still cannot finish Fernando's simple portrait. Almost as soon as I start, I am so weary that I begin to wonder whether it is immoral to draw him.

Mary has experienced a depression of spirits. She delights when Mr. Mann corresponds with her, but her light dims as she reads each line. I can only imagine that he continues to withhold his deepest self from her. If I ever have a lover, I will insist that he pen the most adoring letters.

Mary also spends far more time than is healthy with the

slaves. During a tour we were given of a nearby sugar plantation, we both became horrified by the treatment of those poor wretches, and were assured of the higher quality of slave life on coffee plantations. I can now see why Madame Morrell takes pride in their own slave society, having seen the miserable humanity present at the sugar mills. I have never witnessed such a terrible sight as those walking ghosts who populate the cane fields and tend to the hot cauldrons. How they do not take their own lives is beyond my comprehension, and must speak to the superiority of their tortured souls. After the tour, Mary went to the slave village at La Recompensa, and has wearied herself ever since assisting in planting their personal gardens, ministering in the hospital, and caring for the children. I do what I can, but I see that Mary's involvement with the slaves displeases Madame Morrell, and I wish to remain in her good graces.

How I do tire of Mother's continual reprimands regarding my interactions with men, when Elizabeth forms the most intimate acquaintances with every male within a twenty-mile radius of Boston. I expressed my outrage that Mother continued to allow Elizabeth to distribute my writings so widely and have them read at her salons. Mother should worry less about my violation by the men with whom I keep company, and more the continual exposure of my deepest thoughts and longings. When I speak my frustrations aloud, they are met with Mary's chastisement.

"Sophia, if you truly minded the public reading of the letters that you know Mother has allowed all these months we have been in Cuba, you would stop pouring your deepest thoughts and feelings so abundantly onto the pages."

"How ridiculous of you to say such a thing," I reply. "One would think that my frequent requests to Mother to keep the letters from Elizabeth would be respected and heeded."

"You only put such requests in writing to be able to say you asked, in case you are met with criticism."

"When you say such things, I am burdened to my soul to see how little you understand me."

Mary looks up at me over her letter and smiles, which I find infuriating. Josepha's interruption, however, saves Mary from the tongue-lashing I am about to give her.

"Don Fernando," says Josepha, with a gleam in her eye.

I follow her into my room, closing the door between my and Mary's chambers with some force to convey my feelings.

My cavalier is early, and I am still in dishabille. How it thrills me to know that he is just outside the door while I have not finished dressing, and my hair lies over my shoulders without any confinement.

When Josepha steps out, I am sure to stand just in the doorway where Fernando may catch a glimpse of a woman at rest, something he surely does not see very often. At the opening and closing of the door, I meet his eyes across the walkway, and see his pleasure when he takes note of my state. I will have to make him wait a little longer than usual for our ride, because seeing his face arranged in such a way has struck my artistic sensibilities, and I will be able to finally complete my sketch of him.

Upon my completion of the portrait, the vitality in my blood courses so that after dinner with the Layas brothers, when Louisa organizes the dancing, I join them! Mother will die when she finds out that I waltzed, and find out she will. I do not want to torment her, of course, but to illustrate how well I am. I wonder whether she or the parlors full of women whom she and Elizabeth entertain will believe that little sickly Sophichen engaged in such activity.

In my whole maiden life I have not been able to participate in such a whirlwind of sound and motion, since it usually bruises me to the core. But tonight, after completing a work of art and devouring a chicken dinner from Tomás, and drinking just a smidgen of the wine Madame Morrell so much enjoys, I find myself spinning in three-four time in the arms of Fernando. He leads me through moonbeams with such rolling sweetness I am borne back to the lift and fall of the ocean beneath my feet on the brig. The night breathes in through the doors, insulating me from too much heat and allowing me to drift along with the elegant music.

My head does not hurt a bit after the waltz, though Fernando seems much affected by having me in his arms. I have declined all of his previous offers to dance, so tonight marks something new for us. This shift emboldens me to fetch my completed portrait of him, and when I present it to everyone in the room, I am met with applause and appreciation. Old Tekla surprises me by throwing her broom, leaping into the air, and rushing to embrace me. I laugh with delight as she says, "Ave Maria *santísima*," first squeezing my cheeks and then Fernando's, whom she adores. He embraces the effusive slave with warmth, and I think the ancient woman may have just experienced her life's greatest joy.

I know she wants me to marry him—she has alluded to as much in her incessant ramblings, though I pretend not to understand her. I often dismiss her, but I cannot help but wonder whether Fernando and I are being drawn together for some higher good. When we nestle together watching the pair of turtledoves, just the way Madame Morrell and the doctor do, I find an ease and comfort such as I have never before known. Mary thinks it is her vocation to write about the slaves so the world knows their ills, but perhaps mine is to somehow transform the system through my marriage.

I look to Josepha, who melts into the shadows in the corner of the room, and see a smile on her lips, though her eyes remain dark. She nods at me in appreciation of the drawing and, even amid such joy and celebration, I find a lump in my throat that I do not understand.

6

With just months remaining before we are to leave La Recompensa, Fernando and I become bolder in our interactions, though we still do not dare speak of the future. Our souls settle into a conversation that does not need words, and as his intentions become clear to me, my heart further opens to him.

Then the atmosphere changes.

It begins with a day of blood.

One of Fernando's slaves is killed by a dog, and he and Manuel weep in our company and to the soothing of Madame Morrell, who cries with them. While we lament the terrible lot of the slaves, Tomás walks in even more stooped in the shoulders than usual, his dark face split in lines from his tears and holding a bloody bird. A cat got into the cage and mauled one of the doves, and the other is stained and shivering in the corner. The children come in just when the news is being delivered, and their wails bring us all to fresh tears.

Madame Morrell determines that it will be best to set the widowed dove free, and though we all mourn her leaving us, we know we have to remove her from the scene and further danger. Mary and I, accompanied by the Layas brothers and Josepha, take the Morrell children and Josepha's son to the edge of the forest below the mountains. I hold the quivering dove, who still has a spot of her mate's blood on her wing, and whisper to her that she will be all right. When we find the place I love to visit on horseback, and where it seems that the birds are born of the leaves, we begin our good-byes. I am moved to tears by the gentle caresses the children give her. We pass the dove to each of their little hands and she ends up back in my hold.

"Farewell, sweet dove," I say. "Go find your mate in the mountains of Elysium."

I hold her aloft and wait for her to take flight, but she is not inclined to leave us. I think her silhouette against the warmth of the jeweled sunset will make a lovely painting, and I commit the scene to memory so I can write about it to Mother, and describe the colors for Mr. Allston. For many minutes I hold the dove while the children encourage her to go. Josepha's son, however, nestles into his mother's skirts and is uncharacteristically silent. He watches with large, troubled eyes.

The dove paces along my arm, her small claws leaving little marks on my skin, but still she will not fly. I begin to think we might have to place her on a branch and leave her, when she suddenly cocks her head as if listening for something. The forest is noisy with birdcalls, so I do not know what she hears, but it sends her soaring heavenward into the pink-and-orange sky. Just as she takes flight, Josepha's son runs toward me, crying, "No! *¡Vuelva!*"

He tries to run to the forest to chase the dove, but Josepha lifts him into her embrace and holds him close.

"Shhh, shhh," she whispers, until he settles, and wraps his arms around her neck.

They turn to walk home, and as I watch their shadowed forms proceed, I feel a sudden despair. Fernando tries to talk with me, but I can hardly speak, and he respects my wish to remain silent.

I do not sleep well, and am plagued with a monstrous headache. Fernando looks out at me from his sketch all night, pleading, imploring, so that I have to turn him facedown on the bureau. When I do find a fitful sleep, the beggar girl haunts my dreams.

Perhaps I should take the mist as an omen and stay in bed all day.

When Josepha comes in to rouse me, I scold her and tell her to leave me alone because of my aching head. I must be harsh, because she starts and drops the tea tray to a great clanging assault of noise that sends me groaning under the pillows. My head feels as if it will split in two, and she whispers many apologies as she cleans the mess and exits the room.

I reach to flip the portrait of Fernando back over, and I am so moved and confused at the sight of his likeness that I again have to turn him facedown. For the first time since our arrival, I long for home. The air has changed, and it feels very wrong to be here.

Our imminent departure from La Recompensa that I have been lamenting suddenly cannot come soon enough.

I force myself out of bed and dress, opening the shutters and marveling over how the fog changes the vista. How strange and frightening it looks. It is as if the mountains sense some trouble, and wish to blot the earth from sight.

An hour later, the thunder of horses' hooves calls me from my room, and I join the household on the front porch. A man comes galloping up the avenue followed by many caballeros, and as soon as their presence is made known, Dr. Morrell springs to more life than I imagined him capable. He stands to his full height and meets the men outside. To my shock, he does not invite them in, but begins arguing with the leader by the fountain in such rapid Spanish I cannot keep up.

"What are they saying?" I ask.

Madame Morrell clutches her handkerchief to her face and starts weeping. She shakes her head, refusing to translate.

Tekla wails and runs to the back of the house before she can be stopped, and within moments, all is chaos.

"Mary, keep the children in their rooms!" says Madame Morrell.

Mary rushes to obey, but as we all reach the back gallery, the great cries issuing up from the slave yard call forth the Morrell children, and Mary is not strong enough to hold them indoors.

"Josepha!" I say, grabbing her by the arms, hoping she might be able to communicate something to me, but the shouting makes her eyes go wide in terror, and she takes off like a spooked mare.

I follow her to the gallery overlooking the yard, where her son and the other slave children stand naked for their morning baths. She scoops up her little boy while crying incoherently to the Negress in charge of the little ones. The old woman's face becomes stone—like the very face of the Son Himself upon bearing the world's sins. She corrals the children, who become serious as their mothers and fathers run from fields to pick them up. Mary enters the circle of the slaves, but is unable to understand the language. She looks up at me with imploring eyes. When I see the man and caballeros come around the side of the house with hands on swords and holding chains, I take a step backward to go to my room, knowing I cannot endure whatever is about to happen, but through the mist I feel a pair of large black eyes on me.

Josepha.

She needs help, but I do not know what to do. Any intervention on my part might make the situation worse.

Madame Morrell stumbles sobbing to the piazza, and several slave women clutching their children run to her, begging, pleading.

Don't let them. Don't let them take us away.

Madame Morrell does not say anything. She places her hands on their heads and weeps, but she gives them no other comfort. I look back at Josepha, and a sudden horror seizes my heart. I rush to Madame Morrell, clutching her arm.

"What is happening?" I demand.

"The doctor," she whispers. "The contract. He did not realize it would be now."

"What contract?"

"Twelve slaves. We owe Rodriguez twelve from the sale of the plantation, years ago."

"It is barbarous! He cannot separate the families."

"Don Pedro Rodriguez can do whatever he wants."

"Surely the doctor will find singles, then. He would not allow the separation of families."

"It is not his choice. He has tried."

Josepha cries out, joined by her son, as one of the rough gang members attempts to put her into shackles. She wrenches her arm away and launches up the stairs to where Madame Morrell and I stand.

"*¡Ayúdeme! Por favor! Por favor!*" Josepha begs for my help and I am paralyzed.

"*Bárbaros,*" is all I can manage through my tears. "I am sorry. *Lo siento.*"

I wrap my arms around Josepha with her boy between us, and feel the shudders of their bodies in my very soul. Mary joins me in embracing the pitiful creatures, and issuing blessings and apologies. Our words can certainly mean nothing to these women.

Over Josepha's shoulder I see a fierce man starting after her, until the doctor intervenes and holds up his hand. From what I understand, the doctor tells the men to stop, and that he will see to the rounding up. He issues several commands, and though the women in our arms do not stop crying, they all stiffen and realize that if they do not go calmly, they will be taught a lesson in front of their babes. One by one they quiet, until only the children's sniffles and those of us watching can be heard.

Twelve slaves are chosen that morning and are given a short

time to say their good-byes to their loved ones. Once they are corralled and subdued, Dr. Morrell goes to his room and closes the door. The Morrell children refuse to be sent away and watch the scene in despair. Josepha's boy has to be pried from his mother, who looks like the walking dead. She will no longer meet my eyes as she is led away. She cares nothing for this life she is condemned to live, and I say a silent, savage prayer that she will soon die to escape this hell.

A searing heat begins to burn at the base of my neck, and as the slaves are escorted away, my vision blurs and my entire skull feels on fire. I close my eyes and try to will the pain away, but it will not be gone, and I nearly faint. Eduardo and Mary help me to the parlor settee, where I lay my head in Mary's lap, and Eduardo collapses against Mary's skirts.

"I will never own them. Never. I hate it!" he cries.

His siblings enter the room and crowd around us, adding to Eduardo's proclamations and cursing the men who took away the slaves. No one thinks to curse Dr. Morrell, for whom I experience such hatred that it almost makes me well enough to storm into his room and pummel him with my fists. Mary embraces the children and allows their vehement expressions of anger before offering her balm.

"You will not forget what you have seen today," she says. "You will make sure this never happens again. I know you will."

"But what we intend to do when we grow up is no help to these people," says Louisa. "What about these slaves now?"

"I am confident in my soul that after this short sentence on earth they will experience a most blissful eternity in heaven."

"And they will live in heaven always and forever, and always?" asks little Carlito.

"Forever and ever," says Mary.

Forever and ever. I tell myself, over and over again. Forever and ever. It is all I can say to the children and myself for the remainder of the day, and I retire without dining that evening, wishing never again to set eyes on the doctor or his wife.

Forever and ever.

It is my night prayer, and my morning horse-riding chant, and my hymn for the remaining weeks on the plantation, when I cannot pick up a book to read or a pencil to sketch. It is the focus of my conversation with Fernando the few times I see him after that terrible day, when I make it clear to him that my heart is once again guarded, and he must cease to imagine any future with me in it. It is my consolation all the way to Havana in the rocking *volante*, and in the vice consul's parlor where we wait, and where I cannot look at the slave who serves us tea.

The days before we are to board the ship for home, we are taken to the residence of the Morrells' friends, Don and Madame Fernandez, wealthy collectors of art. Mary arranged the visit in an attempt to restore my spirits and rekindle my artistic sensibilities before we return to our mother. The events that preceded our departure have left me in poorer health than before we arrived, and Mary tries valiantly to lift me, in spite of the fact that she herself has become very pale and empty. How I wish we left a month earlier and were restored to Mother in our bloom. I will lament this also forever and ever.

It is difficult to rally enthusiasm to respond to the art on the walls, impressive though the collection is, until we come to the last piece. A dark canvas peeks from behind a midnight-colored curtain. I look to Madame Fernandez, and she nods. I draw back the curtain to behold a woman. She kneels in supplication, her eyes turned to God, her hands clasped in prayer. Even through the grime and neglect the painting has suffered, her pain oozes from the canvas and draws tears to my eyes.

"Mary Magdalene," says Madame Fernandez. "Humble sinner, begging for restoration."

A force within my artist's soul responds to what I see. It seems as if all human pain and weakness lie here in this fallen woman. All she has left is her prayer, and the area around her heart is the only place of light on the canvas.

"I do not know how we will fix her," says Madame Fernandez.

Near the wall where the Magdalene hangs is a table bearing a small bowl of aromatic oils. Someone must have been preparing to clean the painting just before we arrived. I am seized with an urge to touch Magdalene, but first I caress the slick surface of the oil and allow it to coat my fingertips. I lift my hand to the canvas and touch her praying hands with the oil, rubbing in a circular motion outward from the center. When I draw away, Madame Fernandez gasps. The effect is astonishing. Magdalene's figure has begun to emerge from the darkness. The light of God's touch transforms her in response to her prayer. I dip my fingers in the oil again, almost to my wrist, and bring them back to the canvas, wiping away the grime from the entire figure with a flat palm until she may be seen in her whole glorious, pitiful state, a sinner with nothing to offer, yet somehow more beautiful than the most elegant woman.

I can just imagine her prayer.

Change me, Lord, though I am unworthy.

Forever and ever.

They leave me in the room with the painting that afternoon while I contemplate her. Her crimson robes, her porcelain skin, her dazzling eyes. I hold my journal and find myself noting the colors, the details, the emotions the painting evokes. The air between us seems to ignite a small flame in my heart that I allowed to burn out these past weeks.

In my journal, Fernando wrote the sweetest note to me on our last night in each other's company. He gave homage to our friendship and committed to paper his hopes of a future meeting, though we both knew it would not be so.

I look back at the glimpse of light in the center of Magdalene, near her heart, and remember the beauty to be found even in sorrow—beauty as a result of transformation, an admission of weakness, and a total dependence on the Creator. Even in the darkest hour, our hearts can allow us to see the light.

A thought comes to me, and under Fernando's gentle script I scribble it.

Infeliz de mí! *I see with the eyes that are given me.*

A pledge to always find the good, the beauty, the hope, the light.

Forever and ever.

INTERLUDE

Spring 1864
Massachusetts

Cuba seems like forever ago from inside this carriage to Boston, where I lean against my Nathaniel and he against me. My time at La Recompensa shaped both of us, and I now believe we would not be here together if I had not gone. While I lived my visit, and for the first time opened to the possibility of love, Nathaniel relived it in his imagination when he read the *Cuba Journal*, just before our season of courtship. It is where he fell in love with my heart, where some of the characters in his novels were born, where the seeds for a number of his stories were planted, including Rappaccini and his poisonous daughter, and the dreadful likeness of Edward Randolph's frightening portrait.

I have not allowed myself to remember my stay in Cuba for many moons. Reading through the journal this morning, I could hardly believe these were events I lived. When I first arrived home, I buried the painful memories, and told myself I did so in the name of preserving the light and my own health on Mother's behalf, but now I recognize the truth: I was a coward.

Mary was a coward, too, but not for selfish reasons, like me. She often spoke of a novel she wanted to write about our experiences in Cuba, but she feared that it would hurt the Morrells and their children. Mary will wait until the last of them dies before making public the plantation stories that left their scars on us both.

My agitated husband settles against my shoulder, and I breathe in the aroma of his jacket that holds the smoke of pipes and hearths. Nathaniel believes the family hearth is the true heart of harmony in the world. He does all he can to preserve its sacred quiet, and attempts to suppress all disagreement there—a challenge with a damaged daughter like Una. We ride in peace for several miles, and I am just about to drift off from exhaustion of body and spirit when Nathaniel starts and sits up. He presses his breast pocket and reaches in, turning it inside out.

"No," he says.

"What is it?" I ask in the confusion of interrupted slumber.

He reaches into his side pockets, and groans as he leans forward, feeling in his pants.

"I forgot," he says. "We must turn back."

Dread fills me, for we have gone many miles. If we return to the Wayside, the children will be further disturbed. Nathaniel had to be helped to the carriage on Una's arm, while I consoled our little Rose. When we pulled away, I saw Una bury her face in the crook of her elbow, shuddering from her sobs. We cannot relive that scene.

"What is it?" I say. "I will have it sent to you. What can you need to go back for?"

"Longfellow," he mumbles. "I need it."

I think he has gone mad. Is he requesting the stuffed owl from the Old Manse that we named Longfellow after his old friend? A smile touches my lips, because I think for a moment that my husband has found his mischievous humor of old.

"You jest," I say, and start to again settle in, like a plump dove on a branch, but Nathaniel continues to fidget. I open my eyes and see that he is distressed.

"No, not the owl. I need something. It cannot . . . be sent."

My poor husband is near tears, and I stare at him for a long moment before I see that he will not be settled until we turn back. I lean out the window with great reluctance and command the driver to return to Concord.

Our emotions are all raw today, but again we are bound for Boston, and Mr. Pierce, and the train they will catch heading north.

I offered to go inside to retrieve Nathaniel's mysterious package, but he insisted on procuring it himself. I cried quietly, watching my aged love take halting steps back into the Wayside, half-bent from pain, trembling and weak, and reemerge, again needing Una's assistance to climb back into the carriage. His breast pocket bulged with whatever he had retrieved; I could see that he would not speak of it, and I knew not to ask.

Nathaniel's glassy eyes remain alert as we travel. He stares across time and mumbles about a fox. I want him to talk to me, because a dreadful thought is forming in my mind that this could be our last time together on earth. I swallow the lump in my throat and ask him, "What is this fox?"

My voice stirs him from his memories, and he reaches for my hand. I look down and see that our fingers have become gnarled and spotted. How can these be our hands that used to be so strong and soft, yet still fit together as if one were made to hold the other?

"Did I ever tell you about my fox?" he says.

"No, love, I do not think so. Tell me now."

"It is a sad story. I do not want to upset you."

"You know that I will find the light in the sadness."

"Yes," he says. "In the trip I made alone to New Hampshire, to Mount Washington as a young man, when I took your *Cuba Journal*, I met an ancient fox."

"The same mountains you will visit with Pierce?"

"Yes. But then I was a strapping lad, though incomplete because I had not yet learned the language of love from my dove."

I lift his hand to kiss it before placing it back on my lap. How I adore these moments when the stomach pains do not stab Nathaniel, and he is his old self.

"I saw he wanted to die," he continues. "I knew he wanted to do so alone, but I felt an urge to track him through the understory. His awareness of me impelled his forward progress, but he continued until he reached the crest of a fern-covered hill. He staggered, and then relinquished his power."

I am able to perfectly visualize this scene, and young Nathaniel in it. I could listen to him speak forever.

"He looked at me sideways where he dropped," continues my storyteller, "before placing his head on the fallen leaves. I approached slowly so as not to frighten him, though at that stage I imagined the fox feared nothing on this earth. Up close I could see signs of his many years. In all of my forest adventures, I had never seen an aged animal expiring from natural causes, and I was fascinated. White fur surrounded his face and crusted, milky eyes. His white legs and paws were scarred, and his toenails were broken and jagged. Ribs protruded through his flimsy, sagging skin."

"This is sad," I say. "But it was good of you to stay with him so he was not alone when he died. No creature should be alone at the final crossing."

I squeeze Nathaniel's hand a little tighter. He clears his throat and resumes his tale.

"I do not know if that thought occurred to me at that time, but it seemed important that I sit near him and wave away the flies. I imagined that the fox was grateful, and I followed his gaze to the vista. We were two small mammals in a vast landscape."

"How very transcendental of you, my sweet," I tease.

"It was not nature that moved me; you know I am no transcendentalist. It was the feeling of smallness, of isolation, that I craved. How I wish I felt at home in the crowds of Salem, the salons of Boston. Still, when I am in society, I feel their need and hopes on me like an actual physical pressure. They have always wanted more from me than I am willing to give them, but you know that without my having to say it."

I do. I also sense that sometimes even I am one of this society whom he longs to escape. Company is a burden to those at home in the solitude of their souls.

"Over the valley, a hawk chased a crow away from her nest, and pecked at the scoundrel until it flew away. The hawk cried and circled high above, feathers spread like fingers, soaring in a great arc. She glided close to her nest and then away again, as if pulled in two directions. How she must have relished her moment of freedom. But she swiftly returned to the nest where she was tethered. I remembered wondering if my father felt that way at sea. Pulled to the water while on land, to land while on water, never at home. That is my inheritance—a division of longing."

Nathaniel's seafaring father died of fever after an ocean crossing when Nathaniel still had his milk teeth, and his mother mourned the man all her days. The atmosphere of sorrow in which Nathaniel was raised with his two sisters left a permanent darkness within him. His mother's grief raised a black veil over Nathaniel's soul that he could never fully remove. I shudder at the thought of widowhood, and nestle closer to my husband. He continues speaking, seeming to gain strength from his storytelling.

"The fox made a noise like a sigh, and I allowed the faces of my brethren to recede. I looked at the old one at my side when he lifted his head. I followed his gaze to the crooked branch that extended over the ravine, where a vulture joined two others. They stared at the fox, who had put his head back down, but turned his eye to me. I gazed into its black recesses for such a time that the shadows moved, the sun made its passage. I waited for the fox's signal until suddenly there was certainty in my mind that did not seem to come from me. I pulled my knife from my pocket and sliced a frond of fern to place over his body, a green shroud, and parted the leaves around his heart. I stood over him, drew the arrow from my pack, threaded it in my bow, and shot. The red stained his white fur and spilled to the ground. The hawk again took flight."

I rub Nathaniel's wrinkled hand, which put the poor fox from his misery all those years ago. How sad and beautiful it is that our souls are all connected here in this carriage, where time and space seem not to exist.

Soon Nathaniel is resting on my shoulder, exhausted from illness and the journey, but still unable to sleep. I cannot help but stare with fascination at our old hands threaded together, where one cannot be distinguished from the other.

I imagine mixing a dab of paint on a palette to match our flesh. A drop of lead white, a touch of yellow ocher, a hint of crimson swirled together and spread over our skin to transform us into our young selves. I see it with my mind's eye, and I am borne back to our carriage ride to Concord after our wedding, and then further back, to the days of our prolonged courtship, when I feared we would never truly become one.

7

Autumn 1837
Salem, Massachusetts

As night falls, I am just about to close a volume of Keats's "Endymion," a noble and evocative poem of a moon goddess in love with a mortal man who journeys through worlds and underworlds in search of love, only to end up back with her. I am hoping the lovers will step from the pages of the book and into my dreams, when I feel Elizabeth's heavy step as she lumbers up the stairs. She thrusts my door open and lets it hit the wall. I flinch and grasp my head.

"Must you make so much noise?" I groan from the hammock I have had Father suspend from the ceiling. As silly as the contraption looks in our Salem home, I could not sleep any other way after Cuba. My head pains continue to plague me, and since my youngest brother, Wellington, has died of yellow fever, I find it hard to go through the motions of living, and spend many hours in this hammock.

"Hush, hush," she says, breathless with excitement, her face glowing like a happy specter from the candle she carries. "You must come downstairs."

"Why?"

"Because a man who makes Lord Byron look plain as paste sits in our parlor, flanked by his two dour sisters."

Elizabeth has a tendency to exaggerate when her intellect is aroused. I am doubtful.

"It is the reclusive writer," she continues. "The mysterious one who penned those intensely fascinating *Twice-Told Tales*. You know, the book he was kind enough to inscribe to me after I wrote a letter to him praising his fresh talent?"

My memory is stirred, but my attention is not engaged. If I were to meet every man of learning Elizabeth wrote to in praise and invited to our parlor, I would never cease climbing up and down the stairs. Wordsworth, Emerson, Channing, Alcott— Elizabeth's adoration of these men borders on idolatry, though when she finds out they are just men, she is always disappointed. I suppose she needs a replacement for Alcott, now that they have had a falling-out.

"He would be very intrigued by you, Sophy," she continues. "He would see you as a kindred soul, an artist of high sensitivity who must withdraw from society."

Elizabeth's flattery piques my interest, but for practical reasons I cannot meet this so-called "kindred soul," for I am already in my sleeping gown, and my hair is unpinned. I am stabbed with a sudden remembrance of Don Fernando outside my doorway at La Recompensa before our morning ride, and I fall back in my hammock and insist that Elizabeth leave me in peace.

"Give him my apologies and promises of a future liaison," I say, "but I am not fit for visitors tonight."

Elizabeth stares at me for a moment before nodding in agreement, and taking care to close the door before returning to Lord Byron's handsomer peer.

I blow out my candle and attempt to sleep, but there is no ignoring the low timbre of the man's voice just below me, climbing the staircase and reaching around the door into my room. When sleep finally finds me, his voice is my escort in my dreams, and I think it is the very voice of Endymion himself. It is as if not five minutes passes when I awaken, and feel a longing to meet this writer. I alight from my hammock so swiftly I see stars, and hurry to the top of the stairs, where I listen for his voice. All that meets me is the silence of a slumbering house.

Since returning from Cuba two years ago, I have the disembodied sensation of having left my soul in a foreign land, and I fear she will never again find me.

I lift my pencils and brushes a dozen times a day, but I am soon trembling so that I cannot make a straight line, let alone an original piece inspired by a place I am trying to forget. I have cried many tears over Don Fernando and the wretched state of the slaves in Cuba, and as much as I try to outrun my memories, my letters—bound and published by Elizabeth as the *Cuba Journal*—

have been read so widely that I must recount the scenes over and over again. I attempt to steer the conversation to the foliage, the mountains, the magical aroma of the blooms, and the moonlit horseback rides, but people want to hear of only two topics: slavery and romance.

In addition to that frustration, Wellington's loss to our family, particularly to Mother, has darkened our spirits. My youngest brother was my little pet. It is true that he struggled to find discipline, but just as he discovered his calling—working like Father in medicine—his life was stolen from him. The yellow fever epidemic in New Orleans needed physicians, and Wellington felt called to study there and minister to patients. My brother George had visited him, and wrote that Welly worked tirelessly with the sick, thinking he was somehow immune because of his certainty that he had realized his vocation, and the many patients he had seen back to health. George wrote that it appeared an autopsy Welly had performed led to his infection. Four days after he stuck his gloveless hands in an infected corpse, Wellington was dead.

George—my fellow invalid—calls to me from across the hall, as I am about to make a rare descent to sit at the breakfast table. I am feeling well this morning, even after such a poor sleep, and want to give Mother the comfort of the company of her healthy, living children. Before I join her downstairs, I stop at George's room and lean in the doorway. I force a smile, but it is difficult to look at my ailing brother. George is just twenty-four and the most promising of my three younger brothers, but fate has played a cruel joke on him by inflicting him with tuberculosis of the spine.

This once strapping lad is now pale and gaunt, and is recently confined to his bed because his legs no longer support him. He bears his pain like a saint, and almost never complains. I could learn a lesson or two from him.

"Have you increased your morphine, my dear?" I ask as he winces from a cough, and attempts to adjust his large frame in the small waterbed my father had made to prevent sores.

I cross the room and sit on the chair next to him, sliding my arms under his back and helping him shift onto his side. He tries to turn his head away when he coughs, but he is too weak, and I am hit with the wind of his wet, rancid breath. I draw back, and he apologizes as soon as the coughing ceases.

"Do not worry," I say, pushing his thick, dark hair off his clammy forehead. "At least the air came from your upper region instead of your lower."

He starts to laugh at my vulgarity, and begins another fit. This time I am able to reach under him and fluff his pillow so he is more elevated, which seems to bring him some ease.

The morphine drops lie on his bedside table. I know he is trying to make Father's prescriptions for him last, but he is rationing too meagerly and not getting the full relief that is at his fingertips. I lift the bottle and shiver at my wish to ingest it, but I have had my daily dose, and force myself to pour his. I assist George in drinking from a spoon until it is empty, and the effect comes quickly. I feel my own shoulders relax as I witness his visible relief.

"Thank you, Sophy," he whispers, and closes his eyes. He is soon breathing deeply and regularly, but I am unable to tear myself away.

Another brother will soon be gone. I will have no fellow invalid with whom to yell jokes back and forth across the hallway, no one sicker than me, no man in my life to tease and converse with me. My sisters are so concerned with shaping and educating me that our relationship is often tedious. My other brother, Nat, is preoccupied with his new wife and young babe, as he should be, and has little to do with me. Father cares for me in his strange, quiet way when he is home, but must work as much as possible. George is my small island of love. I do not want to start mourning him before he is gone, but I cannot help it.

I stare at him a moment longer before I am impelled to step into my room for my sketch pad. I wipe my tears with the back of my arm, and once again sit in the chair next to George. Without a thought or prayer, I begin to move my pencil across the paper, and soon, for the first time in months, I have completed a portrait. I look from it to him and know I will use this to create a model—a bas-relief—of my brother that we may have to look on even after he has left us.

Here is a man who is truly ill—a young man who will predecease his parents and siblings. While he lies dying of tuberculosis, I recline in my hammock, acting as if I will die from aches in the head. My shame burns until I can no longer bear to reflect upon it, and I leave George's bedside.

8

Father and I sit next to each other at the table in my room, our heads bathed in candlelight, bent over my illustrations of Cuban flora. He thinks I should try my hand at medical illustration, but the mere thought of such technical work and constant deadlines makes my head ache. I push my knuckles into my temples, and he looks at me with a frown.

"Have you had your doses today?" he asks.

I am confident he has not inventoried his morphine supply, and I wish to lie so I may get more. Father may be intelligent enough to be a doctor, but his incompetence with numbers is the cause of our poverty. I cannot hate him for it, though. He allows his wife and daughters freedoms of education and employment other men would not tolerate, either because he supports it or is too tired to argue it, and he is ever at work, attempting to seek a cure for my condition. My thoughts linger in the fantasy of a morphine haze, but I banish them. If I consume more, George will have less.

I nod my head to indicate that my allowance has been met, and the candle nearest the book blows out from my sigh.

"Curculios," I say, relighting it and turning pages until I find my beetle sketch. "Cuban fireflies. They light up the night as strong as any candle, and are kept in little carved gourds. Enchanting, really."

"Such an exotic garden of strangeness," he says. "Were the beetles poisonous? Any of the flowers? Was there anything that could have been used to help in your cure if the doctor had not been so consumed by his own ailments of body and situation?"

Before I can reply, Elizabeth enters the room.

"Pardon my interruption," she says, "but I wish you both would come into the parlor. Mother is looking after George, and Mary is at a dinner, and I need assistance."

"Why?" says Father. He has a low tolerance for being directed by my sister.

Elizabeth steps forward and closes the door until it is almost shut. "Because Mr. Hawthorne and his sisters are downstairs, and drawing conversation from them is like dropping a bucket in a well of unfathomable depths, and only getting little splashes of water."

"I do not believe you have ever been at a loss for words," I say.

My father exhales a small laugh.

Elizabeth narrows her eyes. "No need for cheekiness, Sophy. I really do need your help. The sisters are as bad as, if not worse than, the awkward brother between them. They clutch his arms for dear life, as if they fear they will drown without hanging on. I can see him physically working up the courage to utter his thoughts, but I do not think he has the capacity for small talk. All I have been able to extract thus far is a short speech about how hard it is to really peer beneath the veil of the soul of one's acquaintances to understand their true motives."

What a thing to say. I wonder if he has read Shelley, who also reflects on the veil of the soul. For a moment, I consider going down with Elizabeth.

"I thought he might be questioning my motives in inviting him," she continues, "but when I began to stammer about how I admire his work, and that I only ask him over to further understand his process, he became very red in the face and worried that he had insulted me. I assured him he did not, but it would be nice to have another soul to assist me in conversation."

I feel for Elizabeth, but not enough to disturb myself. The invisible vise that plagues my brain is beginning to tighten.

"Why do you continue to invite him?" says Father.

"Because I admire him."

"She loves him," I say.

"Enough impertinence," says Elizabeth. "I do not love him— though he is a fascinating man."

"And by fascinating you mean handsomer than Byron," I say. "Good looks make up for many deficits."

"His looks have no bearing on the potential I see in him as a writer, and how I might further his career and reputation through publication and review."

"Your motives sound very pure," says Father, standing and giving me a pat on the hand. "I will assist you only until I feel uncomfortable, which will no doubt be very soon, and then you must alone deal with the consequences of continuously inviting a man to our parlor who is so ill at ease in his own comely skin."

"Thank you," says Elizabeth, hurrying him out of the room without giving me a backward glance.

I stand and creep to the doorway, where I hear Father say, "Here is the writer of whom my daughter speaks so highly," followed by an incoherent mumbling that must emanate from the writer himself. My curiosity is piqued, but not enough to lure me downstairs. Perhaps I will venture into the parlor on Mr. Hawthorne's next visit, which will no doubt occur very soon.

Elizabeth can scarcely go two sentences without mentioning Hawthorne's latest story, the review she printed for him, the way she will help him publish future works. She is forever putting his writings in my hands, and I can see why. Hawthorne's *Twice-Told Tales* has an appeal that I have not found in the work of his contemporaries. He is able to capture some sacred truth about solitude and how it corrupts, though it is inescapable and even desirable. His musings on generational sin are also intriguing, and his strength lies in his pathos.

As an influential and respected publisher and academic, Elizabeth has many friends in many circles, and when she believes in a person, she will elevate him to the highest earthly stature. Her loyalty is admirable, and in this case warranted, though I fear for her disappointment. Mary has told me that Hawthorne has not yet gotten over his former love, a society girl and senator's daughter named Mary Silsbee.

Throughout the winter, I continue to work on the bas-relief of George that he claims is far too handsome to represent him, and which brings much delight to my family, but I still have the feeling of being spiritless. Elizabeth has negotiated the sale of a copy I made of Allston's painting of *Jessica and Lorenzo* for a sum of one hundred twenty-five dollars, which releases me of all guilt for not teaching in my family's schools to earn my keep, but which burdens me with a certain level of recognition among Salem's cognoscenti, who press me to create more. My artistic soul feels that burden acutely, and recoils.

The calendar arrival of spring has not yet displaced winter, and as I sit at my window watching the stubborn piles of snow melt in the first pulse of vernal light, and the cardinals leaping through bare branches, I pray that I may awaken with the season of renewal. How I long to feel the rapture again. How I ache to feel the euphoria from nature permeate my soul. Will I ever again emerge from this wasteland?

My musings are interrupted when I behold a dark figure against the white. He is tall, and his top hat makes him seem more so. He walks with a strange, hesitant gait, almost as if he must coerce his feet to do his bidding. An impressive black cloak moves around him, and he looks like he would be more at home in the night than in the brightness of day. When he draws near the house, he pauses and looks up at my window, the light illuminating his pale face and chestnut hair that is long on his collar.

Nathaniel Hawthorne.

His eyes meet mine and hold my gaze for what must be only seconds, but when I draw back from the window and note the heat on my brow, it is as if I have been sitting at a fireside for many hours. I drop onto my sewing chair and glance around the room, my little sanctuary. My paints rest gaily on the easel; my artwork leans against walls and furniture; my books lie atop one another on desktops and bureaus. My eyes find a paper sticking out from the volume of Shelley I had been reading, and I reach for it. I know this paper—it is my poem "To the Unknown Yet Known." A voice in my head tells me that my soul knew something that I did not when I wrote of my love, a man of letters I conjured, the shadowy figure of an artist, the only man who would do for a fellow creative like me.

I hear the front door open downstairs, and Elizabeth's enthusiastic greeting of Hawthorne, and in spite of the dread I feel about leaving my room, in spite of what I suspect of my sister's feelings for the writer, I cannot dress quickly enough.

I wait on the staircase for many minutes, listening for his deep voice, his bashful laugh. I clutch the banister and talk myself into and out of entering the parlor a half dozen times. My white dress looked so bright and pleasant in my room, but now it seems too plain. Since leaving Cuba, my brown hair has lost some of its auburn tint. It is more becoming worn down, where one may still see hints of the redness, but it would not be proper to appear in such relaxed arrangement, so I have pinned it up and away from my face. But is my skin too sallow after a long winter spent indoors? I pinch my cheeks and bite my lips, willing color into my face, when I hear him speak.

"Oh, no, I have burned it all."

Elizabeth gasps.

"Truly," he continues. "I cannot bear anyone to read my past work. I have even tried to find and destroy as many copies as I can of my first novel, *Fanshawe*. It embarrasses me."

"Shame on you," says Elizabeth. "When future scholars want to see the progression of your style, they will have no juvenilia to aid their understanding. The maturation of the artist as writer is its own story. Would you deprive posterity?"

Again I hear his low laugh. He is modest—a rare trait in a man of letters.

"You flatter me, Miss Peabody. I am quite sure no future scholar will ever seek me. If she did, all she would find is a cheerless room atop my mother's house, where I sat at a stiff desk burning my inadequate word creations."

I can bear it no longer, and force one foot at a time down the staircase and into the room.

He sits on the sofa while Elizabeth stands at the fireplace. When I enter, Hawthorne's eyes meet mine, and he rises. By the holy angels, I feel my soul at once aflame and reaching through my breast toward him. I falter, and he is at my arm, leading me to the sofa. I try to ignore the heat—the fire of our first joining—and lean back once I am seated. I tear my eyes from his to look at Elizabeth, and I see a pain in her face that makes me wish I had stayed in my room. She has no color, and her brow is furrowed. For once it would seem that she is at a loss for words. Hawthorne, however, is animated.

"You must be Sophia," he says.

I gaze at Elizabeth a moment longer, and then turn back to him.

It is hard to find my breath. He stares so intensely from his dark hazel eyes under his dark brow, beneath his dark brown hair. Everything about him is dark, but not dismally so—deeply so, like the most priceless gem. I slide away from him a bit and I am happy to hear my own voice reply in the affirmative.

"Elizabeth has told me so much about you—your art. Your visceral response to creation. Your need for solitude."

"I do need it," I say. "Solitude."

Oh, how stupid I sound!

He does not appear to have noticed.

"Do you find that even when you are in the company of others," he says, "even in crowded rooms, you exist separately? And no matter how you try to join in, you are aware that you never will belong?"

"I am sure Sophia does not feel such a way," says Elizabeth. "She is quite gay in company, but wears herself out with her extreme sociability."

Elizabeth is bitter, and I understand why. It is as if she no longer exists for him. Still, it is not appropriate for her to speak for me.

"I must disagree," I say, not looking at her. "While I try always to be polite and find commonalities while in society, as an artist I often reserve in half my mind a place of retreat from my surroundings. It is there where my soul takes notes for future expression, which I think of as my *innere*—the German word for 'inner.'"

Mr. Hawthorne closes his eyes and nods.

"What a perfect word for it," he says, half to himself, before lighting his face with a smile.

Oh, I have never seen such a transformation on a face! It occurs to me that I could live my whole life trying to illuminate this dark face.

But no! What am I thinking? I am seized by fear and remorse. I am murdering my sister. Though Elizabeth has invited me countless times, she could not have wanted this. She would never have thought that I, the virgin artist, and he, the reclusive writer, would have so immediate and strong a response to each other.

"I apologize, but I have overexerted myself," I say, standing with haste. "Elizabeth has been asking me to meet you for so long, I just had to, but now I must go."

I look back at my sister, who seems to have softened in my agitation. She even makes a move to help me, saint that she is. I wave her off.

"No, no, Elizabeth, you stay with your guest. I hope to see you again, Mr. Hawthorne; good day."

I hurry up the stairs and past George's door, though he calls to me. When I am again in the safety of my room, I close the door and stumble over to my hammock, where I cannot control my tears. My sphere has never been so disturbed by another's as it is now, and I know that Hawthorne must feel the same way.

What can Elizabeth think, having witnessed such an exchange? Will she ever again invite me to sit with them? I know that, try as I will to fight it, I crave another drink at this well.

9

In the ensuing days, I paint with a fever that has not possessed me in many moons.

Elizabeth comes often to my door and watches without entering, or commenting on my exertion. I cannot face her, and what would I say if I could? *Yes, Elizabeth, fate drew me down the stairs to meet the man to whom my soul may converse without language? Destiny spoke through your lips to bring him to me in an artistic partnership of the loftiest proportions?*

No, I will not face her. I will only paint. I must indulge the impulse while it resides within me. I will deal with the consequences later.

Watercolor after watercolor comes into bloom on my easel, and the paintings plant themselves around the circumference of my room, covering old copied canvases. Butterflies emerge from chrysalises; exotic Cuban plants open; birds take flight. The only interruptions I allow are George's requests for company. I carry my paintings to his room, curl up with him in his bed, and tell him stories about Cuba that inspired my art.

"Don Fernando used to collect butterflies for me," I say, attempting to distract myself and the household from the disturbance Mr. Hawthorne has introduced.

"Did you love him?" George asks.

"I love something in everyone."

"I do not mean his humanity, Sophy. I mean, did you love *him*?"

The dying want the truth of the heart. I cannot fool George; nor—I realize—should I. I tell him all the things I keep locked inside that I would not dare mention to others, though I do hold back my feelings about Nathaniel Hawthorne. Hearing that I have loved before seems to bring George some residual joy, since he knows he will never love again.

"Have you ever loved anyone?" I ask.

A smile settles on his dry lips and tears slide from his eyes, which look far away from this room to another time and place. I wipe his face with my fingers and hold his hand in silence.

Oh, how short life is! How fleeting. Why would we ever deny love, even if it has only minutes to bring us peace and pleasure? Who are we to turn away from the very offering of the angels? Perhaps we are put here on earth to be glimpses of heaven to one another, partners to lead one another home.

A touch of watercolor from my fingertips is on George's hollow cheek, and I stare at it, wishing with all my soul that I could paint him to new life.

The interactions of the misses Peabody and that of Mr. Nathaniel Hawthorne increase in person and in writing.

If he cannot be here in form, he sends separate letters to Elizabeth and to me. At first we read the epistles aloud to each other. We make a show of praising the other in her absence or presence. We have never flattered each other so much in all our lives. But it is not long before we plot and scheme to intercept the mail before the other sees it. How we pout when Hawthorne's even, deliberate script is not addressed to she who first finds it! How we torture each other with his words, and even wave off the other sister, pretending she would not get this or that bit meant only for the reader.

And when he comes to our home!

One night, after Father has retired early with his books, and we women sit around the fireside darning stockings, writing letters, and reading, a timid knock interrupts us. Nathaniel and his sisters, Elizabeth (called Ebe) and Louisa, come in like a trio of ghosts and settle on the settee, staring out from large dark eyes like barn owls. How altered he is in their company! How reserved! They strike me as so odd that I have to turn my head away and pretend a coughing fit to stifle my giggles. Mary is able to cover for my lack of decorum by speaking first.

"Elizabeth tells me she first thought Ebe had penned *Twice-Told Tales*."

"It is true," says Elizabeth. "We women must often publish anonymously, as *Twice-Told Tales* was, and the stories have such a delicate and sensitive understanding of humanity that when I heard a Hawthorne penned them, I assumed it was Ebe or Louisa."

"It could never be me," says Louisa in a small voice. "Natty's talent far surpasses anything I could attempt."

Louisa gazes at Nathaniel with adoration, and he gives her a squeeze on the arm, which moves me, and makes me long for his hand on my arm.

"Nonsense," says Ebe. "It is your infirmity that prevents you, not lack of talent in any subject."

"Are you one who suffers in health?" asks Mother, looking up from her mending. She should have been a nurse, so apt she is to care for others.

"I am," says Louisa. "I am a great nuisance to my family."

"No," says Nathaniel.

"You are a great gift to us," says Ebe.

"As Sophy is to this household," says Mother.

Ebe ignores her comment and continues. "Louisa has a gentle spirit, welcome in our house of shadow dwellers."

"You are a family of moon people," I say, and immediately regret speaking such nonsense in a mixed crowd. If it were only Nathaniel, Elizabeth, and me, he would encourage my nature-inspired metaphors, but I realize he will not say a thing with so many around us. It is as if each person adds a weight to his chest, preventing him from getting a word past his lips.

Ebe regards me with suspicion. Elizabeth seems satisfied that I have made a fool of myself. Louisa smiles blandly, and Mary looks on with pity. It is Mother who rescues me.

"My little Sophichen," she says. "Life is art to her. Nature is her sister. Sophy has come to know the world through the example of the seasons, the earth, and the stars. I never properly noticed flowers until Sophy showed me how to view them."

Nathaniel gazes at me across the room, and though he does not speak, I feel his approval pulsing forth. All shame leaves me, as I know that my message and intent have reached the only recipient whom I care to impress.

When Nathaniel and his sisters leave that night, Ebe gives a polite good-bye to the room without individually acknowledging me, Louisa surprises me with an awkward embrace in the doorway, and Nathaniel, after voicing his quiet thanks and good-nights to my sisters and mother, dares to reach for my hand and bow to me.

In the coming weeks, my relief is great when Nathaniel ventures to our parlor without his siblings, though it feels like a feat of acrobatics with Elizabeth present. I imagine myself outside these scenes looking in at the comedic chorus. We each have our own motives, and it is clear to me that *affection* has been born between Nathaniel and me, and *respect* is what exists between him and Elizabeth. Elizabeth's stubborn will keeps Nathaniel and me from being able to talk alone, and I must pretend that is all right with me. When a nagging inner voice tells me that it is not stubborn will, but love that makes Elizabeth behave as she does, I ignore it.

On Nathaniel's most recent visit, we are discussing the merits of various art forms, and those best suited to which sex. Nathaniel believes that painting is the purest form, and praises me for my celestial occupation, much to Elizabeth's aggravation.

"Is not writing a sublime occupation?" I say. "I admire yours greatly."

"No, writing is drudgery, and says too much about the author," he says. "Expression without words, especially through painting, is so much more powerful than the limiting scribbles on the page. It allows the removal of the artist so the onlooker may contemplate without distraction. It is like music."

"I agree to an extent," says Elizabeth. "One cannot help but wonder about the writer when reading his or her words. They seem to reveal the soul in an especially intimate way."

"Which is why women should protect themselves from such exposure, and stay far away from writing," he says.

"But some of the finest writing I have recently seen has come from the pens of women," I say. "My own sister Elizabeth is a fine writer. Would you have her pen run dry in the name of so-called propriety?"

He smiles that brilliant smile.

"I do not mean to insinuate that a woman is not as skilled as a male writer—quite the contrary. It is a woman's special powers of observation and emotion that leave her more exposed than male writers to inspection. If my daughter or my . . . wife . . . wanted to write, I would ask her if she was ready for such public scrutiny. You yourself, Sophia, have said that the notoriety your paintings bring to you burdens your artistic soul. It is merely something to consider."

"I am not the only writer," says Elizabeth, with enough force in her voice to fell Goliath. "Sophy is quite the author herself."

I glare at her. I know she is referring to the *Cuba Journal* and

I am not ready for Nathaniel to read it. A man of his reserve would faint from my effusions, and the passages on Don Fernando alone would have him running from our parlor, never to return.

"Is she?" he asks.

"No," I say. "Only letters, which are not meant for public reading."

"Oh, but they have been widely read," says Elizabeth, relentless wench.

"Really," he says, turning to me. "How have I not seen them?"

"I published them," says Elizabeth.

"Against my will," I say, assuming my straightest posture.

"Oh, Sophy," continues Elizabeth. "You would not want to deny readers your insights in the name of *so-called propriety*."

I sit on my hands so I will not strike her across the fleshy face.

Elizabeth leaves the room and is back in a moment, handing a copy of my sacred journals to the man to whom I want to unite my soul. I feel the heat in the room become nearly unbearable.

"No, Nathaniel, I do not think you should read it," I say, standing and reaching my hands out to take the book from him, trying to keep the hysteria from my voice. If only Mother were here instead of out with Father, she would come to my rescue.

"Do not deny him," says Elizabeth. "Let him see you as you really are."

Nathaniel stares at the book as if it is the Holy Bible, and runs his hand over the binding. I feel shivers on my body as if he has stroked my own skin. He looks up at me with an earnest expression.

"Please," he whispers. "Please, Sophia. Let me."

The room becomes very quiet, and only the crack of wood in the fireplace can be heard. There is a great shift in the air, as if a fatal error has been made in a game of chess. I glance at Elizabeth and see that her smugness has disappeared, and she realizes that her plan to turn him off with my passionate, effusive writings might have been ill-conceived.

"Please," he continues. "I promise I will not judge you harshly. I will only read as an historian. As one interested in another time and place."

That feeling I detected the first time I came in contact with Nathaniel, that common union of unspoken intention between us, asserts itself. It empowers me, and I realize that this diffident gentleman will get to know me safely through the journal. There, my sister will not be able to sit with us, interjecting and asserting her views on every subject, attempting to dam the little streams of affection between us that long to join. Elizabeth senses that once they do connect, we will be a force she cannot control.

"You have my blessing," I say.

The smile again gives him a celestial expression, but not one that is light; it is blazing. His intensity reminds me of the fear I first felt on meeting him at the potential of our union. I am like a mortal confronted with an angel who has told me not to be afraid.

"I must go," he says. "I will enjoy a walk home in the shroud of night, and will light candles at my fireside so I may start reading this treasure. Miss Elizabeth, Sophia, thank you for entrusting me with this book. I will take the greatest care of it."

The thought of his hands on my book while he sits alone in his room is almost too much for me to imagine, and it must also be for Elizabeth. She excuses herself, claiming that she must answer correspondence, and does not acknowledge me as she leaves the room.

I hand Nathaniel his hat, and watch his clean, slender fingers tie his cloak at the neck before I bid him farewell. He brings my hand to his lips and leaves it there a moment longer than he ever has before.

I do not get a wink of sleep that night.

And then he is silent.

In my journals, did I say too much about Fernando? Was I overly effusive with regard to nature? Were my descriptions of slavery too harsh, or did I not say enough? Or is he shocked that I would allow him to read such an uncensored view of my thoughts? Does he think me too forward? Is he angry with me— or even Elizabeth—for introducing him to something that might make him blush the next time he sees us?

I take to bed with a headache that steals my vision and my will to paint. I am certain that he is appalled by what the journal contains.

But perhaps he will be intrigued, enthralled. How often has Nathaniel told us that he prefers to observe people and places from the shadows? He will surely derive great pleasure from peeking in the windows of my heart and soul undeterred.

At last, weeks later, he arrives.

I hear the lift in his voice. He wants me to know he is here, but I am stricken. I do not want to see him. I cannot face him after knowing he has read my ecstasies over men, and plants, and all manner of exotic temptations. The man's ancestors would have had me hanging at Gallows Hill after the very first letter!

I creep to my door and listen. Elizabeth's voice is muffled. Mary is here, and offers to fetch me, followed by more unintelligible speech from Elizabeth. I hurry over to my hammock and in a moment Mary knocks and peeks around to look at me, grinning.

"There is someone here who is quite emotional about seeing you."

I place my hand over my heart and whisper, "Mr. Hawthorne?"

Mary nods, glances over her shoulder, and then back at me.

"Elizabeth seems adamant that you are not well enough for visitors today," she says. "But I thought I would check on you myself in case certain motives in our sister are at odds with the wishes of the two who so enjoy each other's company."

"You are a good woman," I say, bursting with love for my sister, who seems not to judge my friendship with Mr. Hawthorne. Even though her Mr. Mann continues to mourn his wife, dead now for years, he is in Mary's constant company, thus lifting her spirits.

My head is bursting with pain, and a small conviction flutters inside of me that Nathaniel has made me wait for these many days, so I must make him wait. I cannot go running down the stairs just because he has determined that today—after weeks without a word—is the day that suits him to come and see me. No. I will not receive him.

"As much as I long to see our mysterious visitor, Elizabeth is correct," I say. "I am not in any condition to entertain guests, and will not likely be for the remainder of the day."

"This is an interesting game," says Mary, almost to herself. She glances over her shoulder and back at me again before grinning and giving me a wink. She leaves the door open and crosses the hallway to George's room.

What is she up to?

While I wait to see the results of her scheming, I reach for my brush and begin to slide it through my freshly washed hair, which has dried in a soft wave. Pinning it up will only make my head hurt worse, so I stroke it over and over again, arranging it over my shoulders in rivers.

Then comes the sound of many heavy footsteps on the stairs, and the voice of Nathaniel himself over Mary's and Elizabeth's.

"Are you sure he would want to receive me?" says Nathaniel. "Please do not make him feel any obligation. I only want to pay my respects to the brother so adored by such discerning sisters."

"He has assured me that he would enjoy meeting you," says Mary.

My heart races, and I know I should close my door, but it is too late. Nathaniel Hawthorne stands not ten paces from my bed, and just before rounding the corner to meet George, he glances at me, lying on my hammock like a sensuous cat. He tries to look away, but he cannot, and I give him a small smile before Elizabeth's face covers his with a scowl, and she slams my door.

10

Elizabeth enters my room without knocking, wearing a frown and dressed for travel.

"I want my copy of 'Endymion' back," she says.

"Must you go?" I ask.

"You should not have to ask me that."

I feel a stab of guilt. Elizabeth is leaving for Boston to live with our brother Nat, and his wife and infant, to start a boys' school. I believe, however, that it is this dance between the two of us and Nathaniel that has taxed her beyond bearing. She cannot endure it any longer.

"I am sorry you feel you must go," I say, scooting from my hammock and crossing the room to retrieve Elizabeth's book. I remove my poem from its pages and hand it to her. She snatches it and turns to leave.

"Elizabeth," I say, my voice contrite.

How can I speak my apology out loud? For I am very sorry for her. I knew that Elizabeth cared for Nathaniel when I stepped into the parlor that day, but I also knew that she would never marry. Mother has ingrained this wish for us in our minds since we could understand language. Elizabeth has embraced this ideal for the freedom it allows her in occupation and relation, and she encourages me in the same way. How could I have known the harm of two sisters unfit for husbands befriending the same writer? I never could have anticipated the force that was activated the moment Nathaniel and I set eyes on each other. But it pains me to see that Elizabeth is hurt. She has only ever wanted what is best for me, and to be so divided from her now feels like a little death.

"I apologize that you leave so unsettled," I say. "You are very dear to me."

She stares at me for a moment, and then looks away. Dear Lord, there are tears in her eyes. Elizabeth never cries! I begin to feel my own eyes fill, and reach to embrace her. To my relief, she returns my gesture, and we tremble in each other's arms, sniffling until we must pull away to attend to our damp faces with handkerchiefs.

"How ridiculous," she says. "It is not as if I go across the ocean. I can be home for lunch any day I feel inclined."

She places her handkerchief in her skirt pocket and again becomes serious. The rattling sound of George's coughing reaches us, and she shakes her head.

"Life is short," she says. "It would be a shame to ever waste opportunity or . . . love when it presents itself."

Oh, I am crying again. Dear, dear Elizabeth has given me her blessing.

She smiles at me, straightens her posture, and departs.

Nathaniel left a note with Mary for me the day I would not come out of my room.

"*To the queen of the journalizers: Pray accept this lowly serf so he may question Her Highness on the captivating insights of setting and character conjured at her fingertips, but only when it suits said queen in health and in temperament. Most Loyally, N. Hawthorne.*"

I cannot stop my pleasure at his address, and I decide that I will see him the next time he arrives. I am greatly relieved that he wants to see me, and having Elizabeth's blessing has loosened the last of my reserve in dealing with Nathaniel.

The opportunity to visit with him arrives a fortnight later. Nathaniel knocks, and I answer the door with a smile of the sweetest serenity on my face, and my hair and dress arranged almost as well as Josepha could have done. I am shocked that instead of the usual smile I am able to coerce from his dark face, Nathaniel is as stormy as a tempest. He walks into the parlor, where he commences pacing around the room with the *Cuba Journal* in his hand.

"Do you not find the inadequacy of words a tremendous frustration?" he says.

I do not know how to respond to this artist who curses the medium in which he works, so I place my hand on his arm and say, "What troubles you?"

He looks at me from inches away, and this time I do not flinch or pull back. There is a gradual change in his visage, a softening that lifts each of his downturned features like the light of sunrise. When the glimmer reaches his eyes, his entire countenance is open to me.

"Sophia, in your white clothes with your pale skin and diet of milk and bread, suspended in your hammock, you are like a dove, like the very doves about which you wrote. How do you calm me so?"

I look down at the floorboards, overwhelmed by his speech.

"There is nothing I like to do more than calm you," I say.

He squeezes my hand that still rests on his arm, and leads me to the settee, where we sit. He places my book on his lap.

"I must ask you a very important question," he says.

I meet his eyes again, nearly dizzy with anticipation.

"May I take your *Cuba Journal* with me when I leave next week?"

My smile evaporates. "Where will you go?"

"I will not speak of it," he says, his face again darkening, as if a veil is placed over it.

I draw my hand from his arm.

"I have never let anyone have the *Cuba Journal* for so long," I say. "What more could you want with it?"

"I need a friend on my solitary travels, and your voice whispers in my ear when I read your words."

My heart softens, but I keep my exterior cool and narrow my eyes at him.

"Little Sophy," he says with a cheeky grin. "You are a changeling. One moment you are a sweet dove; the next you are a naughty woman. I never know which you will be, and I cannot say which one I like more."

I stand and walk across the room to the fireplace, feeling my anger grow as he laughs behind me. When I turn to glare at him, he is contrite.

"I must be alone for a while," he continues. "So much is confusion right now, and I need to clear my head. There are so many letters from so many of you. I do not trust myself with anyone."

Is his concern for Elizabeth at the root of this leave-taking? I wish I could tell him that she no longer stands between us, but it is too soon—far too soon to speak such words aloud.

He looks at the *Cuba Journal* in his lap and runs his hand over the binding. Again I am covered in chills, and must turn away from him to regain my composure. I cannot stand the thought of being without him for an extended period of time, and the discovery horrifies me.

"I need to write and think without distraction," he says. "But I also know this: I need to have you . . . near me."

This is the first time he has admitted any kind of affection for me, and I wish I could feel nothing but bliss. Instead I am confused and angry and so many other unpleasant emotions. Is this love? If so, I know why the poets are so conflicted.

"Please, Sophia. You have no idea how your journal has fueled a writing fire in me, one that was in desperate need of kindling. I am on the edge of something."

In his gaze, I feel our souls rise up to meet each other, and allow that communion of thought and intention to fill the silence.

If I let him go without trouble, he will see my strength, and that will fuel his growing affection for me and deplete all other distractions. If my uncensored words are in his hands when he is alone, we will be more deeply bound to each other.

"Very well," I say. "Take my little book that holds the essence of my soul with you. Just please come back to place it in my hands after a short time. I will be unsettled until we are reunited."

And unsettled I am.

As soon as Nathaniel walks out of our home, I am overtaken by chills and my hands feel as if they have been submerged in melting snow. My entire body holds a clamminess that drives me to my room, where I stare out the window, down the path Nathaniel has walked so often. I am plagued by the idea that I will never again see him. He is nothing but a shadow in my mind, and I cannot even perfectly conjure his face in my delirium.

I am sure the beggar girl will appear to torment me, and I scan the young summer landscape, but do not see her anywhere. I see only the graveyard below my window, and I know in my heart that Nathaniel will be there before I am given a chance to tell him of my love. He is going to die on his mysterious trip!

It has been days since I have indulged in morphine. I have not had headaches, so I have tried to restrain myself, but now the physical need is back, gnawing from the inside out, demanding satisfaction.

"Mother!" I shout.

She arrives in seconds.

"What ails you, Sophichen?"

I clench my teeth and make my request. "I know I have not needed morphine for days, but I feel an ache coming on."

"You know Father says you should try to suppress the ache."

"I know, and I also know that we must wean ourselves from the need. Only one dose today, and I will be more functional. If I do not have it, I will be of no use to this household, and will only be able to shiver in my hammock."

"You do not need to worry about being of use. You are an artist, Sophy. Your calling is different from that of your sisters or your brothers."

"But I want to help. I want to sit with George at the very least, and if I am overcome like this, I cannot even offer him simple company."

I clench my teeth again, praying she will grant my request.

A film of memory clouds Mother's face. She is a nurturer. Any success this household has experienced has come about because she educated us, cultivated our talents, taught us girls to make lives apart from men. She does this—quite against the standards of the day—with the vehemence of a Puritan preacher. She sympathizes with the holy beauty of a preserved self, separate from others. Elizabeth subscribes to Mother's teachings as if they are gospel, and for most of my life I did too. Until Cuba. Until now.

"Please, Mother. Just today. Tomorrow we will try something new."

She finally nods, though her face is troubled, and when she returns with my coveted antidote, I snatch it from her fingers and drink it down before she has a chance to reconsider. The warm waves overtake me, bathing my head, then my shoulders, then my torso and legs in divine lethargy and peace.

11

D r. Fiske has gone and I am in a state like that induced by morphine, but my own bodily energies have supplied it.

Dr. Fiske is an associate of Father's, and a pioneer in the field of animal magnetism, a therapy that cures one of all sorts of nervous ills. We sit—knee-to-knee—and he rubs his hands down my arms and shoulders. Once my spheres are quieted, he places his hands on my abdomen and maintains periods of silence followed by direction to my body to suppress the head-aches. I must keep our sessions from the public knowledge, because the therapy is quite new and sometimes involves a crisis of body, a most elaborate pulsing and pounding of or-gans that leaves one in a state of extreme rest. The good doctor says this natural mechanism is much preferable to prescrip-tives, and I can see how he is correct.

At any rate, this hypnosis, as it is also known, has cured me of morphine and has left me stronger today than I have been in weeks. It is a good thing, because I am to depart for a late-summer vacation at Marblehead with Mary, to stay with our friends the Hoopers. Ellen Hooper is a poet and her husband, Robert, is a physician, and they are known for their reading parties and pleasant dinners. It will be good for Mary and me to reconnect our sisterly bonds away from home, without the misery of slavery to shadow our stay, and where I may return to my notebooks for painting inspiration.

I have been instructed by Dr. Fiske to take much outdoor exercise, and by Elizabeth's friend Mr. Ralph Emerson to appreciate my unity with the landscape so I may create original art. That the great transcendentalist has condescended to answer the humble letters of Elizabeth's invalid sister astounds me. He is generous to speak to me in his missives as an equal, and I will heed his advice as best I might. I have allowed myself too much rest in Salem. I find it easy to retreat to my bedroom, nurturing thoughts of Nathaniel, whose absence now plagues me like my headaches.

We arrive at the Hooper home on the coast, and are shown to the most royal rooms we have ever beheld. Mary and I squeal with delight at the lavender Turkish carpets, the pale purple-papered walls, the creamy ivory moldings and drapery, and two beds dressed in identical puffy quilts, like amethyst clouds too heavy to float.

Ellen is delighted to have our company, and we chatter like a nest of finches. She tells us that she is overseeing the table settings and menu for tonight's dinner, and insists that we spend the afternoon at the seaside so we are fresh and ready for the party. She procures blue serge bathing dresses and matching bonnets for us, and sends us on our way.

Mary and I walk arm in arm on the crude path through the trees, feeling the fingers of the shrubs grasping our skirts and pantaloons. I take in breaths of the salty zephyrs that have found us here, imagining the wind purifying my lungs and head, and drawing my ailments out on the tide. On the final climb to the beach, I feel my legs coming back to life, my arms pumping, my heart beating with vitality, and all at once the vista opens and the great ocean is before us.

"Oh, Mary! How I wish George were with us! He could find his healing here; I am sure of it. Maybe I will hold my breath until we return and blow some of this tonic at him."

Mary squeezes me closer to her side.

"You are good to care for George as you do," she says. "I am proud to see you ministering to others, and I know you bring our brother great comfort."

"It is he who brings me comfort. There is nothing like the friendship of a man to force me outside of myself and make me see things in new ways."

She glances at me from the corner of her eye, and when I meet her gaze, she grins.

"Just look at the darling families," I say. "And the soaring seagulls, and the dear sailboats bobbing on the rippling waters under the soft topaz sky!"

"Careful, or you will strain yourself, Sophichen. I will be forced to write to Mother."

I pinch her side and turn back to the scene before me. There is a great sloping path leading down to a beach, and I cannot contain my joy; I must run down it. I unthread my arm from Mary's and pull off my slippers before hurling myself toward the water with arms open to the wind. I hear Mary's laugh behind me, and see the ocean's sublimity before me, and when I reach the surf, I splash in up to my knees. Within moments, Mary has caught up with me, breathing hard from her run. I catch the eye of two young men smoking under an umbrella, and the fairer of the two nods at me and smiles. Mary grabs my arm, and we follow the tide line into the craggy boulders on a hunt for sea creatures.

The day moves with alarming quickness, and I feel a slight burn on my nose where my bonnet has not protected me, but I do not care. I call it my sun kiss, and even invite more of his blessing when I lie in the sand, face to heaven, exhaling in time with the waves. Most of the families and seagoers have left, and it is as if Mary and I are alone at the edge of the world.

"Breathe with me, Mary."

She stretches out next to me, and we must look like two great starfish washed up on the shore.

"I must write to Emerson of this," I say. "Have you ever felt such commingling with nature? Can you not feel the presence of the sublime oversoul? I cannot tell where I end and anything around me begins."

"That is poetry," says Mary. "You must paint this."

I feel a sudden separation from Mary when she says these words. I do not want commissions now; I only want to *be*, to exist in this manifestation of my *innere*. Mercifully, she does not speak again, and I am returned to the removed state I crave.

At the Hoopers' table I am reminded of the dreamy Cuban evenings of La Recompensa. A pleasant lethargy, not unlike a morphine trance, hovers at my temples all night, and the conversations pass over me like sea breezes. I must appear to be quite stupid, but I do not care.

Mary and I wear the new cotton dresses Mother helped us sew. Mary chose a pink floral and I found a fern-and-leaf pattern. Our lilac aprons and bonnets complement our dresses beautifully, and the off-the-shoulder leg-o'-mutton sleeves allow for coolness in spite of the summer heat.

Steaming gravies pass under my nose; delicately fried vegetables and succulent fruits melt on my tongue. Flaky pastries and sweets send the saliva rushing to my mouth, and goblets of wine are filled and refilled. I do not feel guilty about partaking when the service is done by pale hands, paid for their labors, and I grow stuffed from the fare.

It is time for the reading, and I choose a chair in a dark corner, next to Mary, while Ellen stands before us and tells us that she will read a piece perfect for ladies and gentlemen who have spent time at the shore, a charming vignette by a mysterious young writer who nearly got himself killed in a duel over an unworthy woman.

"A Mr. Nathaniel Hawthorne."

I jerk to attention in my chair and grab Mary's arm. Her gaze meets mine, mimicking the way I have made large saucers of my eyes. I draw my hand back, and squeeze my fists on my skirts.

Ellen does not elaborate on the firework she has thrown, so this duel must be common knowledge, but what woman could it reference? Not me, of course, surely not Elizabeth. Is there another woman who has been competing for his affections? Could she be why he has so suddenly and sullenly departed human company? I have a small comfort that it is my words he wanted to accompany him on his travels, but it is a very small comfort indeed.

I attempt to pay attention to his essay, "Footprints on the Sea-Shore." What I do hear of his musings on the temporary nature of what we leave behind, the pleasure to be known retreating from civilization, the wisdom of nature, and the ultimate joy on reuniting with society charms me. I will have to read the essay again, alone in my room, but for now I am beside myself with curiosity. I must learn about this duel.

Once the reading is over and the men have retired to the veranda to smoke, Ellen and her friends are surprised to see me, the quietly nesting dinner dove, now animated and involved in all of their conversations. I attempt to steer the discussion back to Hawthorne without appearing too eager—or even desperate—to hear more.

"An enchanting walk to take with Hawthorne through his story," I say. "So well animated, Ellen. You have always infused your poetic tendencies into the very work you read."

"Thank you," she says. "I am delighted you enjoyed hearing

it. I will have actual poetry to read tomorrow, and we will have more guests."

"How wonderful," I reply.

A young woman places her hand on Ellen's arm to ask her a question, but I cannot bear to lose her attention.

"It is interesting so docile a writer might have been a part of such violence," I say.

Ellen and her guest stare at me for a confused moment until Ellen understands my reference.

"Yes, yes, thank goodness Hawthorne did not have to face his friend. It could have ended so badly."

"But the story you hold would have been worth something if it had," says the woman, whom I now wish to strike with the fan she has been waving all night.

"My apologies," I say. "Please fill me in. We are so sheltered in Salem, the news of this averted duel has not fully reached us."

The guest has apparently tired of me, thank heavens, and as she walks away, I draw Ellen into my grasp so she may not leave until the story is finished.

"Have you not heard of Hawthorne's romance with society girl Mary Silsbee?" asks Ellen.

My sister Mary has joined us at the mention of Silsbee, and leans in to get a better listen. Mary once told me that Silsbee is the flightiest flit that ever existed in New England. Her father is vastly wealthy, and she was engaged to a gentleman for some time, but he broke it off. To think that a man with the intellectual depth and material poverty of Nathaniel Hawthorne would be of any interest to Silsbee, or she to him, is both perplexing and troubling.

"It has been all the talk this season," says Ellen, who must begin to realize that poor Salem girls are not frequent dinner guests, and are not privy to society gossip. She has the decency to look ashamed at her assumption. "At any rate, it is said that Silsbee made advances on Hawthorne's friend John O'Sullivan, and when O'Sullivan rejected her, she told Nathaniel that his friend had attempted an impropriety. Hawthorne thought it his duty to defend her honor, and challenged O'Sullivan to a duel. Mercifully, O'Sullivan, being a good friend, counseled the duped writer that he had been tricked by the wily female. Hawthorne was humiliated, and it is rumored that Silsbee has gone back with her fiancé."

I have so many thoughts about this that I do not know how to begin to decipher them. I am unable to speak, so Mary saves me by turning the conversation back to tomorrow's promised poetry reading, and I am able to drift away from the women.

Dominating my emotions is a strange thrill. I did not know Hawthorne had such courage. It takes a man of great character and bravery to go against his docile nature for the protection of others, and I am certain that such violence is against Hawthorne's nature.

While I do feel a hint of jealousy about this Silsbee, I somehow think that Nathaniel must have done such a deed out of duty, rather than love, and that he must have learned many great lessons from the experience. This must be why he wanted to make a journey alone. I am elated that while he escapes the gossip, while he attempts to get to know himself again without out-side influence, it is my journal he carries in his beautiful hands, and my words he reads before he closes his eyes at night. I am certain it is my phrases whispering in his ears, and my ideals permeating his dreams.

I have never been surer of anything in my life.

12

I stand at the window, watching down the street with eager eyes for Nathaniel. I will know as soon as we meet if my conviction that I am his heart's occupation is correct.

It is October, and will be the first time we lay eyes on each other in nearly three months, since his mysterious travels north. He sent a letter that he would return the *Cuba Journal* to me, and I replied eagerly, inviting him to come today. Mother moves between hanging laundry and caring for George and Father, who has now taken ill, and Mary is visiting Elizabeth in Boston, so Nathaniel and I will have privacy.

It is a fine autumn day, and I will suggest a walk outdoors. Since my return from the seaside, I have resolved to spend more hours at exercise than at rest, more time in the moving air of nature than in the still breath of illness and lethargy in this house. I have even maintained my refusal of morphine. Mesmerism has helped my head, and I am nearly as strong as I was in my Cuba days.

I return my attention to Elizabeth's letter, and feel strangely stirred by her latest recommendation that I complete an illustration for Nathaniel's story "The Gentle Boy," to be issued as a small book, financed by Miss Susan Burley, one of Salem's most prominent arts patrons. I will need to draw swiftly, since a publication date has been agreed upon, and the engraver must have sufficient time to work. Elizabeth has enclosed the text for my perusal. I am lost in the reading of this simple yet sad tale, and just as it concludes, I am startled to hear Nathaniel's voice behind me.

"Have you heard of the daguerreotype, Miss Peabody?"

I drop my papers, and in moments he is at my feet collecting them. He turns his face up to me, the autumn sunshine bathing his tanned, glowing skin. The impulse that passes between us is so strong that he closes his eyes. Yes! He has felt it. He kneels with one fist on the floor as if to gain his bearings and says, "It is an invention that presses your likeness into silver, by some magic. How I wish I had a daguerreotype of you standing in the light, my reading angel."

He has called me his angel!

He pushes off the floor and stands to his full height, so I must look up at him. His gaze returns to the papers, where Elizabeth's letter is now on top of the pile.

"I can see by the handwriting that this letter is from your eldest sister," he says. "I know she must have asked you to illustrate my story for me, because it is I who suggested it to her."

I flinch that he has seen her first, and the man not only sees my face, but answers my jealous thought as if I uttered it aloud.

"Elizabeth and I have only written to each other, dove. You are the first Peabody sister I have beheld since my travels."

Dove. I am assuaged.

"How did you get into my house without my admitting you?" I say, a cheeky lift in my voice.

"Your dear mother was in the backyard hanging sheets, and saw me coming. I took a new way to your house, hoping to surprise you. She was going to escort me to you, but your father called through the open window to her, and she left me to find you on my own."

"And is it not heaven to stand here together in the light shafts without anyone between us to divert our attention?" I say.

I am aware that Elizabeth is still between us in the letter, and I pull the papers from his hands and drop them on the table. He swallows like one deprived of water for a long time.

"Come, Nathaniel. I want to walk out of doors with you and hear about your adventures."

It is the first of many walks we take that fall. The first of many excursions in each other's company to artistic salons. The first of many visits in which the shy writer becomes a fixture in our parlor. Sisters, brothers, parents, and friends flit in and out of our company, like birds dipping for drinks in a cool pond, but we exist more and more in a private oasis. I complete my illustration for his story, and he makes his first public recognition of our mutual affection in his eloquent dedication of the book to me. Painters, patrons, and Nathaniel himself praise my illumination of his words through my art, and it seems to me the very symbol of what I prophesied years ago in my poem.

My unknown is now known.

On a December night, he sits in my parlor at the fireside, Christmas cranberries strung on the tree, flickering candles warming every corner of my home, ribbons and wreaths hung in abundance by the dear hands of students and neighborhood children. Nathaniel has presented me with a flower I gave him months ago, pressed into a brooch of crystal for me to wear over my heart. I gave him a volume of Wordsworth's poetry. But my sweet, poor love has never had a piece of art from anyone, and it is all he longs for. Tonight I will draw him and put every drop of my feeling for him in it. I will give it to him as a taste of myself, which I also wish to give to him in body and soul.

"Do sit still," I tease. "You attempt to distract me with your foxy glances and your fidgeting, but I will not be waylaid."

"Did I ever tell you of the fox I met in the mountains of New Hampshire, on my solitary travels?" he says.

"No, and now is not the time. Whenever you speak of your wilderness adventure, you are overtaken by a need to pace, and I want you motionless."

"Then I shall sleep like Van Winkle, and when you finish, you will not recognize me. I will be ancient and white haired, and a mere shadow of the strapping man I now am."

My charcoal sculpts and shades the smoothness of his lower lip, and I am able to complete this drawing in a single sitting. I can see Nathaniel clearly with my artist's eye, and I have no reservation about giving this extension of myself to him, because I know that I have found the one who is meant for me. I use my finger to soften the shading on his lips and around his eyes, and pass the paper to him. He puts his hand over his heart.

"Your fingers flatter me. I know I am not this beautiful, but only become so in your gaze."

"You are wrong. I see you as you are. And I will know your face at every coming age, and it will be familiar and welcome to me always."

He turns at the seriousness in my voice, and stares into my eyes. Clear as if he has spoken aloud, I hear in my mind the words, *I love you, Sophia. Do you love me?*

Yes! I think. *I am yours.*

And then the smile begins, the angelic transformation that lifts his entire face from his forehead to his full, soft lips, basking me in its glory.

January 1839

We are engaged. Secretly.

Once the kisses begin, we are intoxicated with each other. Separation is sweet frustration because it allows us the poetry of love letters and the joy of reunions, but the absences feel like small eternities. How I long to proclaim our love to the world, but Nathaniel is terrified that doing so will hurt Elizabeth, and shock his mother and sisters.

When Nathaniel's father died, Nathaniel became the man in

the house at a young age. Provided for by uncles of varying stern-ness and indifference, Nathaniel enjoyed a unique closeness with the women of his family, though it was assumed rather than expressed. Ebe has an almost unnatural devotion to Nathaniel, and if he tells her he plans to marry and leave them forever, he is afraid of the great pain that will meet them all. In a way, he thinks it will be like his father leaving and dying all over again.

Then there is Nathaniel's wish to earn a steady living to sup-port me, and this has led to his acceptance of a job—with the assistance of my Elizabeth, who knows everyone—as Boston's customs inspector. The salary is fifteen hundred dollars a year, so he will make no fortune, but he may count on the political ap-pointment while the Democrats remain in power, and he will make a name and reputation for himself.

I scheme to get to Boston, where my two sisters and my love now reside, and it is not long before I am studying with the sculp-tor Shobal Clevenger. Though I will be under his tutelage for only a short time, every minute I am not sitting with the master, I will be with my other master, my love, my *husband*, for this is how we now refer to each other—husband and wife—though there has most certainly not been any communion of body to make it so. No, it is our complete mingling of spirit that has married us, with maybe just a bit of kissing and touching to quiet the fires.

Mother must sense my combustibility, because she cautions me by mail as much as she did while I resided in Cuba about how often I see Nathaniel, and how I must restrain my ebullience of feeling. She does not know that her request makes as much sense as asking the falls at Niagara to cease their gushing.

13

I have a friend, Cornelia Parks, who in addition to her talents at mesmerizing me hosts the most fascinating parties. At Connie's hands I fall into an even swifter trance than I did with Dr. Fiske, and without the crisis. Nathaniel is somewhat mollified, knowing that no other man interferes with my sphere, though he dislikes Connie's doing so almost as much.

As the October sun sets, Nathaniel escorts me across the Boston Commons, on our way to a gathering to meet Miss Margaret Fuller, the woman Emerson has appointed editor of *The Dial*. Nathaniel and I are very small compared to large Boston, but it is somehow ours because of the sacred connection we have walking through it. Our boots rustle and crunch the fallen leaves, and the chill in the air encourages us to lean closer. It is as if nature conspires with me to draw in my love.

We pass by a tree with fiery orange leaves, which complement my violet satin gown. Mary helped me select the fabric, which was a gift from Nathaniel, and we sewed it together, pairing it with a simple cream-colored cloak. My family is aware of my relationship with Nathaniel, though we do not often discuss it. Mother has accepted defeat in her campaign to encourage me to a life of chastity, because she sees the fullness of my happiness, and that is what is most important to her. There remains a small strain with Elizabeth, though I have had her blessing, and I fear it will always remain. Nathaniel believes his own family does not have an idea of our love. I think he is foolish to believe they cannot know, but I will not vex him by speaking such a thought out loud. I have learned that Nathaniel is pained by quarrels or negative speech of any kind.

I pause to pat the bark of the orange-leafed tree, and gaze up at its blazing foliage.

"I am sorry you will soon lose your fiery crown," I say, "but I am grateful for your color, which emphasizes my own."

"Yes, thank you, good tree," says Nathaniel, lifting his voice to mimic my own and giving an awkward thump to the trunk.

I shove him for teasing me.

"Silly man," I say. "It is not yet natural for you to address plants in such a way, but perhaps you will allow me to mesmerize you, so I might command your mind to change."

"I would welcome mesmerism from you and *only* you," he says. "I wish you would welcome such interference from *only* me."

"If you would consent to the practice, I would welcome it, but you remain a stubborn skeptic."

"Fine," he says, stopping his walk and closing his eyes. "Entrance me."

"We cannot do it here, but the next time we find ourselves alone in your rooms, I will honor your request."

I give him my naughtiest smile, and he pretends to feel faint until I pull him along, resuming our walk to Connie's house. We proceed in silence for a few moments, and I am nearly overcome with joy to have Nathaniel on my arm. If I die tomorrow, I am convinced that the affection I have known in our courtship is more than others have experienced in a lifetime.

"If I close my eyes, we are in Italy," says Nathaniel, "strolling the Isolino di San Giovanni, bathed in sunset's fire. There, do I sound like you?"

"If you sounded like me, you might mention the angels' breath stirring our hair, and the benediction of the sun shafts."

"You are my angel and my benediction, and your company is all I need to sustain me."

We draw closer to each other, and I can almost see the Italian landscape rising around us. I am overcome with an idea. I will paint this moment for Nathaniel, this moment that feels like a marriage. It will be art just for him, so I may not fear that it will hang on the walls of the Athenaeum. It will be a representation of the mingling of our souls as one, as we walk together on a broad landscape, gazing toward the sunset.

"I long for the days when we may be fully married," I say, "living in creative communion. You will write and I will paint, and the power of each of our artistic mediums will be enhanced by the work of the other, inspiring a fullness of creation not seen since the days of Eden."

"It is nearly too overwhelming to fantasize about," he says. "I never knew such earthly happiness could be mine."

I lift his hand to my lips and press it there. I am eager for more of this talk, but I am met with a heavy sigh.

"What is it?" I say.

"I wish I could simply leave you at the door and fetch you in several hours' time. You know how I detest mingling amongst people."

"It is good for you to part from your solitude," I say. "You are a gift to the world, though you do not know it. And besides, I do not wish to waste a single moment when we are in town together. Our separations make me ill."

"Then come home to my fireside, Sophy." He stops walking and pulls me to him. His lips are at my ear in an earnest whisper. "We can be in perfect solitude and not have the distraction of other human beings."

I thrill at the thought of sharing kisses at Nathaniel's fireside, but I am also afraid of where that will lead. We spent last night in such a way, and it required more willpower to take leave of him than when I gave up morphine.

No, we must socialize.

"As much as I long to do so," I say, "Connie will be hurt if we do not arrive when I told her we would."

"I do not report to Connie," he says, pulling away from me. "She is not my queen, and I worry about the effect she has on you. You are very sensitive and adoring, and I do not want her taking advantage of you with this mesmerism business in which you insist on engaging."

"She has no control over me, and makes me well so I am able to spend more time in the world. Mesmerism is the answer to many of life's ailments, and is certainly better for me than morphine."

"While I agree with you on that count, it simply does not seem proper. When you allow another into your *innere*, you give them an almost sacred entrance into your body. It is indecent."

I pull Nathaniel toward me, and lay my cheek on his chest. "No one may have full entrance into my soul but you."

He rubs my neck, and groans before stepping back to admire me.

"Your hair is so sweetly done," he says. "What is this new style?"

"Grecian braids," I say, turning in a circle so he may see all of me. "Tonight's party will be a transcendental feast in the Greek style."

"What does that mean?"

"I do not know, but I have the hair to support the theme."

We are climbing the stairs of Connie's building, and he steals one more kiss on my cheek.

"You are a little goddess," he says.

Suddenly the door is pulled open, and we are ushered into the crowded house. Connie separates me from Nathaniel, absorbing me into her orbit and leading me through rooms decorated with fragrant yellow roses, busts of Plato, golden fabric draped over tables abundant with oranges, tomatoes, cheese, and flaky dough puffs. I wish to pause and eat a bite from a platter of lamb kebabs, but Connie does not stop until we reach Margaret Fuller, a somewhat dowdy though commanding woman with light hair and blue-gray eyes. Her smile upon beholding us pleasantly transforms her face, and I curtsy to her.

"I have heard much praise of your fascinating conversations from my sister Elizabeth Peabody," I say.

"Elizabeth is your sister—how wonderful," says Margaret. "She is one of the founders of our transcendental society, and one of the brightest minds in it."

"She is," I say.

"And are you the sister who sings or who paints?"

"I paint," I say. "When my head allows it."

"Well, I have seen your painting of a *Scene Near Bristol* at the Athenaeum, and just tonight as I walked across the Commons, I thought how like that warm landscape Boston appeared. I do hope you are well enough to continue your creations. You decorate the world."

Her words touch me so that my face colors, and I whisper a thank-you. I can hardly believe someone thought of my art before they had met me. It is both thrilling and somehow troubling—as if a little piece of my soul is outside of my body, inspiring others. What a great responsibility art is.

I glance around the room to see where Nathaniel has wandered, and I soon find him in a corner where several ladies have him pressed to the wall panels, no doubt praising him for his writing. For a minute or two I am able to observe him without his seeing me, and it is long enough for me to feel overwhelmed by my love for him. Even with him surrounded by doting women, I have no fear or jealousy, because I know that he is mine, made for just me. I could watch him all night, but he is drowning, and I must rescue him. I summon his spirit and think his name, and in seconds he finds my eyes. The relief on his face is so dear that I hurry to him, and excuse him from company.

"Thank you," he says. "It is too much."

"I know, darling. Hold on to me."

He gazes at me but, as I lean closer to him, we are interrupted by a bespectacled man and woman.

"Pardon the intrusion," the man says, "but I must introduce myself. I have heard so much about you, Mr. Hawthorne, though I have not yet had the pleasure of reading your work. I am George Ripley, and this is my wife, Sophia."

Mr. Ripley extends his hand, and I can feel Nathaniel recoil. He is too overwhelmed to speak more. I try to think of why I know George Ripley's name.

"How nice to meet you both," I say. "I am Mr. Hawthorne's . . . friend. Miss Sophia Peabody."

I nudge Nathaniel, who finally reaches for Mr. Ripley's hand and mutters a greeting. I suddenly remember why I have heard of Ripley.

"Ah, Mr. Ripley," I say. "Mr. Emerson says that you are one we should meet. He wrote with high praise of your ideas."

"Emerson flatters me," says Mr. Ripley. "It is he who inspires. In fact, we were discussing the merits of an opportunity in communal living, and he mentioned Mr. Hawthorne by name. Miss Fuller might be joining."

Connie interrupts us to direct our attention to the fireplace, where Margaret will begin her talk. We pardon ourselves from the Ripleys, and I feel Nathaniel relax after we are away from conversation with strangers. I squeeze his arm for reassurance.

While Connie introduces Margaret, she unfolds a tall tripod of a chair that she had been carrying and settles herself with remarkable ease in front of the room of onlookers. Margaret is the epitome of grace and, while Emerson has described her as regal, I imagine her as more of an enchantress or faerie. Tonight she speaks of Greek mythology, but has such a gently coercive way about her, the audience soon contributes, and a full and fascinating discussion ensues.

"When we speak of such things, hours are no longer relevant," she says. "We are of eternal time, connected to the past and future by our full immersion in the moment. Does not this moonlight reaching in through the window remind us of Selene, the moon goddess, and her love of Endymion, and are we not there when we conjure their love through words?"

"I agree," says Nathaniel, to my shock. He can scarcely put a sentence together in a conversation with few, but now speaks before a room of many. How inspired he must be! The group seems to shrink into the shadows, and it is as if the moonlight and firelight illuminate him and this muse before us in holy conversation. "The past forever reaches to us, wishing us to keep it alive, though we often try to outrun it. In this case, however, it seems fitting to preserve a love so beautiful, the love of Selene and Endymion."

"Is their love all beauty, though?" says Margaret. "A man asleep? A man who finds love with another? The poets would have us believe Selene's love was not enough, so he went searching until he ended up back at her feet."

"Love is beautiful even when there are challenges," says Nathaniel. "Those challenges make the union sweeter."

"Perhaps you should try your hand at poetry, Mr. Hawthorne," says Margaret to the room. There is much agreement and many smiles.

Nathaniel's face is flushed. He has never been more beautiful to me. I wish I were Selene, and I could cast a sleeping spell on him forever, so I might arrest the aging process and have him just like this to kiss and love every night by the moon.

"I have always enjoyed that a woman cast the spell in that story," continues Margaret. "That she initiates and leads, and ultimately dominates."

Nathaniel looks at me before he speaks, and I feel many eyes turn to me.

"A woman in full possession of her passion is a mighty force indeed," he says, "and it would be heaven to be ruled by such a goddess."

There are sighs from the women around me, and maybe a groan or two from the gentlemen, but my love for Nathaniel rises up, blotting them all away. Even the sibyl on the chair, who has facilitated this public exercise on the exploration of women and men in love and in learning, is rapt.

The crowd begins to disperse, heading for tables of food, and Margaret remains in her chair, staring from Nathaniel to me and back again. When her gaze fixes on him, I am reminded of a face I once saw, but cannot recall where. Margaret's look is dark, but not quite sad. She stares openly, so I do not think it is adoration, but there is something in her that reaches to Nathaniel as if in supplication.

It is then that I recall the portrait of Mary Magdalene in Cuba, her face conveying a heartfelt prayer. That is how Margaret appears.

14

The air has changed in Salem. I sense it the moment I enter the house.

No one greets me when I arrive. I set down my travel bags, remove my gloves and bonnet, and unfasten and hang my cloak. When I call out, there is no reply, and my solitary voice scatters. I glance out the windows to my left and see the cemetery, where a rectangle of soil announces a newly covered grave. I rub the chill on my arms and note that there are no fires burning in the grates, no pupils or visitors, and there cannot have been for some time, based on the accumulation of dust and dirty bowls and cups that litter the rooms.

I am struck with a horrible thought that George has died and word did not reach me, and I run in a sudden burst up the staircase, trying to keep my breath. As I turn the corner into my brother's room, I startle Mother, who cries out, but George does not stir. My George is not dead but he is barely alive. His face is gray and shiny with perspiration, his body is a mere skeleton draped in wasted skin, and he gasps with a wet, ragged sound as he tries to breathe. Mother rushes to embrace me, and I stare over her shoulder at George. His eyes flicker open and catch mine. They are hard and glassy, but burn with intensity. He lifts his hand and motions at Mother and out the door, and then closes his eyes.

"I am here, Mother," I say. "You must rest. Let me sit with George."

"No, no, I cannot leave little you to this task."

I stand straight and look into her eyes, which are nearly level with mine. "I have never been stronger. Please allow yourself a break."

Mother pulls away and looks back at George. "I suppose I should sleep so I can sit with him this night."

"I shall sit with him. You must rest."

Mother nods her weary head. She goes to George and kisses his forehead, and then leaves the room.

George opens his eyes, and I join him at the bedside in a cushioned chair draped in a sheet, where Mother must have been sleeping these past nights.

"Thank you," he wheezes. "She is so good, but so . . . suffocating. As you well know."

He attempts a smile, but commences with a terrible coughing fit that leaves his lips blue. He is a drowning man. I cannot hold back my tears; nor does he.

"Not long now," he says.

I mark the time that evening by the changing shadows on the wall. Father comes in to administer morphine but does not leave any with me. Mother visits before an early bedtime. Mary is home, and takes a shift while I eat a little bread and butter and prepare for bed, and when I return in my white nightgown, we compose a letter beseeching Elizabeth to join us in our vigil.

I am careful when I climb into bed with George. I do not want him to be afraid or alone for one moment while he waits for that dark angel to escort him to eternity. While George sleeps, I am aware of a shadow lurking, but I do not fear it, and I understand that it is Nathaniel I sense like some sort of hovering ghost.

Moonlight has turned my brother's flesh to stone, and I think of the sculpture I will complete of George that will not be half as beautiful as he is, but which will remind us of him when he no longer breathes the air that we do.

Sleep is beginning to press into me when George's small voice reaches in and pulls me back into consciousness.

"Sophy."

"Yes."

"I am afraid to die." He almost chokes on the words.

I rise on my arm and stroke his hair. "You have nothing to fear. You have a noble soul, and you will be welcome in heaven."

"But have I done enough?"

"You have not been given the blessing of an abundance of years, but you spent them well. You are good and kind, and those who know you, love you."

"Is that enough? I look at you, overflowing with love, revealing the beauty in the world through your art, ministering to others in spite of your own infirmities—that is a life well lived. What have I really done?"

"You have traveled the world."

"For my health," he says. "And great good that has done."

"You have held a good job in a Boston firm."

"As a clerk. I could not feed anyone on that salary."

"We exist in difficult economic times," I say. "You have housed our Mary."

"I needed her teaching wages to make rent."

"My dear brother, I will have far more air than you this night and will answer all of your lamentations with effusions, so you had best save your breath. I adore you and I know with every impulse in my soul that God will bring you, His beloved son, home to rest in a heavenly kingdom, without pain or cares or woes. And when I join you in the final crossing, you will tell me how right I was."

He smiles a bit, and seems more settled, though my words are braver than I feel. "Distract me," he says, after another coughing fit.

I am so tired, I cannot understand how he continues to speak after such a dose of morphine, but I wonder if he is experiencing a last surge of energy before he dies.

"What subjects would you like spoken of?" I say.

"Love. Tell me more of this Hawthorne. When will you marry him?"

I wait a long moment before responding. If Mother hears this, it will add to her burdens. When I am convinced the house slumbers around us, I indulge George.

"He wants to make sure he can support me first before we establish our house."

"A good thing," says George.

"I do not know," I say. "He is an artist, a writer. I do not know if he will ever achieve the affluence he desires to keep me, but when I try to assure him I am used to poverty and that God will provide, perhaps even through my art, he will not hear it. He wants his dove, as he calls me, to live in perfect rest for my health, and perfect ease to paint whenever my soul wishes, never out of necessity."

"An unusual man," says George. "You are lucky."

"I know it. I feel that we were created for each other."

"Then you were."

"We met a man at a salon the other night—Mr. George Ripley. He spoke of forming a utopian agricultural society, a perfect community. Nathaniel is interested in taking part, and inviting me to join him as his wife once the village is thriving."

"How charming."

"I know. And we will live nestled in the hills of Massachusetts in perfect marital bliss."

The fit of coughing that follows scares the conversation from the room, and shortly afterward, my brother has exhausted himself enough to sleep. Now I lie wide-awake, and it is again as if Nathaniel is with me, his voice calling to me on the wind. How I long for the first night when we might share a nuptial bed, in the embrace of Utopia, at the beginning of our artist's partnership. But I recall George Ripley's mention that Margaret Fuller might join his community. In the dark of night, I meet this remembrance with dread. Nathaniel became uncharacteristically open during Margaret's talk. There is something about her that engages his intelligence, and he seemed to connect to her in a way I thought he could only with me.

While the world sleeps, these thoughts distort my calm, and I spend the rest of the small hours of morning in nightmarish realms, haunted by my fear of Margaret's influence on Nathaniel, and by the gasps of my dying brother.

George's is a hard death.

In the ensuing days, Mother is so pained over his suffering that she cannot be with him. Mercifully, Elizabeth comes and gives the rest of us the steadiness and strength to keep vigil. I find a strange energy overtake me in his final hours—one that allows me to ignore sleep and hunger, and attend to the failing man before me.

On November 13, 1839, as the autumn wind pulls the last brown leaf from the tree outside George's window, death takes George as well. It is the only moment of peace in his final days of suffering. A shaft of light pours forth from between the clouds and illuminates his face, drawing his eyes open for the last time. His countenance, which was so sunken and wasted and gray, suddenly seems to have a small life left in it, and his coughing ceases. I watch him breathe his last breaths, smaller and smaller, until his soul leaves his body. His eyes remain open, and a peaceful look settles over him. This is what we are able to show our mother.

Nathaniel writes sweetly to me, consoling words that are second-best to his embrace, which I long for as never before. I feel a renewed urgency to join him in matrimony.

After George's funeral, I sit at my window, and feel that our lives on this earth are but a blink in God's eye. God gave Nathaniel to me, and me to him, and we cannot waste another moment separated from each other.

I will return to Boston. I will tell Nathaniel that, no matter what, we must tell our families of our engagement, marry, and begin our lives together. I know he will be of a similar mind.

15

"*Dove, I know you long to speed time—I do too—but we must not act in haste. There are practical matters that one so celestial as you need not concern herself with, but that must be the business of one as earthly as I. Please do not fret, my darling. We will tell my mother and sisters soon, and the day will come for our marriage, and this entire prolonged courtship will become the smallest trial faced before a lifetime of companionship. . . .*"

I crumple the letter and throw it across the room. He moves like one stuck in tar pits and I long to drag him out by the collar. I am nearly thirty years old! He is thirty-five! At this age, most women have died from having their fourth child, and most men are widowers, and yet we are virgins!

I direct my frustration into my art and create like one possessed. If I could sustain this energy, I might even be able to support us. I have suggested as much, but Nathaniel knows how the process of creation often leaves me ill, and he does not want to rely upon my talents or to tax me in any way. I cannot argue with him, because I do not trust my head to cooperate, which vexes me nearly as much as his reticence.

The bas-relief of George is complete, and I send two paintings as gifts to Nathaniel. I wish I could deliver them to his apartment myself, but with their bulky frames, I could not carry one, let alone two. When the paintings arrive, Nathaniel writes of how I have captured the very essence and moment of our souls' joining, and of his wish that no one but him ever look on them because of their intimacy. He has hung black curtains to protect them from the city's soot and visitors' eyes, but draws back the curtains to behold them each morning and night. He beseeches me to mingle in his dreams so I may be with him while he sleeps.

How I long to make this vision a reality!

The months pass with shocking swiftness, and I am increasingly agitated that Nathaniel seems content to correspond with me and dip into our home for short visits, only to leave me again and again.

"Why can you not visit with me as often as you do your mother and sisters?" I say.

"I do not visit them more, Sophia, but I must see them. I am so divided."

"Then marry me now so we can be together most, and you can go to them when you must, and there will be no more division of spirit."

"I cannot even bear to hold your letters in my filthy hands after working all day at the custom house," says Nathaniel. "I scrub them clean before handling the paper your pure fingers have touched. I cannot imagine coming home to you so sooty."

"Do not be ridiculous. I would take you any way I could have you. If we were told that we could no longer bathe in the water of Massachusetts, I would have you dirty and stinking, and would be happy to do so."

"What a horrid image."

I groan and begin to argue again when he lays his fingers over my lips. I move his hand aside to speak, and he stops the words by placing his mouth on mine, and delivering the most luscious, distracting kiss. When he pulls away, he is serious and his voice is quiet.

"I implore you not to say things that bring darkness between us."

"It is difficult for one like me, so open in my thoughts and words, to suppress anything, especially as it relates to you."

"I do not wish to stifle you," he says. "I only ask that you try to understand me more thoroughly before arguing. There are things I know I must do, without always comprehending why—unspoken impulses that must be obeyed. When you ask me why I must visit here or there, or why my face is shadowed, it taxes me, because there is much about my own nature that I dare not probe."

"I never wish to upset you," I say. "I know that you hold yourself back from embracing life's gifts, and to your detriment. How often do you say I interpret the world for you? I know that our marriage will make you happier and more satisfied. That is why I urge so much."

"I know, my dove."

He kisses me again and leaves, and we make no forward progress.

By the summer, I am frantic. I pace about the parlor with another letter from Nathaniel praising my celestial nature and how my love makes him more worthy of life than he ever could be alone, while all I want to do is strike him with an open palm. Perhaps that would make him awaken from his dreamy musings and see that his angel is a woman of flesh and blood who would like nothing more than to commingle with her utmost passion.

"You wear out the floorboards," says Mary, not looking up from her scribblings.

"I find his complacence baffling. When he is with me, he speaks of his heartiest wish for our marriage. By letter he invokes it. He frets over our separations and how intolerable the gray days are without his dearest dove by his side, and yet he does nothing to hasten the union."

"You know how he wishes for financial security. You cannot rush that."

"What is security? There is no such thing. The only certainly is death and its swift and frequent appearance in our lives. Why not make as much heaven on earth together as we can?"

I am aware that I am speaking to a woman who has waited almost a decade for her love—a man with far more financial stability than mine—and would wait until the end of time. I will find no sympathy from Mary.

I attempt to distract myself in other ways, and find the most heavenly respite in a stay with the Emersons in Concord. Being in the company of Waldo and Lidian, who are so like me in our love of nature, is a joy. I spend hours walking the banks of Walden Pond, visiting friends, wading through the benevolent meadows, and hiking the hills of Sleepy Hollow. When my wanderings take me to the banks of the Concord River, I am entranced by its deep stillness. It is as if nature is trying to reassure me. I reflect on the perfection of its seasons, and remind myself to have hope that time will unite Nathaniel and me at the correct moment.

On the hill behind me is a charming dwelling. I believe it belongs to Emerson's relation, and I think how lucky its inhabitant is to live here by the river, surrounded by fields and orchards, and such a short walk from the village, and the Emersons, and Walden Pond. I would like to live in a house like it with Nathaniel someday.

A movement on the hill draws my attention. At first, I think the young woman I see is an apparition, and then I fear she is the beggar girl, until I realize it is only a farm woman. I watch her walk with her head bent, her severe hair pulled into what must be a painful bun at the nape of her neck, her gown so thin, worn, and stretched it must have belonged to ten larger people than she before coming to hang on her gaunt frame. In spite of the verdant summer surroundings, she is a portent of winter and darkness, and I feel a longing to make her lift her eyes to the beauty of the earth. But I am mute. I fear I would frighten her if I disturbed her deep thought, and before long she is gone from my view, leaving only a chilly wind in her wake.

16

Nathaniel has left his appointment at the custom house and now resides at George Ripley's utopian community, Brook Farm, in Roxbury, Massachusetts.

Nathaniel's April arrival there was inauspicious. A late snowstorm and a severe head cold left him in Margaret Fuller's care. Margaret frequently visits the community, though she is not an official member, and her presence gives Nathaniel much peace, and me much turmoil. Her admiration of and proximity to him test my forbearance.

I travel by stagecoach from Boston to Roxbury, all the while wishing I could ride one of the horses pulling it instead of suffering from the odors of my fellow passengers. One never knows whom one must share a ride with in public transport, and I am unfortunate to be seated between a snoring old woman and a young, portly man with garlic on his breath. I lean over him as much as propriety will allow to take in gulps of fresh air outside the window. Believing I wish to get a better view of the surrounding countryside, the man is gentleman enough to offer me his window seat, which I accept with many thanks.

Eager as I am to see Nathaniel, there is a piece of me that is as anxious to observe his interactions with Margaret, and to look on what will become our marriage home once the community is thriving. Nathaniel thinks that will be soon, and believes the manual farm labor and bucolic scenery will prepare him well for our union and his writing. I certainly hope so, because he has invested two five-hundred-dollar shares in Brook Farm, and that is nearly the extent of our earthly funds. I have recently sold a portrait for a decent sum—a bas-relief of Mr. Emerson's now deceased and beloved brother, Charles. More than the money, Emerson's admiration of my likeness of a man so well loved has filled my soul with confidence and gratitude for this artistic gift God has bestowed upon me. It has also given me new hope that my art might contribute to a household income on a regular basis.

The sun evaporates the morning mists from the gentle hills, and just ahead I see what must be the silhouette of Brook Farm. I can imagine myself nestled here with my love in pastoral society, painting and working in the community that seems so remote yet is in such close proximity to our dear families. I now understand it is God, not Nathaniel, who has made us wait these long months, and for good reason. He has been creating our perfect home.

As I draw closer to Brook Farm, my heart further lifts. This old dairy farm, located along the banks of the Charles River on two hundred acres, will be a model for a new America—one founded on the ideals of abolition, equal education for all, and women's rights. These transcendentalist Unitarians will show the country how we can all serve one another in perfect harmony with man and nature, and I am filled with pride that my husband is at the genesis of such a society.

I nearly jump out of the coach when I behold a figure in the mist watching the road. I would recognize Nathaniel anywhere. He cannot help his eager hand from waving, and I reach my arm out the window and return his greeting until I am near enough to descend from the coach and leap into his arms. He swings me around, and our laughter and salutations echo off the verdant hills. When he places me on the ground, I catch sight of Margaret, who emerges from a door. She raises her hand in welcome and nods, but the shadow from the threshold mutes her expression.

Soon a group has joined us, and after we retrieve my bags, Nathaniel leads me into "the Hive," as they call it, the old farmhouse that serves as a gathering space. I smell warm sausage and the sweet aroma of bread and cream, and I am enfolded into the community. As our breakfast progresses, I am impressed by the youth and vitality of those around me. Most of the residents are young and unmarried, and share equitably in the chores.

"If someone does not like working with the hoe, she may milk cows," says George Ripley.

"And if one does not enjoy ironing, he may slop pig stalls," says his wife, Sophia.

I watch Nathaniel, and feel a heaviness settle in my heart. He has barely spoken throughout this meal, though he wears a pleasant smile. Try as I might, I cannot imagine my Apollo slopping or ironing. He was made to write—not to engage in physical toil. How can he be happy here?

"And what if one wishes to lie on a bale of hay and contemplate the sunrise?" I ask. "What is his place at the farm?"

There is a titter of laughter. Nathaniel stares at his breakfast, but I see a small smile on his lips.

"We all must have time for leisure," says Ripley, "but not until the chores are done."

"Mrs. Ripley has been kind enough to attach book holders to ironing boards so one might read while working," says Margaret. "I have to confess that my page count often exceeds the number of pressed garments."

We share another laugh, and continue our meal until the clearing of the dishes.

Nathaniel rolls up his sleeves and begins to wash plates, handing them to me for drying, and I to Margaret for shelving. Mr. Ripley collects the napkins and table coverings for washing, and Mrs. Ripley wipes down the benches. Others sweep the floor, collect leftovers for the pig, and disperse for farm chores.

"You work together as gracefully as the notes of a symphony," I say. "How natural you all are at utopian living."

"You might not say so if you join us at the barn," says Mr. Ripley. "Many of us have spent more time in offices and classrooms than in cow stalls, but we are learning."

"And we are taking copious notes," says Margaret. "I need my freedom to come and go, so I have not joined on paper, but I share what we learn with other societies and in salons in Boston. I am hopeful that more people will soon join."

"Like me, someday," I say.

Nathaniel looks at me for a moment, but then returns to his task. I imagine that he enjoys washing dishes because he may turn his back on people and not have to participate in the conversation. There is a tension about him, and I am eager to leave our chores to further probe my love. When we finish, Nathaniel takes me by the hand and leads me out of the building, nodding at those we encounter. They nod back at him, but I am sad to see that no real warmth, only politeness, is exchanged. As we pass the barns and manure piles, Nathaniel shudders.

"Come quickly," he says. "It is a relief to spend my day with you instead of shoveling those disgusting hills of dung. And I thought the custom house made for dirty work."

"At least one may breathe in the fresh country air," I say.

"Not when pounds of manure are under your nostrils."

We start along the Charles River. I sense some relaxation in Nathaniel's sphere the farther we get from the barns, but his furrowed brow betrays his inner turmoil. I know better than to bring up my worries to this man who does not like to acknowledge darkness, so I simply give him the news from Boston and Salem, which he receives with interest. Our hike takes us to the edge of a forest where Nathaniel says venerable Indians are known to frolic. He finds an arrowhead, which he lifts, brushes off, and presents to me.

"Maybe it is a sign of good luck," he says.

I pull him close, and he wraps his arm around me.

"Of course it is," I say. "Our union is blessed, and surely will be soon."

"All in good time," he says.

I try not to stiffen at his maddening patience, but he has felt my body change, and does not ask why. I pull away and calm my emotions until I am able to say with a lift in my voice, "I long to see the little abode where we will finally reside together. Where Margaret nursed you back to good health, bless her. Take me to it."

His eyes narrow and he seems about to chastise me when none other than Margaret herself emerges from the woods like a nymph. How she has reached the forest behind us from where she was working earlier, I do not know, and I am chilled at her sudden presence. I have conjured the very woman I do not wish to see. She ignores Nathaniel, however, and comes to me, slipping her arm through mine. I feel her warmth at my side, and I am surprised by both the comfort it affords and by the contrast to Nathaniel's cool torso. I dare to look at Margaret, and see her plain face arranged so kindly that I soften toward her.

"I am glad you are here," she says. "Nathaniel did not seem a whole person until he had you at his side."

I am surprised by her speech, and unable to find my voice.

"Mr. Ripley has many ideals that will be enacted well here, but I know that not all men and women are made for such living."

She glances over her shoulder at Nathaniel, who now trails us with his hands in his pockets. He cannot take his eyes off the grassy path. We walk along in silence, though not peace, and I am confused to distraction. Is Margaret trying to show me that she has no wish to take Nathaniel? To assure me that no trust has been breached? To excuse Nathaniel from yet another place where he does not seem to belong? Margaret saves me from my internal musings by stopping and taking both of my hands in hers. I turn and see that Nathaniel lags farther behind, and still does not look at us.

"I nursed him for you, my friend," she says.

I turn back to her, and when I am convinced of her sincerity, my relief is so great that I feel I will cry. She pulls me into an embrace, and when we release our grasp, Nathaniel is upon us. Margaret turns me toward a tidy row of cottages.

"Nathaniel is strong and ready for his companion," says Margaret. "He speaks of nothing but his dear dove to anyone who will listen. I am happy to listen, because I too am enchanted by you, his sweet artist, and long to see a successful union of heart and mind."

My emotion is great, but I am finally able to speak. "Thank you, Margaret. You have expressed so beautifully what I often think about the true meaning of marriage."

She transfers my arm to Nathaniel's, and we walk to one of the dwellings, where he opens the door. The brightness outside makes it difficult for me to see the room at first. Out of the shadows first emerge my husband's bed and a small desk and chair, where a stack of writing paper and a pencil rest. I can imagine him penning his letters of love and longing to me alone in this room, and I am filled with pity for my solitary husband. There are two tiny windows that do not allow in much light, and a fireplace where I see the remains of burned papers that I know must be stories he started but considered unworthy of being completed. I am moved at the thought of him destroying his work, of doing labor he hates in order to support me. We step in, and once I behold my paintings on the wall over the fireplace, I can no longer stop my tears. He does care for me. He wants me with him always. He does not love this Margaret and she is no threat. In fact, she has gone, shutting the door, leaving us alone together.

When my eyes meet Nathaniel's, I see that his too have a shine, and I fall into his arms, where I am met with a fierce passion I do not anticipate. He kisses me until I cannot breathe.

"How can you doubt me?" he says. "Do I not tell you of my love often enough? Do I not express with every stroke of my pencil how I long for you?"

"You do," I cry. "It is my fault. Being apart from you breeds a doubt that permeates my soul. I loathe our separation."

"I do, too," he says, burying his face in my neck and covering it with kisses that light a fire in me.

Before I know what is happening, we are moving to the bed, and he lies on top of me, continuing to steal my breath with his weight and passion. I answer his kisses as never before, and I am aware of a swelling that ignites something in me that longs for satisfaction. I place my hands in his soft hair and feel him lifting my dress. His motion has become frantic, and I am suddenly overwhelmed by the power of our passion.

"Stop," I say, softly at first and then with more force. "Nathaniel! We must stop."

He becomes still, though I can feel our hearts pounding in unison, as if they wish to escape from our chests. He trembles in my arms and I roll him to his side and bury my face in his plain woolen vest, which holds the scent of the wind in the meadow.

"I do not want to stop," I say. "And soon we will not be able to, so we must marry. As quickly as possible. Then we may rightfully share this room, and quench this longing."

He is quiet, and the throbbing in our hearts and bodies subsides. The room has become clearer now that my eyes have adjusted to the light, and I am struck by how small and plain it is, and how close it is to the people wandering just outside the door—people who could peek in at any moment and find us in bed together.

When Nathaniel speaks, his voice is ragged and tired, and I am again sunk.

"I fear we will never share this room," he says. I look at him and it seems to take a great deal of courage for him to utter what follows.

"I wish to leave the farm."

17

A ten-year-old girl—blind, deaf, and dumb—sits before me, illuminated by the light pouring in from the tall windows here at the Perkins School for the Blind in Boston. She is at once human and spirit, a quiet angel with a presence of calm and innocence. I long to wrap her in protective arms, so vulnerable is she. Her name is Laura Bridgman, and a teacher sits with her, finger spelling on her arm when the girl becomes agitated. A bout of scarlet fever when Laura was only two years old left her in this insensate state, but her intelligence and capacity for learning are legendary. As are her tantrums, I am told.

Samuel Howe, the director, has commissioned me to make a bust—my first fully three-dimensional clay creation—that will be copied in schools for the blind across the country. I feel I am answering a calling in this work. At once I will immortalize Laura and advance my own future, and I hope to replace some of the money we lost at Brook Farm. Like Nathaniel, I had thought our investment was a good one, but we were both wrong. It did not take long for him to see that Mr. Ripley was a man of high ideals and little action, and that communal living was unsuitable for Nathaniel, as it was for many. I did not argue with Nathaniel when he decided to leave, and even supported him in his decision, though it set us further back financially.

Nathaniel does now seem to take more seriously the idea that my art might supplement our income. It seems that this progression—from flat pencil sketches, to oil paintings, to bas-relief, and now this bust—is developing my artistic talents at a fascinating rate. My bas-relief of Emerson's deceased brother brought me the notoriety to receive this commission of a sculpture, if only my pulsing head will cooperate.

I stop and press my wrists to my temples, careful not to get plaster in my hair. I will call on Connie for mesmerism later this day, though I must not tell Nathaniel. I squeeze my eyes shut for a moment and will myself to continue, but the teacher at Laura's side speaks, again halting me.

"You immortalize her well, Miss Peabody," she says.

"Thank you. Do you think she understands what we are doing?"

"Let us see. May I have her touch you and the plaster?"

"It is still wet."

"I will make sure she is gentle."

I nod my approval, and the teacher spells on Laura's arm. The girl becomes animated, and in seconds she is at my side. I am uneasy about the thought of her exploring my body, but realize she will learn something from it, and attempt to relax myself so she does not sense my wariness.

Laura's thin fingers kiss my skin like butterfly wings, and I soon enter a state not unlike mesmerism. She first explores my hair, tugging and pulling so gently I am reminded of Josepha's fingers in my ringlets, and then moving down my face and touching my eyes, and then her own, which she keeps covered with a cloth. She stays there awhile, so I keep my eyes closed, becoming sleepy under the pressure of her fingers. When she moves on, she does not seem to be interested in my nose or my plain mouth, but when she reaches my shoulders she spends time pressing them and kneading them before allowing her hands to travel down my arms, which I now use to reach out to my creation. She follows the curve down to my fingertips, and starts when she reaches my wet hands and the plaster cast. I stiffen, fearing that she will ruin my progress today, when her teacher begins a rapid spelling on the girl's arm.

Laura holds her face down and to the side, as if trying to understand, and a few minutes of spelling pass before she lifts her head and smiles. She places one hand gently on the plaster cast, and the other on her own face, and seems transfixed. Tears wet her blindfold, though she smiles. I feel tears spring to my own eyes, and thank God for allowing me to share in this moment. These small, human discoveries are the essence of earthly joy, and I cannot wait to tell Nathaniel of it.

After a minute or two, Laura pulls away, and her teacher leads her to a towel to wipe the plaster from her fingers while I repair the slight disturbance she has made between the eyes of the bust. While I sit to admire my work, Laura begins to moan and cry. Her teacher raises her hand when I start to stand.

"It will be all right," she says. "Sometimes she has fits of emotion. I can only imagine that her condition overwhelms her."

"I understand," I say, filled with pity for this creature so separated from the joys of the world. I would wither if I could not behold a sunset, or smell a gardenia, or hear the birds sing, or listen to a piano sonata. I am ashamed to find that I am unable to stop my own tears, and I am soon in the full clutches of a plaguesome headache. I reach for a towel to wipe my hands; it is clear that we are done for today.

Suddenly Laura rushes at me and clings to me, her little head resting on my bosom, against my pounding heart. I wrap my arms around her and place my head on hers, moved by the very clear feelings of gratitude and melancholy pulsing from this child. I attempt to convey my feelings back to her, and the physical warmth of our embrace seems to stimulate a cataract of images in my mind.

In rapid succession—almost as if I am dreaming—I feel the embraces of the Morrell children; Don Fernando's lips on my hand; the oil on my fingers from cleaning the Magdalene portrait in Cuba; George's clammy form at my side in his deathbed; and Nathaniel! The moment our eyes first met each other's, his mouth on my neck in his apartment, his *self* swollen toward me at Brook Farm.

These impressions of physical stimulation outside of art bring on a headache like those I get when I create. Will all forms of acute sensory stimulation result in infirmity, or do I become ill because the sensations are incomplete, unrealized, and unfulfilled?

I pull away, blind from the pressure in my head that has surpassed any pain I have ever felt. I hear the teacher's voice call for help, and then it is as if a black veil falls over the room.

18

We have agreed to marry on June twenty-seventh, 1842.

Nathaniel can no longer bear that I must suffer infirmity without his care; nor can he endure our separation. He finally understands that delaying our marriage is burdening not only our lovers' hearts, but also our creative spheres. We are meant to be one, and living apart is wounding our tender spirits because they are incomplete.

Just weeks before the date, Nathaniel finally tells his mother and sisters of our plans. His mother's reaction, which he feared most, is sweet and indicates that she guessed, but his sisters are shocked, and Ebe is especially grieved. My letter to them following his confession is meant as the balm and assurance that their dear Nathaniel will be loved very well by his wife, but it is met with such iciness that the glaciers of the Arctic would grow if exposed to their wintry blasts. I lie in the family parlor—my state of rest following Connie's mesmerism having been severely disturbed—while I thrust the letter from Ebe at Nathaniel. My hand trembles and I cannot contain my emotion.

"She writes that she is much pained and will be polite to me because decorum says she must, but she offers no shred of warmth or invitation. I have never known such rudeness in my life!"

Nathaniel's face is strained and he runs his beautiful fingers over his eyes and rests them on his cheeks.

"I will scold her," he says. "I am very sorry you have been subjected to this. My delay in telling them was only because I sensed the inevitability of their distress. It is our . . . closeness in our house of solitude and mourning that causes them to behave in such a way. My father's absence made them elevate me in the household. They fear that I will not be able to support them if I have a wife and family."

"How can you defend such appalling behavior on the eve of our wedding? This is a time of bliss and congratulation. Even my sister Elizabeth has expressed her pleasure for us, and she might have married you herself!"

Oh, he flinches at this, and I am glad it cuts, shameful though it is to feel this way.

"Only a person of the most selfish nature could put such things in writing to the fiancée of her brother," I continue. "I hope they do not come."

His shoulders slump and he looks so wretched that I turn away so I will not allow my pity for him to quench this anger. I so often restrain my frustration for his sake that my relief at its full expression is profound. He comes to my side and reaches for me. His hands, usually cool and clean, are hot and sweaty. His voice is so low I can barely hear him, as if it requires tremendous effort to utter the words.

"You are right. It destroys me that they have insulted you. I will go at once and reprimand them."

"Please do."

"I will. You must not strain yourself so. Creating that bust has brought such a dreadful return of your headaches—and now this controversy! I cannot stand for you to be ill. You must not allow yourself to be agitated, even if it means that you do nothing but take milk and bread by the fireside for the rest of your days."

"I do not want milk and bread. I want wine and joy. I want our creative communion to begin—you at your desk and me at my easel. Our new Eden. I want it now!"

I pull my hand away, confused as to why I am still so angry with him when he will do as I wish. I have never before felt such sustained impatience with him. I turn back, expecting to see his contrite face, and I am surprised that his countenance has darkened. The blackest storm cloud has covered my sun, and I am chilled to the marrow. He stands and straightens his jacket.

"While we must suffer this airing of grievances," he says, "I have something I must say that I have referenced repeatedly, but which you have ignored, to my great displeasure."

Well! This is something. I cannot imagine how he feels the right to scold me at this time. I do not soften my gaze, but sit up straighter.

"I wish you would stop this mesmerism with Connie," he says.

Nathaniel has spoken each word with such strained deliberation that he is visibly exhausted. As much as it ails me to be in opposition to the man I will finally take as my husband, I will not bend to him.

"If I do not continue mesmerism with Connie," I say, "you will not have a wife, because I will have died from my headaches. Tend to your sisters and leave my head to me."

He looks as if he wants to speak more—his lips tremble and he begins to pace. After a moment, he again meets my gaze. I hear a small voice in my mind that seems not to come from me and so it must be his. It utters just one word.

Please.

His face begs: *Please mind me, naughty Sophy.* His earnestness makes him more beautiful than ever before, and his forehead softens. As much as this conflict hurts my heart, I am in no way in the wrong. I cannot smile for him.

He sighs, smooths his jacket, and reaches for his hat, which he arranges on his head.

"I will go to them now," he says, kneeling before me to kiss my hand. He stays there and gives me a roguish grin. "But know this: Once you become my wife, you will obey me."

With that he leaves me in my mother's parlor. He has spoken lightly, but his words lodge in my brain.

That night, Mother comes to me in my room, where I sit up in bed next to a dying candle, touching the violet brooch Nathaniel gave to me last Christmas. I cherish these interactions because soon I will leave my family for Concord. Mr. Emerson has secured us his late uncle's dwelling—the Old Manse—which has lain vacant for a time following the good minister's death. It is the house I saw on my visit to Concord all those months ago, where I imagined living with Nathaniel in such bliss. But now the prospect of sharing a home fills me with dread.

Mother places a chair at my bedside and her hand on my forehead, which burns with some fever—of illness or love, I cannot say.

"My girl, you must sleep. Your wedding has been so long in coming. You do not want it any more delayed, do you?"

Do I? I am beginning to think I might. I think for a moment that I will not voice my concerns to Mother, so she will not worry, but before I know it, the words are tumbling forth and I am crying in her arms.

"What if I was wrong to accept his proposal?" I say. "What if I break the holy artists' vow? Perhaps I am not meant for marriage after all."

"Perhaps you are not. I never thought you were, myself. Who will take care of you as I do?"

"Nathaniel takes just as good of care of me as you, and almost more so! He wants me to cease all artistic endeavors if they cause me the slightest pain. He does not encourage me to push past my headaches. He wants only my comfort and repose."

"I cannot disagree with him there, Sophia."

"I know, but Elizabeth, for example, never had any trouble pushing me. Mary too. Now that I am to be married, perhaps they will not feel it is their place to encourage me, and I will allow my artistry to wither, and will deny my life's vocation. Is not suffering a calling? Should I not suffer for art's sake?"

"Hush, now," says Mother. "You begin to sound like a Catholic martyr."

I fall back on my pillow, frustrated by this conversation.

"I would be less worried about Nathaniel's care of you getting in the way of your artistry," she continues, "and more of the inevitability of children getting in the way."

"But, Mother, I yearn for children."

She is quiet for a long while, but finally speaks.

"Children are a great blessing and a great burden, as each of you has been to me. You are not a burden I would not want, but you must face the fact that you are not of hearty constitution, and you do not bear your burdens lightly."

"Perhaps if I had the burdens of another to bear, I would not be so preoccupied with my own."

"Perhaps," she says.

I look at my mother and her careworn face. She will not talk me into or out of this marriage. She will tell me the plain truth and leave the decision to me. How I long for her to dominate me with opinions, but she simply plants a kiss on my forehead, pulls the covers up to my chin, and leaves me alone to pass another sleepless night.

"Awaken," says Connie.

I blink my heavy eyelids, and my bedroom comes into focus.

My limbs feel weighted and my head thick, but there is no pain in me, save the ache in my heart that agonizes over my impending nuptials.

"Will you tell him I visited you today?" asks Connie with a smirk, while placing the magnets she has run over my body in a velvet drawstring bag.

"I will. I keep nothing from mine ownest."

"He will chastise you and dislike me further. I know it is because he finds me eccentric."

What she says is true, but I do not owe my friend the truth. Connie's husband left her to seek employment out west during the Panic of 1837. He said he would send for her, but never has. If Connie carries any pain from the separation, she does not share it; in fact, her freedom as a married woman living alone is quite enviable. Still, I will not confirm any of my husband's prejudices to her.

"You are fascinating, and I would not change you for the world," I say, embracing my friend before she leaves me. "Do remember to take your payment. Father left the money on the fireplace downstairs."

"Thank you. And when shall I dress for the wedding? What is the new date?"

"I have sent Mary to Salem to tell Nathaniel that we should wait a week more, just to make sure I am well. I want to be healthy and strong when we wed, so I may begin my life as a wife under the best possible circumstances."

Connie looks as if she wishes to reply, and must talk herself out of doing so, for she remains quiet. I feel a shiver in spite of the warm day.

The following week passes in a flurry of letters and preparations. Our belongings are slowly being shipped to Concord, and while my headaches persist, I feel an opening in my chest that allows room for hope. I have also allowed Dr. Wesselhoeft to treat me with the more conventional means of homeopathy, which pleases my husband. My new doctor is kind and gentle in his care, and I am beginning to feel better.

Nathaniel has sent me a letter full of terrors that plague him in the form of nightmares over my mesmerism with Connie, and the scandal that might ensue to have my name associated with such a controversial practice, but he has ended with promises for patience at my rehabilitation, faith in our love, and exclamations of his own adoration. It cheers me to sense such commitment in this latest epistle, because the postponement has depressed his spirits. In my darkest heart, I am somewhat gratified that he must struggle with impatience during this short time as I have over these long months. Now he knows exactly how his dove has felt all along.

On the ninth of July, we wed in my family's parlor, surrounded by my parents, sisters, and Connie. The reverend James Clarke performs the service for two grown adults who are as nervous as children. Mary and Mother smile while they dab their tears. Elizabeth's eyes are as dry as the wood in the fireplace, and her figure just as stiff.

I feel disconnected from the occasion at its start. Just as Nathaniel enters the room, Reverend Clarke—who has been re- marking on how honored he is to preside over the wedding of one of America's few published authors—must be shocked by my husband's beautiful and youthful appearance, because he be- comes very awkward and nervous, and cannot tear his eyes from Nathaniel's face.

As the service progresses, I allow my *innere* to separate from our surroundings, and coerce Nathaniel's soul to mingle with mine. It takes a short time for him to answer the call, but within moments I sense that we are alone within our spheres. His gaze locks into mine, and our hands seem to melt together. I can feel his communication of love and adoration, and my heart opens like the night flowers from Cuba. I realize that my love walks at night, and I will bloom in his dark and radiant glow, and when I see the shine of emotion in his eyes, my growing elation spills over into the most joyous of tears.

At the conclusion of the ceremony, we hear a tremendous boom of thunder, and in moments the sky has dissolved into great cataracts of rain. I laugh with delight as we race to the waiting carriage, and the door is just barely closed when we col- lapse into each other's arms.

As we begin the ride to Concord, the storm rages around us and shakes our conveyance, but I have no fear, only ecstasy. Na- thaniel is distracted only enough to make passing comments on the rain, but mostly he is at my neck, my collarbone, my lips, my hands—there is not one exposed place on me that he leaves un- kissed. After a short while we become aware that we are stopped in the road, and have been for some time. I hear the call of the driver and rearrange myself so as not to appear too unkempt as we make our way to a stopping post, where we must wait in the carriage while our dear horses rest and recover from the muddy road.

I slide the curtain open so we may watch the summer storm, and then look down as Nathaniel threads his long fingers through mine. He rubs my palm with his thumb in a smooth, circular motion that hypnotizes me.

"Are you mesmerizing me, Mr. Hawthorne? I thought you feared such interference with my mind and soul."

He lifts his hand to my face and pulls me against him, tracing my lips with his tongue and nearly bringing me to crisis. He nibbles my lower lip, and follows with a long, slow, soft kiss. Then he places his forehead to mine.

"No one but I will ever interfere with your mind and soul and body again," he says, his eyes dark with passion.

"Now that you have made me yours, you may be my lord."

"That's my dove," he says, tracing my brow with his fingers before rearranging his face wickedly. "But please do not banish naughty Sophy for good. I want her to make appearances too."

I match his look with a devilish smile and slide my hands into his shirt while kissing his neck.

"You may count on that."

INTERLUDE

1864
Massachusetts

Nathaniel is asleep on my shoulder, dreaming fitfully, while I shift in my seat, wondering whether he can sense my pounding heart, my memories of passion so filling this space that I could suffocate. I press my handkerchief to my cheeks and blot the perspiration on my brow.

How different is this carriage ride from the one after our wedding. How many miles have we traveled together? Have our years of bliss outnumbered our times of pain?

Even in our Eden days, the stain of death spilled like crimson ink over the clean, white pages of our lives. Reflecting back, I am in awe of the great and terrible rivers that delivered the deaths of kin and stranger to us. Water is the source of life, the holy baptism, but can also be the end of it, the drowning. The placid surface of the Concord River that drifted behind the Old Manse—

the river that Nathaniel hated, which I talked him into appreciating just before it stole from us—masked its depths. I could not fathom the turbulence that existed below us on our lazy canoe rides or our winter ice-skating. Had I heeded Nathaniel's good sense, perhaps I could have changed the course of our lives at that time.

My ailing husband sighs and cries out from the pain in his stomach, and I pat his hand to try to soothe him, but he is awake and agitated.

"Are we there?" he asks.

"Not yet, my love."

He takes his hands from mine and reaches up to touch the lump in his jacket as if to reassure himself the thing he needed is still there. Then he wraps his arms around his waist and pulls away from my shoulder to lean on the side of the carriage. I am cold where his body no longer meets mine. It is as if a cloud bank passed over, blotting out the sun's warmth.

"Do you remember our wedding day?" I ask, desperate to reconnect with Nathaniel before we are separated.

He grunts and screws up his face, flinching from pain. I use my handkerchief to dry his sweaty forehead.

"Do you wish me to stay quiet or talk, my love?" I say. "Which will bring you comfort?"

He looks at me, his eyes the only clear and unaltered part of him, though time has taught me of the turbulent depths they conceal.

"Speak if it will bring you comfort," he says. "Though I fear I am beyond it."

"I will paint for you," I say. "I will paint with words something you can hang under the veil inside your soul."

A smile plays at his dry lips. When I mention the veil, I know he is reminded of how he used to hide my paintings.

"I was a dramatic youth, was I not?" he says.

"Perfectly so."

"Where did we hang the engagement paintings at the manse?"

"In your study, remember? Where you could observe them in private."

"No, that is where we hung your *Endymion*."

"I did not make the *Endymion* until I was round with Una."

"Ah, yes. The years blur from this vantage."

"Like the mist on the river in the mornings," I say.

We are quiet for a moment. I drink of our little conversation as if from the wellspring of life. The older I become, the more importance I assign to even the smallest interaction. Fickle, changeable life has taught me to savor any sweetness, no matter how insignificant it might seem.

"I am glad to have this time alone with you in a carriage," I say. "We are fortunate to have each other. When I think of Robert Browning and poor Longfellow—widowers alone in the world—I do not comprehend how they endure it."

"I would not last a day without my dove."

Our friends Elizabeth Browning and Fanny Longfellow both died in 'sixty-one—Elizabeth from her chronic lung illness, and Fanny of a dreadful accident when she dropped a lit match on her dress and caught fire. Henry Longfellow had attempted to save her by wrapping her in a carpet, but the burns were too severe. I shudder at the thought.

"When I recall the Concord River," I say, "I think of how I saw it through the words we etched on the window. 'Man's accidents . . .'"

"'Are God's purposes.'"

19

Summer 1842
Concord, Massachusetts

Under the benediction of twilight, at the gentle prodding of the setting sun's rays, the rain parts like a curtain around our home. As the carriage turns to proceed down the avenue of black ash trees, Nathaniel calls to the driver.

"Halt!"

Nathaniel's face is lit from the emerging sun, and my heart feels as if it has exploded and showered bliss over every inch of this carriage.

"Let us go on foot," he says.

He is breathless with an exuberance I have never before seen in him, and I cannot contain my tears of joy. Nathaniel's eyes leak rivulets down his face. We laugh together at our stupidity, and launch down the drive toward our abode—a friendly house of two floors, where ivy has taken over, and where a dear stone wall leads around to an abundant orchard that borders the Concord River.

Before we arrive at the house, Nathaniel leads me through the muddy earth to the vegetable garden Mr. Henry Thoreau has started for us as a wedding present. After we exclaim over the beans and asparagus shoots, I pull Nathaniel over to the front door, where we remove our shoes and he lifts me into his arms. We burst over the threshold and are greeted by flowers—vases and vases of flowers!—adorning every room like an interior garden. There are notes from our friends tucked in the lilies and roses spilling from baskets and hollowed tree stumps, and the air holds the sweet exhalations of the blooms.

"Eden!" I shout, as my husband places my feet on the floor. I run through the house, ecstatic that my head has clarity and aliveness. "Oh, my Adam, my whole life has been leading to this moment!"

He chases me, and when he catches me, he laughs like a boy who does not know where to begin making mischief. He settles on plucking a lily from a nearby basket, and threads it through my hair. He takes my hand and leads me past the parlor, through the kitchen, and down the slope that runs to the river. When we reach its banks, we marvel over the reflection of the sky in the placid Concord.

"Have you ever seen a more charming stream?" I say.

He wrinkles his nose and grins. "Perhaps my eyes are so dazzled by your loveliness that I cannot comprehend anything lesser, for it looks like a great mud puddle."

I gasp and strike his breast, and he laughs wickedly.

"How dare you insult any aspect of paradise," I say, turning away from him to face the water. "Dear river, please excuse my husband. He is quite stupid with giddiness. Once I attend to him, he might be more friendly and welcoming."

His arms wrap around me from behind, and he kisses my neck so that every inch of my body is alert with longing. I spin to meet his embrace, when the voice of the carriage driver tumbles down the hill and breaks our spell. Nathaniel groans.

"Go, my lord," I whisper. "Attend to and dispose of the mortals quickly so you might have your reward."

"Yes, my lady. My queen. My Eve."

My silly husband kneels, kisses my hand, and runs up the hill in long strides. I press my palms to my burning face and admire his godlike form until he is out of view.

I turn back to the river. Does she wink at me with her sun reflections and the disturbance of jumping fish? I raise my hands to her in blessing and bow my head. In moments, the sun slips behind the clouds and a swift wind raises the skin on my arms, urging my eyes open. With the sun hidden, the river appears murky and foreboding. I regard her for only a moment more before I hurry up to the house to prepare for my first night with my husband.

In our bedroom we have drawn a bath, pumping buckets of water and warming them on the stove, then pouring them into the washtub. We rinse off the summer's heat, and remove the dust and mud of travel—a lifetime of travel—that has culminated in this destination that fate intended for us all along.

The light of thirty-one candles—one for each month that has

passed since our secret engagement—glows over the walls, the flowers, the empty wineglasses, and the bed whose blankets lay open in invitation. I see it all while Nathaniel's hands lather my hair, my face, my shoulders. He removes his shirt, and I am nearly dizzy from his beauty. His arms disappear in the liquid and I accept his explorations with rapture.

I slip out of the water while he slips in, and I make slow work of cleaning his hair and body. Once I finish, I drape myself in my new velvet robe, and wind the music box Mary gave us as a wedding present. Its strange, lovely tinkling fills the air like the music of faeries. I cross the room to brush my long auburn hair until it is smooth around my shoulders.

Watching Nathaniel sit so regally before me, I feel an urge to dance for my lord. At first with a coy smile, and then with seriousness and deliberation, I begin moving to the music, gliding toward him like a harem girl. I lift the robe to cover my face, and then expose it a bit at a time, undulating in ways I could not have imagined. Nathaniel is riveted, and the intensity of his gaze makes it hard for me to breathe. I turn my back to him and allow the robe to slip from my body to the floor. I take a deep breath and then face him, fully aware of my grand state, relaxed from the wine, unafraid and unwilling to wait a moment longer.

He rises, steps from the tub without drying himself, and lifts me to the bed, where we pass the night in a chemical fantasy of the most perfect and exquisite bliss.

20

Awaking from the dream of our honeymoon is a gradual process, brought about by a rainy season, a stream of visitors, and a lack of money. Our perfect obsession with each other, however, delays our full acceptance of reality.

We have an Irish girl to cook named Mary, who also helps us with household tasks. I insist to Nathaniel that we can manage without a servant, but he wants only my comfort, and perhaps a better hand at preparing meals. Three pints of milk are delivered daily, and meat from the butcher three times a week. Though I find the well water fine, Nathaniel insists that it tastes like the slime on the Concord River.

One August morning, I awaken to the gentle nudging of the wind and the shush of rain outside our open windows. I adore our stormy, saturated Eden, though Nathaniel complains about being kept indoors.

"Looks like another day we shall have to occupy ourselves without leaving the house," I say, when he opens his eyes. "Whatever will we do?"

He grins and stretches, then pulls me closer to him and tickles me until I cannot get my breath. Once I have calmed, Nathaniel slides my chemise slowly up my legs and makes lazy love to me while the thunder grumbles. When we finish, we lie with the sheets off, sweating and satiated, staring outside at the glistening leaves.

"Did you take me to an Amazonian rain forest for our honeymoon, and not tell me?" he says.

"Indeed I did. And like the savages, you must remove your clothing and walk around in all your glory, as is the custom."

"Very well," he says, standing up and pacing about the room, delighting me with his fine form.

"Will you keep to custom this evening when our friends come to dine?" I say.

He stops. "Friends, tonight?"

"Do you not remember? I had the butcher deliver an extra cut of beef. Margaret Fuller; her sister Ellen Channing and Ellen's husband, Ellery; Mr. Emerson. I do not think we can expect his wife, poor thing."

I do not need to remind my husband that the Emersons' eldest son died of scarlet fever several months ago. By all accounts, if they did not have their other two children, they would have both perished of grief. As it is, Lidian is a walking ghost.

Nathaniel collapses on the bed, as if he is greatly fatigued.

"Must we always have visitors?" he says. "I suppose I should have known a Peabody would be used to a full parlor, but I thought the noise and chatter vexed you as much as they do me."

"Oh, hush, silly. We have had visitors only three times a week, and never for dinner. It will be lovely to celebrate our monthly-versary with friends."

"It would be lovely to celebrate our monthly-versary doing exactly what we just did several more times throughout the day and night."

"As delicious as that sounds, being forced to wait until our guests leave will make the coupling all the sweeter."

I kiss him on the nose, and pull on my robe.

"Would you like me to draw you a bath?" I ask.

"No," he says. "I am going to walk outside in the rain to Walden Pond, and see if I can persuade Henry Thoreau to join me for a swim."

"On your way, please implore the rain to rest so our friends might not get too muddy. And tell Henry to come to dinner, too, when you see him. The more, the merrier!"

I do not know whether Nathaniel asked the rain to cease, but I certainly did a thousand times today, and just an hour before our guests are set to arrive, the clouds part and give us the most elegant evening light.

On Nathaniel's wet adventures out of doors, I had him collect as many flowers as two baskets would hold, and the result has made a perfect garden of our home. Scarlet cardinal flowers, yellow daisies, pink asters, and white lilies bloom from every table and mantel, and the silver tapers we received as a wedding gift glisten in the front room, where we dine at a lace cloth–covered table. Henry did swim with Nathaniel and returned with him to pick green beans and tomatoes for our feast, but declined the dinner invitation. Henry suffers even more in society than Nathaniel does.

"I told Henry that I would rather join him around a fire under the stars," says Nathaniel. "But he said my wife needs her companion."

"Henry is very sweet," I say. "Though I do not think it good for him to be alone so often."

"Dove, not everyone is meant to be at home in society. Henry is quite happy among the trees and chipmunks."

I light the last taper and stand back to admire its glow. When I look up, my husband is gazing at me, and seems about to say something, but the emotion evident in his eyes has stolen his speech. I give him my most tender smile, and we move toward each other until a knock at the door breaks the spell.

Mr. Emerson arrives with Ellery and Ellen Channing, and Margaret, and we embrace one another and chatter our welcomes and praises. Ellen wants to see every little candlestick and wall hanging, and leads me away to discuss my trousseau, while Margaret joins the men in the front parlor under the great stuffed owl that was here when we arrived, which we have named Longfellow. The owl is an imposing and strange creature whose eyes seem to follow us from one corner of the room to the other, but Nathaniel loves it, so I tolerate it.

After a short time, Mary asks me to call our guests to dine, and presents a steaming and tender beef, a flavorful gravy, rose-mary potatoes, and roasted vegetables. Nathaniel opens two bottles of wine and pours, while I blush under praises of our fine menu, table, and hospitality.

"A toast," says Emerson, once Nathaniel sits. "To the house of Hawthorne, a place warmed by love and the true and perfect union of artists. May your lives together always retain this honeymoon aura."

"Hear, hear," the others say.

I glance at Nathaniel sitting stiffly at my side, and clink my glass on his. Emerson's words feel like a blessing, but Nathaniel seems ill at ease. I hope the wine helps him to relax a bit. I think Emerson intimidates him, ridiculous though that is, and I want Nathaniel to enjoy himself.

"Thank you," I say. "And cheers to all of you who have welcomed us so kindly to Concord. I cannot imagine being more at home anywhere on earth."

We drink again, and the food is served.

Ellery begins talking about poetry with Margaret. I see that Emerson is quiet and somber in his black mourning suit, and feel tenderness toward him for being brave enough to venture into society when life at home must be so difficult. I lean toward him and place my hand on his arm.

"Please give my best to Lidian, and tell her that if there is ever anything I can do—if she needs help with the babies or anything at all, just ask."

"You are very kind," he says, wiping the corners of his lips with a napkin. "While I suffer, her pain seems to have roots far deeper and more intrusive than mine. It is a dark time."

"It saddens me to know how you both hurt. I have watched my mother mourn her lost children. The only comfort I have seen for her lies with those of us who remain. It is good you have the girls."

When I look up, I see that Margaret is watching Nathaniel like our stuffed owl. She is uncharacteristically quiet, appearing to appraise and evaluate all she sees. Nathaniel does not seem to notice. He has scarcely looked up from his green beans. After some time passes, Margaret finally speaks to me. "Have you been painting or sculpting since your nuptials?"

I feel a rush of heat that I may attribute to either the wine or to my discomfort at being the object of her scrutiny. I hear judgment in her question. She is a skeptic, and does not believe marriage can support two artists. I have not created much since we wed, but I certainly cannot explain to her that my husband's body and soul consume me at this time. But perhaps I can suggest it.

"Aside from some sketches of my husband, no," I say. "I have had no time for art, with all of the honeymooning that must be seen to."

My company laughs, except for Margaret. I glance at Nathaniel, who hides his grin behind a napkin. He wipes it away with the crumbs.

"Take care you do not neglect your gifts," Margaret says. "Might I remind you of your intention of making a union of holy artists?"

"Margaret, please," says Ellen. "Sophy is a perfect little bride. Allow her a summer without industry. She will have her life left for creation."

"Pray you do not wait too long," says Emerson. "We must stay at our crafts with discipline in order to reach perfection. Hawthorne, what of you? Do you write every day?"

Nathaniel stares at his wine goblet while he answers. "No. I am a perfect husband and a perfect idler, but a rather imperfect man of letters."

"All in good time," I say, blotting my forehead. "I would prefer to eat beans from the garden, and read books by other men, and take endless walks with my husband over doing any work in this house of love and leisure. I am quite sure the earth would rather her children take part in her bounty now and create later, once she has frozen over and entered her sleeping season. That is when Nathaniel and I work best."

"What a perfect ideal," says Ellen.

After a short silence, Ellery speaks. "Ellen tells me you have a house ghost."

I wish Nathaniel to take part in our conversation, so I place my hand on his thigh.

"Tell them about our run-in with our ghost just a few nights ago," I say.

He takes a large drink of wine and faces Ellery. "Sophia was in the parlor, and heard me thumping about in my study after she thought I had gone to bed. When she went in the room, it was empty. I was asleep in our bedroom."

A gasp goes up from the diners, and I am happy that Nathaniel has affected our guests so. He seems to gain confidence from their reaction and continues.

"Another night we heard the distinct sound of crumpling paper in my study, and went in together only to find nothing. Nothing at all."

"We ran shrieking down the stairs like children," I say. "We could not sleep all night!"

"A charming vision," says Margaret, wearing a tight smile.

Does she find our stories stupid and nonsensical, I wonder, or is she jealous? I do not have time to ponder this question for long, because Mary has entered with dessert.

"Blancmange!" I say. "The only dish I contributed to our feast tonight. I hope it is half as tasty as your spread, Mary."

Our girl curtsies and blushes, and vanishes as if she were the ghost.

After we have eaten our fill, Emerson takes polite leave of us. I watch him walk away, a dark silhouette in the night. Is he a comfort to his wife, or is he ever the orator? Does he pluck lilies from the pond to slide behind her ear or gaze at her with love across the just-lit candlesticks of their home before the guests arrive? Do they weep together in the night, cradled in a sphere of shared mourning? These are the things I think about now that I am married.

I hear that our company has elected to walk out of doors, under the starry sky. The cloudy veil has been removed from the heavens, and the splendor of the full moon captivates. In hushed voices we remark on the enchantment of the illuminated paths that border the river, the leaves glowing silver, and the splashes and cracking twigs that give us a little fright. On our way back to the manse, a cat yowls long and slow.

"Are witches walking tonight?" asks Margaret, raising the hair on my arms.

"Only us," I say, drawing Ellen and Margaret closer to my sides. We share a laugh that we turn into a cackle, and I glance over my shoulder to see Nathaniel's reaction, but his face is hidden in the shadows.

"Perhaps we had best walk fast, with a *Ha*-thorne at our heels," says Margaret. "Lest we end up hanging from the gallows at his judgment."

I laugh to be polite, but I fear she will upset Nathaniel with such comments. He makes no reply, which means either he is hurt or he did not hear Margaret.

"This is a night for spirits and poets," says Ellery. "The moon inspires both."

I slide from Ellen's and Margaret's sides, and slow to match my steps with my husband's, drawing my arm through his. I feel his heat through his clothing, which is always so precise and correct in public, and shiver at the thought that I know him intimately. What a strange and glorious thing it is to have physical knowledge of one such as he—who appears so quiet in company, but who has endless spheres of passion and knowledge to offer. I cannot help but feel frantic at times that he does not allow others access to his depths.

"Am I a terrible bore tonight?" he whispers.

"You could never be a bore," I say. "You entertained everyone with tales of our ghost."

"At your prompting. I was grateful you led me into conversation. I had been trying to find the most perfect entry, but I felt burdened by Emerson's mourning and by Margaret's judgment, both hanging as heavy as drapes around us. Did you feel it?"

"I did, but not as a burden. I wanted to provide an antidote for each."

"That is because you are an angel who wants to bring light to darkness. I am so steeped in it myself, others' darkness seems to cling to my own, like inkblots joining on a parchment. I am a *Ha*-thorne after all."

I am glad his voice is light. If he had chosen to sound sarcastic or gloomy, what a different feeling I would take from this fine night. As it is, I may speak freely, because he will be receptive in this mood.

"You see only darkness in yourself," I say. "But that is not all of you, or even most of you. You give far too much care to your ancestors. You only know of the ones who judged. I am sure there were hundreds more who saw the beauty in the world, who could capture a feeling with a line of black marks on a page, who made their wives so happy on earth it was as if they had died and resided in heaven."

"I will believe it because it comes from your lips."

The house looms dark and watchful over us in the night. As we climb the hill to return home, it occurs to me that I do not want Nathaniel to share any more of his self with others than he does. Perhaps it is my great gift to know deeply one who is so celestial. Reading my thoughts, Nathaniel looks down at me as if he could devour me. In my rising passion, our guests cannot leave us quickly enough.

21

In the late summer, I feel compelled to visit Mother and show her my fine health of body and mind. Departing from Nathaniel is harder than I anticipated, and our leave-taking extends from the bedroom, to the staircase, to the foyer, to the front walk; it ends at the avenue because he is half-undressed. What a sight to sear into my brain!

We pen heated letters to each other during our short separation, but I make my return sooner than expected after he writes that Margaret Fuller is again staying with the Emersons. Nathaniel writes that he nearly stumbled over her laid out on the grass at Sleepy Hollow, and that they passed an afternoon on a gentle hill, under a canopy of leaves, in rambling conversation about everything in the world. I fret and fidget the entire stage trip to Concord, but when I arrive and Apollo himself is on the lane to greet me, arms overflowing with flora and eyes shining with love, my fears disperse on the flight of the butterflies around us.

We pass the end of summer and early autumn wandering the forest, strolling the hills, pillaging the earth and ponds for flowers, sketching pictures and words, and drinking from our shared well of passion. On a particularly glorious fall morning, Nathaniel rows us along the Concord in the boat we purchased from Henry Thoreau that we have christened *Pond Lily*. This is one of our favorite occupations of late, though Nathaniel still insists the river is a mud puddle.

"It is ugly," says Nathaniel, looking over the side.

I reach down and pet its surface.

"There, there," I say. "Do not listen to his insults. You are fresh and lovely as the morning."

He looks over the side of the *Pond Lily* and sees his reflection. My impish Narcissus says, "Ah, behold! The river is handsome after all!"

I splash water, dispersing his image, and flick cold drops over his face. He pulls the oars into the boat and rubs his wet skin over my breast until I am giggling so loudly he places his finger over my lips.

"Shhh, my queen," he whispers. "The villagers will hear us."

"Let them. As an example of what happens when mortals marry for love."

He sits up and takes the oars again, his light countenance disappearing under some dark thought that he soon voices, to my surprise.

"Sometimes I wonder, though, if you would not have been better off marrying for money," he says.

"Hush! Blasphemy!"

"The ugly reality of scarce economics weighs on me. I cannot help but fear you married an idler. My words are stubborn in coming since our nuptials. I am much . . . distracted. Blissfully, mind you, but truly, nonetheless."

"Nonsense. You are producing. Your publisher is pleased with you."

"Pleased and penniless. O'Sullivan has yet to pay me for my stories."

"But there is still a chance we will get our investment back from Brook Farm," I say. "Margaret writes that the place is thriving. She also hints that she would like to visit again soon."

"She will no doubt show up and intrude when she wishes, like last time, when she arrived with her friend Sam and caught us in an embrace through the window."

"Their visit turned out to be a delight."

"Do you think? With her Sam blathering on to us about getting to work and that life is not an extended honeymoon, and Margaret practically forcing Ellen and Ellery on us as boarders?"

"She only suggested the Channings because of how fond we are of them."

"She suggested them because of how poor she perceives us to be—how poor we are."

He looks away from me and at a tree, whose trunk is half-submerged by the high water. It seems out of place and as if it wishes for land but must stand alone until the tide subsides. He rows us near it, and I run my hands over its bark. Several leaves drop into the water and drift like little canoes toward the browning grass along the bank.

"I am sorry," he says, "but boarders cannot be allowed in Eden. I will not have my love with you intruded upon, nor my capacity to work."

"I do not wish for boarders either," I say, though I do have fond memories of my short stays in Boston boardinghouses during our eternal engagement. "But do not discard the idea of guests altogether. The manse has never been more beautiful and welcoming. We must share our bounty of setting with friends and family before winter comes and freezes the landscape. You have said yourself that the outdoors are too grand to ignore. Once the solstice approaches, you may work by the cheery fireside without distraction. Use the present time to collect ideas."

He ponders my words, and soon accepts them with a nod. "You are right, as always."

We continue toward the Emersons' home, where we will pay a visit, remarking over the golden landscape and the turning world. I will regret when these luscious, colorful trees lining the river will cringe in the cold, when we will not be able to fill our bellies from our orchard and garden, but must ration our meals, and find our heat at stoves and fireplaces. I shiver at the thought.

Nathaniel is quiet on the remainder of the trip. When we reach our destination, he pushes the boat onto shore and carries me to dry ground before pulling the vessel farther up the bank. He takes my arm as we start along the wooded path. In minutes we are being scratched by thickets and brambles, and have lost our direction. There is a chill in the forest, and my feet feel the cold reaching through my summer slippers. Nathaniel leads me with one hand while he holds back branches and vines with the other, becoming stormier all the while. He is so easily frustrated by the minutiae of life. While I attempt to stifle my giggles, he growls and grumbles and is about to insist we turn back when we stumble upon a clearing and nearly run into Emerson's ward, Henry Thoreau himself. Henry's face glows with a warm smile.

"A wood nymph!" I say. "See, Nathaniel, I knew we would find one."

My husband's handsome face is contorted in frustration and his usually pristine clothing is torn and soiled, but when he sees how smudged and ridiculous we both are, he laughs. Henry joins in our amusement and leads us to a path we never would have discovered on our own.

"Thank heavens we found you," says Nathaniel. "I have finally mastered the art of navigating the *Pond Lily* through the Concord, but these woods still seem inhospitable. I had a better knowledge of the wilds of New Hampshire than I do of these small forests."

"Have you taken the time to stop and listen to what they tell you?" asks Henry.

"No, I have not. I leave all communication with vegetation to my bride."

Henry smiles. He is a delicate soul, one made of spiderwebs or the veins of a leaf. His stillness is like the river; his craggy face and brown hair are like tree bark. If I did not know him, I might miss him in the woods, because he is one with it.

We emerge from the forest and approach the Emersons' house. It rises in a stately manner before us in the Federal style of architecture, its large rectangular shape balanced by identical chimneys on either side. Now that Henry is in residence, his touch is evident all around the grounds, which flourish with young trees and autumn flowers. Just as he has planted and nurtured our garden, he has done the same with the Emersons' land. In spite of the gentle day, I think how strange it is that a dwelling may look so tidy on the outside, but hold such sadness within.

"Do you think they are fit for visitors?" I say. "I know grief is an unwelcome guest that crowds out those in the flesh."

"It will be good to have your lightness brought into their home," says Henry.

He opens the door for us, giving it a gentle knock to alert the Emersons to our arrival. Lidian emerges from the parlor, clad in black, her face white and drawn. She greets us quietly and manages a small smile.

"Thank heavens Henry found us wandering the woods," I say, "or we may have been lost forever. No offense to you, Nathaniel."

"None taken," he says. "I am hopeless in the forest. In the town too, for that matter. The farm, the river, on land, at sea . . ."

Emerson's two remaining children—three-year-old Ellen and infant Edith—play in the parlor where Lidian leads us. A portrait of little Waldo, their deceased son, watches over the room, and I notice Lidian touch the likeness before sitting down on a chair. The girls take turns on a rocking horse before an audience of unblinking dolls. Lace curtains allow the sun to illuminate the room, and oil lamps stand at the ready for nightfall. The tables and mantels are populated with busts, statuettes, and candlesticks, meticulously shined and evenly placed, without a speck of grime. It is all so tidy.

"Please excuse Waldo; he is working," she says.

Nathaniel's face flashes dark with what must be envy. Seeing that Emerson may work undisturbed by visitors at his wife's protection will no doubt fuel my husband's desire for seclusion. I find it rude that Emerson would ignore guests for work, but I remind myself that once the creative impulse takes over, it is difficult to extricate oneself from it.

"Nathaniel, how about a turn around the garden?" says Henry. "I have bulbs for you."

Nathaniel seems relieved at the suggestion. Our own garden has captivated his interest so much that I know Emerson's will bring him pleasure. He can also enjoy Henry's quiet fraternity, away from this house of grief. He looks at me, seeking my blessing, and I nod. When the men have gone, I turn to Lidian. How aged she is since the first time I met her, during my courtship with Nathaniel. When I stayed with the Emersons back then, Lidian was bright and fresh and full of ideas; now her eyes are shadowed, her dark hair is graying, and the sadness she bears over her great loss visibly weighs upon her. I kneel at her feet and enclose her hands in mine.

"Lidian, what can I do?"

She begins to cry, and holds a handkerchief to her mouth while looking out the window at the men.

"If you could just make the world spin backward . . ."

"Oh, if I could . . ."

She looks down at me and a smile finds her lips. Edith crawls over and uses my dress to pull herself to standing. Her precious face is inches from mine, and she touches my tears with her finger and mumbles baby talk. I hold out my hands to her, and she reaches for me, so I lift her in a whoosh and delight at her giggles. She waves her arms when I hold her still, so I again lift her. Ellen comes over and wishes for such a frolic too, so I indulge her, but I must stop after one lift because she is much heavier than Edith. The girls resume their floor play, and Lidian resumes her crying. I reach for her free hand and rub it between mine.

"I wish I could muster the energy to play with them," she says. "Poor Edith has scarcely known her mother to smile."

"Your smile will return like the spring," I say. "Mourn your boy, but rest your love and hope in your other babes. They are so dear."

She nods and looks out the window, where Nathaniel and Henry have disappeared. She speaks almost to herself. "I do not know what I would do without him. . . ."

At first I think she is speaking of her husband, but the way she gazes out the window suggests she means another. Before I have more time to reflect on this utterance, Emerson enters the room with a scowl that deepens when he sets eyes on Lidian. When his gaze meets mine, he arranges his face politely.

"The great sculptor Sophia Peabody Hawthorne graces our study."

"You are far too kind," I say.

"And where is the writer husband?" he asks.

"He is outdoors with Henry," I say. "Shall we all join them? It is such a charming day."

Lidian moves like one unsure of her footing, but I soon help her outside with the girls. Emerson has put on his hat and joined the men in the garden, and we open blankets to sit upon. The Emersons' cook brings out the tea service, and we pass the time nibbling apple tarts and pointing out birds to the girls. The men soon join us, Nathaniel now more at ease, sprawled on the grass leaning on one elbow, and Henry at Lidian's right side. Emerson sits apart from us on a bench.

"If we could just freeze this moment," I say. "Nothing could ever eclipse the perfection of an autumn day."

"While the autumn does enchant," says Emerson, "I have the strange longing for a snow-covered landscape and a cheery fireside by which to read."

Nathaniel runs his fingers along the threadbare cuff of his worn jacket. I noticed a hole in the socks he put on this morning, and it makes me die a small death inside to see one so fine as he—a man with the countenance of a king—dressed in the clothes of a poor writer. Ralph Waldo Emerson, a man making money on lectures and widely published works, a man with a small fortune in the coffers from his first deceased wife, can look forward to winter, because he will always be warm and full. As much as I longed to come here, suddenly I wish to be at home, reassuring my husband with my touch.

"There is already a chill in the woods," I say. "The first whispers of winter, crouching among the dryads. Henry, we will need you to escort us back when we go, if you do not mind."

"I would be glad to," he says.

We chat of small things for a bit longer, but the conversation feels forced, our individual troubles blocking the communion of our spheres. Nathaniel is tense and quiet, and I have again noticed the special warmth that glows not between Lidian and her husband, but between her and Henry. I can see that Henry is a comfort to her, and wonder if this makes her husband envious or relieves him of a burden. I cannot imagine finding peace in anyone but Nathaniel.

On the boat ride home along the meandering river, we are silent. Nathaniel has withdrawn into himself, and I know better than to probe him. He needs space to consider his emotions and determine whether they should be acknowledged. I cannot help but think of the Emersons. Once a man I nearly worshiped, the Emerson of our previous acquaintance is now altered in my opinion. In his treatment of his wife and even of my husband, I sense that he feels himself superior to others. There is a coldness in him that I did not notice before, which I now feel like the wind buffeting against us on the Concord.

Nathaniel shuts himself in his study for the rest of the afternoon, leaving me alone and frustrated. Mary is late with our meal, and the chicken is tough, so I cannot help but snap at her. Nathaniel is so deep in his *innere* he does not notice. Later that night, while he leans on a pillow on the floor reading Shakespeare and I mend his torn socks by the fire, stewing in what I feel is his abandonment, he speaks so suddenly that I start and drop my sewing.

"I never knew I could be so happy on earth," he says.

I am perplexed that his brooding has resulted in such a proclamation, and in spite of the quick tenderness I feel for him, I set
my face sternly.

"I am glad to hear that," I say. "All these long hours you have
kept silent from me, I was sure you were forming a quarrel."

He closes the book and comes to me, laying his head in my
lap and rubbing the sides of my legs.

"I know, my dove, and I am sorry you have to bear the burden
of a writer who hates words, a lord who has no occupation, a
hapless toiler without real success or learning or notoriety of any
kind, beyond a handful of stories that will go unremembered in
the space of a decade."

Softened, I lift his face to mine and run my fingers through
his hair.

"You must never apologize for being my heavenly reward on
earth."

"But look at Emerson! He has money, a fine home, speaking
and writing engagements, children."

"Inherited money from one dead wife; a miserable living wife;
a hoary cold heart . . ."

"Do you really think so?"

"Of course. Lidian is fragile as a locust shell. There is no
warmth between the two of them."

"Perhaps we just do not see it," he says. "I cannot express my
feelings in front of anyone but you. I know what society thinks
of sullen me."

"Yes, but anyone can look at my adoring eyes to see our affection. Lidian is hollow. Her eyes are blank."

I continue to stroke his hair, and he goes quiet and looks into the fire. How his face shifts and changes in the light. I lean down and kiss the side of his neck at his collarbone, and he reaches up and guides me to the floor where his pillow lies, and where he takes me with great tenderness.

22

Winter has come on with a vengeance, and our dear Old Manse has become a chilly abbey, where we remain cloistered near airtight stoves, wearing fingerless gloves, and marveling over the swelling in my breasts and stomach now that the physical manifestation of our love grows within me. My sickness has subsided, though Nathaniel continues to dote upon me in the most ridiculous manner, and I am pleased to feel a return to lustiness following those weeks of nausea.

One morning when the wind has let up and the sun gives us gentle relief, Nathaniel goes to chop wood, leaving me inside sewing flannels. I sit under our owl Longfellow, and direct commentary on my thoughts to him as a peace offering. His eyes still stare at me coldly. Through the leaded panes I see the naked branches like fingers reaching toward the winter sky. Now that the orchards are barren and we cannot sell our produce, Nathaniel works at the woodpiles, trying to think of ways to keep us from starving. Desperate as we are, I cannot help but thank God for our abundance of love. I am enthralled not only by Nathaniel's physical beauty—so apparent as he rolls up his shirtsleeves before raising and lowering the ax—but also by his expressions of love. Though his diffidence in public is painful, he is open and effusive with me in the privacy of our home, and I will never starve for that alone. His love satisfies every aspect of my being.

I am alarmed to notice how thin he has become. He pushes his portions to me at meals for the nourishment of our little one, and brings me treats from the breadmaker in the village when he returns from the post office or the reading room. I must refuse him in the future and insist he satisfy his own hunger.

Nathaniel ceases his chopping and wipes the sweat from his brow, stopping to turn his face up to the benevolent sun. Seeing him in the light, I am seized with inspiration. I place my sewing on the table and hurry to get my sketch pad, which has remained blank for many months. Before I know what has come over me, I am scribbling away at a plan for a painting, and do not notice Nathaniel until he shakes his head like a dog, spraying me with snowflakes and wetting my drawing. I scold him and close the pad so he may not further damage my creation, and swat him away from me.

"You scamp!" I say. "Where did this snow come from?"

"I had just had the thought of how hot I had become, and our dear sister tree obliged me by shivering in the breeze and showering me with snow. There, I sound like you."

"You are not like me. If I intruded upon your work and dribbled drops on your writing, I would never hear the end of it."

His face is contrite. "I apologize. I saw some boys racing over the hills toward the river for skating, and was overcome with my own mischief. Forgive me. May I see what you have drawn?"

I hesitate a moment, aware that if I tell him my plan to paint, he will caution me to avoid activities that might induce my headaches, but excitement overcomes my reserve and I open the pad before him.

"Endymion. Loved by a goddess, father of multitudes, eternally youthful. You, my love. I want to paint it."

His eyes grow dark as he runs his hands over the page, and he begins to warn me, but I touch his lips with my finger.

"Shh. I will stop if my head aches even the slightest bit. But you must know that I am alive as never before. Our child has given me double vitality. My every nerve is tingly and receptive. I feel as if I could"—I look out the window toward the Concord, the sun glinting off her glassy surface—"skate on the river!"

"Ha!" he laughs.

"No, really." I stand, overcome with the need to exert myself. "Dr. Wesselhoeft would agree."

"Is it safe?"

"Of course," I say. "Let us go observe the boys. Our study will make us better parents to our growing babe."

Nathaniel helps me into my coat and boots, and we commence a walk in the winter sun, leaving Mary to prepare our dinner. It is such a pleasure to know the industry of the household continues in another's hands while we may enjoy each other and the outdoors, though I do not know how much longer we will be able to afford help. Our spirits are high, and we walk without trouble over the rough surface of the frozen river, though the boys tease us and threaten to make us fall by skating too close. One of the boys apologizes, and I tell him that I will call on his mother to tell her what a good son she is raising.

"What is your name?" I ask.

"William Hunt."

"Hunt. Your parents live on Monument Street."

"Yes, madam."

"Half the village is made of Hunts," says Nathaniel as we leave the boys and continue our exertions. "They must have ten children."

"We might have ten children in our house of Hawthorne," I say.

Nathaniel exclaims in horror. "Let me figure out how to feed one little Hawthorne before we have ten."

"We will," I say. "Your best writing is about to come. I sense it."

"I am glad. All I feel is a need to kiss my wife, and drink hot cider by the fire, and read books written by greater men."

Over hills and through groves we travel. He becomes silly and drops into a snowbank to make angels. While he faces the sky, however, he notices we have lost our sun.

"Dove, let us return to our hearth. I am afraid you have been out too long."

"A good thought," I say, reaching around to answer the pressure in my lower back with my palms.

He is up and at my side, using his own hands to knead my back. He pulls the scarf from my neck and kisses me there, whispering promises of a most satisfying rubbing of my entire body once we finish our dinner.

Our return to the manse takes longer than I remember the journey out, and by the time we reach the Concord River, though I try to conceal my discomfort, I am weary and chilled to my bones. The sky is gray, and all hint of sun has left. The hoary gusts are back, and blast us on our descent to the ice. I have never wished for a warm bath so mightily as I do at this moment. We are silent as we tread with care over the frozen river, arm in arm, slipping in places where the boys had not skated. On our way to rougher ice, my boot finds a slick surface, and before I know it, I have fallen, nearly pulling Nathaniel down on top of me. I flinch as a sudden and terrible pain grips my abdomen and renders me breathless.

"Sophia!"

The pain becomes an intense cramp, and I am nauseous and feel a growing dread as my underclothes are filled with sticky wetness. I smell the metallic tang of blood, and once Nathaniel helps me to my feet, I feel it oozing down my legs. Red drops begin to color the frozen river, and I let out a sob. Nathaniel sees and goes pale. He hurries us to the bank, where he lifts me and summons I know not what strength as he runs with me up the hill toward our house.

I have become feral and inaccessible since the accident that took our unborn child.

I slink around Nathaniel's study like our cat, aimless, distracting, unable to settle down to work or conversation. It was my fault. If I had never indulged in silly impulses—if I had not put our baby in harm's way—this never would have happened. Nathaniel grieves, but not as I do. He never felt the ripening, the quickening from the inside. The witness of an event has no access to the true emotion of the one who lives it, though he thinks himself capable of imagining all feeling. He scribbles in our common journal now, giving voice to our sufferings in a way he cannot compel his throat to do.

I am curled up in his study at the window, leaning my head on the frigid glass, twirling my ring on my cold, shrunken finger. Tears slide from my eyes as I silently accuse and question the river.

How could you, after all I have done for you? My blessings and benedictions. My defense of you against my husband. Is this your revenge? Or is this the consequence of the witch's condemnation? Nathaniel's ancestor, the Salem judge who ordered the women hanged, was cursed by one of the accused before her death. Are we suffering from her dark magic?

I shake the ridiculous thoughts from my head, and glance at my husband. He sits not three feet away, but it might as well be an ocean. Why does he not touch me? Why does he still work when he sees my pain? To lose my husband to writing after losing the baby to the icy river compounds my anguish. Day and night, I rise from our bed to wander the house, and the only thing I may count on is finding him bent over the desk he has installed in the corner, facing away from the window, scribbling in his notebooks, oblivious to any human or specter who wishes to haunt him.

He is not the only writer. I will put down my own words.

In a savage motion I use my diamond ring to scrape the window that looks over the Concord, but my hand does not obey my mood. As if mesmerized by a spirit outside of myself, I write:

Man's accidents are God's purposes.
Sophia A. Hawthorne, 1843

Nathaniel is at my side now. When I finish, he takes my hands and wraps them around his neck, and leans into me in the embrace I have been longing for. Tears fall and I feel his wordless sympathy, his frustration over his inadequacy and inability to change the situation. With what must be great effort he speaks. "He or she will come back to us."

I am confused. Does he mean when we dwell in heaven? He sees the wrinkle in my brow and continues.

"Our child meant for us will come back. I am convinced we did not lose this babe. He or she is just . . . postponed. I do not know how I know it, but I do."

I find his strange words comforting, and I am warmed that he tries to console me.

"When you are ready," he says, "we will try to bring the baby about again. Only when you are ready."

I look back at the river, muted in the gray day. The stillness in her currents newly freed from the ice and the absence of light on her surface gives her an appearance of lowliness and shame. I am overcome with the need to move forward in spite of what has transpired.

"Draw me a bath," I say. "Pour me a bit of wine. Let us look to the future."

23

I may always count on the spring to bring freshness to life.

My sister Mary is set to finally wed Mr. Horace Mann, and then they shall be off to Europe. When I lament my prolonged courtship, I am reminded of my poor sister's circumstance, and how much longer she had to endure a treading of water. A decade! Year after year of waiting for Horace to grieve the untimely death of his first wife, cultivate his career, and finally realize he would be a better man with Mary as his wife. I recall Mary's darkest days with a chill on my skin—days when she said she thought of taking her life because it was no life. Days she spent scribbling tales of Cuban slaves who have never stopped haunting her. Maybe she will finally find some peace.

Mary writes that she is the happiest woman on earth. I cannot help but smile to myself, because she could not possibly be while I am alive and married to Nathaniel, but it gives me pleasure to see these words, and I wish nothing but the utmost love and joy for her nuptials. How gratifying it would be to someday see such words from Elizabeth's pen.

As for me, I endured a brief separation from Nathaniel to visit Mother, leaving my poor husband behind to much lamentation at the manse, but my stay restored and buoyed me beyond words. Nathaniel and I are secluded here, and when one's sole company is of the celestial variety, it does a person good to mingle with other mortals.

But how I go on.

Mary's news and my visit with Mother are nothing compared to the ecstasy of my married state. I am as ravenous for Nathaniel as he is for me, and to think that we will live our lives forever dipping into such deep and satisfying wells of pleasure is almost too much to comprehend. And now that the weather has become mild, he has left his corner desk to join me in the world.

On the freshest, dewiest day of the spring, I kiss the cook's cheek and scoop up a basket for flower picking. I think I will start for the bridge that will take me over the river and to the fields beyond. First I make for the vegetable garden, where Nathaniel clears the weeds and leaves to prepare for our spring sowing.

Nathaniel is bent over, facing the house, to my dismay, for I do admire the other view of him. I giggle at the thought, and when I do, he stands and breaks into an open smile of pleasure. When I come closer, my mischievous love rushes to me, lifts me in his arms, and falls over sideways with me into a great pile of brush. I scold him gently, for I am happy to lie on the earth as the gentle zephyrs of the equinox prompt it to arise, with this man who would have found such silly behavior unthinkable before we met. He brushes a tendril of hair from my eyes.

"Where are you going without me, my little wife?"

"Over hills and dales in search of new flowers."

"May I come with you, or must I continue toiling in overgrown Eden?"

"You may come with me if you promise to do unspeakable things to me in the evergreen grove."

He laughs low into my neck, which vibrates in my every pore. "Of course. You need not ask; it may be your assumption."

He pulls away and lifts me to standing, taking great care to brush my dress and hair free of weeds. I do the same for him, when I notice a shadow on the bridge that assumes a girl's form. In a few moments, I see that she is the young woman Martha Hunt, the village schoolmistress. On this day of great verdure and spring pleasantry, she is an echo of winter, a gray smudge on nature's living painting. I want her to look at us so I may wave and greet away her dismal facade, but she keeps her gaze down. I resolve to try to visit her the next time I am in town, though I have hardly spoken to her. As quickly as she has appeared, she is gone, leaving us to wonder whether we saw an apparition.

We debate the matter only as long as it takes us to walk three paces, for we have already found a purple crocus and the shoots of a daffodil, and abandon all thought of winter in any form.

On our stroll home through the bent rays of afternoon, after we have mingled most satisfyingly with each other in the seclusion of the pine grove, Nathaniel leads me to the Concord instead of back to the manse. The waters have swollen so that they reach into our orchards and lanes, and nearly lap over the post where the *Pond Lily* is tied. I cannot help but pull back and drop Nathaniel's hand.

"Come, Sophia," he says. "It is time to make our peace."

I look at the water, an amiable reflection of the gentle sky visible on its smooth surface. Little birds dip for drinks, and the flooded trees reach up to their full height as if trying to dry off their trunks. A wind at our backs brings the smell of roasting meat from the house, making my mouth water. I look back at the manse.

"We will not be long," he says, reaching for my hand. "Let us renew our good feelings for the Concord River."

The breeze seems to nudge me toward the water and my husband, and I decide to obey. He helps me into the boat in silence, and situates me comfortably with my flower basket before untying us and pushing away with an oar. The moment we are away from land, I feel as if I will be sick. I grasp his arm, nearly upsetting the oar into the water. He pulls the oar into the safety of the boat and lets us drift without persuasion while he reaches for me.

"You are so cold," he says, rubbing my hands between his strong, callused palms. I am distracted by his laborer's hands, and turn them over to touch the hardened blisters he has earned chopping endless cords of wood and working in our garden.

"Your hands should be smooth. Author's hands, not farmer's hands," I say.

"I am no farmer," he says. "These are Adam's hands."

"When did this happen?" I say. "When did you inhale my optimism from me and reflect it back, while I dwell in dark places? Is this what you felt like before our marriage, my love? Was your mind a dark chamber of fear and reticence? Is this what it is to be you?"

"I am only the moon reflecting your light," he says. "Even now. Only clouds obscure your full brilliance. Let us blow them away so you may shine forth."

I summon the courage to peer over the side of the boat and into the river. There, as always, is my image reflected back at me. The blood that dripped on the ice that day has been absorbed, and new growth blooms on the banks. I feel my communion with the ripening world revived after the dark months. I plunge my hand into the chilly water, where the last of the ice chunks floated only a week ago, and it feels clean—cleansing. I think of the words at the end of the *Cuba Journal*: "I see with the eyes that are given me."

At once I am reborn. The light again winks on the river. My husband is himself. I am myself. I find that I am laughing without knowing why. I splash him, and he splashes me back. We stay on the river until the shadows lengthen, and the cool evening air reminds us that winter has only recently departed.

24

That summer I conceive again, and we are ever welcoming visitors, who both fill my days with joy and distract Nathaniel from his writing. Living with my husband, I observe that authors are forever unsettled. He longs for solitude to work, but when the words do not come, he acknowledges that interaction with people stimulates his ideas. He never minds Henry Thoreau, but is ambivalent about Emerson, who is so self-assured. He enjoys Ellery and Ellen Channing in small doses, delights in his sister Louisa—the only member of his family to bestow her warmth upon us—but is agitated by Margaret Fuller.

While Louisa is visiting, Margaret is staying with the Emersons. She comes to call when Nathaniel is out rowing with Henry, and I observe how Louisa becomes even more shy in Margaret's direct and imposing company.

"What are you creating?" Margaret asks as she walks with

Louisa and me through Sleepy Hollow. We are making a swift outing before the building clouds become a summer storm, and we are confined indoors.

Without thinking, I smile and pat my stomach, looking at Louisa and then Margaret. Louisa draws in her breath with a smile, but Margaret does not hide her displeasure. I have a sudden worry that Nathaniel will be upset that I have shared our news.

"Do not tell Nathaniel I have hinted at what we suspect," I say.

"I promise," says Louisa. "But I will not stop smiling about it."

"And you, Margaret?"

"Of course I promise," she says. "But soon you will be able to talk and think of nothing else. And then what will happen to your art?"

"My art is here," I say. "Our love is a garden with many plants. This little bud will only add to the rich and varied landscape."

"How nicely put," says Louisa.

We climb a tall hill, and at the crest I am winded but alive as never before.

"I know what will happen, Sophia," Margaret says, surveying the slopes shaded by evergreens and deciduous trees. "It happens to all women. You will be the one who has all the duties with the child. Your husband will work to escape the squalling infant. You will resent him because you have no time to yourself."

Louisa's eyes are wide. I can see that she is stunned to be in company with Margaret, who speaks so freely, never censoring a single thought. I, however, feel strangely serene under Margaret's scrutiny. I know how unhappy she is in love, how she is forever disappointed because she falls in love with men she cannot have. She watches her friends' marriages, imagining herself as a substitute for the wife under observation, and even sometimes intrigues the men to consider her. Ultimately they never make Margaret their choice, and she is bitter for it. But I pity her, so I will not turn on her.

"My mother fears the same fate for me," I say. "But Mother does not have a husband like mine. I do not know if anyone has a husband like mine. What I create and do not create is the result of my impulses—not another's. I cannot help but think it will be the same once we have our babe."

"I hope so," says Margaret. "For you do not want to end up the little marker at the side of the grand headstone, where future writers and readers will lay their offerings, honoring only the man published and not the woman who supported and even made his work possible."

The wind rises, and the first rumble of thunder can be heard low in the distance. I ponder Margaret's words as Louisa and I part from her and hurry back to the manse. By the time we arrive at the lane, the squall is in full power, and we are soaked through. After we run into the house, breathless and dripping, I have Mary heat water for a bath for Louisa. I urge her to bed early, so she will not catch cold from the elements.

I do not share Margaret's words with Nathaniel that night, but I cannot stop pondering them in my heart.

As I stand before the easel holding my oil painting of Endymion in our downstairs studio, I breathe deeply, desperate to distract myself from the headache that has taken root between my eyes.

Months have passed. Instead of visitors, we now have letters, but they are a poor, cold substitute for the presence of the ones who pen them. Louisa has become very dear to me, and is a true comfort in her correspondence. It is gratifying to me and to Nathaniel how Louisa and I have grown in our affection, though his mother and Ebe remain reserved. Margaret writes regularly, and has become more kind and supportive of my pregnancy, though she also continues to encourage my artistic pursuits. Elizabeth and Mary can be relied upon for thick letters, and I am overjoyed when I learn that Mary, too, is expecting. But no one writes or encourages me to paint more than Mother. She says that art will distract me from the nausea that has become severe. Even more important, what I produce could become a source of income for this house, for it is no secret how we struggle.

I have set to my task with new fervor, but creating has brought back my unwelcome youthful companion: pain. Hours of concentration beget hours of suffering. I dare not share my infirmity with Nathaniel, because he will beg me to stop, which I will not do. *Endymion* is reaching a form of color and depth like nothing I have ever painted. I am convinced this is because this Endymion is Nathaniel, and I have tasted the rich, intoxicating beauty of love's full communion. My feeling is all over the canvas, and will no doubt emanate from it, stimulating its viewers. I have not yet shown Nathaniel, or anyone.

My mind flashes to the portrait of Mary Magdalene in Cuba,

and the dreaded blurring at the edges of my sight begins. I fear I will have to stop before this headache does me in, and I have to tell my love of my artistic illness. My hands shake, but I will myself to stay until I have used the paint I have mixed. I cannot waste a thing when we have such light coffers.

I squeeze my eyes shut and then open them, and look on the browns that make up the painting. I do not want to use bright colors because of cost, in part, but largely because I want emotion to enlighten the painting. *Endymion* will be expressed on a palette like that of Mary Magdalene, reflecting the same wish for light, but from a different source. While Magdalene longs for light directly from God, in my painting the longing for light will be derived through man, for the benefit of love in all creation.

The child moves in my womb, and a pain shoots down my inner leg. I am happy to be sick and in pain for this miracle, but oh, how the body is burdened. I use the paint as quickly as I might without sacrificing the quality of the work, and finally stumble to the window to open it and let in the air. The first chilly November wind following our Indian summer fills the room and helps me to breathe. The cold gives some relief to my head, but not as much as the pressure from my knuckles.

"Sophia!" I am startled by my husband, who comes in and grasps my arms. He pulls me away from the window and closes it with haste. "You will catch your death!"

His sharp hazel eyes take in my paints, the canvas, and my hands clutching my head.

"The headaches have returned," he says.

"No, it is simply because I am hungry."

"Dove, you must not do anything that brings you pain."

"But it brings me more joy than pain."

"I will do my utmost to bring you joy. You must stop this if the headaches again plague you."

"But does the writing not torture you at times? You love it and crave it in spite of that. You must write. I must paint."

"Why? Why now? You have been content to happily recline in our home and receive visitors for more than a year. Why this sudden urgency to paint?"

I know it is in part because of my creative longing, and, more darkly, Margaret's prophecy, but I am ashamed that the largest reason is because we need money. To say it would wound Nathaniel, and I cannot bear to hurt him. He is tortured by his publisher's lack of payment, and the irrecoverable loss of our investment in Brook Farm. I understand better now why he was so reluctant to marry me—because of the pressure to support us. How I wish I were a wealthy heiress so my love could compose as many or as few words as he would in a day, and we could be free of this burden.

I turn away from Nathaniel, but he reads my thoughts; I can conceal nothing from him. He walks to stand in front of *Endymion*. I cannot help but look back at him for a reaction, and I am moved. Nathaniel's eyes grow glassy with unshed tears. His mouth quivers and he places a hand over his heart. When he finally speaks, his voice is low and husky.

"It is beauty. The very definition."

I feel my joy rise up like a swollen river, but just as I am about to reach for him, I see that he becomes stone.

"You will not sell this. Not for me, not for us. No one else may look upon it."

"You cannot be serious."

"I have never been more serious about a thing in my life. This is the most intimate, the most revealing portrait of our love that has ever been made. It would be a violation of our mutual trust to hang it in another's parlor for the appraisal of strangers."

"But it could help us. It could free you to—"

"No. I am sorry, but I cannot allow it. I admire you and what you try to do for us, but this is too close to my heart. To our spirit."

I am raw. I cannot be angry with him, because he has acknowledged what I knew about the intimacy of this painting, but I resent that he has made this decision and I will not be able to persuade him otherwise.

"I will not stop painting it," I say.

"I cannot force you to stop, but I do hope you will consider your health and the health of . . . us all before you pick up that brush again. Especially because it will be a hidden work."

I can endure this no more. I turn to leave, but I am overtaken with such dizziness that I am forced to lean on Nathaniel's arm while he helps me up the stairs and into bed. I curl up on my side, away from him where he lies next to me. He rubs my back, trying to make me feel better and to mend what is rent between us. I scoot farther away, and after a short time he leaves me alone. I hear him walk to his study and close the door, where he will write without pain or limitation, and where he may do what he wishes with his work.

I am bitter.

I cannot help but wonder what Margaret would say.

I am listless and feverish in the following weeks. Bouts of melancholy seize me like never before, and my mind is a maze made of hedges from which I cannot find the way. My thoughts spin in circles, and I am unable to concentrate. If my old friend Connie Parks lived nearby, I would summon her for mesmerism in spite of Nathaniel's discomfort with the procedure.

Nathaniel tries to resurrect me. He is pained that he has caused me distress, though he is emphatic that the work not be sold. I suppose he would rather that we starve. My illness has strained him so he cannot write, and our home is a dreary place. I emerge from our room for mealtimes, then creep back upstairs, taking the place of our Old Manse ghost. Nathaniel is the other specter, haunting his study.

After our supper one December evening, I pace the upstairs hall. Nathaniel sighs with frustration in the study. I know my distraction is making him half-mad, but I cannot help myself. After some minutes, I work up the courage to resume painting, and head downstairs. As soon as I step into the studio and behold my unfinished masterpiece, Nathaniel slams the door to his secretary, and there is a great shattering on the ceiling above me that must be the bust of the goddess Ceres destroyed.

All time stops, and with it my beating heart. It is the sound that pierces me—like all the knives and forks that tormented me in childhood, the slave bells, the cart and carriage noise from the roads, the plaguing clamor of my youth to which I was so sensitive. All of that noise concentrated in the shattering of the bust makes my head feel as if it is exploding, and I am at once screaming on the ground, feeling as broken as the sculpture.

I do not know how long I wail, or how Nathaniel gets me upstairs to bed, or how he calms me, but I awake to the dawn inching through the window, illuminating the still-clothed and sleeping form of my husband, and warming the room with sunlight we have not had since autumn.

My eyes are swollen and my nose is stuffy, but I sense the light is trying to show me something. I get up as carefully as my large belly will allow, wrap a shawl around my arms, and walk downstairs to the studio. I could cry with joy when I see that *Endymion* is aglow and beckoning, and resolve then that I will finish this work whatever the cost, and even if it is never seen by the eyes of another mortal. The only way out of this dark forest is to walk straight through it.

25

We look on this most glorious creation in wonder.

"It is a she," he says in surprise.

"A red-haired she."

"Like a little faerie."

"Our faerie queen, Una."

He smiles. "Una. Purity. It is the perfect name."

"Una Hawthorne."

"And what a dear little sack she wears," he says.

"I made it using the silk flannel Louisa sent. I cannot wait until Lou meets our girl."

Una scrunches up her little face and cries. Nathaniel pretends to be horror-struck.

"Does it always make that sound?"

"Often to always."

She makes a terrific gaseous explosion. He screws up his mouth.

"Does it always do that?"

"Often to always." I laugh.

"An unladylike and troublesome creature," he teases, running his hands over her tiny head. "You must begin her education immediately. Call your sister Elizabeth for help. We should waste no time taming this wild thing."

"I will. And her first lesson will be to ignore every word out of her silly father's mouth."

"Excellent advice," he says.

He smiles, but soon his face becomes shadowed, and I wonder what troubles him.

"Do you want to hold her?" I ask, offering up the little bundle before she becomes squally and insatiable, as I know from her meager forty-eight hours of life she is apt to become. He looks very much as if he would prefer not to hold her, but wants to appease me. He takes Una from my arms in a great jumble of blankets and nervousness, but finally settles and begins to walk her around the room.

"Here is your mother's velvet robe that makes her look like a queen. Here is a volume of Shakespeare, which you will learn to read as soon as possible. Here is a magazine that contains a story from the man holding you. The payment made to him for it should cover the cost of the periodical itself, and no more. And here is your mother. The sun around which you will join me in orbit."

My mind lingers with distraction on the mention he has made of being paid so little to write. He places Una back in my arms, and I barely notice the kiss he plants on my head before leaving me alone to feed Una, who is greedily sucking the night-gown covering my breast.

Nathaniel will not allow me to lift a finger except to write to our family and keep them up-to-date on every utterance and motion Una makes, and to check on the progress of her cousin, Horace, born to Mary just a week before Una entered the world. Poor Mary has had much difficulty with nursing, as has Ellen Channing, so I give them my best advice, and have even fed Ellen's half-starved infant. Between my abundant breasts and Dr. Wesselhoeft's excellent care, Una has already outgrown her colic and thrives in the most satisfying way.

When Nathaniel is not slaving at the manse, he slaves at his desk, for the muse has chosen now, of all times, to pour forth her gifts. Una and I enjoy his celestial presence during the day, at least, so I forgive him our cold bed at night. Today the first breath of autumn has arrived to tease us with its relief from the summer, and I sit in the shade of an ash tree while Nathaniel harvests tomatoes.

"Perhaps I could hire myself out as a wet nurse," I joke, while Una pounds my neck with her dimpled fists. She is at my breast sucking merrily. "Ellen's baby seemed drunk when I finished with her the other day. Poor Ellen has had a terrible time with her milk."

"Is it proper to allow your friends' babes to suckle you? They cannot bring any illness to Una, can they?"

"I am sure it is all right, since that is how babies have lived for centuries. Besides, the little thing looked quite underfed. It was an act of charity."

My husband's forearms glisten with sweat. I feel myself wanting him more than ever lately, but he keeps putting me off. I watch him like a she-wolf and allow my shirt to open, exposing the breast that is not currently in use. I clear my throat and grin at Nathaniel, but when he sees me, he does not respond as I wish, and looks away, returning to his task. I slide myself back into my top, mortified by his reaction. Does he find me repugnant now that I have borne a child?

"You know I would love to take you," he says, as if hearing my thoughts.

"No, I do not know that."

He stops his work and looks at me. When he sees my embarrassment, he comes and kneels before me, taking my free hand in his.

"I am sorry to have distressed you," he says. "Of course I want you, but during the day you belong to her, and during the night I have to belong to my work."

"I understand," I say, speaking a bit of the truth. "But Una will nap soon; we can steal time then."

"My dear, when we consummate our love it pulls all of my energy out of me, and I need it. We are starved for money, and these stories, they are pleasing to me and seem to have a demand all their own. They are my own infants, and I am afraid that if I neglect them, I will lose them."

When he thinks that I am appeased, he pats my hand and returns to the garden, but I feel no better.

That night he is a madman, tearing apart our boxes of storage, searching for something, and rambling about someone named Rappaccini.

"Why are you thundering around the house, mumbling about Italians?" I say. "I have just got the baby to bed."

He comes into the room where Una has just fallen asleep and pulls out drawers without even trying to be quiet. Soon she fusses, and when he sees her, it is as if he forgot who and what she was. He has the decency to give me an apologetic glance. I grumble and go to pick her up to rock her back to sleep.

"What are you looking for?" I ask.

"Your *Cuba Journal*. I want to read about all of those flowers and your descriptions. I have snippets in my notebooks, but I need the whole thing."

"I think Mother has it, or a friend of hers."

"Argh!" he yells, and runs his hands through his wild hair before leaving me to the baby and slamming the door to his study.

I sit alone in the dark with Una, trying to calm my agitated little one, and can hear Nathaniel pacing again. As frustrated as I am with his thoughtlessness, I cannot complain to the man who has become a near farmworker by day and scribbler by night. I must encourage him so he can get down these stories. Perhaps if he finishes and they are well received, we will not have to be cast out of this home we dearly love but can no longer afford to rent.

That night, by the light of a tiny candle, I write to Mother, asking her to secure and return the *Cuba Journal* at once, and then to Elizabeth, telling her that the writer is active and productive, and to prepare Boston for what I am certain will be a collection of stories that will lay the foundation for my husband's legacy. I only pray he might publish his work before we are evicted from Eden.

Winter at the manse is made warmer by my little one. I stand with her at the window in my studio of empty easels and blank canvases to point out the ice-encased trees and blanketed landscape. Una mimics my words in her baby talk, and is very interested when I scratch the glass with another message.

Una Hawthorne stood on this windowsill

January 22nd, 1845

While the trees were all glass chandeliers.

A goodly show, which she liked much, tho

only ten months old.

I am content to fill my days with my child, though I feel some measure of guilt for neglecting my art. Though Una's learning is my new canvas, a living creation that consumes all my energy, Margaret's voice seems ever at my ear. I quiet it by thinking that there will be time later for oils and pencils.

Nathaniel's story "Rappaccini's Daughter" was published in O'Sullivan's *Democratic Review*, and his *Twice-Told Tales* were reissued, but neither of those worthy endeavors has reaped enough for us to pay our debts. My love has recommitted himself to seeking a government appointment.

In truth, the charity of family and friends keeps us afloat—that and our extreme love for each other. We often ask how we can be so happy and so poor, and the answer lies in our contentment. Nathaniel is back in my bed, and without the gardens to consume him we live peacefully, though hungry and often restless, in our home. I think if we starve or are evicted, I will not cry, for these years of happiness at the manse are more than the average person can claim for a lifetime. I do worry about Nathaniel, though. I must work the way one labors at a well with a water bucket to keep him in good spirits. If I may draw one easy smile from him a day, I feel as if my work is accomplished, and very often I am able to draw two or three.

May brings us a welcome visit from Nathaniel's Bowdoin College friend Franklin Pierce. Franklin is a successful lawyer and former senator, and has recently been appointed by President Polk as federal district attorney to New Hampshire. One would think his credentials would subdue Nathaniel into silence, but he is the only man of his position I have seen my husband welcome with a warm embrace, a pat on the back, and an ease of spirit. I attribute this to Franklin's kind and engaging manner, and their history of friendship. Franklin has no pretention, and is happy eating cold chicken and whortleberries on a picnic blanket, with Una using him as a plaything. He also partakes of the drink quite a bit, and while I do realize he is on holiday, I wonder if he becomes so often drunk as a habit. I have no judgment of others on the subject of addiction, however. Even years removed from my own morphine struggles, I get a thrill at the thought of the drug. I also know how Franklin is suffering. Though he and his wife, Jane, have a young son, they have lost two others. The first boy died just three days after his birth, and the second in 'forty-three at four years of age from typhus. Franklin says Jane is a bruised soul whose only light in life now rests in her little Benjamin.

It is late evening, and Franklin cannot stay with us long. He plans to depart in the morning to return home to New Hampshire, and he and Nathaniel are already silly from wine. They look like brothers in the shadows. Both recline on our picnic blanket on the hill overlooking the Concord River. Both have dark hair and wear white shirts rolled up at the sleeves. But my half of these men is much thinner than the other—gaunt from poverty.

While Franklin patiently endures Una's climbing on him, I study him and try to imagine how one goes on in the face of such tragedy. But here he is, doting on our wild daughter, sharing laughter with us, lifting up my husband's sagging spirits.

"We must find an appointment for you, friend," says Franklin.

"I do not think anyone will have me."

"Good God, man, you are the best of what is out there. Intelligent, creative, diplomatic."

"I try to tell him," I say, attempting to lift Una from Franklin.

"Let her be," he says. "I am charmed by your little faerie queen."

"Oona," she says.

"Yes, Ooooona," he echoes, drizzling clover and grass in her hair. She smacks it away, and again dives at his stomach, eliciting a groan.

"Una!" I say, pulling her away, but Franklin is on his feet and has my girl in his arms. He throws her high in the air, to my horror and her delight, and soon the night is filled with the sounds of her delicious laughter. When they both tire, Una crawls into my lap, and Franklin resumes his place on the blanket. Nathaniel lights the oil lantern, sets it on the ground beside us, and refills our three glasses with the last of the wine.

"If you would not accept a post in the government," says Franklin, "you know Longfellow would write you up a good review if you publish something. He greatly admires your work, and always wishes to promote it."

"I do have some stories coming together. I will write to him once they are complete."

"I have read some," I say. "They are brilliant, though the loneliness and suffering of his characters never fail to startle me."

"Nathaniel does have a penchant for anguish, but he writes it well, almost as if he is looking into the reader's own dark heart."

"Well, that is it," says Nathaniel. "I am not writing from my own heart, but to reflect to the reader him- or herself."

"You may try to convince yourself," I say, "but you do not fool us."

A splash in the river draws our attention down the hill, but the new moon does not allow us to see anything except shadows.

"It must be difficult to write dark fiction here," says Franklin, "in such idyllic surroundings, with such a woman at your side."

"Good Franklin," I say, taking a long drink of wine. "Always so kind."

"It is," says Nathaniel, reaching for my hand. "She is very distracting."

He gives my side a squeeze, which causes me to laugh. Nathaniel hushes me and points to Una, who has fallen asleep. I kiss her red curls and inhale her sweet scent. When I look up, they are both watching me. I feel a great closeness in our spheres, and wish to console Franklin, who clearly longs for this domestic tranquillity.

"I wish you and Jane peace," I say.

"Thank you," he replies.

"We cannot comprehend the depth of your suffering," says Nathaniel. "We had a small suffering when Sophia miscarried our first child from a fall on the ice."

"Oh, no," says Franklin. "I am sorry; I did not know."

"No, do not apologize," says Nathaniel. "I only tell you so that in sharing our pain, we might somehow ease yours. Does that make sense?"

"Perfect sense," he says. "There is comfort in knowing others have suffered similar pain, though I would not wish it on the worst of my enemies."

When our glasses are empty, and my back aches from holding my sleeping girl, Franklin is kind enough to lift her from my arms while Nathaniel gathers our things. I follow Franklin into the house, making sure he does not stumble with Una, and I direct him where to lay her. He kisses my hand and hugs Nathaniel before walking on unsteady legs to his room.

The next day, we escort Franklin to town to catch the stagecoach, and are sad to see our friend go. As we return to the Old

Manse, walking with Una under the boughs of the ash trees, we are each silent, desperately trying to think of a way to keep our beloved home that we can no longer afford. Nathaniel retires to his study, and I let him write without distraction. I teach Una about her sister flowers in fields and forests. We let our cook go, because we cannot pay her.

Every night in bed, Nathaniel and I cling to each other, hanging on for dear life.

26

At first I think the banging on the door is in a dream.

Nathaniel and I celebrated our third wedding anniversary that day by writing all of our cares of poverty on paper that we folded into little boats and launched down the river. Then we took Una to Walden Pond for a picnic with Henry, eating sweet treats sent by Louisa. Finally, we reenacted our wedding night in the light of the moon, and were asleep in each other's arms by nine o'clock. So it comes as a great shock to us, who have just crossed over into slumber, when the pounding begins and will not be ignored. I pull on my robe and peek at Una, who sleeps on, mercifully, and then follow Nathaniel to the front door, where Ellery stands breathless and trembling.

"What is it, for God's sake?" says Nathaniel. "Is it Ellen?"

Ellery shakes his head, attempting to catch his breath before speaking.

"There has been a tragedy. On the Concord River."

Nathaniel and I look at each other, and I feel something shrink inside of me. He puts his arm around me and turns back to Ellery. "Go on."

"We need the *Pond Lily*. It is the schoolmistress, Martha Hunt. It would appear that . . ."

Ellery stops and stumbles while taking a seat on the steps, wiping his perspiring head with his handkerchief.

"Pardon, Sophia, but I do not know if you would like to hear this."

I draw closer to my husband. "I am composed for anything you might say."

He stares at me through the dark for a moment, and then continues. "It seems Miss Hunt is missing, and likely has . . . courted her death in the river."

"Who told you this?" asks Nathaniel.

Ellery gestures out the door, where I now notice figures on horses and foot; among them I recognize General Joshua Buttrick, who lives near the Hunt family, and another person who appears to be a youth. I step away from Nathaniel in an attempt to better see, and the moonlight reveals William Hunt, the boy we saw ice-skating on the river the day of my miscarriage. Martha's brother. He is pale and ghostly. I place my hand over my heart, stricken by thoughts of my dead brothers, George and Wellington.

As Ellery apprises us of the details, his voice sounds far away. "Her family did not see her this evening, and when they asked around the village, they realized she never made it to school this morning."

"Oh, no," says Nathaniel.

"Yes. And General Buttrick found her bonnet and shoes. It appears that she has taken her own life."

I cover my mouth. The girl cannot yet be twenty years old.

Action resumes around me. Nathaniel kisses me and tells me to stay in the house. I am silent, because I know I will disobey him once he is out of sight. He joins Ellery and the men as they hurry through the orchard to the river. Once more I check Una, who sleeps soundly, and start out the back door.

The heat of this stifling July night presses around me. I look up to see the stars embedded like tiny diamonds on a great black cloth. The moon is a pearl. The peeping insects in the trees and the shush of the wind remind me of Cuba. In case I am seen by the clusters of men along the banks, searching for a sign of the girl, I wrap my robe tightly around my body, though I am hot enough to fling it off. I have knotted my hair, but the curls have escaped and are stuck in sweaty tendrils to the back of my neck.

I stay in the shadows and watch my husband and Ellery launch the *Lily*. I implore God to let this be a mistake, or let them find her soon; let it not be a suicide. Who can bear the thought of a young girl in such depths of melancholy that she takes her own life?

Oh! The dangers of solitude!

Something catches my eye—a movement on the bridge like a shadow that disappears as soon as I have seen it. Dread and terror fill me. First I think it is the beggar girl, but then I realize it must be the apparition of Martha herself, as we saw her all those months ago.

I never did visit her.

In spite of a sudden wish to run back to the house and hide away from this scene, I cannot leave. I weave my way along the secluded path and track my husband. From the whispers of men I learn that Martha was seen pacing the banks of the Concord for hours this morning.

"The poor thing must have agonized over whether to do the deed," says one.

"She has been prone to melancholy," says another. "She has tried this before, but was stopped by her sister."

Yet another man—her father, perhaps—speaks. "It is that ghastly narrative by the slave Frederick Douglass. Reading it tortured her."

Good heavens, what a tragedy!

Safely protected in the trees, I remove my robe and wipe the sweat from my neck. I have been out here no longer than twenty minutes, but Nathaniel has moved too far from me to see, and I cannot stray farther from Una. With reluctance, I make my way back to the house. Somewhere a hawk cries, and I hear shouts. I look back at the river but I can see no men at our bend. They are farther down the Concord. I stop and stare at the black surface of the river, where the moonlight makes strange lines like claw marks in the water. It is as still as death. Then I hear a terrible cry. They must have found her.

I find that I am running over the grass. My slippers are soaked from the saturated ground, and though my milk has almost ceased, my breasts are leaking through my nightdress. When I get closer to the house, I fling open the door and hear my poor Una sobbing upstairs. Her screams suggest she has been crying for some time. Now I am weeping, too. I take the stairs two at once and scoop up my poor, sweaty babe, whose red curls are stuck to her face and neck; she blazes from her fear and anger.

"Poor thing," I say, with visions of both Una and Martha in my mind.

I do not sit in the rocking chair, but tear open my chemise, popping the buttons in my haste, and press Una to me while I stand. Though she rarely nurses anymore, she latches on with such force that I grimace from the pain. There is a great searing burn as the milk lets down, followed by tremendous relief.

Once my nerves have calmed, I walk with her to Nathaniel's study at the back of the house, and gaze at the river through my scrawled writing and the other notes we have scratched on the glass. I wonder when the terrible thing will be birthed from the Concord's waters, and how my husband will bear seeing the consequence of a solitary life ended in tragedy.

INTERLUDE

1864
Massachusetts

Nathaniel was haunted by the recovery of the girl's body—the grotesque birth of her stiff corpse from the river. They found her handkerchief along the banks and poked into the black water until they hooked their ungodly catch and dragged her to dry land, where she looked like a statue of agony in death. The way Nathaniel described her clenched hands raised above her head and her bent knees called to mind the Magdalene painting from Cuba. I pray now that God had mercy on the poor creature.

Years later, to free his mind of the tragedy, Nathaniel wrote of the nightmarish scene in *The Blithedale Romance*, but I wonder whether his soul was truly exorcised. What Nathaniel did not write was that two more Hunt sisters lost their lives in the Concord River; the first took her own life several years later, and the second accidentally drowned, or so they say. There would be more drownings in the future of those we loved and knew best. I cannot think of them now.

"What troubles you, dove?"

Startled, I am unable to respond at first.

"I hope you are not filling your sweet head with worries of my old body," he says.

"While your old body is always on my mind, the shadow comes from my remembrance of poor Martha Hunt and her sad family, and all the river took from us at that time. And of all that water has taken."

His eyes darken. I know he sees their faces in his mind.

"I have not thought of them for some time," he says, so quietly I almost do not hear him.

My mind returns to the months after the suicide, when we were evicted from the manse, and how my heart broke, both for our loss and for my burdened husband. There is a daguerreotype of Nathaniel from that time that brings tears to my eyes. His face is so gaunt and his eyes so haunted, one would never realize that we had lived in secluded bliss within the walls of our marriage house, with only the cares of the world at large to trouble our hearts.

But I did not allow myself to dwell on our shame. It was in Salem, where we returned for Nathaniel's appointment at the custom house, that I learned to keep secrets that would save us. It was in Salem that our Una, increasingly spirited to the point of wildness, became a Pearl by her father's pen, and where Nathaniel learned to expose his uncensored depths in a novel that would make him known throughout the new and old worlds.

27

Summer 1846
Salem, Massachusetts

I read the words over and over again, but they still do not make sense. Nathaniel has handed me a copy of the *New-York Tri-bune* in which Margaret Fuller—our so-called friend—describes my husband's story collection, *Mosses from an Old Manse*, as thin and lacking clear insight into the human condition. My indignation has me sputtering and boiling like a pot on the stove.

"How could she?" I manage to spit through gritted teeth. "After all of our troubles, our near destitution, our friendship! This is a betrayal. A jealous betrayal because she cannot stand that we are in love, and our family grows, and you are just beginning to make a name for yourself as a writer."

"I too am surprised, but as a published author, I suppose I must prepare for critical reviews of my work."

"But this is not scholarship. This is blindly personal."

"It is not all bad. She has nice things to say about some of the stories."

"She should praise all of them, for they are each brilliant. She is ruffled that her book on modern women was widely criticized, while all she has seen are good reviews of your work."

My seat is still sore from our son's birth weeks ago, and I have strained my exhausted head with my outburst. Una looks up at me with large eyes and stands like a little schoolmistress.

"Oo should no yell, Mama."

Nathaniel and I cannot help but smile at our commanding little tot. I open my arms to her and she runs to my lap, injuring my body a bit in her jump, but not enough for me to flinch too awfully. The babe sleeps on in the nearby bassinet; we have not yet named him. If our daughter is the angel of light and passion, our son is the angel of tranquillity, praise God, but no name seems good enough for our little prince, so that is what we call him.

"I should not have shown you," Nathaniel says, lifting Una from me. "Henceforth I shall only share the good reviews. In the meantime, I will burn this paper, and with it the last embers of our friendship with Queen Margaret."

His voice has many layers. He pretends he does not suffer, but I hear the deep hurt, the bitterness and regret. I am angry with myself for stoking the fires of his frustration, and vow to emphasize what is good and positive.

"I should not have erupted," I say. "You are correct, Una. Let us only speak of the light. Mr. Channing praised your book highly. Franklin Pierce and Mr. O'Sullivan adore it. You never disappoint Mr. Longfellow. You will have a salary of twelve hundred dollars a year at the custom house, and our debts are nearly paid off."

"And I am now the proud father of two perfect cherubs," he says.

"What's a terub?" asks Una.

"It is a spunky wee angel borrowed from heaven for earthly enjoyment, though it does have a streak of mischief, a dash of turbulence, and a force like a tempest at times."

"I don't know what oo say," says Una, with all of the disgust of a haughty woman, and demands to be put down, much to her father's amusement.

I remind my daughter that she must be polite and respectful, but the little prince stirs at my speech, taking my attention from Una, and from worry over the reception of my husband's work.

The weeks and months of rearing young children blur together as if in a silvery dream, compounded by the beginnings of our gypsy life. I am content, but never settled, blessed with an abundance of sensual stimulation and closeness, but distracted by I know not what.

We finally named our boy Julian. Nathaniel is partial to Julian from Shelley's work, because of Shelley's frustrations with the so-called limitation of words, but I think of the nobility of Shelley's character Julian, in his belief that man can make the world better. Either way, our friends and family think us strange for giving our children unusual names, but we believe it makes them special.

I could never have anticipated that I would reside under the same roof with Nathaniel's mother and sisters, but that is exactly where I find myself. We must economize, so it makes little sense for us to keep separate lodgings, and we start in a small house together in a fine Salem neighborhood. Soon, however, with so much time spent in such close quarters, we determine that a larger home in a less fashionable section will better serve, even if we cannot afford to furnish it.

Fourteen Mall Street is a great, slim, rectangular-shaped thing, long from one end to the other, but thin so that the sunlight will heat the rooms in the cold months. In our three-story abode, our family will have use of the first floor for our chamber, the nursery, the handmaiden's room, and pantry. It will save us money to only have to use wood to heat one floor of stoves, and I will be able to see the children playing outdoors wherever I am in the house. Madame Hawthorne, Ebe, and Louisa will have rooms separate from ours on the second floor, and we will meet only if we choose to. Nathaniel has the luxury of the entire third floor for his study, where he may work without the noise of children or callers in the parlor to disturb him.

As taxing as the moves and cohabitations with his family have been, I am pleased with the energy of this time. Nathaniel has begun to put on weight, so he no longer has a gaunt, feral appearance, and has slowly settled our debts with his custom house pay. He has also been appointed secretary of the Salem Lyceum. He invites our friends to lecture, and when they come, other friends do as well. Emerson, Thoreau, Channing, my sisters—we see them with some regularity, and Nathaniel is a bit more at ease because he has steady employment, and more of a name for himself through his contributions to journals and reviews. I do wish he would accept more of the invitations from society to speak and to dine, but he refuses, and tells me that his evenings are for me and the children, and not the wealthy and the intellectuals, who want to gawk at the man who writes the dark stories.

It is difficult for Nathaniel to find time to write, having to work all day and attend to his family in the evening, but he makes up for it by always having a journal at his fingertips. He jots notes to himself here and there, but the long passages mostly detail the observations he makes of Una and Julian.

The winter of 1848 is the first I can remember when Nathaniel is not miserable, but he is restless. I know by the way he stares out windows, does not hear me when I speak, and often seems startled by human company that stories are forming in his mind.

One night I awaken to find our bed cold. I wrap my shawl around my arms and check the children first, who sleep soundly, before creeping up to the third floor. There I see Nathaniel working at his desk by the light of a single candle. He has left the fireplace cold, either to conserve our wood or because he did not want the idea that took him from his sleep to slip away on the night wind. He wears his nightshirt, and has a blanket wrapped around his legs, a scarf around his neck, and fingerless gloves on his hands. His brown hair appears black, and the flickering candlelight changes the shadows on his face so that he looks like a haunted man. I wish to go to him, but I cannot bear to disturb him; nor can I tear myself away. I will impress this moment upon my consciousness, for it would make a divine painting, if I were ever again to return to an easel.

Only the whistling winds outside and the scratch of his quill on the paper can be heard. When he pauses to dip the quill in the inkpot, he lets out his breath as if he has been holding it, and lifts his head to stare at the wall across from him. I slip back farther into the shadows so he does not see me, and watch until he places his quill on the desk and rubs his eyes with his fists. He turns a page in the journal lying next to his papers, and reads with great interest until he suddenly picks up the quill again, fills it with ink, and resumes his scribbling.

He has shared his journal with me, and it is full of observations of Una's temper tantrums and comments. While I attribute her mercurial nature to her young age, he ascribes more sinister motives to it, and half jokes that she could be possessed. I wonder what Una can have to do with what he writes with such determination. Perhaps it will be a children's story, one that will not reflect the darkness of the human heart, one that will not wake me in the middle of the night with fear for what my husband conceals under the veil of his soul.

28

Summer 1849

While I am in Boston in July, visiting Mother and Father with the children, enjoying time with family during the day, and reading the sultry, beseeching correspondence from my husband in the evenings, a letter from him arrives that interrupts our peace. Zachary Taylor, a Whig, has won the presidency, and with a telegram notifying him, my confirmed Democrat husband (though antipolitical to the core) is terminated from the custom house. I return with haste to Salem to support my love in his despair, and enter a war. The Whigs, led by that serpent Reverend Upham, bash my love for claiming to be a simple writer while actually being a political climber; the Democrats defend his honor and innocence. The politicians fight like mongrels over Nathaniel's ousting, and my love loses.

While Nathaniel calls on our blessed friends who lent us money, wearing his shame like a cloak, I bring the children into the sunny parlor to show them an old treasure box. Una and Julian bend their heads over the dusty lid of my paint kit, and exclaim as I open it. Inside, brushes rest like bones in an old tomb.

"You both are young, but not too little to begin to learn about art," I say.

I allow each of them to pick up a brush and caution them to hold their tools with reverence. I show them the colored powders, lay newspapers over the floor where they will work, and allow their dimpled hands to assist in the mixing. Soon, while they delight over the life they bring to the paper, I remove a shade from our lamp, place it on the secretary, and begin to paint a mythic scene on its surface.

Nathaniel finds us late that afternoon splotched with color and aglow with creative inspiration. I have no ache in my head, but only in my neck from bending over my art. When I show him the lamp shade and explain that I know a lady who will pay no less than five dollars to purchase it for her reading room, his eyes become glassy.

"My angel," he says. "Your kind supplication of our friends has saved us. I am both mortified by my circumstance and gratified that we have so many who love us. And now, to have you doing this . . ." His voice catches.

I place a kiss on his trembling lips.

"All will be well," I whisper, as he takes me in his arms.

He believes me.

Though it is late in the evening, it is nearly one hundred degrees. Nathaniel's mother and sisters decide to join us on our walk to the confectioner's on Buffum Street, where we may purchase ice cream for mere pennies. Ebe walks ahead with Una, the only member of our family besides Nathaniel with whom she cares to interact. Nathaniel strolls just behind, holding Julian's hand on one side, and Louisa's arm on the other. I trail them with Madame Hawthorne, who though sickly has asked to join us. I am glad, because I have been harboring silent fears of her declining health. Over these years I have become fond of her, and fear how the children and Nathaniel will mourn her when she no longer lives on earth.

"I am pleased you joined us," I say, hiding my alarm at her frail arm. She wears, as always, an old-fashioned black mourning dress for the husband she lost almost forty years ago, but we are all without sleeves in the terrible heat. With her arm laced through mine, I can feel the way her wrinkled skin hangs off her bony frame.

"I am glad I am able," she says. "I fear the time when I will not be strong enough to join you, so I must take this opportunity."

"No," I say. "Do not speak of such things."

She smiles and stares ahead at her family, addressing me without meeting my eyes.

"I am grateful for you, Sophia."

Her voice is quiet; I almost cannot hear it above the clatter of horses in the street, the mariners yelling from the docks, and the seagulls crying overhead. Tears prick my eyes at her words. She so rarely utters her thoughts aloud.

"And I for you," I say, giving her a gentle squeeze.

"You have brought him into the light," she says. "I would not have thought it possible."

I am barely able to mutter a thank-you, and must pause to wipe my eyes. She speaks no more, and though my family is happy enjoying the novelty of ice cream and a walk through town, I cannot help but feel dread, because Madame has uttered the words of one who will soon say good-bye.

Within days, she begins to fail.

I run back and forth between her bedside, to fan away the dreadful flies in this hellish heat, and the nursery, to keep the children away from her illness. Nathaniel's sisters take turns with me—Louisa helping during the day and Ebe at night when she prowls the world—and soon I am also taking shifts at Nathaniel's bedside, where fever and despair seem to be killing him too. I press a damp cloth to his forehead, praying over one invalid and the next, willing myself to remain calm and not to imagine that my children will succumb as well. Nathaniel is often incoherent and rambles about his aching ear and his pounding head.

"How did you bear your headaches?" he whispers. "I never understood the magnitude of your strength until now."

I try to quiet him and reassure him that all will be well, but I am aware that the woman who bore him is not long for this earth. I fear what her loss will do to Nathaniel. He is in awe of her, and she of him, but I cannot say whether the two of them have ever expressed these feelings out loud. If Nathaniel were well, I would encourage him to do so before it is too late.

The days pass in the darkness of decline, and the children become more and more unruly. They are disturbed by the drawn countenances of those who are normally so bright with them, and are left so often alone that they fight and fuss and make a terrible racket. As soon as I empty Madame Hawthorne's chamber pot and hang the laundry, Julian has spilled my writing ink on Una's dolly, and her flare of temper can be heard from Mall Street to Herbert. I try never to shout at the children, but it is hard to restrain myself when Una kicks Julian's little shin with all her might. Ebe finally emerges to help, and removes her favorite to the upstairs room with kisses, much to my frustration at this indulgence of my daughter. Louisa comes downstairs just as Nathaniel appears in our chamber doorway. He is still flushed and looks dreadful, but he is at least standing, and I praise God aloud for that.

"Natty," says Louisa, "I am afraid the end is not far."

Nathaniel looks as if he will collapse at this news, so I help him to his mother's room, which already has the stink of death. It is a stifling chamber on this brutal summer day, and I command Louisa to open the curtains and the window.

"Are you sure the air will be good for her?"

I give her a look that demonstrates how little such a thing matters at this time, and she nods and obeys me. The window sticks, so I hurry to help her, and when I turn around, I am moved.

Nathaniel kneels at his mother's side, grasping her gnarled hand and crying. Louisa is much affected, having so rarely seen such emotional displays from her brother, and rushes out of the room. Ebe's figure soon darkens the threshold. She must have left Una with Louisa, for she is alone, but when she sees her brother's devastation, she too must go. Nathaniel's pain is almost as hard to bear as the death of his mother.

She whispers words to him that further break him until he sobs and places his head on the bed. He replies, but I cannot understand him, and I hope they have spoken aloud their love for each other. I know Nathaniel curses the inadequacy of words, but with this display of feeling, his mother will have no doubt of his devotion.

When she becomes still but for a slight, staggered pulsing of her chest, Nathaniel lifts his head and looks out the window where our children now run in circles on the grass below. He looks back at his mother and then out the window, his face a tempest of confusion and despair, his heart divided between the great truth that is reinforced with each passing year of our lives: One hand is open, overflowing with an abundance of joy and vitality; the other is a fist, clutching a void so desperately that the nails dig holes in the skin.

Following his mother's death, Nathaniel sinks into a terrible blackness of spirit. He is unreachable, and the entire household falls ill. As we struggle to survive this chaos and recover, Elizabeth comes to rescue us.

I nearly cry aloud when I see her aging, round figure walking up to the house. We have been polite with each other these years since my love and marriage to Nathaniel, but I have always felt a chilliness because of her first loving him. I meet her at the door in a quivering state, and the angel hesitates not one moment before scooping me into her ample bosom in the kindliest embrace I have ever known.

In just days of having her near us, the veil of mourning begins to lift.

She stands behind Una, holding my daughter's hands, instructing her on how to cut her roasted chicken.

"There," says Elizabeth. "Now you will not have your mother always do every little thing for you. You are growing. You must do more for yourself."

Una's five-year-old eyes are wide and accepting of Elizabeth's confidence in what she should be doing. I also know Una is glad to have a knife in her possession—something I would never allow under normal circumstances with one so quick-tempered as my daughter.

"I will, Aunt Lizzie," she says.

Nathaniel looks on with warmth. Though he is still pale, he joins us at table and does not need to rest as often.

"Such charming manners," says Elizabeth. She praises Una's moments of good behavior, because she has observed what else my daughter is capable of. My girl has grown even more mercurial with the passing weeks, but I believe that is because of the death and illness in the house. I am certain she will calm down once we are all in full health.

"Me too," says Julian, face sloppy with gravy and bread crumbs.

I wipe his little cheeks with a napkin and brush my hand over his hair.

"Yes, you too," says Elizabeth.

My children continue to show off for Aunt Lizzie through

the remainder of the meal, and once the dishes are clear and their nursemaid removes them to prepare for bed, Elizabeth joins me and Nathaniel in the parlor. Almost as soon as we sit with our books, she removes a letter from her dress pocket and clears her throat for our attention.

"I have received a letter from Mr. Emerson with the most shocking news," she says.

"What is it?" I ask, surprised that Elizabeth was able to hold back her gossip for an entire meal. Nathaniel continues to read his book. He knows Elizabeth always thinks her news is shocking, but rarely does it measure up to such a description.

"It is about Miss Fuller."

That has Nathaniel's attention. He closes his volume of Shakespeare and sits forward in his chair.

"Old Queen Margaret," he says. "What muck has she got into now?"

"A scandal," says Elizabeth. "She is living with a man in Italy, to whom she may or may not be married. *And they have a child.*"

I cover my mouth and Nathaniel draws in his breath.

"No," I say.

"Yes."

"But when? How?"

"I know nothing but what I have told you, but you may count on my trying to find out much more."

We are all so agitated that for the rest of the evening, we are able to chatter about nothing else. We invite Louisa and Ebe into the parlor and share the gossip, which I fear will shock Louisa's delicate self to fainting, but she is able to control herself.

"Imagine," says Louisa. "The woman who so criticized you when you were expecting, having her own child. I wonder if she still attends to her art."

I laugh at Louisa's impertinence, and almost immediately feel guilty for talking about Margaret in such a fashion. For her to have conceived a child with a man, she must surely be in love, and love is what has always been sorely lacking in her life. While Ebe and Elizabeth discuss the probability of Margaret's marrying this man, I turn my gaze on Nathaniel. He stares out the window, wearing a look of distaste, though I do not know whether that is because he is scandalized, or is as unsettled as I am about the whole business. In a moment, he turns and gives me a tight smile, but I cannot read his thoughts.

We are not able to speak of Margaret in the coming days as Elizabeth packs to leave us. The house is full of constant bustle, with friends visiting to pay their respects and offer comfort in our mourning, and Nathaniel retiring early and sleeping like the dead in his rehabilitation. On the day of Elizabeth's departure, I give her my warmest embrace, and cannot help my tears.

"We would all have perished without you," I say.

"How ridiculous," she says. "You would have brought them through it, Sophy."

"She would have, but we are grateful." Nathaniel steps from the front door and reaches for her hand to kiss it. She glows from his attention, and leans in to give him a hug. I cannot help but smile to see the two of them together. Elizabeth has grown portly, and her hair has turned almost completely gray. Nathaniel, however, looks unchanged from the days when we courted, aside from the lines that have settled around his eyes. It is amusing to imagine that if the two of them had joined, what a strange, mismatched pair they would now make.

The children tumble out of the house and give Aunt Lizzie kisses and waves as she climbs into the stagecoach bound for Boston. Nathaniel wraps his arm around my waist and we watch her until the carriage is out of sight.

Nathaniel has healed in body, but a persistent gloom surrounds him. He is frantic at the ledgers, trying to find ways to support his sisters and his own family, so that after weeks of watching him agonize I must break the promise I made to myself and confess my secret.

Since Nathaniel received his first pay from the custom house, I have been in charge of our finances, and unbeknownst to him, I have set aside a large sum of his every payment as savings in case of disaster. Now that his mother has gone and left his sisters in our charge, and her meager assets barely covered her funeral, I must tell my love that all will be well.

The night is gentle—the first we have had in many weeks that bears the suggestion of the autumn to come. Nathaniel writes of his mother's death to friends near and far, and the light of the moon and the candle on his desk give him a celestial bearing. Even though the stoop in his shoulders reveals his burdens, he is ready with a smile when he sees me in the doorway.

"It is late," I say. "Come lie in my arms."

He rubs his eyes and runs his hands through his hair, making it wild. "As soon as this letter is concluded. I promise."

I walk over to his desk. I have brushed my hair and plaited it for bed, and have already changed into my nightclothes and washed my face and neck with cool water. I place my hands on his shoulders and begin to knead away the tension that sets him like a Roman statue. He allows his head to fall back and sighs with pleasure as my hands creep down his back and around the front of his chest.

"I have something to tell you," I whisper in his ear from behind him before giving his perfect lobe a nibble.

"If you tell me you are with child again, you might become a widow, for my heart cannot take it."

I give him a pinch on his sides, and he flinches.

"No, not yet," I say. "I hope you do not think me cruel for what I am about to reveal, but I promised myself I would not share it with you until we were desperate."

"I can certainly attest to our desperation, but I fear what you might say."

"There is nothing to fear," I say. I slip the key from the ribbon on my wrist and lean down over him to open the door at the bottom of the desk. With a flourish, I slide it open and say, "Your treasure, my lord."

The candlelight glints off the surfaces of the stacks of coins, and in seconds I am in his arms being swung around in a circle.

"Sophy! Did you pillage a ship of pirates at the dock?"

"Yes!"

"Stop teasing," he says, placing me on the ground. "How did you come by this? Are you the girl from Una's storybook who spins straw into gold?"

"It is but a portion of your earnings, saved each payday from the custom house. We have lived like misers, and this is the result."

He makes an O with his mouth and walks over to the drawer.

"But how can that be? I barely made enough to keep us fed."

"You barely made enough to keep us fed with the amount of income I allotted our household. This is our savings, and a little from my painted lamp shades."

The man bursts into tears before me, and comes forward, pressing his lips to mine with the same urgency as when we courted. I respond eagerly, tugging at his shirt and feeling his body come alive in ways we have not experienced for months. I worry that his sisters will hear us, so I pull back and motion my head toward the stairs.

"Sophia, what would I do if you ever . . . How did I live before you?"

"God is with us," I say. "And now you may do as you have always wanted, without the shackles of government employment or the directives of other men. You are free to write your novel."

29

Spring 1850
Massachusetts

Just two weeks after its first printing of twenty-five hundred copies, *The Scarlet Letter* sells out, and soon becomes an international success.

Earning the praise of his contemporaries brings about a deep and quiet satisfaction to Nathaniel. Finally he can hold up his head in the company of men of worldly success and position—men like our brother-in-law, Horace Mann; Ralph Emerson; and Henry Longfellow. Though not rich, we can pay off our debts and assist Nathaniel's sisters. Above all, Nathaniel is most grateful to have succeeded in scouring the tarnish from the surname his ancestors stained.

But his termination from the custom house and subsequent unemployment, his mother's death, and our illnesses have all taken a toll. Nathaniel's boyish cheekiness evaporates. His playful mischief is difficult to resurrect. His shoulders have lost their angles and begin to stoop. The spell of enchantment that has so long preserved his youth now seems to evaporate.

I too feel like a wilting flower. Childbearing has spread and softened my body, and gray streaks begin to dull my auburn hair. I long to paint again, but between Nathaniel and the children, I am so blessedly, constantly *needed* that time itself slips through my fingers like water.

Shortly after Nathaniel's mother's death, Salem suffocates us. The memory of our last walk with Madame and the room of her death haunt us so that we cannot wake from the nightmare. While Louisa is a pleasure, Ebe's darkness seems to encourage Nathaniel's, and I want him away from her. We decide to go inland toward the mountains to rent a little house in Lenox, where Una and Julian may romp unhindered in grassy fields. Now that Nathaniel is well-known, he cannot walk down the streets of Salem without being forced to endure multiple conversations, and the post has begun to deliver the oddest and most unsettling confessions of all manner of adulterer and criminal. It seems that readers make assumptions about the authors of books full of strange secrets and confessions.

In the Berkshires we will drink of the fresh mountain air to purify our bodies of illness and our minds of fatigue. Nathaniel will not have to restrict his walks to the dead of night, because we will be more isolated, and here, undisturbed, he may begin his next novel.

Undisturbed.

It is a word worth pondering, for the very wish for it, the definite utterance of it, leads to its elusiveness. It is a state we pursue in our daily lives—in our hourly lives with young children— lamenting that we cannot achieve it, but it is in these small lamentations that true blessing exists, for it means there are no great tragedies prowling at our doors and hearths.

I ponder this while attempting to unpack and organize our possessions in this little red house Nathaniel calls our Scarlet Letter, fend off Julian, who is hungry every moment of the day, and entertain Una, who is a monster when she cannot play out of doors. The rain has arrived in a great drenching deluge, and I hustle the children inside and help them change their soaked clothing, all the while watching out the back windows for my husband, who left on a solitary walk to Monument Mountain an hour ago. I peer over the luscious green grass, but the precipitation prevents me from seeing all the way to the lake and mountains, and I am startled when Nathaniel enters the house from the front walk instead of where I anticipated he would emerge in the back. He is as soaked as a river plant, and his hat wilts over his slick hair, which is plastered against his neck and face. His gaze is on the floor and he removes his hat with care and runs his hand through his hair, shaking off the water before looking up to meet my eyes. I see an unspeakable darkness that I know cannot come from the weather, and I am frightened.

"What is it, Nathaniel?"

His mouth opens to form a word, but he cannot find a way to start speaking. After a moment, he reaches inside his jacket to his breast pocket to extract a letter, and hands it to me before walking to the window and leaning on the sill with his back to me. When I see Elizabeth's script, my hands begin to tremble. I remove the paper and let the envelope drop to the floor. A newspaper clipping falls out, and Una snatches it up and walks toward the hallway to try to read what it says.

"Una, bring that back to me," I say, scanning Elizabeth's familiar handwriting.

A great loss . . . a terrible tragedy . . . who could have predicted or wished such an awful end to her . . . the poor child . . . may God have mercy on all their souls.

Una lifts the paper to me and I see a headline that does not make immediate sense.

SHIPWRECK AT FIRE ISLAND, NEW YORK

I take the paper from her hands and scan the article, my eyes shifting from top to bottom in search of my connection to the wreckage, but I see nothing. Relieved that it is no one in my family, I start at the top of the paper again, and read with interest about the ship *Elizabeth* returning from Europe, which ran aground in a terrible storm just before reaching the mainland. As the boat disintegrated, its passengers jumped overboard, and most of them perished, including those on the list of names printed below. The names mean nothing to me until I reach one.

MARGARET FULLER OSSOLI

I suck in my breath and stagger to the nearest chair. Julian and Una look up at me with wide eyes, and I attempt to control my emotions, but I cannot help the tears that start as I reread Elizabeth's letter.

Emerson had learned of the wreck and dispatched Henry and Ellery to join in the search and look for Margaret's body, but they had no success. From the survivors, they learned that Margaret's husband drowned and her son had gone overboard, so she refused to leave the ship even though certain death awaited her on its splintering planks. A sailor had attempted to save the boy, but both of them washed ashore with no life left in them. Margaret's body had not been found.

It is too much to bear. I squeeze my fists to my eyes and take deep, labored breaths. I do not know how to reconcile my bitterness and anger for Margaret these years with my deep sadness at losing a woman whom both of us once loved. To think of watching her husband and child die, and choosing to die herself!

Nathaniel's head is down and pressed to the window. His shoulders rise and fall. Julian has stuck his thumb in his mouth, but Una comes to me and places her hand on my arm.

"Do not cry, Mama," she says. "Whoever has died has gone to God."

30

All of these deaths have done something to Nathaniel that I would not have expected: They have forced him back into life.

The summer following our arrival at the little red house becomes a time of great abundance. We cannot drink enough of each other and of our healthy children, the fresh lake, the pure air, the fragrant flowers. We raise chickens, and ride horses, and take in feral cats. We climb mountains, and Nathaniel teaches the children to swim in our lake, honoring our unspoken understanding that none of ours will die by water. Nathaniel also becomes close with another young writer who has achieved success and acclaim with his published works, Herman Melville.

Nathaniel met Herman at a picnic and hike with friends in Pittsfield. They were apparently overtaken by a tempest that sent them all into a cave for shelter. There my forty-six-year-old husband found an admirer in thirty-one-year-old Herman. To my surprise, Nathaniel liked Herman so much that he invited him to stay with us for a few days while Herman looks for a place to live nearby with his young family.

The children rush out the front door when they hear the galloping and barking that accompany Herman's arrival. I cross to the window to see the man throw his strong leg over his horse before it has fully halted, and tie a massive dog to the post. He and Nathaniel embrace and slap each other on the back as if they have known each other for years instead of weeks, and Una and Julian run to Herman and beg for rides on the canine.

"Let him water his animals first," says Nathaniel, which sends Una off to the well pump.

"Where are your wife and boys?" asks Nathaniel, as they walk to the house.

"I left them with friends," says Herman. "I do not want anything to interfere with my time with the great Hawthorne."

I watch my husband dismiss his comment with a wave and a bashful smile, and cannot take my eyes from the visitor, who cannot take his eyes from Nathaniel.

The men have been embarking upon mountain hikes over difficult terrain, and the children are disappointed to be left behind, as am I. I envisioned more picnics and leisure with our guest, but one so young as Herman cannot be expected to sit still for long. I wonder how his wife endures his restlessness.

At the dinner table in the evenings, Herman is polite to me, but it is clear that he is here to worship Nathaniel. Herman is a strapping, bronzed man whose youth is a reminder of our own. Just being in his presence seems to revive my husband, as if Herman's company is the antidote to the sad events that forced us from Salem. But Herman's effusions are like the sun on a blazing summer day—a warm delight at first, followed by a hot discomfort.

"*Mosses* stirred a longing in me that I have not felt from fiction in some time," says Herman, devouring the strawberries and cream placed before him. "It is as if you know my soul."

Nathaniel's face flushes. He has run out of ways to thank this young man, and shifts in his chair in what I recognize as a growing unease.

"Truly," Herman continues, "it is as if you have burrowed some dark and beautiful seed in my heart's dirt that produces the greatest abundance of growth."

Nathaniel's eyes seem to beg my assistance, so I attempt to speak with Herman. I know from our short acquaintance that trying to converse with Herman about matters of family, horses, or weather is fruitless, and the only subject he will engage in with enthusiasm is the magnificence of Nathaniel Hawthorne. While I would never tire of such a subject, after just three days my beloved is burdened by Herman's admiration.

"What high praise," I say. "It is gratifying to see that you perceive my husband's depths, and what his writing inspires in the reader, the challenge he poses to view our fellow mortals with an eye not of judgment, but of deep understanding. Especially understanding of our own hearts, and how we all bear the capacity to produce great evil, but also great goodness."

"Indeed," says Herman, finishing his third glass of champagne. "His writing is as fine as that of the Bard himself!"

"I must stop you in your kind lunacy," says Nathaniel. "While I am grateful for such praise, you cannot compare me to Shakespeare. It is a form of blasphemy."

"Nonsense," says Herman, his eyes growing wild and strange. "You underestimate your talent, and because I have such admiration for you, I will not hear a word spoken against you, even if it comes from your own lips."

I see Herman clench his fist and feel an iciness creep into my blood. I watch him the way one would a tamed circus bear, with a mixture of awe and fear. This is a man who has lived below brig decks with sailors and in jungles with savages. His passions are as rich in color as the most striking tropical foliage, but like the jungle, his beauties seem to conceal danger, and he is not a man I would want to cross.

"Hear, hear," I say, standing and lifting Julian from his chair, who protests because he has not finished his strawberries. I sit him back down, and Una reaches over to feed Julian the last bite and wipe his mouth with a napkin.

Una glances at Herman and then at me. "I will take him, Mama. We will read books before we go to bed."

I am grateful for her assistance and praise her for it; secretly I am glad the children will not be here if Herman becomes drunker. We will all be relieved when he no longer resides with us.

But he has apparently enjoyed his time with us so greatly that he has found lodgings just six miles away. Nathaniel makes light of it, saying that it is good to have one's admirers so close, but I hear the uneasiness beneath his words, and wonder how long he will endure Herman's attentions.

I instruct our African cook, Mrs. Peters, to set a place for Herman at dinner. He has been at our table with regularity throughout the autumn and now winter, and we never know which Herman to expect: the jovial young man or the brooding writer. Mrs. Peters has come to help us, since I am again with child, and Nathaniel will not have me exert myself in any way. He confessed to me one night that he'd had terrible visions that this babe would do me in, and while I assure him that I have never felt better with a pregnancy, I obey his wishes to rest to calm his heart.

When Herman comes into the house, he has already stomped his boots and shaken the fine coating of snow from his coat. He presents a basket of oranges to me that he procured from a ship on his visit to Boston, and tells me that he hopes they will remind me of pleasing times in Cuba, which, to my surprise, he has been interested to hear about. I can hardly believe that anyplace I have occupied without Nathaniel would hold the slightest draw for him, but I am relieved to see that he seems light in mood.

Mrs. Peters accepts the oranges with suspicion and commences a great scrubbing of their poor skins before agreeing to peel them for our meal. Mrs. Peters is as loyal to us as a Cuban house servant, but we can all rest easy knowing she is paid wages instead of living in servitude. She is imposing and moral, and the children mind her far better than they do me. She is a comfort to me when Nathaniel is on his rambles or working on his new novel, though I cannot help but feel her reserve. Can true affection ever develop between our races, or will we ever be wary of one another? Our country simmers like a covered pot over the issue of slavery, and while Nathaniel and I do not approve of owning slaves, we cannot imagine what a division or even a war between the Northern and Southern states would do to our young nation.

Nathaniel, Herman, and I discuss these topics after the children have been put to bed, while Mrs. Peters cleans dishes in the kitchen. Nathaniel has wrapped my arms with a shawl, and we sit around the hearth. Winter has come without mercy, and as charming as our little red house is, an unwelcome wind from the mountains finds all the cracks in walls and window frames.

"My mother and sisters are violently opposed to slavery," I say, "but they have no practical suggestions for how to phase it out."

"I still find merit in the idea of sending the Africans back to their continent, though the idea is losing fashion," says Nathaniel.

I hear a cabinet slam and wonder how much of our conversation Mrs. Peters overhears.

"But what of those blacks born in America?" says Herman, his voice deep and husky. He has become low during the evening, and his mood pulls at one like a current under the sea. "Africa is as foreign to them as it is to us. It does not seem fair."

"No, there must be a better solution," I say. "But when I think of the young men in the States at war over it, I cannot endorse it."

"Nor I," says Nathaniel.

"Nor I," says Herman.

This silences us for many minutes. My sister Elizabeth would call us cowards, and maybe we are, but I can think only of my children and my home, and the thousands of homes like ours, and how it would be a tragedy to open the crusted-over war wounds of a country such a short while after its independence.

The wind rattles the panes and whistles eerily out of doors. It is a prowling wolf, looking for a way into our house. I wrap the shawl more tightly around me and embrace my swollen stomach.

"I have the strangest feeling of Margaret Fuller in the air tonight," says Nathaniel.

His observation causes the hair on my arms to rise. Why would he say such a thing? He turns to me and must sense my thought, for he addresses it.

"Talk of slavery makes me think of her," he says. "She could not endorse the novels of a friend, but she could promote the *Narrative* by Frederick Douglass, and stir up the tempest of the antislavery movement, which prowls the civility and domestic tranquillity of our nation like the wind outside our doors."

"Do not speak ill of the dead," I say.

Herman shifts with apparent discomfort in his chair.

"Since her death, I have tried to forgive her," says Nathaniel, "but I cannot. And my ire grows. She was a woman who lived however she wished without care for another, without putting the needs of those around her before her own selfish opinions. We are breeding a nation of such thinkers and individuals— intent on personal expression at all costs—and that will lead to war. I might be a more successful writer if I did not seek to address human truth, but rather spewed out my own limited opinions without care for reader or critic or any kind of propriety."

I am shocked by Nathaniel's outburst. He usually reserves his opinions for me, behind closed doors, and always with extreme reluctance to commit to an ideal. There are no simple answers, and he does not have the optimism to see around the struggle. The older I get, the more like him I become. We have lost so many through death that I cannot think it prudent or moral to stir up tempers that would lead to war. My sister Mary would tell me to think of the slave families and the futures of our children. She would say our salvation depends upon it.

Nathaniel paces the room, but stops before the painting *Isola San Giovanni* I made during our engagement. The piece he used to hide behind a black veil in the privacy of his rooms he now allows to adorn our parlor so any visitor may look upon it, though he still conceals *Endymion*. Has he become more comfortable in his love, or has he forgotten the intensity of feeling that inspired the work?

"Forgive me," he says. "I am unwound from politics. Franklin Pierce needs me to write his biography, to establish himself firmly as a Democrat. He believes we cannot have war at any cost. Slavery will gradually disappear, family by family. Blacks will be freed a generation at a time and become employed, like our Mrs. Peters. Laws can be made prohibiting any new transactions involving human property, while allowing the old owners to finish what they have started, though they be damned. If we shed blood for this cause, there will be a curse on future generations. The races will never reconcile. Pierce will keep our nation from a war that would only bring about the swifter resolution of something that would otherwise work itself out eventually. But I am reluctant to write about such matters in a biography."

"Such a book will lose you more than one friend," says Herman.

My stomach quakes at the thought of such a loss for a man who has so few intimates. I watched how the troubles in Salem before his removal from the custom house pained and aged him.

"But what about *The House of the Seven Gables*?" I ask. "You must finish it before you move on to another work, especially one so controversial."

"*Gables* is complete," he says. "I will commence reading it aloud to you tomorrow night, and it will be published in the spring. My writing Franklin's biography is not a project set in stone. We just started discussing the idea."

"But does Franklin not understand that you are a fiction writer?" I say.

Nathaniel meets my gaze.

"What could be more fictional than biography?"

Just after *The House of the Seven Gables* enters the world in the spring of 1851, so does our little Rose. Cheered as we are by the new babe, sales of the novel, about the generational stain of sin, lag, so Nathaniel writes a storybook of myths for children, *A Wonder Book for Boys and Girls*, and it meets with surprising success.

While I sit feeding my tiny Rose, I spend my days watching Nathaniel through the windows at play with our children. No task is beneath him, and he approaches every act with such tender attention. He lies in the glowing sun while Una and Julian cover him with grass. As soon as they finish, he jumps up, pretending to be a monster, scaring them into thrilling shrieks and chasing them around the yard. Then they visit the henhouse and the nearby barns. Once the sun becomes too hot, they make for the lake and forest with baskets for collecting flowers and other natural treasures. They deliver them to me fresh every day, and our tiny home is grandly decorated from the abundance of flora. Una must be careful in the sun, but Julian is so brown, Nathaniel jokes that he could belong to Mrs. Peters. She does not acknowledge the joke as amusing, but I can tell it charms her, because of how the corners of her lips lift when she turns away.

Herman continues to visit often—very often. While Nathaniel loves his friend, Herman's incessant intensity, his probing matters of publishing and politics, God and life's meaning, and his inclination to melancholy burden Nathaniel. Herman writes his whale book but is plagued with insecurity about it. I have read his earlier work and assure him of his talent, but I am well acquainted with the doubts that dwell so near the hand that is impelled to create.

My artistic power is a snuffed candle. It is impossible for me to conceive of lifting my paintbrushes for anything but color time with the children. I have tried to keep my hand active through sketches for Una and Julian, or to send to Mary's three children—yes, she now has three—but there is no heat in my ventures. I suppose I am glad not to be plagued with the delicacy of brain from such activity, but sometimes, especially at night, I miss it like an old love, and wonder whether we will ever meet again.

Mother wrote to me in her last letter on the subject, offering much comfort. The woman who was so adamant that I never marry or compromise my artistic gifts seems to have come around to another way of thought entirely, for she believes that in a partnership like mine with Nathaniel, one must support the other instead of both being consumed. She reinforces my belief in Nathaniel's genius and the necessity that his work be shared with the world. I must keep our home and spirits up if he is to be productive, and it is a worthy sacrifice to make for posterity. It is strange to see such words from my mother's pen, so altered are her views. Despite her advice, I hope my own artistry does not dry up completely.

My loves are now returning from a sojourn, but I see that Nathaniel's face is flushed, and the children are hot and exhausted. Rose has been inconsolable today, and I know her cries reach them outside when Nathaniel lifts his head and wrinkles his brow. He will not be able to write due to the heat and the noise, and as they enter with their complaints and requests for nourishment, the walls of our little house press closer.

I do not know the exact moment we feel compelled to leave Lenox, but we seem to arrive at the idea simultaneously. Perhaps it is when I knock my knee on the hobbyhorse and almost fall with Rose, or after gasping through an entire summer without the relief of sea breezes, or when Herman sends a letter that embarrasses Nathaniel.

I recline in our bed, giving Rose a good feeding before tucking her in for the night, as Nathaniel washes his face and hands. It is as hot as a Cuban kitchen house, which suits us far more than the misery of winter on the mountain, but we must open a window to allow the wind to bring us oxygen. I hear the leaves outside shiver, and delight in the sound.

"If the signature on that letter was not that of a man, one would think I had a mistress," says Nathaniel.

"Please do not say such things."

"I do not mean to be vulgar, but I cannot help but recoil at such a display of emotion."

"You know Herman regards you with the greatest affection. He dedicated his book to you. He never hides his feelings. Why are you now so aggrieved?"

"It was my letter praising *Moby-Dick*. That I would write to him of enjoying it so affected him that he went on to proclaim that our hearts beat under the same ribs, and our souls are in direct communion."

"Oh, my!" I say. "But you feel grateful when a fellow writer praises you, especially one more advanced and well regarded than yourself. Surely you understand Herman's rush of feeling. He has been so long at his novel, and so worried about its reception."

"I know, but he goes too far."

Nathaniel has removed his shirt and I cannot help but feel a fire at seeing my husband, still in such fine physical bearing, so near to me. I give him an impish look and he shakes his head.

"No, dove. Please. Though our babes are fine and perfect, Rose is the last. Let us at least get her out of booties before we even think of such a thing."

He blows out the candle on the night table and removes his pants in the dark before crawling into bed. He does not cuddle into me as usual, but pulls over to the far edge. The noise he makes awakens Rose, who fusses but is too full to drink more. I cannot get her to stop, so I am forced to climb out of bed.

Nathaniel turns over. "Do you want me to walk her?"

"No," I snap, and leave behind a chilly wind in my exit.

31

Autumn 1851

Though we have lived in Lenox for only eighteen months, our parting is emotional.

Herman must sense that his constant attention is part of the reason we are leaving. His heat and his need became too intense, and I would have cautioned him if he could have heard me, but he is not one to take advice from women. The night before we go, he visits us to bid farewell. He cries and embraces Nathaniel, but mercifully does not stay long. Once he has gone, Nathaniel releases his breath as if he has been holding it for many months.

As we load the baggage wagon the next day, Mrs. Peters comes to me in a rare display of affection, and pulls me into her bosom. When she draws back, I wipe my eyes.

"You have squeezed out my tears like a clothes wringer," I say.

Nathaniel also embraces her. "Thank you for your care of us," he says. "We will not forget you."

She nods her head and takes leave of us.

As we pull away, we cannot help but look back over our shoulders. As tightly as we were all packed in the house, as burdened as we felt by winters and young writers, it was our home, and where we brought a babe into the world. Every time we settle in a place, I think of Mr. Emerson's words the first night he dined with us as newlyweds, when he toasted our house of Hawthorne. Wherever we go, I wonder whether we have finally found the place where we will lay our foundation. I suppose I will have to keep wondering.

"Oh, Mama, the cats!" says Julian.

Five felines that have prowled our gardens and barns, and enjoyed our leftovers and petting, line the fence post. One of them runs her black paw over her face.

"She's crying," says Una.

"No," I say, moved that the children are so affected. "She is waving to us, wishing us well. Wave back!"

Their dear little hands rise and we watch the cats until they are out of sight, and we may turn to the future. Before we decide where to settle next, we will stay at my sister Mary's house in West Newton, which is empty since the Manns have gone to live in Washington now that Horace has been reelected to Congress. We will be just streets away from where Mother and Father now reside, and Nathaniel is glad to be closer to Boston and the possibility of another salaried job. He believes Franklin has a good chance of winning the presidency in the upcoming election, and might secure him a government position. No matter how successful his writing, it never brings in enough to keep us out of debt. Nathaniel is convinced that he will not have to abandon writing, fortunately, even with steady employment, now that he has a firm grasp of crafting novels. He even has an idea for a new romance based on his time living at Brook Farm.

At the train station, the children are thrilled when the mighty locomotive pulls in with much noise and bursts of steam. I plug my ears until the whistle stops, imagining that my young self would have fainted at the thought of traveling in such a loud conveyance. Once we embark upon the short ride to West Newton, it occurs to me how near Brook Farm we will reside.

"It will be advantageous for you to visit the old farm and recall impressions for the novel," I say.

"I think so too," he replies. "Though I have many unfavorable associations with it, since we had to sue Mr. Ripley for our investment."

"How helpful it would have been if he had actually had the means to repay it."

"Indeed."

We stare at the cloudy November landscape, and I cannot help but recall the day I visited Brook Farm. How long ago that was, though it seems as if not much time has passed. To think that Margaret no longer breathes the air of this earth is painful. I hope she rests in an Elysian dwelling, somewhere beyond the common cares, with her husband and son. Will she figure into Nathaniel's new work, since she was so frequent a visitor to Brook Farm?

"I am pleased to hear you are pursuing a new work of fiction," I say. "Political writing is dangerous and pins one down like an insect on a board. I was never comfortable with the idea of you writing Franklin's biography."

"I do agree, to an extent," says Nathaniel. "But you must know that the biography will still likely be written."

"But how will you do so while remaining politically ambiguous? Franklin will not be popular among our liberal Northern friends, and you may be perceived as proslavery."

"It is a danger, but Franklin is a dear friend, and I align with him in light of my ardent wish to stay away from war. But it is no matter. I will write an introduction to the biography excusing myself and disclaiming all political assumption. I will make it clear that it is a work meant to honor a great friend, not to put forward a cause."

"You must prepare yourself for a backlash either way," I say.

"Yes," he replies. "But writing it will mean Franklin owes me a favor, and that could lead to employment."

I wish to probe Nathaniel further to ascertain whether his wish for steady employment is a sacrifice for our family or a real hope of his own. I cannot think that my seraph, meant to illuminate humanity through his writing, is fit for public office. But I cannot continue our conversation, for we have arrived.

We pass the winter unsettled and ill at ease in our surroundings. Nathaniel becomes consumed with his new novel, leaving me to the children. I educate them at home, but we must take a break from our studies when Mother becomes ill, and I have to stay with her. There are times I fear she will die, but after an extended affliction, her health begins to return.

At the end of a particularly exhausting day spent caring for Mother, fretting that I will bring her illness into my house, and returning on snow-covered roads to our chilly home, I am pleased to see a letter from Mr. Emerson. It seems the old Alcott place, Hillside, is for sale, and the price to buy it is not outrageous. I cannot help but become wild with excitement. I pace all afternoon until Nathaniel descends from his study, pale and exhausted, and I thrust the letter into his hand.

"Concord! A return to Eden!" I say.

His eyes scan the letter, but his face is not as animated as I had hoped.

"We have never been able to purchase a home in our lives," he says. "And purchase means settled. As much as I long for grassy meadows and rivers for our children, I do not know if I am capable of rooting myself in a single village."

My heart falls. I am desperate for rooting. Since the birth of our children, we have been on the road like gypsies, moving every time we make just enough friends to miss them. He senses my disappointment.

"Dove," he says, "let us visit the house and see if it is fit to live in, but let us consider renting instead of purchasing."

"I will consider it, but I ask that you consider purchasing instead of renting. I am tired, Nathaniel."

It seems as if the whole of our vagabond existence, the exhaustion from nursing Mother, and the pressure of our inadequate finances falls upon me at once, and I burst into a sudden fit of weeping. Nathaniel takes me in his arms and escorts me up the stairs past our worried children. They gather around me in the bed, a party of faces I adore, asking Mama how they can help her. Their gentle coos and whispers are the last thing I hear before falling into a nightmare-ridden sleep.

While I am ill, Nathaniel is a gentle and inexhaustible nurse. He stays in the room as much as possible, forever scribbling—what, I do not know. He reads Shakespeare to me and the children in the evenings, and works with Father on keeping Mary's house and landscaping in order for their return. After a week, he comes to me with the celestial smile that pulls me out of my misery, and the news to accompany it.

"My publisher writes that the most recent issuance of *Twice-Told Tales* has been a success. Thousands of copies have sold. They will advance us whatever we need to purchase Hillside!"

"But you said you do not wish to be settled," I say.

"Perhaps not for an entire lifetime," he replies, "but if we can purchase a house, we will always have a home to return to, no matter where we travel."

I embrace Nathaniel, trembling with love for him and for all he does to bring about my elation. I am certain no wife has ever been happier.

Una enters the room, followed by Julian.

"Is Mama all right?" asks Una with a wrinkled brow.

Though my face is bathed in tears, I show her my smile to calm her heart.

"Papa has found us a home, and one you will love."

"Will it have trees?" says Julian.

"And neighbors?" says Una.

"And cats?" says Julian.

"And a studio, and a study, and a garden, and a guest room!" I say.

The children run to the bed and wrap their arms around our necks, and we are in a loving huddle until Una realizes little Rose is lying in her cradle away from us.

"Rose!" says Una, launching herself out from under the blankets and over to the baby, who is roused from her sleep. Una scoops up her sister and carries her to the bed before climbing back in with us. Una leans into Rose, who reaches for Una's face and smiles like an angel, though she was just awoken.

"Here is the rose flower on our little shrub," says Una. "Our Hawthorne bush, where we will always be like branches together."

32

We move into the first home we have ever owned, and are greeted by Ralph and Lidian Emerson and Henry Thoreau, who are delighted at our reentrance into Concord society.

The Alcotts called this ancient house the Hillside because of its situation at the bottom of such a landform, but we have changed the name to the Wayside to honor those soldiers who marched past it on their way to the battles of Lexington and Concord. I have also begun the extensive renovations that will be needed to resurrect the old girl, as I affectionately think of her. I have hired men to paint and build, and on my own I have torn down dry-rotted wallpaper and supervised Una as she hung paper in Nathaniel's study and in the dining room. I place *Endymion* in his study, and the work has never been more at home as on the wall of this old house. It is as if it always wanted to grace this room, and glows with a new feeling. I have had a sapphire carpet laid in the study and an emerald rug in the dining room. It is shocking how a splash of green is like a spring bloom pushing through the brown earth, bringing vitality to the house. The carpets and paints draw out the colors in the Italian landscapes and the Grecian busts as becomingly as in a museum, and though the exterior of the Wayside still needs much work, I am proud to greet guests here.

"I must admit," says Nathaniel, "I did not think it possible to make this drafty clapboard frame habitable, and suspected we would fare better in Thoreau's Walden cabin. I never should have doubted the magic of your touch."

"I will tell Louisa you said so," I say, holding up a sheet of stationery. "I miss your sister dearly, as do the children. I told her she must visit us now that we are settled, and I will not hear of any more excuses. We might even encourage her to live with us permanently, instead of with distant relations in dismal Salem."

"Good thought," he says. "And please send Elizabeth my thanks for the books to add to our home library. Your sister is very kind to remember us."

It remains unspoken that Ebe continues to remain aloof. I have given up hope that we will ever have a close relationship. She has taken up a small dwelling alone at the seaside, with a rent not too burdensome for us.

"Mary sends her and Horace's best," I say, pulling her letter from the stack. "They are pleased to see you gaining recognition for your work, and see our purchase of the Wayside as proof of our prosperity."

"It will only take one visit for them to see that we prosper in love, but not wealth, but if I had to pick one over the other, I would choose the former."

"Indeed."

Julian comes to the door with his face and hands covered in mud and a smile that graces his cheeks from one side to the other. He brushes his curls from his forehead in a gesture so like his father's, I press my heart at the thought of how grown-up he is getting.

"I have dug up a hawthorn bush!" he says.

"Not from our neighbor's yard, I hope," I admonish.

"No, Mama. From the hill behind the Wayside. We may plant it in our front yard like we are planted in our own house."

In the doorway behind Julian appear Una and the Emerson children, Ellen, Edith, and little Edward. Lidian also enters the frame, and I am pleased to see her so lively. I know one child can never replace another, but she seems to have found a new vitality now that another son has been born to her and Mr. Emerson.

"I hope you will join us at our gathering this Saturday," says Lidian. "There will be many important and learned fellows who would love to mingle with Mr. Hawthorne."

"Thank you," I say. "I am sure we will be happy to attend."

Just as I think with gratitude how blessed we are to have so many friends, and such ample society, I catch sight of my husband in the corner. He appears trapped, his face pale, his eyes shadowed. Unease vibrates off of him. I know that he fears there will be no stillness, no solitude in Concord.

As politely as I am able, I usher the group to the front yard for the ceremonial planting of the hawthorn bush. I squeeze Nathaniel's arm on the way out and note that he feels as stiff as stone.

All is hustle and bustle as we prepare for Louisa's visit. She writes that after her trip from Albany on a Hudson River ferry, she will see the sights in New York City, and then take the train north on July twenty-eighth, to spend several weeks with us celebrating our housewarming.

Nathaniel's *Blithedale Romance* has been released, and his publisher says he thinks they will sell out of the first printing. While I am very glad to hear this, I quake and shudder a little at what readers will think. *Blithedale* is nearly an autobiography, and Nathaniel's chronicle of his time at Brook Farm and the devastating suicide of the Hunt girl resituated within the frame of the story are most unsettling. While Nathaniel read the novel aloud to me over many nights, I could not help but feel disturbed that Margaret Fuller was present on every page. I am further upset by the knowledge that my husband has begun working in earnest on Franklin Pierce's biography, and I fear that his friend's unpopularity among abolitionists like Emerson and even my own siblings will cause strife in our family.

I have distracted myself from dwelling too long on such thoughts by weeding the front gardens with the help of the children, and planting rows of dear flowers to welcome Louisa. After each blossom is laid in the earth, each of my angels and I kiss it and welcome it to our land. The children are charmed by the practice, and it settles my nerves.

Once I have swept the front walk and fluffed the sofa pillows, scrubbed the children to shining and checked on tomorrow's dinner, I can finally rest and enjoy my excitement. Nathaniel reads aloud to us from his *Wonder Book* while I mend the baby's socks. It is a pleasure to hear his deep, warm voice animate the text. There are no stories on this earth, even his own, that cannot be made better by his elocution of them. We put the children to bed with wishes for a blessed sleep and prayers for Aunt Louisa's safe delivery to us.

Nathaniel is in good spirits the morning of her arrival, and while I dress for breakfast, he has the audacity to pat me on the behind. I am shocked and delighted, and when I turn to scold him through my smile, I am moved to see how like his Old Manse self he looks.

"You have lost years overnight!" I exclaim. "It seems I have married Endymion after all."

I turn and regard myself in the looking glass, frowning at my wide hips, my spongy midsection, and the sneaky lines of gray hair that seem to reproduce overnight.

"I am afraid you have married a mortal after all," I say. "I look very much my age."

He comes up behind me and gazes at me over my shoulder in the mirror.

"My love, your face could not be more handsome, your eyes more kind, your figure more inviting than they are now. You are only improved since the first time I set eyes on you. Then you were a mere girl; now you are a woman."

He kisses my neck, and I relish this moment. Something out

the window distracts me, however, and I am surprised to see Nathaniel's old custom house friend William Pike walking up to the house, wearing a grave expression.

"What is Mr. Pike doing here?" I ask.

Nathaniel follows my gaze out the window, and in our reflection in the mirror, I see his smile evaporate.

"I cannot imagine," he says, and in a moment, we are separated and his warmth is gone from my body.

While Nathaniel puts on his jacket and steps out of the room, I walk to the window and call down to Mr. Pike.

"Welcome," I say, motioning him toward the house.

He raises his hand and nods, but looks very morose. I am filled with dread, and hasten to finish dressing and pinning my hair before hurrying downstairs. Soon the children have joined us as Nathaniel opens the door to Mr. Pike and offers him a seat, which he looks very much like he needs. I instruct the children to play on the pine path, and Una, sensing my unease, leads her siblings away, hushing their questions.

"Please," says Nathaniel, as soon as they have gone. "What is wrong?"

Mr. Pike looks from my husband to me before he utters the terrible words.

"Louisa is dead."

Nathaniel mutters a strained cry. I begin to sob.

"It pains me to bring you this tragic news," says Mr. Pike. "A most horrific occurrence on the Hudson. The boat on which she traveled, the *Henry Clay*, apparently entered into a race with another vessel. At some point it caught on fire and split in two, and the passengers had to jump overboard and swim for their lives. Louisa was one who did not make it to shore."

I am breathing so fast and so hard I fear I will hyperventilate. My husband gasps and stands to lean on the mantel before staggering to the stairs. I move to follow him, but he holds up his hand and climbs to the second floor.

"I am so sorry to bring this news," says Mr. Pike. He places his face in his hands.

In a moment, Una trails her siblings, who will not be kept away. When they see me in tears, they run to me for comfort and I must tell them. I break into fresh sobs, especially when I see their quivering lips and pained faces. Only little Rosebud does not understand, though she is sad to see her mama so upset. She crawls into my lap and buries her head in my dress. Una and Julian sit dumbfounded, sniffling and wiping their eyes at intervals, trying to comprehend that they will not get to see their beloved auntie Louisa now or ever. Just when I think I will collapse from grief, a thought seizes me.

"At least she is with Grandma Hawthorne now," I say. The idea brings me such comfort that it is as if a breeze has moved through the room, and Louisa's spirit has blessed us all with this knowledge. "She will never be ill, or cold, or tired, or sad in any way again. She will be in heaven with her mama. Is there any more restful place?"

Una stops crying and nods her head, but Julian cannot stop his tears. The poor dear has never known such sorrow.

After a time, I know we must eat the breakfast that has been prepared, which we imagined would be partaken amidst joyous chatter and is now accompanied by tears and lamentation. I know better than to fetch Nathaniel, and I wonder how long he will remain upstairs. Mr. Pike cannot be persuaded to stay and eat, and leaves us with condolences and apologies.

"I want Papa," says Julian, after Mr. Pike has gone.

"You must leave him," says Una. "He has lost his sister and needs to be alone."

I am quieted by my eldest daughter's insight. Though not yet ten, she is a wise girl. Julian is only six, and must think on this awhile as he eats his eggs. Soon his face brightens.

"I know," he says. "I will tell him what Mama said. Aunt Louisa is with Grandmama in heaven. That will make him feel better."

Julian jumps from his chair and runs out of the dining room to the stairs. Una makes a move to stop him, but I place my hand on her arm. We listen as Julian's footsteps pound above us, but then all is quiet. In a minute or two, Julian returns with a hanging head.

"Papa is gone," he says.

"I am sure he is outdoors," I say. "Probably walking his path. Let us finish, and I will keep a plate for when he is ready to come in."

The rest of the day is passed in heavy silence, and I am weary by the time I tuck the children into their beds that night. I cannot help but imagine Louisa and her terrible watery death, the passengers screaming and burning around her, and the awful decision she made to jump, hoping that someone would rescue her while her skirts became so saturated with water that they pulled her down to the depths of the Hudson. And will her body ever be found? Will she be rigid and blue like Martha Hunt, or lost at sea like Margaret Fuller? What is the source of this legacy of drowning among our friends and loved ones?

Nathaniel has been gone for hours, and I begin to worry. I step outside into the twilight, where fireflies wink in the grass, and the first stars appear against the pink and indigo wash of sky. It would have been such an enchanting night to introduce Louisa to the Wayside, and this thought nearly undoes me.

I redirect my attention to finding Nathaniel, and soon his figure appears as a silhouette on the hill behind the house. He moves among the trees, so removed from me that he is like a ghost. I take a step toward him, but something stops me. He wants to be alone, and I cannot bear his rejection of my comfort, so I will leave him on the hill to pace and mourn in solitude.

Louisa's body is found, and Nathaniel travels to Salem for the funeral. Because of a miscommunication he misses the service, but is able to stand at her graveside and pay his respects with Ebe. It is probably for the best. Nathaniel is not one for a minister's sermons.

The ensuing months, while we are supposed to be settling in our home, become darker and drearier. In spite of robust sales of *The Blithedale Romance*, Nathaniel cannot outrun his depression of spirits. I send him to the seaside to visit Ebe, and while he comes back in good physical health, I fear for the heavy veil over his soul.

I am devastated in January of 1853 by the death of my beloved mother, and it is only because of my grief over not being able to attend to her in her final days that Nathaniel takes a break from his work. He comforts me with exquisite tenderness, and our little family resumes reading books and playing games by the fire. None of us needs to speak aloud how fleeting life is, and how we must enjoy one another to the utmost every minute we are in good health and one another's company. We are still unsettled, however, so when Franklin Pierce is elected president and an appointment is offered to Nathaniel, we do not dismiss it outright, but rather weigh the benefits of traveling to foreign places in hopes of refreshing our minds and hearts. President Pierce would like Nathaniel to be the U.S. consul in Liverpool.

"England, Sophia," says Nathaniel. "Just think of how often we have gone there on the words of Shakespeare and Wordsworth and Shelley. Imagine visiting the land from which my ancestors set out centuries ago. Here is our chance to unite the future with the past, and escape the pain we have here."

"But what of the children?" I say. "Shouldn't they grow up in their native land? Might it not be unsettling for them to be wrenched from their birth soil and made to travel over an ocean to foreign shores?"

The thought of Louisa's and Margaret's deaths by drowning sits between us for a moment until Nathaniel shakes his head.

"Perhaps our crossing and safe landing will right a wrong in our spheres. We will bring good from bad, and in the process our children will be granted an education through experience instead of just through the books with which you instruct them in small Concord."

My heart begins to open to his reasoning, but I am still unsure.

"Dove." He is at my side now, more animated than he has been for months. "Think of the creative stimulus. You will explore new landscapes that might become art. I will observe humanity that might become story. Our artistic fires will blaze once again!"

I think of my dry brushes and my longing for any kind of rekindling in my marriage, be it on a canvas or in bed. Nathaniel and I have become boarding mates. Our torch of passion is just a candle since little Rosebud came into the world, and the deaths of Louisa and Mother have snuffed the last flame. The thought of our love's resurrection is tempting, and when it is partnered with the idea of our creative renascence, I cannot help but feel a soaring in my heart.

33

Before stepping on board the *Niagara*, I experience such dread that I do not think I will be able to climb the gangplank. While Nathaniel pulls me along, I cannot dismiss the feeling that Margaret and Louisa are moaning on the wind. The first day at sea is a nightmare of motion, but upon arising the next morning to clear skies and smooth waters, my soul finds rest.

During the weeks we spend crossing the Atlantic, the grief that has hold of me loosens on the breezes, and I am reminded of my favorable journey to Cuba. Introducing the children to the wonders of marine life and cloud formations consumes my days, and dreams of verdant fields and English gardens fill my nights. Watching Nathaniel pace the decks, hands clasped behind his back, I think how at home he is on the sea, and that his father must walk with him.

Upon our arrival, however, I am depressed to see that there is no poetry in Liverpool. Shakespeare did not write of this wretched, dirty city. In fact, I fear that his words about all of England were only a fantasy, for the reality is Dickensian—gray skies, damp air, frigid people. The children wither in the city where there is no grass for frolicking and no fresh air to breathe, and a cough takes root in my chest.

Nathaniel's reputation from *The Scarlet Letter* and *The House of the Seven Gables*—which were pirated and sold throughout England—in addition to his appointment as consul, have made him famous here. Although we receive many courteous invitations from important people, we have to decline almost all because of my ill health. Nathaniel is far too diffident to appear among strangers without me at his side, and I have the sense from our neighbors that he is gaining a reputation for aloofness.

My cough spreads to the children, and there is not a wink of sleep to be had in our small hotel rooms. Nathaniel is the only one in good health, but he suffers much on our behalf.

"Perhaps I should resign," he says.

"How ridiculous," I protest. "It will get better."

But my cough grows worse, and we finally decide that the children and I will die if we stay in the city. Nathaniel makes arrangements for our crossing of the River Mersey, and reserves rooms at the Royal Rock Hotel, where we will live until we find a more permanent residence. He will commute to and from Liverpool each day.

My spirits are low as we pack up our belongings yet again and transport the children to the ferry station. I hold Rose, whose cough frightens me, and allow Una and Julian to cling to my skirts. We must look like candidates for the workhouse, so pale and weary are we. I look up at the sky, imploring the sun to break through the relentless clouds, but it remains hidden.

The Mersey is as murky and brown as the Concord under unfriendly skies, and I cannot help but wonder what we could have been thinking to relocate our children here. They have behaved admirably under the circumstances, but how much can they be expected to endure? How much must we all endure? I am so melancholy by the time we approach the shore of Birkenhead that I do not know how I will settle our family at the hotel.

"Mama, Papa, look!" Julian is exuberant for the first time in weeks, and I follow to where his finger points.

A shaft of sunlight penetrates the gloom and shines on the ferry station. The clouds break in spots here and there, as if God were throwing on lamps to illuminate the town for our pleasure. Nathaniel and I look at each other and his face breaks into a wide grin, the effect not unlike another shaft of sunlight. We disembark with new vitality, and are further heartened when we arrive at the hotel, a charming angular building of old stone lined with pretty flowers and walking paths. Well-dressed men and women carrying frilly umbrellas nod to us in greeting, and the chill leaves the air. As soon as our bags are settled in our rooms, the children beg us to take them to frolic in the nearby park. There, Nathaniel and I draw together as we watch the little ones scatter about, half-mad with excitement to have grass for running out of doors. Rose is charmed by the stalls of smelly donkeys, and their handler allows her to pet their noses.

"You have not coughed for twenty minutes straight," says Nathaniel.

"Nor have the children," I say.

"Praise God!"

"Mr. Hawthorne, are you becoming religious?"

"I will become anything to have you all restored to me."

He kisses my head and we settle on a bench where we may watch the children play.

"It pains me that you will have to go to that dirty city every day," I say.

"Do not worry. I will be happy in spirit, knowing you are so well situated."

"We should look for a permanent place close to the ferry so we may walk to this park after you have gone each morning, and be here to welcome you home each evening."

"That will be grand."

"You sound like an Englishman!" I say.

He laughs. "I do feel a deep ancestral contentment in these lands, but I have not forgotten America. Being thousands of miles from my native soil has made a patriot of me, in spite of the political bickering that divides our nation."

"Do not tell me you want to return home already. Cough or not, I might not ever again consent to move."

He does not reply, and I am left to wait and wonder how long we will stay before my husband sets his sights for other lands in his endless quest for a place he feels at home.

A luxurious carriage conveys Nathaniel and me to Poulton Hall, the country house of the president of the chamber of commerce,

Mr. William Barber. He lives at the stately redbrick ivy-covered estate with his two unmarried sisters and, rumor has it, many ghosts.

They greet us in the magnificent entrance hall sparkling with diamond-cut chandeliers and wall sconces, and I cannot help but spin around and gape at the mirrored panels, damask curtains, and gilded wallpaper. The misses Barber are delighted by my reaction, and must think me very quaint. They are all as in awe of my husband as I am of their house, and they soon forget me to praise him for his writing.

"It is a thrill to have a man of your talents in our home," says Mr. Barber. "You do us honor with your visit."

"Yes," says Jane, the younger sister. "We know you are selective of the society you keep, so we are grateful to be considered worthy."

"I am afraid Nathaniel has a reputation for being stingy with his company," I say. "But I must take the blame for him. My ill health has prevented him from venturing out much. He is a devoted caregiver."

"How honorable," says Ann, the older sister. "I can see why being in your charming company would eclipse any gathering."

I bow to her compliment, though I know she is just being polite. I am a toadstool in this house of English roses, but it is no matter. I am happy to be out with my husband, enjoying the hospitality of a wealthy English family.

While the women praise the genius who wrote *The Scarlet Letter*, I meet Nathaniel's gaze to see that he is comfortable, and when he gives me a small smile, I slip away to peruse the adornments of the four-hundred-year-old home. I am joined by Mr. Barber as I approach a fox reclining at the foot of the carved stair.

"Extraordinary how he sits so still," I say.

Mr. Barber smiles. "My dear, he will not move. He is stuffed."

I cover my mouth and feel my neck redden as my host laughs.

"I am delighted you thought him real. He was real enough before I shot him. In fact, I hope to add to my menagerie after my upcoming trip to Scotland."

"My apologies for being so simple," I say. "I hope you will excuse me."

"I could not be more pleased with you, Mrs. Hawthorne. It is not often one meets such a warm and humble spouse of such a famous man."

"You will find my husband far more interesting than me, if not in conversation, then in writing. He is usually very shy."

We look over at Nathaniel and Mr. Barber's sisters, who are laughing at some comment. Ann slips her bangled arm through Nathaniel's, and begins to lead him to the back of the house, while Jane calls to us.

"Come, we will stroll the gardens while we still have light. Then we will introduce you to the ghosts once the sun goes down."

I am surprised by Nathaniel's ease in attending the sisters, and cannot help the pinched feeling in my stomach. How tall he stands now that he has been praised for his work. How much more at ease he is than the man who was pressed to the wall by female admirers in Connie Parks's home, all those years ago. While I am glad for him, I dislike the jealousy arising in me.

Mr. Barber offers me his arm, and we follow my husband and

his admirers. The women are stately and elegant, and attired in muslin and rich silk. Jane wears a luscious black velvet jacket, and both are adorned with as many jewels as the chandeliers. I glance down at my frumpy brocade and stand a little straighter. Concord fashions will not do in English society, and I hope my husband's income will allow us to dress as befits his station. Once we are corralled out of doors, my mind is lifted from trivial matters of dress and filled with the splendid beauty of the garden. Here is the England we had anticipated—the wide avenues, the luscious grasses, the fragrant flowers, the elegantly cut hedges. All dark feelings in me are replaced with calm, and when we approach one of the old oaks lining the lawn, I cannot help but walk over to it and place my hands on its great, sturdy bark, much to the enjoyment of the Barbers.

"Mrs. Hawthorne is a great lover of nature," says Nathaniel. "The trees and flowers are her sisters."

"A living Beatrice Rappaccini," says Ann.

My, how she has prepared for this meeting!

"My own," says Nathaniel.

I am touched that he would say such a thing, and smile over my shoulder as the rare setting sun warms my face. His eyes find mine, and I am at once reassured, knowing I am beautiful in the gaze of my love.

On our trip upstairs, Nathaniel takes my arm before the sisters are able to claim his, and as a result, they lead us like tour guides through the halls of their haunted house.

"This is the Martyr's Chamber, where a woman was locked and tortured for her faith."

We step inside and walk to a tiny attic window where barely a thing can be seen except sky. I am moved by how awful it must have been to die in this small room.

"Starved!" says Ann so close to my ear that I jump. "Wasted away to nothing. She cries at night."

"How dreadful," I whisper.

Nathaniel narrows his eyes and gazes around the chamber as if committing it to memory. I will not be surprised if this place finds its way into his fiction. We are soon heading down a hall that leads to at least twenty rooms, when Jane stops short, and we nearly run into her.

"Here!" she says, pointing to the crimson carpet with great gravity. "Here is where a man slit his own throat and died."

"Found by his children," says Ann.

I shudder and glance at Mr. Barber, who seems to be enjoying himself immensely. I, for one, would like to return to the elegant downstairs rooms to get away from these horrific spots.

"Speaking of children," continues Ann, "it is said that three hundred years ago, some were murdered on this very floor, and they can be glimpsed in the moonlight, searching in vain for their dear mother."

I am sick of these stories, and relieved when we are again in the parlor taking digestives. I realize my hosts are trying to make a memorable experience for us, but I have never been so eager to return to my children, who are being minded by the nursemaid. The hour of our departure arrives, and we board the carriage, waving to and thanking our hosts. Once we turn off their drive I shudder.

"I am so happy we are not spending the night in that house of horrors."

"That was fascinating," says Nathaniel.

"But disturbing," I say. "Did you get the feeling that the misses Barber wanted to be written about?"

"Most definitely."

"They are very elegant, but a bit frightening."

"Yes," says Nathaniel. "Is it any wonder they have not found husbands?"

I laugh and snuggle against my love, and do not separate from him even as we retire to our bed for the night.

34

We pass a year in a succession of dinner parties, house tours, and visits throughout England and Wales. Nathaniel is so busy he has no time for writing, but he does not fret, because his *Tanglewood Tales*, which he had written earlier, and the reissue of *Mosses from an Old Manse* keep his literary fame steady to growing. My husband thrives on ale and beef, and thinks himself suited to England, though he continues to complain about dirty Liverpool and the personal financial burdens he must bear for the consulate. Support for shipwrecked sailors, half-mad vagabonds, and seamen's funerals must be paid for out of his own pocket while he awaits reimbursement, which does not come, and the American papers are unafraid of finding fault with him because of his ties to President Pierce, who is considered an ineffectual leader.

Nathaniel is loyal to Franklin more as a friend than as a political ally, and for that reason he refuses to turn his back on him. Nathaniel trusts Franklin implicitly, even when he signs bills that stir up the antislavery cause. The reality is, Franklin has no heart for the presidency since his son died in a gruesome railway accident just before he took office. The tragedy of the Pierces' losing all three of their sons weighs heavy on us. I cannot imagine their sorrow. By all accounts the man has become a shadow, haunting Washington with about as much weight as an ancient ghost that people have ceased to fear, doing anything he can to keep his wife from succumbing to her grief.

My sisters assault us with abolitionist pamphlets and papers until I must insist they stop sending them. Una began to read one such paper and launched into a myriad of questions about a subject I have no wish to discuss with her. The innocence of my girl must be preserved at all costs, and teaching her about an abominable system with abominable supporters and refuters will do nothing but erode Una's soul by exposing her to the evil in the world.

Our second winter in England has brought a return of my bronchitis. My cough is nearly the only thing I will remember from my time here, because it permeates every minute of the day. The children's education suffers because their invalid mother cannot teach them. We have taken to sending Una out for lessons in French and dancing, among other subjects, and Julian frequently accompanies his father to Liverpool for life education. At least little Rose is too young to need studies, though I feel sorrow for her that I do not possess the energy I had for her siblings. In truth, our time in England is not satisfying the urge we thought it would, and my worsening health due to the damp weather is a heavy burden for us all. Nathaniel often wishes to resign his post, especially after a consular bill passes decreasing his income. It seems we are never going to be wealthy. At least the income from Nathaniel's books allows us some measure of comfort.

As we welcome in the New Year of 1855, we receive word from Elizabeth that Father has died. My husband breaks the news to me in my sickbed, and stays with me all through the night as I weep because I could not attend him or Mother in their final hours.

"We are orphans," I say. "Is there anything sadder than an orphan?"

"But think of your words of comfort in death: Our loved ones may be together in heaven, never again to know another day of sickness or sadness or suffering."

I do not answer him. This blow has made it harder for me to have faith in those words, though I have uttered them countless times, because we have no guides on this earth now. It feels very blustery to stand on the hill as the oldest generation.

"Shall we go, dove?" Nathaniel asks. "Why do we stay? Allow me to resign. Let us return to America and allow our roots to dig deep into the soil, for better or worse. I was a fool to drag you here."

"You did no such thing. I wanted to come, and I am certain that it is not right to return to America now. It would cost a fortune, and our country is a hotbed of anger and civil fighting. We cannot protect the children from it if we return, and if we go we will have to choose a side."

Nathaniel holds my hand and looks to the window, where the black, foggy night obscures his view. I follow his gaze for a moment and quake at the thought of being out there in that frigid dampness. The mists of England are so deep and penetrating they must be the very feeling of bodily death. I have regular dreams of dying here, and dread the nightmares as if they are prophecy.

I turn back to my husband, my sun. He is so stately and handsome, and grows more so each year. There is not a finer-looking man in all of Christendom, and his beauty of character and nobility outshines even his face. He is a living work of art—a sculpture whom God has breathed to life. This thought of sculpture makes my fingers twitch, and I think of how satisfying it would be to make a bust of Nathaniel—to run my hands over his face and then shape cold clay into its form. I feel a surge like lightning through my body, but a coughing fit soon chases away the artistic impulse.

"One thing is certain," he says. "I will never allow you to pass another winter in England. We will find a place for you to reside on the continent where you may recover. I cannot bear when you are ill."

These fantasies of my love in marble or clay consume my inmost thoughts, and linger like a pleasant dream. The spring and summer allow for a return of my physical health, though my spirits continue to be depressed and unsettled. As we face the autumn, we decide that we cannot risk my health again.

Nathaniel's friend and former publisher John O'Sullivan now

resides with his wife, Susan, in Lisbon, as the U.S. minister to Portugal. At his invitation, and after much agonizing debate, we determine that I will go with Una and Rose to stay with them, and Nathaniel will keep Julian with him in Liverpool. We have not endured a separation like this since our courting days, and that was torture.

After we again pack our belongings and book our passage, Nathaniel escorts us to Southampton to sail for Lisbon on the steamer *Madrid*. He cannot speak from emotion, and I cannot shake my growing frustration. I know I consented to this arrangement, but I am unreasonable right now because of poor health and my dislike of our never-ending gypsy lifestyle.

There are many tearful good-byes among the children, but Nathaniel and I cannot look at each other. To do so would mean a total collapse and the full wrenching realization of having to return to writing sterile letters instead of folding into the warmth of each other in bed each night, and greeting the day together each morning.

As the steamer bellows into the harbor, I feel as if I could scream with it. I have a premonition that this will be our last meeting, and either one or the other of us will not survive our separation. It is a feeling I have had for weeks, ever since Una told me about her dream in which her father died. Our nurse-maid takes the girls on board, Julian is occupied with kicking rocks, and Nathaniel is in conversation with the captain, beseeching him to care for us. After the men shake hands and part, Nathaniel returns to me, and I meet my love's eyes. We reach for each other at the same moment, and I cannot stop my tears.

"This is not natural," I say. "We are never supposed to be apart."

I know my husband will not speak, because he never can under such circumstances. I pull back and clasp his arms as hard as I can.

"Promise me. Promise me we will meet again on this earth."

He presses his lips together so he will not cry.

The steamer bellows again, and I hear Una call to me.

"Promise," I say. "You must, or I will not leave. I would rather die here with you than apart."

I am aware that Julian is staring up at us.

Nathaniel swallows and utters, "I promise. We will not leave this earth unless we are in the company of the other."

35

Autumn 1855

TO NATHANIEL HAWTHORNE, LIVERPOOL

Lisbon, November 1855

My Dearest Husband,

How can I reconcile the healing in my lungs with the withering of my heart?

If not for the girls, I would curl up in bed, blind to the vivid colors of the royal palaces, deaf to the regal music, dumb to the raptures that try to leap from my lips at the vivid newness of life in this foreign place.

How could I not draw you to me as my equator? How could we have thought the tropics of our love would not carry me through this illness?

I have tried three times to start this letter while withholding my depression of spirits, but I must express myself, for our separation feels very final. How can it not when we have not suffered a separation like this for thirteen years?

Please rest in the knowledge that John and Susan's tender care of us is sweet balm. Since we cannot orbit you, our sun, we orbit John, and he glows with the status we afford him. He stretches out on the floor to play marbles with Rose. He asks Una about her lessons and thoughts on all subjects. And with me, he sits in a chair near the fire, patting my hand while I pour out my soul's grief over your absence. I sense that his old guilt over his late and missed payments to you, which partly led to our eviction from the manse, lie at the root of this attentiveness, but because we are in comfort and my lungs improve by the minute, I do not care what motivates him.

John's mother lives with them and is a lovely grandmother figure for the girls, though her health is poor. In our evenings by the fireside, I cannot help but think of our mothers and fathers, and how our children are at a great loss for not having them. Just last night, Mother was so strongly about the atmosphere that I could not help but cry. John gave me his handkerchief to dab my eyes.

But enough of this darkness. Now that it is released, all of my correspondence will be full of light and love and reports of our improving health. I will paint pictures for you with words, and will report on what we eat and wear, and remark on all the fine kings and queens with whom we share our evenings.

Please give my love to Julian, and tell him his mama misses him so much her eyes could pop out. (He will like such vulgarity.)

Thine Ownest,

Sophy

TO SOPHIA HAWTHORNE, LISBON

Liverpool, November 1855

Dearest Wife,

I have never felt relief such as that upon beholding the letter from your hand, and was borne back to our courtship days, when your letters were all I had to light my way. "A splendor among shadows," as Shelley said.

Please, dearest, I beseech you to allow yourself to glow. Imagine my distress upon reading your words that your innere *light is so dim and flickering. I cannot endure the winter in wretched Liverpool without your light. Let it shine. I am glad you released your sufferings to the winds, and it is my strongest hope that they will scatter and allow you to bloom without their burden. I could see the glimmer of it as your letter progressed, and ended in such cheekiness. (Julian laughed so hard he fell over backward in his chair. Imagine his own mother using words she often chastises him for using!)*

In truth, I cannot feel fully pleased that O'Sullivan's handkerchief and warm hand are your ballast, because it should come from me, but I am glad that you have some comfort in this world. I imagine his old guilt gives him great energy for caring for my family, as it should. We know that O'Sullivan has never had a head for business, though he desperately wishes he had.

Rest assured that your absence in Julian's life has inspired many women to help in his care. He receives escorts to church, dinner invitations, and even dancing lessons. The boy has more occupation at female hands than he cares for, and in that I am happy. His only complaint is about the miserable coldness of the place, but the complaints only come when he sits still, which you well know is only for about six to seven minutes out of any given day.

There is no rest for me without you. The bed is cold and empty, and the pillow is no rival to your heavenly bosom, where I am frantic to lay my head. I have placed my forehead on this paper for you to press to your breast.

I have also added a note that I have kissed for little Rosebud. Tell her not to drop it, but if she does, she may seek its replacement on her mother's fair lips.

I must stop thinking of you, or go mad.

Give my best love to Una, and thanks to O'Sullivan.

Thine Ownest . . .

TO NATHANIEL HAWTHORNE, LIVERPOOL

Lisbon, December 1855

My Sweet Angel,

I once told Elizabeth that you were an angel God gave to me to light my way on the earth. She no doubt thought it was nonsense, but you are, and you must be told until you believe it.

You will be much delighted to hear that I have not coughed in two weeks. My lungs thank me for this stay, though my heart scolds me for any improvement in my health at the expense of time with you.

Do you care to hear about the sparkling place settings at the palace, the ostentatious clothing of the royals, the succulent feasts that are fattening us like shiny hens? I am still the plain dove among parrots, but I am happy to be so simply me in this place, because I am never made to feel outside of anything.

John escorts Sue and me to dinner on each arm, and involves us in the conversations as best he can. He has picked up Portuguese with admirable ease, and I know some phrases. When I cannot communicate perfectly well, I am able to use Spanish or French, depending upon my dinner companions, to enjoy an ease of fraternity.

Rose has been quite the spirited one. One moment she pets the embassy dog with gentleness, and the next she has swiped the holy hat of the visiting monsignor, and I must chase her up the staircase to retrieve it—a most embarrassing trial! Mercifully, the people are kind and pleasant, and even following Rose's naughtiest moments, John or Sue or the clergy themselves are all reassurance and delight.

One shadow has befallen this house. John received word that his beloved brother died, and we have entered into mourning on his behalf. Do not worry that the girls must be a witness to such sadness in life, for at four years old, Rose is only occupied with what is in her immediate sphere, and Una, at eleven, is nearly like a woman. I fear you will not recognize her when you next see her, for she has crossed over, and maintains the dignified manners and seriousness of a lady. I am sure her letters have given you a clue.

I confess that I begin to have stabs of longing for home, and by that I mean the simplicity of Concord and the Wayside. I am glad that my brother Nat occupies it with his family so the walls do not grow cold, but I long to reestablish our Hawthorne bush there and allow it to take root. I know this is months—nay, years—off, but it is a beacon in the quiet and sad times of the heart. Those little moments of melancholy sneak up on me like a cat on silent paws, but retreat just as quickly, leaving me wondering where they came from in the first place.

I took your kisses and head rests from your last letter with eagerness. Just seeing your handwriting nearly brings me to . . . Well, I will not write it, but you understand my meaning.

Pat Julian's head for me. Embrace your deepest self, imagining my arms and hands.

Thinest,

Naughtiest,

Sophy

TO SOPHIA HAWTHORNE, LISBON

Liverpool, December 1855

Naughty Sophy!

I have not seen such writing since I lived in Salem and we had not but kissed! Imagine my shock and pleasure.

I hope the handkerchief you used to blot your passionate brow did not bear the O monogram.

I am distressed that my girls are a party to O'Sullivan's grief, and it makes me regret more than ever that I sent you away. What could I have been thinking?

Oh, yes, I wanted you to live!

Well, I will continue to gnash my teeth and mourn your absence, but your frequent letters will help the wounds. Please send them more often—even once a day. Spare me no detail of your life. I want to know every morsel eaten, every conversation spoken, every breath breathed.

Spare no expense if you wish to adorn yourself or make the girls' wardrobes suitable for royal society. You deserve such costumes, and will bloom in them. Our finances are in good order, as long as we stay on the continent, which we must continue to do. I do know that Pierce will not likely receive the nomination for the next election, and at that time I will resign the consulate, and we will travel the continent together thoroughly, before returning to our mother land.

Your sister Elizabeth returned the abolitionist pamphlet I had once returned to her. She hopes it will influence me, and wishes for Una to be schooled in the circle of hell that is slavery. I have explained to Elizabeth the inappropriateness of exposing unsullied young girls to treachery in the world, and would think that—in spite of having no children—having educated them for years, she would understand how detrimental that would be to Una's development.

It saddens me that you refer to Una as a young woman, because she is still just a girl to me. An imp. A little Pearl. But she is not.

I really cannot think of anything at all but your lips, your hair, the low sweetness of your voice. You are a welcome ghost, haunting and tormenting me at all hours of the day and night. I run my hands through my hair, trying to conjure the feeling of your fingers in it. I inhale the scent of the dresses you left, but all trace of Sophy is gone. The winds of the waterways assault me, chilling my bones to the marrow, relentless in their reminder that there is no warmth for me while you are gone. The thought of you smiling over your sewing at O'Sullivan's fireside, sharing laughs with those who are not me, is torture, especially when Una writes that O'Sullivan is second only to me in your heart.

When this separation is over, we must never allow it again. How could I have done this? I am frantic, dove.

Please take the tenderest care of yourself and the girls. I have horrid visions of men delivering black telegrams with news of death and permanent separation. The visions make it so I can barely work.

Send me a letter as soon as you receive this. Rub it on you. Include a lock of hair. Give me anything of yourself that can fit in an envelope.

And burn this correspondence, as I have done with your letters.

Thine Own-Ownest

TO NATHANIEL HAWTHORNE, LIVERPOOL

Madeira, January 1856

My Splendor, My Sun,

O'Sullivan—or rather John, as we call our friend—may be second to you, but if first is at the feet of the god himself, second would be in the darkness of a cave at the foot of Mount Olympus. No god has ever been jealous of a mortal, and I do not recommend starting a new tradition.

(See—I nearly blaspheme to offer my assurances!)

You are my one and only, and I should never have to make that clear, because it is the very center of my being. But if I must say it, sing it, write it, play it, or paint it so you understand, then I will be glad to do so at the start and end of all of our correspondence.

We write to you from Madeira—the most gloriously splendid island I have seen since Cuba—where we travel to further help my lungs, and see to the health of John's mother. John did not think you would mind his taking us on a further voyage, and I report to you that our journey was safe and has dropped us in Eden.

Promise Julian I will paint him a picture with words of the shiny, fat green leaves, the shocking pink vegetation, the rustling palms, and the sapphire and topaz waters. The peak of Pico Ruivo is always shrouded in mists, but looms mightily in the way of the mountains of Cuba. There is a peace about the people here, which one could attribute to living in paradise (or the wine!), and all is calm and ease. The only shadow is the vacancy of you and Julian. We will have to return as a whole in the future.

In your next letter, please include a note for your naughty Rose. She has become quite thorny, slapping and scratching her sister, and having fits and tantrums unbecoming a lady. Perhaps hearing her father's thoughts on her behavior will improve it, for she can be quite the little savage! Just when I am at my wits' end with her, she throws her little arms around my neck and says, "I'm sorry, Angel Mama!" and so covers me with kisses, I cannot help but laugh and grant forgiveness.

Tell Julian that I am glad he is feeling better and growing so much he must have new clothes every other month. Tell him not to leave his childhood behind too quickly, because Una has already abandoned hers, and we will all grieve heartily to lose two children to maturity during our separation.

I have included a separate, sealed note (written by Naughty Sophy) that speaks of my passions for you and how it will be when we are once again in our nuptial embrace, and I have even illustrated the missive in the margins. Read it quickly and burn it so I am not humiliated for generations to come at the hands of scholars wishing to understand Nathaniel Hawthorne's creative process. I did not even sign it.

Most Affectionately,
Thy Dove

TO SOPHIA HAWTHORNE, MADEIRA

Liverpool, March 1856

Dear Sophia,

I cannot help but express my anger at O'Sullivan for dragging my beloved girls on a journey when they are supposed to be safely situated in Lisbon, and would appreciate notice preceding instead of after such travels in the future. I am grateful to providence that you are happy and safe, but I am agitated that my loves are even farther from my cold bosom. Will you ever be close to me again?

Thank God for the coming spring, to end this winter of misery. Your letters alone have kept me from throwing myself off the cliffs, and I allow reports of your joy and health to seep into my soul and nourish it. Pray, do not worry over Julian being negatively affected by my sullenness. He is the most jovial and remarkable boy, and does well to lift his gloomy father's spirits. He might look like me, but his good nature comes solely from his mother. He is sometimes naughty—also like his mother—which has led to my tossing him over my leg to administer a sound spanking, but I know that soon he will be large enough to do so with me, so I must find a new means of discipline.

I am happy to hear that Rose is behaving better. I told her in my last letter that I would gobble her up if she did not mind *her mama. Please enact the pretend gobbling on her to show her I am not one to be trifled with.*

I wrote a separate letter to Una, praising her talent at correspondence and to show her that I understand she is no longer a child. Her letters are very much enjoyed by Julian and me, and I can hardly wait to see the young lady she has become, though it fills my heart with something like grief, and not a little dread.

You need to know that I am ill. I have had a cold, but it is more than that. It feels like a sickness of the mind and heart that will not be made right until I am again at your side. When I am not with you, it is as if I am drawn of pencil and erased—a faint outline on a paper. Without your touch I have no color. I am but a shadow—a weary ghost wandering in search of resurrection that he cannot find. Our reunion cannot come fast enough. June cannot arrive soon enough.

We will come together and join ourselves, never again to be separated. I will leave the consulate and we will travel throughout the continent, ending up in Italy—the land of our courtship dreams—to live the very essence of the art you painted for me as an engagement gift. We will become that art, and I will again know what it is to live life in color.

Thy most loving husband

36

Winter 1858
Italy

Rome turns her back to us when we arrive. It is a painful thing to enter the city of your imagination, where you have always told your artist's heart that it would be at home, and find no welcome. I have the feeling she does not want us, though we want her. Every statue is faced away; every fountain stands frozen in time. I wish to take a flaming torch to the ice hanging from places that should be bubbling and splashing like brooks, whispering ancient secrets to us. Rome in winter is a sarcophagus of marblelike bone—dark and dead, sterile, rigid. Even the ghosts have abandoned this place.

The journey was difficult. After Nathaniel resigned the consulship, we settled our affairs in England, which took longer than we expected, as such things tend to do, and moved on to France, dragging bags and children with us, impatient at every stop for Italy, our self-proclaimed promised land. We met new friends and old, including Herman Melville, whose brief, awkward visits with us in England marked the end of his relationship with Nathaniel. Through Elizabeth's correspondence, we were saddened to learn that Ellen Channing had left Ellery for cruelty, had been persuaded back to him, and then died following the birth of their fifth child. Our trunks became more weighted, as did our souls, burdened with memories of those we had lost, and the losses of others.

We exist, however, in a kind of panicked reverence to God. In spite of our travels, illnesses, and sufferings, our Hawthorne bush has not lost any branches. We are together and know that we will never part again. This is the joy of our frozen winter. This is what my eyes will see and my heart will feel, and I will radiate it to Nathaniel and the children until they believe it as I am beginning to do.

A flock of doves on the wing wakes me before the church bells have begun their serenade, drawing me out of bed and to the window of our apartment in the Palazzo Laranzani. My bare feet are cold on the tile, and my worn white nightgown is too thin to afford any warmth, but I am compelled to know what the birds want me to see. I move my gaze over the dome of St. Peter's, the elevated saints, the clay-tiled roofs where smoke ascends like incense to the gray marble sky. I watch and wait, and I do not have to wait long. A shaft of light, such as one Julian calls a ray from heaven, reaches down to the rooftops and is guided by the travels of clouds until it rests on the dome. Then, almost all at once, more light begins to beam down, a ray here, a line there:

an illumination. In the space of mere minutes, all of Rome is in benediction from the blazing pink-and-orange sunrise.

This is God's assurance.

I hear a noise on the bed behind me, and turn with the light warming my hair to see Nathaniel awake and staring at me with the most tender look of adoration. I move toward him and the light reaches my love, turning his pale skin pink, as if the Great Artist has touched a marble statue with paint and breathed life into him.

Nathaniel does not fall in love with Rome with the speed that I do.

His puritan soul is shocked to its inmost core at the nudity depicted in sculpture and paint. He cannot identify with the grandeur of the robustly healthy body because he is too busy shielding the eyes of our children and averting his own from the abundance of breasts, bottoms, and male genitalia, which all give me the profoundest delight.

My health has never been better, and in spite of the chill and my reluctant and gloomy husband, I drag him and the children from gallery to gallery, basking in the rapture of beholding the art and architecture I have so long studied and imagined. Nathaniel has begun insisting we leave the children with their nurse, Ada, a charming young American woman we all love, so we can explore the galleries without compromising their innocence, and I consent, not because I agree, but to enjoy my husband alone. My return to health and these stimulating surroundings have awakened me, and I enjoy exchanging squeezes and pats with Nathaniel as he professes his endless shock.

Today we visit the Capitoline Museum sculpture gallery, where the massive *Dying Gladiator* is the focus, but whose *Resting Satyr* draws our attention. This charming likeness of a faun—a creature that looks human at first glance until the pointed ears and tail are observed—seems to have such a youthful air of relaxation and exquisite comfort about it that even Nathaniel resists commenting on the dangling manhood at his eye level.

"Here is something I can appreciate," he says.

Our arms are linked, and I pull him closer to me so our sides are touching, warming me from head to foot.

"Does he not offend your ancestral prudery?" I say.

"Strangely, no."

"Why not?"

"Perhaps my mind is expanding to allow an appreciation of form. This faun is pleasant. Unsexual. He conveys ease like that of Eden and shows the lighter side of the animal nature of humanity."

I shiver when Nathaniel speaks of sexuality, and he steals a glance around the room before touching a kiss on the side of my neck.

"Rome is thawing you," I say.

"And the spring," he adds. "And my relief from the dreadful cold that was my companion all winter."

"I will further the thaw in our chamber this evening," I whisper in his ear.

"Then I will wish away the twilight and urge the hastening of the night."

I am light-headed and must separate from Nathaniel. His low laugh follows me, and I think how pleasing it is to hear his high spirits. How young I feel! We could be in Concord at the Old Manse during our Edenic days.

That night we dine alfresco on cheese, fruit, and nuts purchased from street vendors, and follow it with wine. We grow a little stupid, and whisper silly things to each other as we stroll the city streets, all the way to the Fountain of Trevi. The moonlight winks at us on the frothy waters and illuminates the impressive and imposing figure of Neptune, god of the sea. We stand before it, arms entwined, feeling the chill of the spray, smelling the fresh water, and listening to the hypnotic cascades. It seems a great reward for the trials we have endured to stand here in Rome together before this magnificence. It is early spring, so there is still a nip in the night air, and we are eager to return home to our bed. Nathaniel leads me away, but not before a figure standing near the fountain catches my eye. It is a solitary woman whose face is so white in the moonlight she could be a statue. I feel a bone-deep shiver as the image of the beggar girl assaults me, and becomes the face of Margaret Fuller. I halt my step, and Nathaniel turns to me.

"Are you all right?" he asks when he sees my face.

I squeeze my eyes shut for a moment, and then dare to look back at the woman. She is clearly not Margaret, but there is a sorrow and a longing about her that remind me of our old friend. I do not want to bring her memory between us, though, so I arrange my face into a smile.

"Of course," I say.

We continue for home, and I am able to suppress the past and enjoy my husband. Time seems to hold its breath. His hands travel over me like a sculptor's, molding, kneading, bringing me to new life. We are one as we have not been in many moons, and when we finish, we cling to each other, and he falls asleep in my arms.

But sleep will not come. I am haunted, and fear what always follows my visions. I sense there is something coiled in the darkness, waiting to steal our perfect happiness.

37

Though life is abundant and thriving around us, I am forever glancing sideways, trying to catch the darkness before it catches me. Why must happiness's twin, despair, forever lurk nearby? Why can we not throw ourselves with abandon into the arms of joy without ever watching over our shoulders?

I know it is partly because of the hollow grief we feel over being exiled from our home country. The political turbulence there reaches us across an ocean, rocking our foundation like an earthquake. I curse the devil who ever started slavery as much as I curse my sisters for their epistolary diatribes. One cannot escape, even though thousands of miles separate us.

When Nathaniel and I are able to pull the veil over our sadness, there is great joy to be found. The children are in excellent health, Nathaniel and I are like new lovers, and my artistic self is inspired daily while he works at a novel he calls *The Marble*

Faun. A source of greatest pleasure to us is a colony of American and English artists we have met in the elegant rooms atop the Palazzo Barberini of sculptor William Story and his wife, Emelyn.

Though it is our first Sunday salon with the Storys, we feel as if we have known them for ages. Emelyn extends her cool hands, drawing us into the magnificent apartment where one can view enchanting palms through arched windows. The gold damask wallpaper, creamy marble fireplaces, heavy green drapes, and frescoed ceilings are like elegant theater sets, housing a cast of fine writers, painters, and musicians. Some we know from Boston, others from our travels in England and France, and all are at ease in this fine place where our ideas and philosophies are free to mingle. Each conversation feeds the artistic soul like a banquet, but no others in our acquaintance set us more at ease than the poets Robert and Elizabeth Browning.

Elizabeth rarely comes out in society, as she is an invalid with weak lungs and a morphine dependence, but her doting younger husband remarks that the Roman air has given her new vitality, and he is pleased to have his talented wife at his side. Elizabeth has more fame from her poetry than anyone else here, but her warmth is abundant, and the way she elevates even the humblest of us shows her generous spirit.

Once the men have retired to the balcony overlooking the Fontana del Tritone to smoke, and we women have had our tea poured by servants who seem to emerge from the frescoes and then become absorbed back into them, Elizabeth addresses me.

"Emelyn tells me of your great talent in art. She said you are known in the New World, and that your paintings hang where they might be viewed."

"That is very kind," I say, "though my work must be dusty indeed, for it has been many years since I have created anything worthy of public display."

"You will no doubt be inspired in Italy, where the heart of art beats in the world."

"I am pleased that I have been able to complete many sketches while traveling the halls of galleries and palaces, and without a single headache."

"Do you suffer?" asks Elizabeth. I know there is nothing an invalid likes to hear of more than the health woes of others, which might somehow illuminate or at least justify her own.

"I do," I say. "Much of my youth was spent nursing the hurt in my skull following artistic creation. I was on morphine for years."

"So you know how I feel," she says. "Dependent, foggy, unsettled."

"Oh, yes," I say. "If I could wish away your infirmities, I would drop every last penny I have into the fountains of Rome with your name on my lips."

"Thank you," says Elizabeth.

"Someone once said a similar thing in these very rooms," says Emelyn, staring off at some memory. "It was Margaret Fuller, just after she married Giovanni Ossoli, and she worried for her son's health during a smallpox outbreak. She said she would drop every penny she owned into the fountains to keep him from illness or any suffering a day in his life."

I shudder, thinking of the night I imagined Margaret's ghost at the fountain. I was aware that Margaret had known the Storys—everyone who visits Rome knows the Storys—but I was not aware of the degree of their acquaintance. As much as it hurts, I want to hear more about Margaret and the little family she had and lost, especially while my husband is engaged with the men, safely out of hearing. I reach for Emeyln's arm and gently implore her.

"Nathaniel will be disturbed, for we have a complicated history with Margaret—one of deep friendship and betrayal. But now that she is gone, and in such a tragic way, I feel only pity for her. Tell me what you know about her."

Emelyn places her hand on mine. She glances at the men, and back at me and Elizabeth. "I will tell you this, with confidence: Margaret was a changed woman in Italy. I had known her in Boston, and thought her arrogant and off-putting. But here she nursed soldiers wounded in political uprisings, spared no sacrifice to assist others, and bloomed in the glow of love from her soldier Giovanni and their son, Angelo. She was a testament to the graces of perfect love in an imperfect world, and though she met a terrible end, her life was not a tragedy. She was greatly adored and admired, and can any of us hope for more?"

With Emelyn's last, sweet utterance, the men return to the parlor, and Elizabeth and I hide our faces to wipe our tears with embroidered napkins.

Tonight in private, I think I will tell Nathaniel of Margaret, but by the time we are home and I work up the courage, he is sleeping soundly. I decide not to interrupt his slumber, and instead lie awake, thinking of Emelyn's words, allowing them to wash the stain from my memories of Margaret, and to permeate my being with their sacred truth.

Elizabeth Browning tells us that summer is best passed in the countryside, and suggests that we visit Florence to secure a villa. She resides there for her health, and welcomes our family to her beloved Casa Guidi to entertain us with her spirit stories, and to recommend nearby properties we might inhabit. Una is taken with the frail and lovely woman, Rose becomes awed in her presence, and Julian is fascinated by their little son, Pen, though he is more a plaything than a playmate. The child must be ten years old, but is as airy and slight as a butterfly.

While we search for a country house, we take temporary rooms at the Casa del Bello on the Via Fornace in Florence. Nathaniel is in as fine spirits as I have ever seen him, partly because the surroundings are like living history, but mostly because of how inexpensive it is to live here. We have abundant space, a private study for Nathaniel where he has recaptured his muse, servants to relieve us of drudgery, and as much red wine as we wish. The children are in ecstasy over the private garden, and run and spin like little dervishes, with the exception of Una, who is becoming a graceful and watchful young lady. At fourteen, she quivers on the verge of womanhood with that mixture of reserve and recklessness that so characterizes the age. Sometimes she will turn cartwheels with her smaller siblings, but more often she wishes to sit with and listen to the adults discussing all manner of art, politics, and religion. While I am fascinated and pleased to see our girl blooming into a woman, I often see Nathaniel gazing at her as if he does not know what to make of her.

It is an evening in June, and we sit on the balcony of the Casa Guidi with the Brownings, watching the fireflies like tiny star drops that have fallen in the emerald grasses. The night inches over the sky, bringing the quarter moon to its glorious splendor in the deepening color. Ada has taken Julian and Rose to bed at our apartment, but we have allowed Una to stay with us. Nathaniel is relaxed and quiet, because he has had a good day of note taking in preparation for earnest work on his novel, and I have enjoyed the pleasure of sketching all afternoon. It came to me earlier today, as our Rosebud chased tiny purple butterflies in their zigzag patterns over the grass, that she was lovelier than any cherubic statue, and therefore worthy of being committed to paper and, hopefully one day, to paint. I enjoyed tracing her cheek, which retains some of the roundness of babyhood.

"Did you know Sophia is a master of the highest order?" Nathaniel says, his tongue loosened from wine.

"I have heard of Sophia's talent, but do elaborate," says Elizabeth in her serene voice. She looks out from behind rows of dark ringlets, and fingers the branch of pink roses I have brought to her from our terrace. "I want to know more, and it is good for Una to understand her mother in terms of art."

I feel such warmth toward Elizabeth. It is painful to observe signs of the illness that wastes her body, but she bears her condition with grace, her contentment shining forth from her blue eyes. It is an honor that she admits us so freely, when she is so often taxed by social interaction.

"I should not be elevated among the likes of you," I say, staring down at the folds of my pink muslin skirts.

"Sophia is humble," says Nathaniel, "but her talent is abundant. It is a shame she has not had the opportunity to pursue it these years since the children were born."

Una's eyes grow wide at this utterance, and I hope she does not take offense. Nothing has brought me more pleasure than to nurture our children.

"Art is a state of being," I say. "Just because my paintbrushes are dry does not mean I am not creating."

"But have you sacrificed a portion of yourself at the altar of family?" asks Elizabeth.

At first I do not answer her question, which sounds like one Margaret Fuller once asked of me, because I must ponder its origin. Margaret would have asked the question with scorn, but Elizabeth asks out of curiosity, inserting no judgment.

"I suppose we must agree on the meaning of sacrifice," I say. "And whether it has a positive or a negative connotation."

"What is your connotation?" asks Una.

Now they all look at me, and I wish we could talk of the seasons or the night or the music drifting to us on the breezes from the church across the square. I am entranced by its hypnotic quality, and it is as if I am mesmerized. I do not wish to explore these murky waters. I must be growing more like Nathaniel.

"Sacrifice seems to me to be a state of the highest and holiest order," I say, no doubt influenced by our very Catholic surroundings.

Nathaniel stares at me in the moonlight. He glows like a celestial body, silent and looming.

"But perhaps the universe has sacrificed by taking you from your painting," says Elizabeth.

It pains me to acknowledge it, but I do sometimes imagine what my life would have been if I had never entered the parlor that day to meet Nathaniel. Such thoughts come on the difficult nights, when Nathaniel is cross, the children needy, and the blank sketch pad seems to accuse me of neglect from across the room. Would I be a world-famous painter by now if I had not chosen domesticity? Would I want such a thing, when the pressure and act of creation often brought me such physical misery? I do sometimes mourn the death of my single artist's existence, but almost never.

"I have provided the universe with light through my children," I say. "Their good effect will extend farther than any hanging canvas I might have produced."

"And you still might produce," says Robert. "It is never too late."

Elizabeth begins a coughing fit. She apologizes and holds up her hand when Robert stands to help her, but she cannot get her lungs to stop their spasms.

"I beg your pardon," says Elizabeth, "but I must go to bed."

"We will see ourselves out," I say. "Good night."

We all stand and Robert leads Elizabeth away, while their servant escorts us to the front door. The terrible sound of Elizabeth's cough follows us outside, and even down the street, for we can hear it from their open window. Nathaniel pulls me close to his side and looks up to the Brownings' room before gazing at me with a troubled expression. Una takes his other arm, and we make the short walk home. Just before we arrive at the Casa del Bello, Una speaks to me.

"You should paint again."

"Perhaps I will," I say, reaching for her hand. It is warm and pulses with youthful energy. "Maybe you will paint with me. We can paint oil landscapes in the lands that inspired me before I saw them with my own eyes."

"Do," says Nathaniel. "I am eager to see such a creation at this juncture, now that you have so much more of life's wisdom."

"Should I paint a copy or my own creation?" I say.

"Do not ask us, Mama," says Una. "It must come from your own heart."

I ponder her words as we enter the apartment and prepare for sleep. When I crawl into bed, I watch the stars through the window and try to hear my heart's impulse, but all that consumes my thought is the sound of my husband's breathing beside me, the creakings of the apartment, and little Rose's cries from across the hallway. When she does not quiet on her own, I go to her and lift her into my arms.

"Shhh, what is it, Rosebud?"

"The white woman scared me," she says.

A chill rises on my neck in spite of the languid summer heat.

"It is all right," I say, though I am unsettled. "It was only a nightmare."

Rose snuggles into my neck, and I sit with her on the bed, rocking her back and forth until she falls asleep. I lay her down and cover her with a sheet, full of love for my little lamb in the clutches of night terrors—feelings that will not be assured away while the rest of the world rests.

Though I do not sleep a wink, I am relieved when I see the morning light inch its way across the floor, sending the dark spirits who roam in the night scurrying for the shadows.

Rose does not speak of the white lady again, and I am soon so occupied with our move to the countryside, I forget the foreboding I have felt since my visit to the Trevi Fountain.

38

There is a large, ornate gate at the entrance of the Villa Montauto on Bellosguardo Hill, just one mile from Florence but seeming to exist in a world its own. Count Montauto rents his ancient castle to us for a price so low it is nearly a gift. We must promise only to pay on time, and to fill his crumbling estate with laughter and energy—two stipulations we should have no trouble fulfilling. The young gentleman is his ancestral home personified, having an air of faded dignity. Like the flaking frescoes that adorn the substantial walls, the count looks as if he badly needs a dash of color—a curious thing for a man not yet advanced in years. I imagine that he must have some romantic tragedy in his past that has aged him before his time.

Standing in the large, square entrance hall, gazing up at the wide stone stairs leading to endless rooms, taking in the muted wall paintings of fauns and nymphs that must have once been so grand, I have a sudden image of myself on a scaffold, adding new color to that which is lost. I am so overcome with this idea that I voice it to Nathaniel, who indulges me.

"Signor, fetch the lady a ladder and a jar of paint."

The children laugh at the thought and begin to run through the hall; even Una cannot help herself. I caution them and Ada attempts to round them up, but the count lays a gentle hand on my arm.

"Please, signora," he says. "Their joy is what I had hoped for."

Ada joins us, and I see that the count admires her loveliness. Our Ada is a gem, and we treasure her beauty of person and soul. There could be no better guide for our children, and I do not think we have to worry about the admirations of gentlemen, for she is devoted to a fiancé back in America whom she mentions with every other breath.

We tour the house to see that it has been prepared, and are happy to meet the dear old couple, Tomaso and Stella, who oversee the property. The stone floors are swept and shining, the curtains of white muslin look fresh and new, billowing in the breeze, and the immense and ornate furnishings are fluffed and dusted so they rest like heavy jewels in each room.

The tower that characterizes the Villa Montauto is what drew Nathaniel here in the first place, so we all follow him to the ancient structure, where two owls and the ghost of a monk are said to reside.

"The climb is difficult," says the count, "if the ladies would prefer to stay behind."

"Oh, no," I say. "We are quite accustomed to walking and hiking, are we not?"

Una and Rose nod, though they look unsure about exploring such a dark and haunted bit of architecture. Ada laughs and takes their hands as Julian charges ahead, brandishing the wooden sword he carries on his person at all times.

The stair is wide, and barred windows allow in a bit of light at each landing. We come to a small, decrepit chamber that the count informs us was the prison that housed the holy monk during the days of Catholic persecution; it is where he continues to reside in his death. I get a chill as we pass, but it is an exciting feeling, and I am not yet winded from our climb. We pass several more rooms at landings along the way, and now that we are above them, the windows are no longer barred, and I catch glimpses of the landscape I am beside myself to view in unobstructed glory. I am beginning to find breathing difficult, but I try to hide how tired I grow. Oh, to be as young as the children, taking steps two at a time, and still able to remark along the way!

When we reach the top of the stair, we disperse along the summit of the tower and share a collective intake of breath. In all my life, I have never seen a landscape like this one. From the loftiest heavens to the deepest depressions, here is the magnificent splendor of creation. I thought I knew Eden until I viewed the vineyards, fig trees, and olive orchards of the Arno Valley. From the highest church spire to the most mean peasant abode exist all states of the world and nature in harmony and proximity.

The sweet lakes supply the rich and fertile hills and fields, and the gentle ringing of convent bells competes with the song of birds and the music of travelers, so abundant in these parts. Here the artist knows he has found the source, and even if history obscures his talents from posterity, he knows that he has existed among and contributed to the well from which all other creatives will drink.

I gaze at Nathaniel, who holds his hand to his heart in a pose I know conveys an ultimate feeling he cannot express with language. He looks at me and we share a moment of satisfaction that impresses itself upon my own heart so that it burns.

"Do you see how all the weather exists at once," says Una in a voice so quiet, she does not break the spell, but enriches it. Una has learned to introduce an idea without spoiling the mood, and later, I will tell her that she is her father as he would like to be, for he has not yet mastered the art of subtle and poignant observation. It is what most eludes him.

I see what she has noticed—how a storm drags its robes over the valley, while a wash of sunlight blesses an assemblage of houses, and yet another cloud bank shades a field in need of relief from the summer sun. I can see before us the very truth of existence: Life is at all times and all at once a magnificent and terrible pageantry. This must be how God sees the world, and why He is not overwhelmed by the darkness as we small humans are: for He can see those enjoying the light at the very moment that others are in the deepest despair, and He knows how swiftly the weather moves over the land.

It is a summer of enchantment that passes so quickly I fear it is a dream.

We have such an abundance of space, we have all taken suites of three to four rooms each to call our own, where we may arise at our leisure and return at day's end, after we have enjoyed dinners, and friends, and stargazing, and the talents of the traveling musicians. We eat figs from the trees, eggs from our chickens, and drink wine that Tomaso calls sunshine, for it is golden and sweet and casts a wavering reflection when sun passes through it. The heat and the languor have brought Nathaniel's writing to a halt, but while this perturbs him, he is not unused to taking the summer months off from his work to allow his ideas to simmer. I assure him that when we return to Rome in the fall, the chill in the air will keep him busy indoors at his writing table, so he must enjoy his physical life now.

And enjoy it we do.

Nathaniel and I have separate sleeping chambers, but we spend many nights in one or the other's abode, taking pleasure in each other in such perfect privacy, we have even dared to walk about without our clothing, like animated statues. Nathaniel's person is much leaner and more beautifully preserved than mine, as he is still a living Apollo, but he loves the roundness of my form, and delights in it as Bacchus at the cask.

We awaken late from a night of love, and I slip across the stone back to my chamber to dress, clutching a wilting red poppy in my hands. Nathaniel traced the flower over my body like a paintbrush last night, and I will press this little beauty to keep always, to remember our passion. I pull on the lightest morning dress of pale blue, for today we will view galleries full of the Virgin, who has won the heart of this heretic through her solemnity, purity, and endurance in the face of great trials.

There is nothing so golden as the sound of merry laughter from one's children, and that is my joyful welcome this perfect morning. I descend the stairs to the loggia, where the air flows, opening one's chest, and the scents of peeled oranges and flowers enchant me. The valley is shrouded in mists, and I must stop and view it before joining the group at table. Ada is sweetly adorned with an orange blossom in her fair hair, and her blue eyes and dewy skin are as lovely as the landscape. I am quite sure Julian minds her so well because he is in love with her, as we all are.

"I could paint you," I say to Ada. "I see a girl—perhaps a princess—looking out over an Italian landscape she has married to inherit, which welcomes her as if she were a native plant."

Ada blushes and thanks me, and Una stands to retrieve something from the corner. She returns and presents me with tubes of oil paints and a small canvas.

"From me," she says. "I asked Papa to help me secure it for you, now that we children are older, and you have more leisure."

I am so moved by my daughter's offering that I am rendered speechless. My girl has intuited that she and her siblings need me less, and she gives the gift to fill my time and satisfy my impulses when they cannot. I was speaking from fancy when I said I could create original art. But perhaps I can try now that I have lived for many years and understand all of life's passions, joys, and hardships.

Nathaniel joins us and scolds Una kindly. "I wanted to be here to see her receive it."

"I still glow from the gift," I say. "Though I am afraid I will disappoint you if I do not use it right away. I still feel as if there is so much to see, and the quality of the art around us intimidates me from touching a brush to the canvas."

"It is a gift," he says, "so there are no restrictions or instructions on its use. It is merely a suggestion if you need a new way to pass your hours that might bring you more pleasure than ways of old."

I relish the sparkle in his eye while he says this, and once the children have scattered to the garden with their nurse, I whisper to him that I do not think it possible to experience any more pleasure than I do now.

At the end of a slender avenue lined in hedges, roses, and fig trees, I find my Rose on a secluded bench. A cat sits near her and allows her to pat its back, while it keeps its eyes squinted shut. The entire scene would be charming except for the dark look on my little one's face. She glances at me as I approach, and then returns her eyes to the cat. I sit next to her and pat her back the way she strokes the feline.

"I think I will pick this rose from the garden today," I say, giving her a ticklish pinch on her side, but she barely flinches. "What is it, Rosebud? How can you be sad in paradise?"

She sighs, but seems reluctant to talk.

"Are you sad that we move around so much?" I ask.

She shakes her head in the negative.

"Has Julian been pulling your braids or leaving ghastly spiders in your rooms?"

She shakes her head no, but a smile begins to lift her pink lips.

"Did Ada make you study your arithmetic all day instead of allowing you to frolic in the gardens?"

She shakes her head no again, and then turns to me and locks me in an embrace that knocks the air from me. I feel her forehead, but it is not feverish. She is as cold as stone, and I move her away so I might look at her more clearly. My little one has been growing at an alarming rate, and it occurs to me that she might feel left out, since her older siblings are so very independent and are encouraging my independence through art. Perhaps she senses that her childhood recedes every day, as we do, and is fearful of its passing.

Even if Rose feels this way, I realize that it is a conversation above what she is capable of enacting, so I simply say, "Can I do anything to comfort you?"

She looks aside and then back at me, and with great effort she finally speaks.

"I have the bad dream a lot."

"What bad dream?"

"The white lady."

It is as if all sun contracts from our summer garden. My child has inherited the beggar girl, and while I do not know what it means, I recall the dread I felt and continue to feel whenever she appears to me. Whether she is an apparition or a manifestation of some deep fear, it matters not. She is as real as the fear she inspires. I pull Rose to me and try to warm her with my embrace.

"Do you know that I used to see a white lady, or a girl mostly, in my dreams?" I say.

Rose pulls away and looks fascinated that her mother could ever see a thing that would frighten her.

"It is true," I say. "And I have always feared her. But do you know what has recently occurred to me?" So new is this thought that it comes to me as I utter the words aloud. "She is a reminder to me to enjoy all that is beautiful in my life. I need not be scared of her. I should feel very sorry for her, because she does not know the joy of life as I do. I must never become like her, but must persist in seeing the good things around me."

Rose's face relaxes a little, but she is still somber.

The cat has grown bored, and jumps down from the bench before slipping away into the foliage.

"Come," I say. "Let us follow her. We will have an adventure today, and see only what is good."

Nathaniel joins us in our jaunt to the Pizzi and Uffizi galleries, where I continue to teach him to see with my artist's eyes. He is naturally drawn to the visual arts, and after staring at the work of the masters for only a short time, he can be seen placing his hand over his heart.

Standing before the most perfect canvases, I feel as if my *innere* and that of the original painter are one, and that all time has fallen away around us so we may share the moment and the deeper meaning. This happens for me only with the very best work—art inspired by lofty and holy persons aware of their partnership with elements and spheres not of this earth. Raphael's *Madonna della seggiola* is one such work. In it, the Virgin clasps the Christ child to her in the sweetest maternal embrace, but underlining the tender scene is a shadow in the look of the mother and the child, and a desperation in the way she clasps Him. It is as if she understands she will lose Him someday in the most terrible way, so she must cling to Him while He fits in her arms. Simply looking at the painting, a mother wishes to clutch her children to her and never let go, yet a measure of comfort lies in knowing there is a mother who endured trials long ago and may walk with us in our own.

The children have gone ahead with Ada, so my impulse to touch those I love is fulfilled in Nathaniel. I take his arm and feel the heat of his body. We stand for many minutes before starting away, but not before either of us has taken parting glances at the Virgin.

"Do you ever get the feeling that if the corruption were removed from the Catholic Church, it might be a perfect religion?" he asks.

"My dear, there would be no way to separate the corruption from the Church; therefore I do not know. Why do you say such a thing?"

"The art, to start. Gazing upon the likes of this Madonna, one understands more about the gospel than one could from an hour-long sermon given by one of our ministers."

"I am sure some priest somewhere has gone on for too long as well," I say.

"It is a certainty, but let us also take confession. If a stiff puritan like me could pour out his deepest guilt and sins to a priest and find a measure of peace and even atonement on earth, it might make a lighter man of me."

"Your words are shocking," I say.

Nathaniel has not attended a church service in many years, and I fear that spending so much time viewing Catholic cathedrals and Catholic-inspired art has made a convert of him.

"You need not fear my subscription to the faith," he says. "I only recognize that there are merits in some of the practices I witness."

"I can agree with you in terms of the art, but I am not in line with your feelings on the other elements of the faith. Or rather, the priests would continue to repel me even if I agreed on the positives. Men who do not interact with women have nothing to soften them, and their ignorance leads to misunderstanding."

We exit the gallery onto a piazza, where a group of young priests passes. I fumble and drop my fan, and one of them leans down to pick it up, and places it in my hand. He smiles kindly and proceeds to join his brethren.

My children run ahead of them, aiming to scare a group of pigeons into the air. The young priests join Julian and Rose in chasing the birds into flight while Una watches with interest. She is a vision as pure as the art from the gallery, wearing a face of pleasure and serenity like the Virgin; her flushed skin and red hair color her like a painting by Raphael. Nathaniel stops beside me, and we stare at our beautiful creation smiling up at the sky with the birds rising around her.

In the middle of the night, a violent wind, like the crashing of an ocean wave, assaults the villa. It persists for an hour, lashing and howling like an angry spirit, and I wonder that Rose or the other children do not awaken and join me in my bed. I half wish to run to theirs, and am so restless I light my candelabra and creep to each of their chambers to see that they are all right.

Rose is curled into a ball with her bottom sticking in the air and her hair wild and sweaty around her cherubic face. I pull off her quilt and allow only a light sheet to cover her body. It is a miracle she is not awake, the wind rattles her windows so. When I check on Julian, I smile to see that he holds his sword in one hand and his leg hangs off the side of the bed. He looks as if he has just come in from a medieval war, and will return to the battlefield the moment he awakes. I think I will lift his leg onto the bed, but decide against it, for fear that he might start and jab me with the wooden weapon. In Una's room, I see that she has pulled the curtains closed to keep out any shred of light, so the only thing visible is the grotesque human skull she found in the tower and brought to her room. It sits leering at me from her writing desk, a Shakespearean prop of magnetic and frightening association, and tomorrow I will insist she return it to its original resting place. If there is a ghost in the villa, I am sure it does not appreciate the removal of its head from its rightful room. I pause outside of Nathaniel's chamber, but decide against going in to sleep with him. He seemed much fatigued this afternoon and evening from our long walk in the summer heat, and I hope he is getting a satisfying rest.

I go back to my room alone, and listen to the tempest. When I do sleep, I dream dreadful nightmares of evil spirits rattling the panes, trying to get into our home and wreak havoc with my dear, unsuspecting family.

39

Elizabeth Browning's friend Miss Blagden is a spiritualist who holds regular séances at her villa. I am enthralled by Elizabeth's belief in the spirit world, and have engaged her in endless discussions about it, while Robert and Nathaniel rolled their eyes and attempted to explain away the unexplainable. Sadly, the Brownings cannot be here today because they have decided to summer in France. Elizabeth would have enjoyed Miss Blagden's sessions with us and would have offered explanations to make her pronouncements coherent and plausible. Without Elizabeth, we are left a bit bewildered.

Nathaniel watches alone, outside the circle, standing with crossed arms and a frown, as Ada holds a pen and, at Miss Blagden's instructions, attempts to act as a medium for the spirit who has joined us. The last thing I see before the curtains are drawn are Una's large and watchful eyes gazing in at us from the courtyard. She wished to stay and observe, but I told her the séance might scare her. She reminded me that she slept next to a skull before I forced her to remove it and fears nothing, but I still banished her to watch over the younger children while we dabble in the supernatural.

As we adults sit in the heat and the half dark, hoping for the touch of our loved ones from beyond the grave, one of the ladies shrieks, "Something grabbed my skirts!"

Suddenly all of those seated at the table experience the terrible thrill of a *thing* disturbing our persons. I jump in my seat and brush the feeling away, wondering whether it is the power of persuasion tingling my legs, or an actual ghost.

"It is the spirit of a child," says Miss Blagden. "The hands are small."

Several of the ladies, who must think it could be one of their little lost babes, turn and dab their eyes with kerchiefs, while I shudder at the thought. Before long, icy chills tickle the tendrils on the back of my neck. I turn and look over my shoulder, but there is no one there. Oh, how glad I am that Una and the other children are frolicking in the garden, for they would be frightened if I had let them stay! My eyes catch Nathaniel's where he stands in a veil of shadows. I wish I could see what he is thinking, though I suspect I know. He surely thinks this is all nonsense.

Ada's hands flit across the paper, and Miss Blagden uses the light of a candle to read the words aloud.

Sophichen.

I gasp, as does Nathaniel. This is the way my mother used to refer to me many years ago. Ada could not know. I begin to tremble, and tears well in my eyes.

Next Ada writes, *"Infeliz de mí."*

My *Cuba Journal*! To see with the eyes given me—the eyes of hope.

Nathaniel looks perplexed, as though he remembers the words but cannot place where he has seen them. By the savior, my joy has turned to fear. What will be written? Is this Fernando? Has he died? Or is the spirit in our midst Mother? As if in answer to my thoughts, Ada begins to scribble with more speed, and I am certain it is Mother.

"Write it. Lift the veil."

"Write what?" I say. I have been writing in journals about our travels, but am I to publish them as I did the *Cuba Journal*, or am I to write something else?

I know how Nathaniel disapproves of women exposing their inmost souls on the page, so he would surely insist the opposite. There is whispered chatter all around me, but I ignore it. I am thirsty for my mother's counsel.

"Please," I say, addressing Ada's pen without care for how silly I must appear. "What do you mean?"

I am desperate to know more, but the pen remains still.

I think of my loved ones—my father, brothers, Louisa. I begin to cry.

"Are you all together?" I say. "Mother, are you with Father? George? Please!"

Some of the women weep with me, and Miss Blagden rubs my back. I hear the door close, and see that Nathaniel has gone. He will probably scold me later for allowing something he sees as a farce to distress me so. My soul feels rent in two; I wish to follow him, but I must have more interaction with Mother. My head begins to throb and my dress sticks to my back from the heat. I am parched for water, but I utter my questions without ceasing. I must have more! But the pen is still and Ada is exhausted. There are murmurings of disappointment among us, especially because I am the only soul who received communication.

"There, now, Sophia," Miss Blagden says, patting my hand. "We will try again another time."

I nod, but my heart screams, *No! We are running out of time.* We are already planning our return to Rome in the fall, and I feel the desperation of the journey's end beginning to weigh upon me. If I could, I would live forever in Italy, in eternal communion with the masters of art and in the very presence of history. My entire life has been leading to this place in time—it is as if I inhabit the sketches and paintings I created all of those years ago, and I cannot bear the thought of leaving them.

I flinch from the light when the curtains are opened, and I am disoriented and weak. My husband has left me, so I have no arm to hold. I feel my way out of the room, leaning on the backs of chairs and moldings, until I am finally outside in the garden. The air fills my lungs with freshness, and I begin to feel better, but I will not be restored until I have conversed with Nathaniel and received his loving assurances.

I hurry forward, taking the turns along the garden paths, wondering where he and the children have gone so fast. The sounds of a rushing fountain and faraway convent bell cover my calls to Nathaniel, and I do not want to further project my voice, because it might frighten them. After a few more turns, I am relieved to finally behold the objects of my search. I think I will let them know I am here, but the pretty scene they make stops me on the cobbled stone. Una has her arm through Nathaniel's and the two study a fountain where a forlorn marble nymph leaks water into a basin through a cracked urn. The mosses have kindly adorned her form so that a father and his daughter may look upon her together without blushing. Julian and Rose chase butterflies on a nearby knoll.

I cannot enjoy the scene entirely, however, for my family is separate from me—almost farther away than my deceased family. They look like figures on a canvas, hung on a wall, part of a world I cannot inhabit.

This is our last week in Florence, and we make one final visit to the Uffizi.

I stand before Dolci's *Magdalene* for a long time until Nathaniel comes to me and touches my shoulder.

"Shall we go on ahead without you?" he asks.

I do not answer for a moment. The woman's look of supplication is captured as perfectly as that on the Magdalene I cleaned all those years ago.

"Seeing her like this," I say, "it is as if not a day has passed since I beheld the stained painting in Cuba."

"Italy has a way of doing that," he says. "The past crowds out the present."

"Is that why this summer has felt like a dream? I thought it was just the morning mists on the Val d'Arno. The exquisite happiness. The days suspended in time."

He reaches up to smooth the hair on my forehead, and I am touched by his tender gesture.

"You speak poetry that would please even the Brownings," he says. "There is a piece of me that wishes to remain here, except for a restlessness that has begun. I tire of naps and séances, and I feel a building of words and a rising of story that cannot be fully accessed here in this garden of earthly delights. All I can manage are fragments I shall use for further creation."

He kisses my hand, but the place he has touched feels colder instead of warmer. I know that when the weather cools, so does my love, for that is when he writes. I manage a tight smile.

"Do go on," I say through pursed lips. "I want to stay and attempt a sketch so I might have a basis for creation as you will, to occupy my Roman winter."

He holds my gaze for a moment, but when he understands my tension and feels my bitterness, he leaves me.

I will not allow any frustrations during the coming weeks to spoil this time in heaven, so I disperse my dark thoughts and find a bench. I reach into my bag to pull out a pad and pencil, but when I press the tip to the page, it has no point. I open the bag to see whether I have a penknife, but it is not there, so I must suffer with the blank page and hope my memory supplies what I need.

We sit in the tower of the Villa Montauto for the last time, absorbing as much splendor from the rich night as we can. The moon wanes but it still possesses some of the glory of its recent fullness, even illuminating the faraway tower where Galileo spent so many evenings. He would be riveted by what we see, for a comet has been making its lonely, blazing path through the sky for weeks. It has been growing in brightness, and behind it is a tail like a flaming feather.

"Where is it going, Mama?" asks Julian.

"On its way to crash into fiery communion with some massive star, I hope."

"You wish it destroyed?" asks Una.

"No, love, only to be a part of some greater glory, and not to travel alone."

"But it has such magnificence on its own," says Una. "If it were part of another celestial body, it would be forgotten, or at the very least unnoticed."

"No," says Nathaniel, pulling my hand into his. "It would be enhanced and add to a greater light."

This is the way he repairs me without touching the wound, so I feel no sting from the pain, only the relief of the healing. I do not know whether I am the comet or if he is, but it does not matter. Our communion is what is sacred.

As we climb aboard the carriage piled high with trunks the next day, endless travelers on this earth, Nathaniel and I look back at our beloved abode. The persistent morning mist shrouds the villa, save the tower, which stands with dignity over the scene. I imagine our Hawthorne ghosts on the summit as we were last night, and emotion rises in me at the thought that our summer in Florence is receding and we will never have it again. Our children grow older and time marches forward, so we must engrave these days in our memories, or write them on pages with inadequate words, or sketch them on paper that will never capture the full flavor of the first living of them.

But I remind myself that this year has been richer and fuller than any before it, and since the day I first saw my love, the years have grown in blessings in ways I could not have imagined. I will look with hope toward a future that continues to beckon, and I will blaze forward, burning these moments on my heart so that I may live them eternally.

40

The splashing of the Trevi Fountain can be heard through the open window of our snug apartment in Rome, overlooking the Piazza Poli. The autumn has been kind, and we have not experienced any despair, but rather a lifting, buoyed by our surroundings and the society of the Storys.

We delight in touring the galleries, the ancient sites, the gardens and cathedrals, and the children have grown much in their education from experiencing the world instead of simply reading about it. Poring over a text about the Colosseum is nothing compared to standing on its dirt, once red with blood, while the crumbling walls tower over us. Feeling the cold shadow of the looming Pantheon is so much more moving than trying to comprehend its greatness from a reproduced pencil sketch.

Still, in spite of our love of Italy and our frustration with the simmering political landscape of America, Nathaniel and I think the children will soon need to return, or they will find themselves inhabitants of nowhere. As one who has borne the burden of feeling isolated even in a warm and familiar society, Nathaniel does not wish our children to suffer the same restlessness. I have already started making plans for our return, though we will stay on until the spring.

For now, I am recording all of my artistic impressions in my journal and sketch pad so I might copy and paint later. I must drink in my surroundings as much as possible as preparation for when they will be but a memory.

The ringing of the bells of St. Peter's calls my eyes from the pages of my journal, and I notice that night falls fast. My heart pounds at the thought, because Ada and Una have not yet returned from their museum visit, and the air is not safe. Though the season of malaria is nearly concluded, Roman residents know to be home by six o'clock. I close my journal and step out to the parlor, where Nathaniel paces at the window.

"They are not yet back?" I ask.

"No, and I fear I will have to venture out to find them."

"I wish you would," I say. "Ada must have lost track of time or their way, and I cannot bear to think of them out late, for more reasons than one."

Nathaniel pulls on his black cloak, and I am moved by the impressive figure he still casts. He is out the door within moments, and I hurry to the window and watch his dark form striding across the piazza. I have a flashing memory of the first time I beheld Nathaniel, when he walked toward my family's house in Salem and lifted his face to the sun. That moment struck me so that I had to back away from the window. My soul knew what was coming, and in spite of every difficulty we have faced, I would not trade one moment of our lives together.

Julian and Rose are reading by the warmth of the Franklin stove, and I join them with my copy of *Jane Eyre*, but I am unable to concentrate. I chew my nails, wiggle my legs, and again cross the room to the window. A chilly breeze drifts in, and I hasten to pull the shutters closed and lock out the elements. Though I admire the tranquil evening that touches everything with an amethyst glow, I cannot enjoy it.

"What's wrong?" asks Julian.

I turn to him and attempt a smile. "Oh, I am just full of a mother's worry. Ada and Una are not back yet."

"They will be here before you know it," he says. "Una said they wanted to sketch the Palace of the Caesars."

"You must run, then, and tell your father, for he set off in another direction!"

Julian jumps into action like a little soldier, and pounds down the narrow staircase, while I call after him to hurry back if he cannot find his father. I watch him run on sturdy legs until he is out of sight, and am suddenly angry with myself for sending more members of my family into the elements. Rose joins me at the window and wraps her little arms around me. She is such a slight child; I am easily able to lift her, though she is seven years old. She rests her soft cheek against mine, giving me some comfort.

We hasten to open the door when we hear the ringing, but it is only the man who brings our dinner. We have no kitchen for food preparations, so we take all of our meals on delivery from the delightful *ristorante* nearby. Rose helps me set the table, and our stomachs rumble in anticipation at the aroma of beef. Just as we pour the last glass of water, Julian calls to us and bounds up the stairs. Una and Ada follow, and finally Nathaniel.

"I do apologize," says Ada. She wrings her hands, and her pretty forehead is wrinkled with worry. "We lost all track of time because we were so caught up in our sketching."

"I found them first," says Julian.

"We would have beaten the dark home," says Una. "There is no need for alarm. Besides, after October there is no fear of Roman fever."

"I am sure there is not," says Nathaniel. "But let us not court danger while we are in the Eternal City, and spoil our dream of Italy."

"It will not happen again," says Ada. "I promise. I hope I did not worry you too awfully."

Ada reaches for my hand, and I squeeze it so she knows she is forgiven.

"All is well," I say. "Besides, I can sympathize with getting lost in a drawing and not noticing the passage of time."

We all agree and settle like a flock of birds around the dining table, where we enjoy our meal and one another's conversation. We finish the night around the card table, as we always do, and retire early. Nathaniel wraps his arms around me in the moonlight, and we lie in each other's warmth, whispering of our travels and the future, and of how very much at home we feel this time in Rome.

As I sit alone in the early morning, journalizing on the art I have seen, sipping coffee and watching the rain streak down the windowpanes, a noise draws my attention to the doorway. What I see there so startles me that I stand, upsetting my cup and sending it tumbling to the carpet.

"Una!"

My girl is glassy-eyed and spectral, and makes a move toward me with outstretched arms. I barely reach her in time for her to faint into my grasp, and I am horror-struck at how she burns.

"Nathaniel!"

He emerges from our room in moments, confused from sleep and frightened to see me on the floor, crumpled under Una's weight. Ada soon follows, and covers her mouth. Nathaniel is at my side. He lifts Una in a gallant motion and carries her to the sofa in his study. He rests his cheek against her forehead and then jerks back as if seared by a hot iron.

"Ada, go to the Storys' immediately and see where we might find a doctor," I say.

She wastes no time racing to her room and dressing. She pulls her hair into a knot as she hastens down the stairs, and lets the door slam on her way out.

I kneel beside where Una lies.

"Fret not," I whisper. "Help is on the way."

Una rocks her head back and forth, and she quakes fearsomely. I reach for her forehead and force myself to leave my cold hand on the burning heat, hoping to bring her some relief. She leans toward me and opens her eyes to slits, where a single tear slides down the side of her face.

The ensuing months are a blur of sleeplessness filled with Una's awful cries and tremors from the Roman fever, moments of lucidity punctuated by madness, doses of quinine administered every two hours by the intense and capable Dr. Franco. Our friends visit and comfort us, bringing food, flowers, and conversation to our stale rooms. Nathaniel is beside himself, sick with a lesser form of the fever, and working like mad on his newest romance. Even Ada contracts the illness for a time, but Dr. Franco is happy to nurse our beautiful governess back to health. Ada's recovery gives me hope, and Dr. Franco is so confident of his cures and care, so noble and assertive, that I half believe the disease fears so worthy an opponent.

I sit in a constant vigil at Una's bedside, and find a strange energy in nursing her that has never before possessed me. I can go for days without sleep, and it is a good thing, for Una wants only my care. She becomes inconsolable if I leave the room for even a few minutes, so I have set up a bed in the study, and take all of my meals there.

When Una is well enough, Nathaniel brings the other children into the room and we attempt to entertain her with cards or novels. When she is in her fits, he keeps the other children far away so they will not be frightened. Julian is frustrated by the upset to our household, for he is a boy of energy and vitality, and our depression of spirits in conjunction with the chill of winter burdens him. Rose watches with large, dark eyes, but rarely comments aloud. She has become more withdrawn than before, and I fear that her sister's illness will permeate her tender soul.

In the midnight hours, Rose sometimes comes and sleeps in the study, or rather, she lies with me, because we both have trouble sleeping. On one such dark night, she cuddles with me, and I run my fingers through her fine hair.

"The white lady in my bad dream was Una," she whispers.

"Why do you say that?"

"Una has the look of her, and she scares me."

"Una cannot help her fits, Rosebud. It is a symptom of the Roman fever."

"Will she die?"

My throat seems to close and I squeeze my eyes shut and breathe deeply until my nerves are steady.

"I do not think so," I say. "Do you see how Ada is better, how Father has beat the illness?"

"But it was not the same with them."

Rose is right. They never burned with such intensity, or turned purple in the face, or became so saturated with quinine— the drug of succor that also threatens to kill. But Una is young and she is strong, and I have a feeling in my heart that God will not take her from us.

"Your sister will make it through this illness, but we must pray for her every minute of every day."

"Will God listen?"

I do not know. Here in this city so populated with churches and statues honoring the savior, so influenced by the saints and holy people of history, it seems the best place to seek intercession. But there is also a heavy feeling of death and coldness in Rome, and I fear that the darkness here could consume us if we are not vigilant.

"God always listens," I say. What I do not utter is that His answers to our prayers are not always what we ask.

Franklin Pierce becomes the answer to one prayer; his arrival in Rome saves my husband's sanity.

Our winter of illness has reached its icy roots deep into Nathaniel's soul. Gray has overtaken his hair, which has begun to recede on his lined forehead. The man who was rarely ill is now incessantly plagued in his lungs and in his stomach. He despairs over his daughter, his writing, and our finances, and I am so consumed by caring for Una that, for the first time since our meeting, I cannot comfort him.

Franklin has brought his wife, Jane, to vacation in Rome, though they spend much time apart. She keeps to her rooms, and he keeps to ours, and I am grateful for his tender and amiable presence.

Late one March evening, when the temperatures are still low enough for Nathaniel to pull on his winter cloak for his walk, I leave Ada at Una's bedside while she sleeps to tuck Rose and Julian into bed, and to fetch a plate of beef they have set aside for me. I am just crossing the room with my cold supper when Nathaniel enters with Franklin, who bears two bottles of wine. Though lines extend around his eyes, his hair is grayer, and he has put on some weight, Franklin is still impressive in his appearance. I touch my hair, which is escaping its loose bun, and run my hand over my soiled, wrinkled apron. What a fright I must look.

"Franklin," I say, placing my plate on the side table while my stomach growls. "If I had known we would be graced with your company, I would have taken a moment to make myself presentable."

"You are always a figure of grace and loveliness," he says, placing the wine on the table.

He gives me an embrace that loosens my stiffness with its warmth. I stare over Franklin's shoulder at my husband, who also looks as though the simple company of an old friend who has suffered trials relieves some of his own burden. He hangs up his cloak and hat, and comes to fetch Franklin's.

"Please do not allow me to interrupt your dinner," our friend says, pointing at the plate. "But do join us with a glass of wine."

I peek into Una's room to see that she still sleeps before agreeing. Ada looks up at me from her book and down at Una, but waves me off to show that she is happy to stay. Franklin walks to the door, and when his eyes find my sickly girl, he frowns and places his hand on my back. Even across the darkened room, one can see how fast Una breathes, how fitfully she sleeps, and how wasted she appears. I pull the door so that it is almost closed, and escort Franklin to the fireside, where Nathaniel has poured three glasses of wine and has set my plate on a small table next to the wingback chair nearest Una's room. Franklin joins Nathaniel on the settee.

"How is Jane?" I ask.

He takes a long drink before answering. "Jane is . . . Jane. She is a sad woman, rightfully so."

"But you are not a sad man," I say.

"I am," he says. "But I am capable of placing that sadness in a secret place so I may live in the day and tend to my grief alone at night. If I could not do that, I could not exist. But I do not want to talk about the Pierces. I want to know about Una. Is she improving?"

"Not enough," says Nathaniel. "Sophia works tirelessly at her side, scarcely sleeping or eating a thing all day and night, but every time Una's fever breaks and we have a whisper of hope, the cursed illness returns with a vengeance."

"And likely will continue to do so throughout her life," I say. "Dr. Franco tells us that if one survives the initial infection, it is likely to reassert itself through the weeks and months and years to come, though not with such severity as it does now."

Nathaniel adds, "If we can just get her to the place where she exists more in health than in illness, it will be a great relief on us all, though none so much as my wife."

He looks into the fire while he speaks. His words are kind, but shallow of feeling. We are all ghosts to him while Una suffers, or rather, he is a ghost to us—separate, blurred at the edges, inaccessible.

"There is no agony like that of watching your children suffer," says Franklin. "We would all gladly take it on for a lifetime so our young ones did not have to endure even a moment of discomfort."

"Indeed," I say, chewing the cold beef that I must force down with the wine. I have no appetite.

"I know that there is nothing I can do or say to ease your burden," says Franklin. "But please allow me to keep you company, even if it is only to share a drink at the fireside or a walk through the city. Do not ever feel as if you must entertain me or be anything but what you are, while you endure this hardship."

"Thank you," says Nathaniel. He wipes his eye with the sleeve of his jacket and turns to his friend with a quivering smile. Franklin reaches for Nathaniel's hand.

I stare at their joined hands, and push away my unfinished dinner. My husband and I have not had such ease of contact between us in weeks, and in just one night with his old friend, Nathaniel's shoulders have relaxed, his smile has returned, and he has spoken a string of words. While I appreciate Franklin's presence and offer, I cannot stifle my jealousy, though I am ashamed of it.

Una's cry brings me to my feet, and I nearly upset my glass of wine. Franklin stands with me, but I motion that he should sit, and I leave the men so I may attend to my daughter.

Over the following weeks, while Nathaniel and Franklin spend hours touring the city, taking in the sights, reflecting on the gloomy state of politics in America, and simply existing with each other, I attend to my daughter's health. I obey every instruction from Dr. Franco, even the latest, most distressing directive to cut off Una's hair. When Nathaniel hears this prescription, he turns stony and leaves the room. I hear an intake of breath from the corner, where Ada shrinks. The doctor vexes and stimulates Ada with his amorous attention, so she is forever hovering in the shadows, unsure of whether to show her sweet face.

Una is in one of her fits, and mumbles incomprehensibly. I almost dread when she regains full consciousness from this mutilation, for she is a girl at the threshold of womanhood. Her hair is a crown. Her body has begun to develop, but her sheltered mind is still very young. There is, and has always been, however, a deep wisdom in Una. She has an intelligence for life's truths that surpasses her limited years, and I know she is Nathaniel's favorite child. She is so much like him.

"Would you like me to do the deed, signora?" asks Dr. Franco, laying his large, dark hand on mine. "I know this will be difficult. I could even stay. This night will determine the outcome of her illness."

"No, Doctor. Una wants only my care and attention. I will do whatever needs to be done to save my child."

He stares at me with a creased brow, and then nods and stands to pack his bag. I feel affection for this man who has so faithfully attended to us day and night. I wish I were wealthy and could bestow a large sum on him. Instead, I stand to escort him out, not missing the look of longing he gives to Ada. It does something to me to see this wanting that cannot be satisfied, and I realize that part of his attention for my daughter comes from his love for our governess. She will not have him, however, because she is spoken for, and while I am sorry for him, I cannot help but think that if he really cared for Ada, he would not burden her with his desire. It is disorienting to have such distraction, and I suddenly wish him gone. He lingers, though, and when he speaks it is with great effort.

"Signora Hawthorne, you know it has been months."

"Yes, and I am so grateful we have had you to care for Una."

"She has endured much, and I am afraid that more quinine will be fatal."

"I know, Dr. Franco. We have discussed this."

He stares at me from under dark eyebrows, his lips pursed, and perspiration on his forehead.

"I am sorry, but—"

Una cuts him off with her screech, and I rush to her bedside to hold her through a fit of convulsion. She feels sticky and clammy, and spittle comes out of her mouth. After a few moments, she becomes deathly still, and her skin is the color of marble—so gray she could be a statue in a gallery. I look back at our doctor and know what Dr. Franco was going to say, though I cannot bear for him to voice it. He thinks she will die.

"We shall call you tomorrow if necessary," I say, with more sharpness than I intend.

He turns to leave the room. Before he goes he looks at Ada once more and then at me.

"I am sorry, signora. Deeply sorry that I could not . . ."

He does not finish, and soon he is gone.

Ada lets out a sob and joins me on the bed, where she runs her hands through Una's sweaty hair. I feel like one in a nightmare as I rise to fetch the scissors. Nathaniel stands by the window in the parlor, looking old and worn. I hardly know what to say to him, but I must prepare him.

"This evening and the night will be critical," I finally manage.

He covers his eyes with his hands, but I have no consolation for him. I reach for my sewing shears and leave him alone.

In the room, Ada still cries over Una, whose chest barely rises and falls with breath. I have no tears in me now. For the first time in my life I am angry with God. Bitter and angry, and unwilling to give up.

I steel myself and lift Una's tangled, matted auburn hair in my hand. Without hesitation, I begin to cut it off, and soon it is shorn to her head. I gather the hair and throw it into the wastebasket, leaving only a lock for myself. Ada is so beside herself I must escort her to bed. I tuck the covers up to her ears, and run my hand over her silky hair, and then her forehead so she knows I do not blame her.

"If I had never taken her out," says Ada, the sob in her throat choking her words.

"No," I say, shaking my head. "You are not to blame."

"I do not deserve your kindness."

A strange brightness gilds the city and creeps into the room, turning it gold. I look up at the glass of the window, and I am reminded of the windows we etched at the Old Manse. I will use those words to console Ada, though I do not know whether I believe them anymore.

"Man's accidents are God's purposes."

I leave Ada to rest, and when I enter the parlor I am surprised to find Robert and Elizabeth Browning there with Nathaniel. Elizabeth carries a bouquet of lilies that she places on my writing desk.

"He came to us," says Elizabeth, pointing at Nathaniel. "He told us that the end might be near."

I try to catch my husband's eyes, but he stares at the floor. It is as if he inhabits another world from me, and I am chilled at the thought that I have no impulse to enter into his sphere until I know Una is either recovered or dead. This separateness gives me almost as much pain as my languishing daughter.

"Life's sufferings are a mystery," says Elizabeth in her low voice.

I take the seat nearest her, sitting heavily from fatigue. She reaches for me, and I clasp her slender, cool hand in mine. I am astounded at the comfort her touch affords, and it is as if she has opened a great dam. My tears fall, and soon I am weeping.

"Good, Sophia," she says. "You must release the burden. You have been so strong, so hopeful during this ordeal. It must be balm to your soul to cry."

I pull my hand away, and use my handkerchief to wipe my eyes, relieved to unleash the pressure that has been building up for so long. I did not want to allow myself the indulgence of tears for fear they might never stop, but soon they do, and I am left feeling lighter, though still very sad.

Nathaniel and Robert have gone to Una's room, but they come out shortly, looking ashen and shocked.

"You are a comfort to me," I say to Elizabeth. "I know your health makes it difficult for you to leave your villa, and your generosity in visiting us and offering your kindness will never be forgotten."

"Think nothing of it," she says. "You are not alone. We will hold you in our hearts, even when we are not here."

We embrace, and Julian and Rose come tumbling into the room from their chambers. Rose stares at all of us with wide, dark eyes, and when she sees me, she looks very troubled. Elizabeth kneels down to speak to her.

"The lovely Hawthorne Rose," says Elizabeth. "A rare variety. How fortunate your parents are to have you growing in their garden."

"I am a knight, guarding the garden," says Julian, which brings smiles to the company.

"You are," says Nathaniel, placing his hand on Julian's shoulder. "And will you help me to escort the Brownings home, my knight?"

"First I must get my sword!"

While he runs, Nathaniel reaches for Rose and lifts her.

"What about you, Rosebud?" he says. "Will you come with us?"

She nods and rests her head on Nathaniel's chest. I reach for her cloak and tie her into it while she is in her father's arms. When I glance up, the desperation in his gaze threatens to unmoor me. I stare at him a moment, fighting my tears, and try to hear his thoughts, but there is no understanding past my own distress.

Once they have gone, I return to the sick chamber, my prison. I have scarcely ventured out for months, and only recently have I discovered that spring has come, since I no longer shiver indoors, and Julian brought me a bloom. I sit vigil with Una all night, aware of the world outside the door only when I hear my family return and the silence following their going to bed. I watch Una's chest in a state of mounting panic. Her breathing is labored, and it sometimes seems as if an eternity passes before she takes her next gasp. After midnight, heat begins to emanate from her wasted body like a torch. I lay my hands on her head and flinch at the temperature, which feels higher than ever before. I snatch my fingers back and pace to the window, stuffing my knuckles into my mouth so I will not cry aloud. I open the shutters, no longer caring what foul air I let into our rooms, only wishing for the fever to reach me and take me with Una into death. The sky has clouded over and no stars are visible. I have never felt so alone and abandoned by God. I begin to weep and whisper frantic prayers and petitions, bartering with God about what I will give if He gives, what I will sacrifice if He allows my Una to live.

I beg and pray and bargain all night, and I am in a state beyond human exhaustion when the first light of day begins to add color to Rome. The transformation from the sepulchral city at night to the resurrection of dawn is profound, and my heart stills to see it. I am reminded of the weather over the valley in Florence—all at once dark and light, stormy and bright. I imagine reaching for the sun, and wishing the clouds away, and as I do, I am seized with a vision of the Raphael portrait of Christ at the pillar, depicting the very moment of His loneliness and lamentation at being abandoned. It is all human loneliness and suffering. It is my suffering. He has lived it, and as Elizabeth Browning said, I am not alone.

Gradually, like the rising sun, the burden slips from my soul like a robe to the floor. I feel bewildered but peaceful, and I know in my heart that whatever happens to Una is right. If she lives, I will never cease thanking providence, but if she does not, she will never again know suffering, and one as stainless and pure as she is will be ensured an eternal communion.

My comfort is such that I am again in tears, but elated that I have come to this realization. I look at Una and see that she is very still. Summoning my courage, I come nearer, and when I reach her bed, I lay my head on her chest. It rises and falls beneath my ear, and I lift my face to hers. I cry aloud when I see that her skin is no longer flaming red, but pale pink, and as warm as spring sunshine.

She will live!

A sound in the doorway draws my attention, and my husband is there. He is spectral, but when he sees my face and I nod my head, smiling through my tears, a look of profound joy and relief changes his entire countenance. I rise to embrace him, who has been as lost to me these months as my daughter has been.

41

Summer 1860
Concord, Massachusetts

How small the Wayside looks on our return from the world. We step out of the railway wagon and are greeted by our friends Ralph and Lidian Emerson, Ellery Channing, Henry Thoreau, my sisters Elizabeth and Mary, now a widow, and Mary's three children. I can see in their faces how shocked they are at our altered appearances.

I descend first, plump, gray, weak from the relapse in my lungs I experienced in England after we left Rome. I have lived through hell and come home to my small though dearly beloved Concord. I settle on its branch, content to never again leave. Nathaniel descends after me—wearing his new mustache, and topped with entirely white hair. His stomach has never been the same since his illnesses abroad, and he walks somewhat hunched. The only thing unchanged about him is his eyes.

The children follow us: Rose, nine years old, stepping carefully out, slight and darkened from her fair babyhood. She resembles me most, I think, though she is not prone to raptures as her mother is. Then Julian jumps from the carriage, fourteen years old, strapping and handsome. He is as tall as his father is stooped, and sometimes when I glimpse Julian from afar or pass him in the house, I see Nathaniel as a young man—bursting with vitality and cheekiness. Julian possesses a confidence Nathaniel never had; there is no diffidence about my boy. He is of this world and will do well in it. Finally, Nathaniel waits for his sixteen-year-old Una, and holds out his weak arm for her weaker one. I do not imagine the intake of breath from our loved ones as she steps out. She is gaunt and her hair, which was long and tumbling when we left Concord years ago, has not yet grown out to reach her shoulders; it is an auburn as faded as dust. Roman fever is a creeping and savage illness that often returns with fevers and terror. I know it will plague her for the rest of her life. The dark circles under her eyes mirror her father's, and seeing the two standing together here, so changed and wrung-out, breaks my heart.

But we have made it home safely, and for that I am grateful. I close my eyes and turn my face to the sun, allowing my thanks to pulse out from me to God for letting me keep my family with me on earth, no matter what their state. Now that we are home, on our native soil, I will tend to our Hawthorne bush until it blooms again. I will tend to us all and restore the health of mind, body, and soul for which we are starved.

The carpenter's banging makes Una shriek and moan. We have begun renovations on our little farmhouse to make it more like our beloved Villa Montauto. We are adding wings and piazzas, but most special will be the tower, like that in Florence. It will become Nathaniel's study and his retreat from the world, where he may write in solitude amid his family.

Una's fits of temper since her illness grow more frightening, and I am no longer strong enough to subdue her physically. She acts like a two-year-old again, but now she is bigger and stronger than me, so when she starts to yell and cry and throw things, I am helpless to stop her. When she was small, I could carry her to a chair and hold her close until she calmed. Now I can only drag her to her room and lock her in—a most drastic and upsetting measure for us all.

The fits come without warning. One moment Una sits in the grass reading a book or sketching with the Alcott girls; the next she screams from the pain in her head and spirit like the madwoman in Mr. Rochester's attic, and her father must suffer the embarrassment of dragging her indoors so the neighbors do not get more fodder for their gossip against us.

Though we have been welcomed cordially, there is tension between us and our neighbors. Nathaniel refuses to side with the North or South as the country marches to war, and my sisters overwhelm our post with antislavery missives and essays and chastisements like blasting cannons. They reprimand us for not taking a stand in writing and professing our views in public, and I scold them by return mail until I promise not to communicate with them if they do not cease fire!

The children have gone to bed after a particularly awful day of Una's fits and carpenter problems. The workers are nearly finished, but Nathaniel has noted—and I agree—that the changes that were supposed to make our home look like an Italian villa have made it look like the queerest old haunted house on the block. The tower does not loom impressively—it juts up like a strange afterthought. There is no symmetry or timelessness to the dwelling now; it is an awkward jumbling of mismatched architectural features.

Nathaniel sits in a chair by the fireplace, frowning over another of Mary's letters of condemnation.

"How can she think that God would want man to take up arms against man for any cause?" he grumbles.

"I do not know," I say.

"I would think that losing her beloved husband would make her inclined to seek to save others from a similar pain, especially from one delivered by a musket ball!"

"One would think."

"Thank God I am too old and Julian is too young to fight, should it come to that."

"Thank God indeed."

He stops his rant to look at me, and when he sees how I rub my head, his face softens.

"Dove, I am sorry. You toil and work so hard, and when you sit down to rest at night, I have nothing to give you but my tempers and frustrations."

"I am strong enough to bear it," I say. "The burdens are heavy with or without your acknowledging them, and truthfully, I would rather have your words than your silence."

"No," he says. "Saying them aloud only cuts us deeper."

"I cannot agree. Speaking them releases the inward pressure and helps us to endure, because we know that we are not alone."

He smiles. "We have been having this debate since you were the artist invalid of Salem, and I was the stormy, obscure writer."

"And now my daughter is the invalid, and I am no artist, and you are famous, though you would rather not be."

"Sophia," he says. "How unlike you to be so dark. Has it finally happened? Have I stained you with my blackness? My soul should be damned for it."

"Do not say such things. In all the world, you are my consolation and my companion. There is no moment I have shared with you that I would undo."

I see his eyes glisten in the candlelight, and he smiles at me with such tenderness that the day's cares become only a faint memory.

"You have always been beyond what I deserve," he says, looking down at his lap.

"I feel the same about you. It must be our shared adoration of each other that has made our love so perfect all of these years. Even when it was not."

We let this sit between us, and after a short time settle together on the settee and stare at the picture of *Isola San Giovanni* over the mantel. My eyes move down to the hearth, and my thoughts drift to the image of a young girl and a slave man.

"Louisa Alcott sat here with me for tea last week," I say, "and told me the most interesting story."

"About what?"

"They harbored a fugitive slave here when she was just fourteen. The man remained for a week, on his way from a brutal farm in Maryland to freedom in Canada. She taught him letters with charcoal on this very hearth. She said that she did not understand the true meaning of hope and courage until she met him, and that though he is long gone and she does not know what became of him, she feels a sensation in her soul that he is well."

Nathaniel is silent.

"Do you think we leave an essence behind us?" I continue. "Even when we are alive? Do you feel the man here? I think I do sometimes."

"The walls must hold on to something of us when we go. But maybe I do not really believe that, and that is why I help you etch windows, and write in journals, and disrupt our family to add onto this queer old house. Is it a kind of quiet desperation to be remembered, even when I do not wish to be thought much of now?"

Our hearth fire pops, startling me.

"I had a dream about the slave woman Josepha, who had to leave her son in Cuba," I say. "She did not speak, but I felt her blaming me for not intervening. Do you think it is true? If we do not take a side, are we as guilty as the slavers?"

Nathaniel sighs. "Dove, how can we be on the side of war, no matter what the circumstances? How can we support a cause that obliterates moments like this—moments that husbands and wives and children share at their firesides? If there is no time to sit together in such places, there can be no hope for the future."

I have never felt so confused in my life, and I simply cannot face this issue anymore. Not right now, while my Una is so broken. I have to start with healing in my home before I can consider further regions. It is as if Nathaniel reads my mind, because when he speaks, it is of our daughter.

"What are we to do with Una?" he says. "She cannot be around this noise and renovation any longer. Do you think your sister Elizabeth would have her? She is so fond of Una, and could see to her education, since we cannot afford a school."

"Only if we sign on the line with the Yankees in blood."

"How about Mary?"

"She feels the same way Elizabeth does."

"But she is nearby and her love for us is greater than her frustration. Can you call on her tomorrow? Tell her what you have told me about the slaves, fugitives and dreams. Show her that we turn the matter over in our hearts, even if we cannot make a decision on it."

"Yes, I will do so. It is time anyway. Our letters have become so cold. If we sit in each other's company, we will never express the recriminations we do on paper. We will reach an understanding, and maybe she will help us with Una."

And help us she does.

Mary has always been the best Peabody sister. Her compassion outweighs her judgment, and she can always be counted upon for her intercession, not unlike the savior's mother, with whom she shares a name.

Una has been permanently damaged, but by allowing her changes of place between our home, Mary's, and even Ebe's, who has favored Una since the days we lived together in Salem, the years pass for us in a kind of manageable existence.

Rose takes lessons with her cousins and the Alcotts, and has an inclination toward writing stories until her father sees her doing so, and erupts in a temper that shocks us all. She has not picked up the pen for fiction since then. Julian is accepted at Harvard College, far enough away for him to achieve some independence, but close enough so that he may visit whenever he chooses.

Nathaniel works on his manuscripts in his sky parlor, sketching what he hopes will be his best work, spawned from a lifetime of travels and experiences. But after we hear of the first shots of the war being fired at Fort Sumter in 'sixty-one, and then learn that Louisa Alcott is called to join the nursing units at the Washington hospitals, and then suffer the death of our friend Henry Thoreau, Nathaniel lays down his pen.

It is May of 1862, and I stand with Lidian Emerson at Henry Thoreau's graveside in Sleepy Hollow, more than a year after the war began. Emerson listens to Ellery, who gestures large and cries openly over the loss of his friend. I cannot help but think he disturbs the forest air, which must wish to be still with the passing of one of its sons. Nathaniel stands alone at the crest of a hill with his back to the mourners. That is the way Henry would have wanted us to behave at his funeral—in quiet, solitary reflection under the dome of the sky and the canopy of leaves. A sob escapes Lidian's mouth, and I draw her to me.

"I know," I say.

I do know. I know that Lidian will mourn Henry at least as hard as she would if her own husband were under this mound of earth. She loved Henry, and he loved her, and Henry's friendship with Emerson suffered these past years because of it, and because Emerson became so much a man of the world while Henry burrowed deeper into its soil.

"I was the reason he left Walden Pond," says Lidian. "I needed him while Waldo toured with his lectures. Henry was my dearest companion."

I lift my handkerchief to her eyes and dab the left and the right.

"Everything he did was an offering. Everything a gift," she says. "If he planted a row of beans in your yard, it was to feed you, and so you did not have to soil your hands. If he filled your lamp with oil, he did it so it would be full in case you wanted to read all the night through without stopping. If he embraced you, he held on longer than anyone else, so a full communion of soul and warmth could encircle the two of you, and you would remember exactly why you embraced in the first place."

How tragic that Lidian must confess these whispers in a mourner's ear instead of proclaiming them at a podium. I again gaze upon my husband before raising my eyes in gratitude to the heavens. How cold and empty my life would have been without my companion.

"For a man so at home with nature and so often separate from mortals," I say, "your friendship with Henry was the greatest gift of his short life. Love is what allows the giver to make a treasure of every small offering."

I wrap my arms around Lidian and allow her to cry. Emerson notices us, but looks away, as if he cannot bear to see his wife's grief over his friend.

That night I help Nathaniel into his sleeping gown. His stomach hurts him so that it is difficult to stretch his arms up high, but I do not mind caring for him so closely. He is ashamed at his lack of strength, and apologizes as I tuck the covers up under his chin.

"I wish the ground had accepted me today, instead of Henry," he says.

"Oh, please do not speak such things aloud."

"But I do. Life is more hard than easy, and I am tiring. I envy Henry, now embarking upon the good sailing, as he said."

"Are you trying to break my heart," I say, "or do you feel this with such conviction that you cannot help but utter it aloud?"

"The latter," he says. "But I will stop if it distresses you."

I blow out the lantern and crawl into bed with him, scooting closer as he tucks his old legs and body behind my own.

"I cannot mourn a man like Henry too greatly," I say. "I feel that one so in tune with nature's spirit will slip easily into Elysium. But I will grieve for Lidian. I think Henry might have occupied as much a space in her heart as her husband."

"Perhaps more," says Nathaniel.

I pull his arm tighter around my body, and have trouble sleeping that night, knowing how cold Lidian must be in her bed.

FINAL

Spring 1864
Massachusetts

I am seized with panic as our carriage enters Boston and turns down Charles Street, where Franklin Pierce comes into view.

Nathaniel and I have not said enough. I do not know what secret he holds. He promised we will be together when he dies!

"My love," I say, clutching the lapels of his jacket.

The words back up in my throat and choke me. There is so much to say and no time left to say it.

"Sophy."

Now he cries, and I know this will be our final parting.

No, no!

"Please," is all I can utter, and I know from a lifetime of his insistence on silence, of his hatred of words and their inadequacy, that he will not have any parting comfort for me.

There is nowhere Nathaniel Hawthorne should die except wrapped in my arms. I say this to him with my mind, and I know he receives my thoughts, because he shakes his head and looks down at his lap.

He must look at me. We cannot waste one minute!

Franklin is at the side of the carriage opening the door, and I grab it from his hands and pull it shut. He is shocked and I do not care.

I push my face into Nathaniel's breast and sob.

Oh, God, do not let this be the last time I hold him. Please.

He trembles and cries with me, and holds me in his feeble arms. His white hair tickles my face, and I inhale his sweet, clean scent laced with traces of an old cigar and the breath of the pine trees at the Wayside. I try to content myself with his embrace and accept all of the love he has for me, which has been so abundant, so perfect, even—as I have told him—when it was not perfect.

Our love is a work of art. It is the great masterpiece of my life because it has been rendered over decades. It has been made of blood and tears and love and laughter and despair, and a million tiny moments that in isolation seemed small, but as part of this vast canvas convey a depth of feeling as has never been seen before and might never be seen again.

I feel his words before I hear them, and I am so startled he speaks aloud that I pull away to see that I am not deceived.

"I have been seeking myself and my place in distant lands for so many years," he says, "when all I had to do was look at the horizon of your mouth, your eyes. I am home and I have always been since I have had you."

The words are cool water on my heated skin—an anointing. Worth waiting a lifetime to hear.

"Then come back with me," I say. "Do not leave."

"I must go. I feel . . . called."

"Then promise me you will come to me when this journey is over, and never again leave."

He looks out the window. Franklin has turned away with his hands behind his back. I feel affection for him for doing so, though I am jealous that he will escort my husband on this trip.

"Do you not know that I am always with you," says Nathaniel. "Even when my body is not. Our spheres are always in communion with each other, and will be until the last sunset."

I do know this. I will remind myself every day.

"Do you remember the first time we met?" he says. "When you came into the room in your white clothes, descended from your invalid artist's loft? You joined me, a mortal, from your heavenly spire. Do you know that was not the first time I saw you? The first time, you sat in a window holding a sketch pad. The window framed you like a picture, and I thought how like a work of art you were, and how I would never have something so perfect."

He touches my gray, coarse hair and runs his hand down my plump, lined cheek, wiping my tears with the backs of his fingers.

"You are still a work of art, my dove."

I take his face in my hands and kiss him, relishing the tickle of his mustache and the softness of his lips. We embrace again, our perfect love sitting like a warm weight between our hearts.

After a few moments, Franklin has turned back and sees us pull apart. He opens the door to help us out and says some kind words to me, but I only nod my head. I cannot speak. They start away, but Nathaniel turns back to me, weeping, and with considerable effort he kneels before me.

"If you ever want me, go to the pine path," he says. "I will roam there always."

I lay my hands on either side of his head in blessing, the way I have done with the children. After a few moments, Franklin helps him stand. I do not watch Nathaniel as he hobbles away on the arm of his old friend. Instead I return to the carriage and stretch out on the seat, where the scent of pine lingers, and I inhale it in deep breaths until I am home in Concord.

When I arrive at the Wayside, I note the dark tower my husband has left. I cannot greet the children yet, so I creep to Nathaniel's path. The walk is still and windless, and feels empty without my husband's form filling it. I pace the path for hours as the sky burns a pink-and-orange sunset. I wait and watch, but there is nothing of Nathaniel here but the footsteps he has left behind on the ground.

I step in them with my small worn slippers, stained from the dust of London and Lisbon and Rome, and countless other cities, one at a time.

Not two weeks have passed since Nathaniel's leaving, and I am unable to settle.

I have replaced him on the path, walking back and forth at all hours of the day and evening, waiting for a sign of him. The pines are still and the air is clear. It is as if the world holds its breath.

Una is home with me, and has been a remarkable comfort. She senses my need for calm, and has not had a fit in some time. At night we read together and sketch with Rose, and Una has seen to arranging our meals with the cook, and our invitations to friends' houses. I am grateful for her assistance and distraction, because I am numb and unable to concentrate on anything. Also, I have experienced a sudden weakness and unsteadiness of frame. I feel as if I am pulling a heavy load behind me like a plow horse, and I have to frequently sit down until I regain my strength.

On the day my love had planned to arrive in New Hampshire, I am frantic for a word from him. Franklin has been in contact through short missives, but it is not enough. I cannot bear this. I wring my trembling hands and search out my eldest daughter until I find her in the sky parlor.

"Una, write to Julian in Cambridge. Tell him to meet your father and bring him home."

"Father would not wish it," she says.

She leans on the windowsill with her back to me, where Nathaniel usually stands sentry. I can see the outline of her bones through her thin, worn dress, and note the slight hunch of her shoulders. I cannot reconcile this muted person with the young child of such vitality and passion who inspired the impish character Pearl. In spite of Una's physical deterioration, her travels and trials have given her a deeper wisdom and a gravity that I welcome, now that Nathaniel is not here. But with a grown daughter, every exchange is heavy with things unsaid and the unspoken assertion of her will against mine—the burden of her judgment.

"He always wishes to see Julian," I say. "He will allow Julian to persuade him to come back to Concord."

Una turns to look at me with her dark eyes, and hesitates a moment before speaking.

"Perhaps he does not wish to come back to Concord. It is so small and closed."

I start to protest, but I hear someone calling from downstairs. Dinner is ready.

She walks past me without looking at me, and descends to the dining room. I follow her, a little angry and confused about her meaning. With Una, one never knows whether she speaks of present matters or some larger issue, and I am in no mood for such discourse. I hold my tongue, though. The threat of her tantrums keeps me silent.

I fear that we are a family of half conversations. Nathaniel's silence, Una's elusiveness, Julian's absence, Rose's quiet. Sometimes it seems I am the only one who makes any noise, and it is exhausting to exist in such a way. I feel a powerlessness like when Nathaniel left before our courtship, and did not return for months. I knew he carried my *Cuba Journal*, but our separation was not on my terms and did not end with the expediency I would have wished. He found some great meaning for himself that he was happy to communicate on his return, but I was left having to catch up from my nesting branch. I resented it then, and I resent it now, and I do not know how much longer I can endure it without a flare of temper.

I stab my chicken and try to control the rising heat in my body. My hands tremble so that I have to hit the plate several times before sinking my fork into the meat. Una now sits with her posture erect, and takes slow, deliberate bites. Rose looks from Una to me with large eyes. None of us speaks, and just when the silence becomes unbearable, there is a noise on the piazza.

Una rises as if she cannot flee quickly enough, and I hear her open the front door. I stop stabbing and turn my head to listen, and there is suddenly a commotion and a cry. Rose reaches for my hand, and in a moment my bitterness evaporates. We stand at the same moment to see what has happened, but before we can leave the room, my sisters are there, darkening the doorway.

It is from Una's lips that I hear the words from the other room.

"He has died!"

For a terrible moment I am filled with hatred for my sisters. Elizabeth has always been jealous of our love. They both judge us for our silence on the war, and our strange house, and my being absent for our parents' deaths, and Una's madness. Was it not Elizabeth who once told me that Emerson thought Nathaniel and Bronson Alcott together might make a whole man?

"No! Do not say such a lie!" I say. "He is coming home. . . ."

But before the sentence is complete, I am broken.

I release Rose's hand and crumple to the floor, where there is a flurry of hands and hushed voices, soothing, petting, embracing, leading me to the couch in the parlor, wiping my tears with their handkerchiefs. Elizabeth kneels beside me, a considerable effort for one her age, and her face is all kindness and love. I am ashamed of my impulse to anger, but I still cannot comprehend this news. I shake my head, and feel tears seep into my ears and down my neck. Oh, if I could drown myself in these tears!

"Sophy, you poor girl," Elizabeth says. "How we suffer to bring you this tragedy. Cry it away. Cry it all away."

Mary kneels beside her and takes my hand. "There never was one so loved as Nathaniel by so devoted a wife. You gave him a little bit of heaven on earth, and now that he is there, he will wait for you and bless you more than he ever could here."

Her words ignite more sobs. I am unworthy of such kindness from them.

I force myself to sit up and call my daughters to my sides, tucking their bodies into mine. They both cry on my breast, and I think what a sad tableau we make—a room of women in grief. But soon, among the shadows of our mourning, I am aware of a warmth that comes from the light of our spheres. We are joined in our pain and love, and in our wishes to assuage one another. If we were a painting, we would have light in our centers, though shadows surrounded us.

Nathaniel was that light to me, and I to him. That is the sweetness that lives in this pain.

When I am calmer, I finally understand why Nathaniel left—it was to spare me the grief of seeing his body without a soul. Now I will forever remember him as he was when he was alive. He will exist to me as the young man I sketched by the fire in my parents' house, whom I watched chop wood at the manse, who allowed his children to cover him with grass, and who stood on ships' decks, as natural at sea as the father he lost to it all those years ago. He will be the rower in the *Pond Lily*, the writer at the desk, and the dark form pacing on the pine path, more at ease with the trees than with men and women.

"He has spared me the image of his death," I say. "He has spared all of us so he may forever live in our memories. That is how much he loved us."

Elizabeth buries her face in her hand while she cries.

I pull her and Mary to stand with me and the girls. As we embrace, the light coming in the window from the fading day rests on the canvas of *Isola San Giovanni* that I painted. Our small figures against the vast landscape are joined and young, and are facing the future. I can hardly wait until our figures are together again on the fields of Elysium for eternity.

I never set eyes on my love again.

Franklin arranges for Nathaniel's body to be held and delivered to the church on the day of his funeral. Una and Rose help me arrange my hat and veil on the morning of the service. Franklin and Julian hold my arms on either side, escorting me. The reverend Clarke who married us all those years ago, and who was in awe of my husband then, is in awe of him now. The Church of the First Parish is filled with the great people of our time: my sisters, the Alcotts, Ellery Channing, Ralph Emerson. Franklin sits with our family, and sixteen men bear Nathaniel's casket out of the church and to the carriage, which takes him through town one last time to Sleepy Hollow. We lay him to rest on a gentle hill, under a canopy of leaves.

At the reception after the service, I try to smile at the well-wishers and take in their kind words about my husband's genius, what his work means to them, and the little ways they interacted with the elusive author. But the longer the day wears on, the more I feel how much Nathaniel would have been frustrated by near strangers trying to claim a piece of him. Aside from Franklin and a very select few, Nathaniel could not bear entering into acquaintance with many, for he could not simply talk of the weather or village gossip. To befriend Nathaniel was to encounter a celestial individual, and he allowed only people of deep thought and genuine humility to enter into his sphere. I believe there were depths to him that even I could not access, so to hear these small stories of seeing him at the bakery or glimpsing him at Walden Pond tires me the way it would have tired Nathaniel.

After two hours I can take no more, and slip through the crowds to sneak outside. As I step out on the piazza, I am surprised to see Elizabeth and Franklin with their heads bent together in private conversation. They do not see me, and I do not want to be seen. I turn to find another way outside, but Elizabeth's words stop me.

"He told me he never wanted to live to see sixty years of age."

Franklin nods as if he has heard these words before, but I have not. I slip into the shadows to hear what she could mean.

"Do you think he hastened it?" she asks.

Franklin clears his throat. "I will not say. There is evidence, but it is no matter. My friend would have died that night anyway."

I feel as if I cannot breathe. A fist has closed around my throat, and I press my chest, taking great gasping gulps. A horrible memory rises—that of my weary husband insisting we turn back to the Wayside so he can get something that he put in his coat. I shake the thought away. He would not have!

"I stayed with him until he fell into a fitful sleep," continues Franklin, "and left the door between our rooms open, in case he cried out. But it was not he who cried when he passed. There was a strange screeching, like a dog but higher and throatier—maybe a fox. It awakened me, and left me so unsettled that I got up to check Nathaniel. When I found him, he was utterly still and peaceful."

Franklin's voice breaks, and Elizabeth reaches up to pat his back.

I step forward, and when they see me, their faces go pale. I open my mouth to speak, but there are no words, so I step off the piazza and rush to the pine path. They do not try to follow me, and for that I am grateful.

From where I walk, I see the mourners leave over the next hour, and I stay there until the evening light changes, finally sitting on the bench where Nathaniel and I used to view the sunset.

Nature enfolds me in my grief. She settles my heart and allows me to push the words I overheard away from me. They do not matter now. They are separate from my part of Nathaniel's death. Now I must welcome his spirit wholly into mine, so we are never again separated.

I hear it before I feel it—a sudden rushing like a wave, or the sound of the rainfall on the mountains of Cuba. I turn my head to the sky and see the pines begin to rock above me, and all at once I am engulfed in a warm, sweet wind that lifts my hair and fills my lungs. I take deep breaths and suddenly feel Nathaniel. He is there. Dark and quiet, calming and radiating love. He is everywhere around me. I cannot contain my tears, and I stand to walk in the wind, to inhale every morsel of this gift.

The light has gone on in the tower of the Wayside. I see Una there, looking out toward where I stand. I know she cannot see me, but she knows I am there, the way that I know Nathaniel is here, though I cannot behold him. It is time for me to return to my children and offer them support in their grief. I must let Elizabeth know with my embrace that all is well between us, and I will endure this hardship.

When I return, everyone has gone and left our little broken Hawthorne bush alone. Once the children retire, I creep to the room where our letters and journals still lie beneath the floorboards.

I pry up the wood and remove each item, caressing every artifact before laying it on the table. I kiss the paintbrushes and pressed flowers; I embrace the journals my husband touched; I inhale the love letters he wrote to me during our long courtship. I will immerse myself in his words so I may relive our lives, and rekindle mine as it was before I entered into communion with him. It will be enough now that Nathaniel has finally found his true home.

After all this time, I now know that some people are not for the world. They are messengers, passing through avenues and city streets, on mountain paths, over verdant fields, and in quaint villages; holders of secret, universal truths, and bearers of the knowledge that the rest of us need to progress: in song, on canvas, in pulpit, and on the page. The tragedy is that many of them do not understand that they are bearers of truth, and in their sacred nature are forever isolated from those of us at home on the earth.

Nathaniel called me his angel because he dealt in the celestial, but I could not be a bearer. I have often felt at peace in the world, and happy to observe and experience the beauty around me. I look with fondness at distant horizons, but until now, I have not been in a hurry to reach them.

Nathaniel was wrong about the limitations of words. In that most holy book, it says, "*In the beginning was the Word, and the Word was with God, and the Word was God.*" Words are the bridge to the Eternal. They hold the power in the cosmos to conjure, transport, condemn, unite, destroy. If Nathaniel had understood that the words were arrows in his bag instead of barriers, perhaps then he would have found his peace.

The candlelight shines on the artifacts from our lives on the table before me. I imagine the stories trembling for my attention and longing for me to piece them together so they make sense, so they spell the true romance of the years we spent together.

I recall the words Ada scribbled at the séance from my mother.

"*Write it. Lift the veil.*"

I know the power of words and the way they reach off the page to the reader, dissolving all borders of time and space. I understand how words expand the minds digesting them, allowing those who sit in quiet rooms to embark upon grand adventures with people they could never meet within the circumference of their own lives. For those who do not fear the vocation, it is our charge to put down the words, one after another. To make a case. To make a story.

It is clear what I must do. I must use words in ways that, despite his greater gifts, Nathaniel would not, because he feared that he would expose too much of himself. I must share his life, because the world needs his story, my story.

And in our story, the romance of the Hawthornes, I will have the final word.

AUTHOR'S NOTE

Sophia Peabody Hawthorne did write after her husband's death, or rather, she copied their letters and journals in order to keep her husband's legacy alive, support her family financially, and remain in spiritual communion with Nathaniel. She worked closely with his publisher, James T. Fields, to release their common and travel journals, but she was full of doubts from start to finish; she worried that Nathaniel would not have been pleased with her for publishing their personal writings, and was disappointed with the cool reception the works met. Those who thought they would finally be able to peel back Nathaniel's veil remained unsatisfied. Sophia's omission of what would have revealed intimate details of both their elations and trials, particularly her own contributions to the journals, resulted in documents that were too reserved to satisfy public curiosity.

Sophia traveled with her children overseas to Germany to see to Julian's education with more economy, and eventually moved to England, where she became ill with a form of pneumonia. Una kept vigil at her mother's bedside the way Sophia had with her all those years ago. In February of 1871, Sophia died with Una and Rose at her side, and was buried at Kensal Green in London. Una died in 1877, in England at the age of thirty-three. In 2006 she was reinterred with Sophia in Sleepy Hollow Cemetery in Concord, Massachusetts. Sophia now spends her eternal rest with her husband, Nathaniel; her daughter Una; her sister Elizabeth; and their friends the Emersons, the Alcotts, Ellery Channing, and Henry Thoreau, on a gentle hill under a canopy of leaves.

ACKNOWLEDGMENTS

My fascination with the lives of writers from the past continues, and I am thankful to God and to many people for their support, encouragement, and inspiration.

To my publishing team, Ellen Edwards, Kara Welsh, Craig Burke, Courtney Landi, Kevan Lyon, and Lisa Bankoff: I am so grateful for your guidance and partnership on this novel.

To those who supported and kindled my research: Janet Somerville, for gorgeous photos of Florence; Lucia O. Ditch, for patient assistance with Spanish language translations; the Department of Special Collections at the Stanford University Library; and to the staff of the Library of Congress in Washington, D.C.

To my family and friends, particularly my three sons, Robert and Charlene Shephard, Richard and Patricia Robuck, Kristina McMorris, and Kelly McMullen: Your loving support means more than you can know.

And last, to my husband, Scott Robuck: I could not have understood my characters or their particular kind of love without you. You are a gift to me, and in the more than twenty years we have spent together rests an eternity of blessings. I am so pleased that your story intersects with and completes mine.

SELECTED BIBLIOGRAPHY

From Concord to Boston to Salem, walking in the steps of my characters provided the first and greatest inspiration for the novel, which was deepened by the writings of Nathaniel and Sophia Hawthorne. Their journals, letters, poetry, art, and fiction provided the fabric upon which this narrative is based, as did the writings of Sophia's children; her sisters Elizabeth and Mary; and their friends the Alcotts, Ellery Channing, the Emersons, Margaret Fuller, and Henry Thoreau. The scholarly work available on the Hawthornes is equally fascinating for those who wish to know more about these captivating people and their contemporaries.

Here is a short selection for further reading:

Hawthorne, Julian. *Nathaniel Hawthorne and His Wife*. Boston: James R. Osgood and Company, 1885.

Herbert, T. Walter. *Dearest Beloved: The Hawthornes and the Making of the Middle-Class Family*. Berkeley: University of California Press, 1993.

Lathrop, Rose Hawthorne. *Memories of Hawthorne*. New York: Houghton Mifflin and Company, 1897.

Mann, Mary Tyler Peabody. *Juanita: A Romance of Real Life in Cuba Fifty Years Ago*. Boston: D. Lothrop Company, 1887.

Marshall, Megan. *The Peabody Sisters: Three Women Who Ignited American Romanticism*. Boston: Houghton Mifflin Co., 2005.

Valenti, Patricia Dunlavy. *Sophia Peabody Hawthorne: A Life, Volume 1, 1809–1847*. Columbia: University of Missouri Press, 2004.

Wineapple, Brenda. *Hawthorne: A Life*. New York: Random House Trade Paperbacks, 2003.

Wright, John Hardy. *Hawthorne's Haunts in New England*. Charleston: The History Press, 2008.

ABOUT THE AUTHOR

Erika Robuck is a contributor to the fiction blog Writer Un-boxed, and she maintains her own blog, Muse. She is a member of the Hawthorne Society, the Hemingway Society, the Historical Novel Society, and the Edna St. Vincent Millay Society. She lives in Annapolis, Maryland, with her husband and three sons.